RED BIRD SUMMER

Disclaimer: ...on. Names, characters, organ... ...e a product of the author's imaginatio... ...ally. Any resemblances to actual persons, living... ...to events or locales, are entirely coincidental.

AUTHOR'S NOTE

With one exception noted in the last paragraph below, this book is entirely a work of fiction, including the characters and events, and some place names (Hing Long Lane, Flower Road and Ong Hing Terrace).

At the time the events in this story took place in the 1970s, Kowloon Walled City was still in place but the Hei Ling Chau leprosarium had either closed down or was in the process of closing down. The Hong Kong Police Force's Narcotics Bureau was located in a run-down part of Central South in the 1960s but whether this was still the case in the 1970s is unknown to the writer. The Narcotics Bureau did store drugs on site but whether this claim can be verified is dubious.

There was once an entire wall of heroin, as described in the text, stored in the Hong Kong Police Force Narcotics Bureau offices, in the ladies' toilet. This is a personal memory and gave rise to this story, but of course I would never insist upon its authenticity.

In **RED BIRD SUMMER,** Pearl Green and Karen Henderson are two successful Hong Kong women, whose old friendship brings them back together after many years to set up an archaeological project for Pearl's philanthropic organisation, the Hong Kong-based June Bowen Foundation. Karen, an archaeologist acclaimed for her work in Southeast Asia, is injured during a robbery at the Hong Kong Archaeological Museum. One of a number of stolen objects is associated with Pearl Green's past. The Museum Director, Albert Ho, is professionally jealous of Karen and convinces himself that Karen stole the artefact for Pearl. He hires a shady new arrival to Hong Kong – BJ Cresswell – to get it back. The lives of Pearl and her friends come under threat. Pearl seeks help from three men: her father, the powerful Sir James Gates; the mysterious Hong Kong businessman, Yip Yee Koon; and the British former China watcher, Peter Benson. Together, they masterfully untangle the many threads of murder and intrigue that run through this story.

Although **JAN PEARSON** draws material for her books from her memories of living in Hong Kong during the 1960s, she has lived in Australia for most of her adult life and these days enjoys rural living on the scenically beautiful Far North Coast of New South Wales in Australia.

With an initial background in earth sciences and a twenty-year career in various policy roles, Jan has now turned to writing, drawing from her imagination, memory and life experiences. Like *Tiger Autumn, Red Bird Summer* focuses on her beloved Hong Kong. Each book won a Publication Prize in successive years in the competition for the international Proverse Prize.

RED BIRD SUMMER

Jan Pearson

Proverse Hong Kong

Red Bird Summer
by Jan Pearson.
Published in Hong Kong by Proverse Hong Kong, November 2015.
Copyright © Proverse Hong Kong, November 2015.
ISBN: 978-988-8228-02-7

1st published in pbk in Hong Kong by Proverse Hong Kong,
January 2014.
Copyright © Proverse Hong Kong, June 2012, January 2014.
ISBN 978-988-8227-12-9

Distribution enquiries to:
Proverse Hong Kong, P.O. Box 259, Tung Chung Post Office,
Tung Chung, Lantau, NT, Hong Kong SAR, China.
E-mail: proverse@netvigator.com
Web site: www.proversepublishing.com

The right of Jan Pearson to be identified as the author of this work
has been asserted by her
in accordance with the Copyright, Designs and Patents Act 1988.

Cover design by Elbert Siu Ping Lee and Artist Hong Kong.
Printed by CreateSpace.

All rights reserved. No part of this publication may be reproduced, stored in a retrieval system, or transmitted, in any form or by any means, electronic, mechanical, photocopying, recording or otherwise, without the prior written permission of the publisher or publisher and author. The book is sold subject to the condition that it shall not, by way of trade or otherwise, be lent, re-sold, hired out or otherwise circulated without the publisher's prior written consent in any form of binding or cover other than that in which it is published and without a similar condition including this condition being imposed on the subsequent owner or purchaser. Please contact Proverse Hong Kong in writing, to request any and all permissions (including but not restricted to republishing, inclusion in anthologies, translation, reading, performance and use as set pieces in examinations and festivals).

British Library Cataloguing in Publication Data.
A catalogue record for this book is available from the British Library.

For my sons Nicholas and Andrew

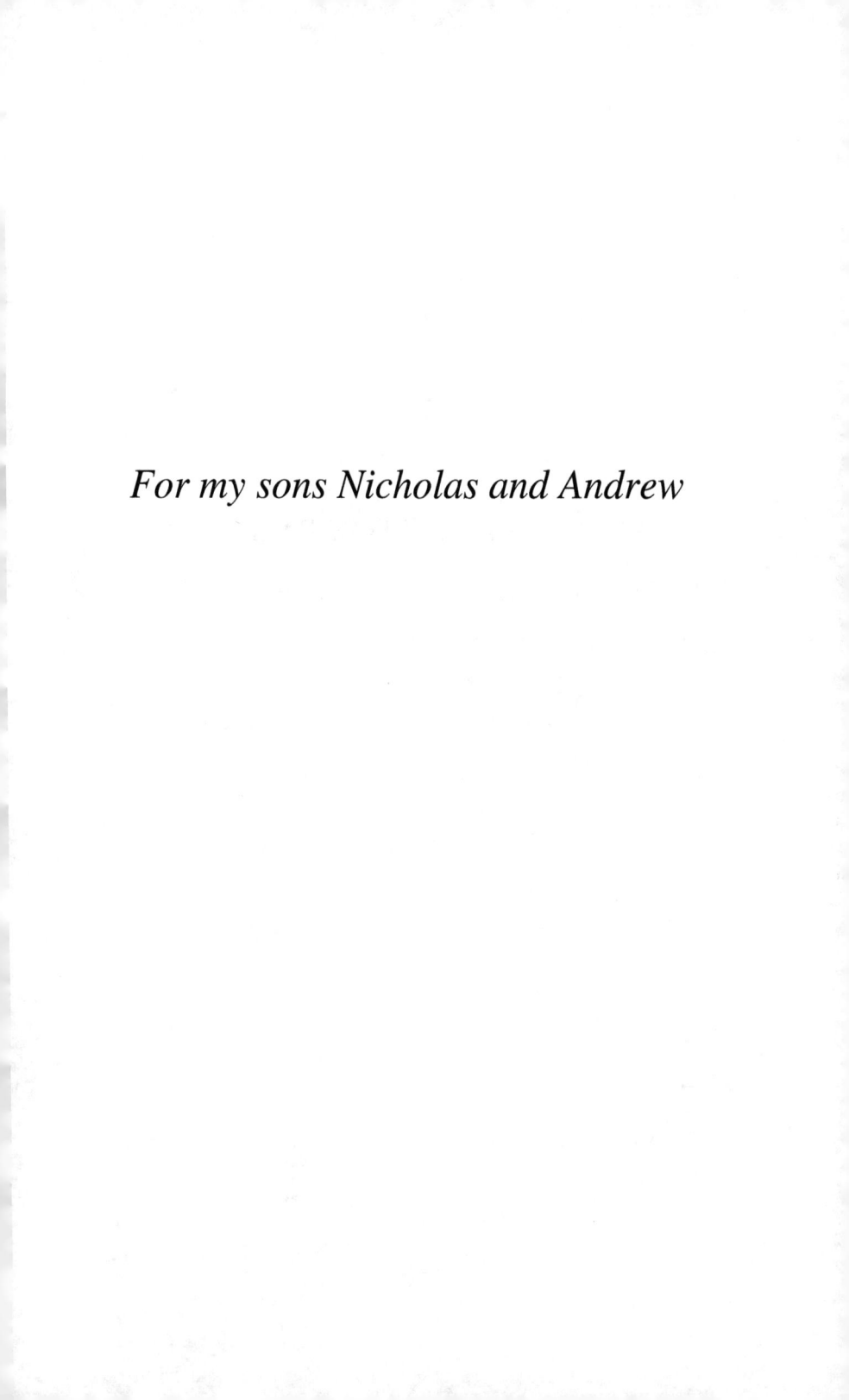

I

RED BIRD RISING

The Hong Kong Archaeological Museum
Wednesday 3 August: 6.30am

Karen Henderson held her breath. One last piece of patterned earthenware to persuade into place – the most difficult – she had to have the confidence to tap it in firmly. The rubber-headed archaeologist's hammer might be the best tool for the job. She exhaled and just did it. The object retained, no, gained, form and the piece stayed in place. Glue was not going to be the last necessary resort after all. She leaned back in her chair. The bowl sat with squat complacence on the battered work-table, so clearly true to its original form, even to the slight dip in the edge, that she smiled at it with a familiar fondness. It had taken five years of toil to have this moment, to savour everything the pot represented: its own past and her future. It stood as irrefutable evidence of trading activity in the waters around Hong Kong many hundreds of years earlier than had ever been established before and its presence here, in these waters, was far rarer than its provenance or function. It would simply throw marine archaeological research in south-east Asia into a spin.

Kaz heard a noise off somewhere, soft, like mice scratching the highly polished floors in the galleries beyond the archive room. She was alone in the museum and reckoned on having another hour before the first staff arrived for the day's work. She updated her notebook and sketched the potsherd that had completed the Qing Dynasty pot's rebuild. She was in the museum's archive room, the lower of the two circular stone storeys of monolithic sandstone blocks. The tower is attached to an equally stout but single level stone structure that makes up the four public galleries of the Hong Kong Archaeological Museum. Formerly the British Navy's Armoury, the building's rugged structure sets off the delicate glass-cased museum displays perfectly and even the archive room is beautiful, lined with chest after chest of wine-red rosewood offsetting the creamy sandstone walls to stunning effect.

Suddenly there was another noise close by. It was something being dragged. But before Kaz could turn to call out to whoever else was in so early and invite them to come to inspect her handiwork, she reeled from a thudding blow to the back of her head, and sprawled, bleeding, across the expanse of the room's pitted, ancient work-table. A wallop of dazed fear at the impact became disbelief in slow-motion as Kaz saw her pot raised in the air and then casually hurled across the table. It shattered on the flagstone floor and the last thing she registered before she slid into unconsciousness was a smooth-skinned hand taking her room-key from the work-table. Seconds later, as the door closed, Kaz was unconscious, and locked in.

Wednesday 3 August: 1.00pm

Pearl was having difficulty understanding what had happened at the museum. She was in her office in downtown Hong Kong just as she was every working day, sitting at her ugly, ex-army desk with Kaz beside her in what passed for a visitor's chair. Kaz was rambling a bit, just one of several good reasons perhaps why she should have been in bed, not flitting around in the late Hong Kong summer heat with a bandaged head and a probable dose of concussion. Pearl had minced no words in telling her so.

"I am not going to give up my plans for today, Pearl. Albert went puce when he found I'd been in the archive room before museum hours without clearing it with him first. That noise. I should have taken more notice. He would have taken my keys away as punishment he said, if the thief or thieves hadn't thoughtfully relieved me of them. And now I'm being given pretty strong hints that it was my fault – 'Are you sure you locked the outer door, Dr Henderson?' – that sort of thing. I thought I'd try to look useful by bringing *this* around for you to have a look at."

Dribbles of sweat were starting to seep through the heavy gauze bandages that the Hospital Registrar had insisted on dressing her head with. The building the two women sat in was yet another colonial building, the old Fire Services HQ on Connaught Road facing the harbour. The building belonged to Pearl in its entirety. She had inherited it from her mother and during the past ten years had converted the former garages into ground floor offices. It was an immense space, built for the original purpose of housing Hong Kong's fleet of fire trucks; the ceiling was more than twenty-five feet high and the air-conditioner, which was useless, had long been turned off. All it did was stream water down the harbour-facing sandstone wall, which only added to the humidity. Kaz wiped her face and thought of surf and surging white waves kicking up mounds of silver white sand. Pearl didn't notice the heat. Hong Kong summers send many expatriates to their homelands (wherever home is) with a cooler or kinder clime, but Pearl Green was a lifelong Hong Kong resident and stoically ignored the best that a hot August Hong Kong day could throw at her.

She took the envelope Kaz handed her and extracted a black and white photograph, looked at it tight-lipped for a second or two and slapped it back down on the desk. Kaz remained silent, but watched her carefully. Pearl's thick, mothy-brown eyelashes hid her expression but there was a rasping note in her voice that betrayed how she felt: "I haven't seen this bloody thing since the day my mother died."

Karen put the photo back into its envelope and returned it to her briefcase. She lit a cigarette, hands shaking as she did so. "You do recognise it though?" Pearl nodded. "I'm sorry if I upset you, maybe I'm not thinking clearly. I had no idea that it was associated with your mother's death until I read the archive notes, and naturally, I was very curious about it. It went missing with the theft of the bestiary collection from the first gallery.

"Albert is furious and a full security review is under way to find out how the thieves got in this morning. If I wasn't absolutely sure that I'd locked the outer door I'd be confessing at this very moment just to get him off my case."

Pearl did not smile. It was just like Kaz to try to laugh off something as serious as this theft. If anyone ever mentioned *her* little treasure trove though that was different ... Kaz was very single-minded about some things. She said, "I'm not surprised he's miffed, with twenty million dollars worth of borrowed antiquities gone." Her voice was harder than she'd meant and she changed the subject: "Perhaps you should take the doctor's advice and take it easy my dear. You are very pale."

"I'm fine, the hospital doc gave me the all-clear. I had to get back to the museum to see if I could salvage my pot; I was terrified that someone would just scoop it all up and throw it back into the workbox with all the other pieces. That's when I saw this." She gestured at the photo. "The staff had made up an inventory of the stolen items and when I saw the notes that went with the little artefact, I offered to talk to you about it. Better me than have Albert Ho on your case. Really, he's going ballistic about this. You'd think he bloody well owned the collection himself."

"And your skin is going all blotchy. And will you *stop* going on about that thing. People can get really ill after sustaining a head injury, you know." Kaz drew heavily on her cigarette and Pearl waved the smoke away. She felt silly for being so abrupt, and said, "I *can* give you some background on how this thing turned up if it helps you get back on side with Dr Ho.

"I first saw it the day that mum died. One of the tremors that shook the health clinic rattled a ceiling panel loose and it must have been up there. It was on the floor next to her when I – we – found her. With the way that the buildings are all so interconnected in the Walled City, this object could have been carried into the ceiling from practically anywhere and probably by rats."

Pearl shuddered at how the memory of seeing that pin beside her mother's dead body also invoked her fear of rats. Pearl insisted on wearing boots all year round and now she swung out of the chair so quickly and planted her booted feet on the floor with such a thump that Kaz double-inhaled and choked. Pearl smiled at last and looked at her friend fondly. Kaz said: "I'm sorry, Pearl. I really had no idea about the pin's history and I'm sorry I made you think about it all and also about the rats. I know how you hate them. This object is nothing at all like the other things the thieves took. They targeted that fabulous Tang Dynasty bestiary collection, which has been on display in the first gallery. That is another reason why Albert is so furious. It's the first loan from any mainland museum to our museum. He's going to have a lot of explaining to do. Incidentally, there's no useful information about this little pin on record except for this photo taken in 1964, and these few notes. I don't understand why the museum even accepted it."

Pearl thought she knew why. "The Police offered it to the museum when mum's case was closed and I think Albert accepted it more as a tribute to her than anything else. They told me about it during my final interview with the officer who had charge of the case. I wondered afterwards if they thought I wanted it." She shuddered at the memory. "As if I could ever ... what do the notes say about it?"

Kaz dug around in her bag and found the curator's notes. "Umm ... 'the object is a decorative round metal pin, with gems/gemstones set at each compass point around the circumference; comprising diamond; onyx, sapphire and ruby; made of iridium, an unusual material for such work and previously unknown in Asian decorative pieces. Provenance: unknown.' It was in the archive room in a storage box. I don't think it has ever been displayed. The whole thing is interesting, don't you think?"

"Not particularly. Did you see anyone when all this happened?"

"No. All I saw was a hand. A man's hand. Very smooth. It was a tactile encounter, you could say. I think this pin is interesting because the archive room is stuffed with precious objects and they chose this. Did they come into the room to put me out of action or did they come in for this object? If they knew where this was kept, that means it could be an inside job. But I can hardly conceive of who or how or why if that is the case. I'd rather think they quickly opened a couple of drawers after dealing with me and grabbed the first portable thing that came to hand."

Kaz carefully felt the back of her head. It was beginning to throb badly. The Duty Registrar at the hospital had reassured her that the wound was superficial, which is why, he cheerily informed her, it had bled so much. Apart from being told she would possibly experience some slight concussion, she had the all-clear.

"The bestiary collection was excavated from a ship too."

"And so?"

"My field work of course. The bowl I had just finished restoring was excavated from *my* wrecks. Don't you find that significant? Perhaps this theft has something to do with my research, maybe it's a warning about my work at Squid Cove and maybe ...."

"Ah yes", said Pearl, a little vindictively cheerful now. "I see it all. The thieves stole the collection because they know you are a marine archaeologist which somehow threatens the sanctity of your site. And then what did they do? They stole the pin for good measure because they know we are friends and that it has been connected with me in the past? Woo-ooh. Double threat. What are we supposed to do? Never sleep again?

"Bullshit."

"Quite. How was the pin missed?"

Kaz was miffed. "The archive drawer was left open. But even if they had tidied up and vacuumed before they left, it would have been missed when the next inventory was done." She fidgeted with the bandage. Her hair was escaping the bandages and felt revolting. She could feel the sweat starting to run down her temples and she shivered. "These things rarely show up again after a theft like this. They go into private collections, anything from the scale of a private museum to a shoebox. Secrets. Archaeology conceals as well as reveals."

She pulled at the bindings again. She was clearly uncomfortable and Pearl could see that more than a throbbing headache was troubling Kaz. But it was no good being too inquisitive. Kaz was pretty good at keeping her own secrets. It was Pearl's turn to observe her friend and she was all too aware that all was not well. *I suppose when the thief or the thieves smashed Kaz's reconstructed pot early that morning, they didn't care that they were destroying the result of five year's work.*

"They can't destroy the result of all your slog, Kaz. That remains for all to see in your research and now in your book. Something you can be so proud of: At thirty-two you have a reputation that most archaeologists only dream of achieving by retirement age, if they are lucky."

But Kaz was off somewhere else entirely. Try as she could, today, which should have been a day for celebration of the first visible proof to support her work, everything had fallen flat and here she was, sluggish, hot, sweaty and hungry and thinking longingly about her former husband, Drew. Not to mention sitting near her dear friend Pearl who looked everything she did not at that moment. Kaz sighed.

*

"I said – hullo? – Kaz? I want to talk to you about working for the June Bowen Foundation if you can squeeze it in between the demands of fame and wealth. – Kaz?"

"Oh sorry, Pearl love, I feel a bit woozy. Say it again?"

"I said it's time to eat," shouted Pearl.

*

The yum cha palace roared with the lunchtime pandemonium of people eating and food carts shoving their way through the aisles, with long queues of hungry customers waiting for a rare seat. "The foundation is doing well, Kaz."

Kaz nodded her aching head carefully, ate a whole *ha gow* with some difficulty but managed a long swallow of San Miguel beer without apparent pain. Did she need the lecture? Pearl droned on about the investment base, the property portfolio, how she had been approached to float the June Bowen Foundation on the stock exchange and how she had told them all to push off. Kaz wobbled in her chair.

"You need to go to bed."

"No. I'm probably in shock, that's all."

"I would be deeply moved if you were ever shocked by *my* language Kaz. Concentrate, woman! I have a proposal for you," Pearl said, a little pompously. "Will you eat chicken feet?" She took two servings from the trolley.

"That's it? Chicken feet?"

Pearl ignored her. "I don't think that you should have another beer either if you are serious about remaining conscious. – Where was I? – Oh yes, the Foundation's next five year goal is education and I want to set up a scheme to give a number of students an opportunity to achieve their higher education goals. Naturally I thought of you when I wondered who would be the best person to run it. I want to capitalise on your expertise to give the foundation enough credibility to fund scholarships, so obviously we will be offering them in the field of archaeology. Will you run it for me?"

Kaz's jaw loosened. Pearl was much amused. A waitress pushing a trolley of food past them decided to let the offer of *siu bao* go. These *gweipor*s obviously had enough energy already without needing more. With her beer bottle tilted at an alarming angle and the bandage descending towards her eyebrows, it was not Dr Henderson's most sophisticated moment. Pearl took the bottle from her. "I'll have the beer while you get your jaw sorted out." The waitress glanced back to see Pearl pouring beer into her empty teacup. Her decision to pass these *gweipors* by had obviously been the right one.

Wednesday 3 August: 2.30pm

A taxi took Kaz and Pearl back to the Fire Services HQ in afternoon heat that had become crushingly hot. Kaz had decided not to return to the museum. She kicked off her shoes and pushed up the sleeves of her cotton top. She hadn't given Pearl an answer and Pearl waited, eyebrows arched enquiringly. "OK, Pearl. You know how much I'd love to be based in Hong Kong permanently again and this job seems perfect but, at the moment? In another year or two I could be more useful, surely?" Kaz sounded more formal than she needed to.

Pearl nodded in agreement. "You are right of course. Your career is hot. I also realise that my offer can't compete with a job in a top UK university but it would be a great career move for you, longer term, as well as being good for the Bowen Foundation, of course. Your work here will probably be your life's work. How are you going to manage if you are based in England? You need to be in Hong Kong and if you accept my offer you can still do your work and achieve something worthwhile as an educator as well. Think about it please, Kazzy. The job comes with a damned good salary and I'm throwing in a fully maintained apartment as my personal contribution.

"People will fight to join your Board, given your academic reputation. There will be miles of support for you. Admit it. It's a brilliant idea and this is our time. This is a brand new age, Kaz, for god's sake, and we are women with the capacity to make our mark."

"Let me think." Two things came into Kaz's mind, the first being that it was a long time since Pearl had called her Kazzy and the second being that Kaz had never thought of herself as being a woman of a new age, for god's (or anyone else's) sake. Why didn't she think like that? Maybe it was just the way Pearl went at things. Pearl had left girlhood behind the day her mother was killed. Making and shaping the June Bowen Foundation in honour of her mother's memory was her life's work. They both had obsessions. Pearl's life was work.

So is mine. But work is Pearl's only life. She wondered if Pearl ever thought of living differently. She didn't travel, never took holidays, never did anything for herself but have the odd casual fling and endless pairs of boots made. She even met her social obligations out of a sense of duty, rarely for her own enjoyment. If the opportunity Pearl was handing to her today had come along two years back, would she and Drew have divorced, or would he have moved to Hong Kong too, well able to make his own way in an academic community which he knew from student days? Would their marriage have lasted if they had consolidated their interests in Asia instead of dividing their careers between countries?

"If I accept, the job has to be separate from my post-doctoral work. I have to maintain the integrity of the site."

Pearl waved the comment away: "goes without saying."

"If I'm right, the next phase of work is going to blow marine archaeology out of the water, and – except for you – I won't share it with anyone or anything, and that includes official Bowen Foundation business. Not yet." Pearl's face hardened. Secretiveness in her friend she acknowledged, but exclusivity was new.

Kaz understood the look: "My reason for keeping the site secret is sound, believe me. I am almost sure that what appears to be a small reef supporting the wrecks is in fact a deeper layer of even older vessels. If I'm right, it means they are very ancient; that the Chinese were making trading voyages beyond their own river and estuary systems way earlier than anyone dreamed. Long before even Jorge Alvarez's account of his journey to China in 1513, and even before the great Chinese explorer Zheng He, for instance. *If* I'm right."

The significance of these ancient mariners was lost on Pearl. Kaz continued her tutorial: "whether the layers constitute a time line or a series of sea-faring collisions is impossible to tell yet, but I'll lay all the proceeds from my book that it's not a natural formation. – You haven't read my book have you?"

It was not the turn Pearl expected the conversation to take. "Um, how come that's a problem?" Kaz pursed her pretty mouth in reprimand.

"I know you. All you ever read is fashion magazines."

"Well," said Pearl, "I read the beginning and the end. You know I don't have much leisure time ...."

"Where is Squid Cove?"

"I don't think you exactly spell that out, do you? Just that it's south of here." She waved her arms airily to the south, in the general direction of Macau, Singapore, the Philippines, Australia ....

"Spot on. If I had revealed where it is, the site would be stripped bare by now, by salvage-divers, treasure-hunters, anyone with a pair of plastic flippers and a set of goggles who can stay under water for two minutes. *That* is why my book is selling so well. As well as being a subject of great academic interest – as I'm sure you'd agree it was if you'd read the bloody thing – it is also a mystery story." She walked unsteadily across the vast room to the window. The afternoon sun had polished the harbour to copper and it outlined the edges of the bandage so that it looked like a helmet of fire. Inside the wrappings, her head now felt like it was on fire too.

"At book signings, people ask me to inscribe the flyleaf map. My publisher says that's because they think I will subconsciously sign my name over the site. Needless to say, Squid Cove does not exist. That doesn't stop one particular day-tour operator though. He takes people to the uninhabited end of Cheung Chau Island and tells them that's where the wrecks are. See what I'm up against?" She shook her head.

"Then there are the difficulties with the site itself, particularly in recording the placement of materials. Everything is likely to have been moved around – by settling, water action, storms, tidal surges, fish – you know what water's like."

"Kaz ...." Pearl feared the tutorial would become a lecture.

"Let me finish, Pearl. I've wanted to tell you where it is for some time. Someone apart from me needs to know and now, if we are going to work together it would be a sign of bad faith for you not to know. I liked what you said about making a difference ...." There was a knock at the door and she stopped in mid-sentence. Danny Tsiu waited outside, a stack of folders in his hands. He looked expectantly at Pearl and glanced at his watch.

"Danny, hi! Come in. Kaz, you worry too much. Just say yes. Do some research. Do we confine the scheme to Hong Kong students or go regional or even further? Think about it. Let me know quickly. I want to get on with setting this thing up."

"I have thought about it and of course I'll do it. That's what I was about to say too. How could I pass this up?" Kaz kissed Pearl and hugged her. Pearl smiled. Danny looked at his boss's radiant face, papers forgotten. Pearl was smiling, really smiling. It was a rare event and when it happened, it was a show stopper.

But Pearl hadn't finished. "The apartment. It's Dr Benson's old place on Upper Albert Road. It's very nice and it's stuffed with the loveliest antique furniture. Benson had excellent taste. Sit down Danny, please. Kaz and I are nearly through here and I've lots to tell you."

"Dr Benson's place. Didn't he come back to Hong Kong after all?"

"No. He lives in Japan, took up Zen Bhuddhism after *he* had a nasty knock on the head, as I recall." Kaz ignored her. "His apartment came up for sale two years ago." Pearl's jaw tightened a little. "My mother was at his apartment the day before she died and I was supposed to meet her there. But it didn't happen." She flicked at her hair, dismissing a thought. "So when the place came on the market, I was curious enough to have a look. There was a framed photograph of mum in the sitting room and when I saw it, I felt as though she had waited for me after all. So I bought the apartment."

Kaz gathered up her briefcase in a bright attempt to look busy. She could have cried. She dropped a quick kiss on the top of Pearl's head. How easy it was going to be to leave England, especially since her father had died, as well as the divorce ... all she had to do was turn down the Cambridge job and pack a few boxes. She felt the tears coming after all. She wiped her hand across her face as though tired:

"Right. I'll be back next week then. I'm going back to the museum if I dare and then I'd better clean up for this conference. Turning up looking like this won't cut it with the New Archaeologists, I can tell you. Very sophisticated, they are. And I'll let the Curator know that there is no additional information that you can give about the little pin artefact then, shall I? A flat in Upper Albert Road? Well well, even my mother would have been impressed." She waved farewell and left the room. She had drawn new energy from the conversation and it exuded from every pore. Pearl smiled again. She hadn't seen Kaz look like that for a long time now. Kaz was back.

Wednesday 10 August: 7.30pm

The Boeing dipped and Kaz willed her stomach not to lurch as the port wing dipped so steeply that it seemed to disappear beneath the belly of the plane. The 707 was positioning itself for the hair-raising theatre of landing at Hong Kong's Kai Tak Airport. At the approach, it took a long swooping bow over the roofs of the jumbled landscape of Kowloon's buildings. But the pilot's run was too short and he long-looped the aircraft back out to sea to execute an even steeper approach. Kaz sighed. Yes. Just another Kai Tak landing.

Kai Tak Airport occupies an extended peninsula of reclaimed land in Kowloon Bay and the landing approach is said to be one of the scariest in the world, for the crew as much as for the passengers. Most buildings in Kowloon are restricted to three stories in height, and as the plane dipped its bulk earthwards for the second approach, the people in the top floor apartments were clearly visible. To land successfully without ploughing into the airport buildings, the pilot had to touch down as near the interface of airstrip and harbour as possible. This manoeuvre was never pleasant. The landing strip had been built for smaller aircraft than the relatively new 707s. As the pilot brought it down with the familiar jerk of tyres hitting the ground as the brakes were simultaneously applied, there was loud cheering and clapping from the passengers.

A veteran of more than fifty touch-downs, Kaz let go of the small ebony scarab she wore around her neck and joined in the celebrations with a rather mannish whistle. She cleared Customs without any problems and stepped out into the oppressive evening heat. The streets were crowded and although there was nothing but the familiar noise and street bustle of Kowloon at night, she felt uneasy. She felt, and Kaz even almost apologised to herself for being so dramatic, as though she was being watched.

She reminded herself that it was only a week since the museum incident. She had left Hong Kong for London on the early flight the day after and the week that followed was a blur of packing boxes and rearranging her life, such as it was, in England. She put her uneasy feelings down to fatigue and when the driver of the first taxi that came along was happy to take her over to Hong Kong Island, Kaz got into the cab gratefully. The thought of lugging her heavy suitcases on and off the Star ferry after such a long flight had little appeal. She settled into the smart, obviously very new vehicle. She would go to her new flat, have a shower and ring Pearl. Maybe she would come around for a drink. Then tomorrow, she would start organising office space, resources .... Kaz dozed and by the time the vehicle reached Garden Road she was asleep. Did she feel the jab of the needle before sleep became unconsciousness? Even if she did, she was certainly unaware that the driver had changed direction and was weaving his way through the evening traffic towards The Peak, instead of turning right from Garden Road to her destination in Upper Albert Road.

*

At eleven o'clock Pearl started to worry. Even if Kaz had been held up in Customs she should have reached the flat in Upper Albert Road not much after nine o'clock. On the other hand, Kaz may have spent time with a Customs Officer. She was notorious for carting odd bits and pieces around and often roused the suspicions of Customs officials. Pearl rang the airport. The flight had landed at 7.30pm, and all baggage was cleared. Pearl yawned, went into the kitchen and poured herself a beer. She sat on one of the settees in the vast living room and picked up her personally inscribed copy of Kaz's book, the title of which was simply: *South-East Asian Marine Archaeology*.

She had not realised how carefully Kaz had concealed her excavation site until their conversation of the previous week, and was becoming increasingly curious about where it could possibly be. She browsed the text again for clues. It was crowded with material about the small islands that lay to the south and south west of the Hong Kong Island group. Squid Cove could be anywhere.

She looked at the flyleaf map again and thought about the pathways of the typhoons that sweep through the South China Sea most years, and ransacked her memories for stories about islands that had been ravaged and those that had been left undamaged by the passing wind-driven nightmares of weather. Kaz's wrecks may have been sheltering in such a location when they were caught by the ravages of some ancient wind-blow.

Pearl remembered that there is a typhoon-shelter at Cheung Chau. She flicked through the text and studied the index for entries about Cheung Chau – lots, but all related to archaeological finds made on the island at different times when the land was re-worked for agricultural purposes.

She went to the long, antique, architect's desk that her mother had bought for next to nothing in a junk shop in Hollywood Road. It stood behind the sofa, its various parts mysteriously adapted for many functions. Pearl lifted up the middle section so that it became an easel and clipped a map of Hong Kong to it. She fetched Kaz's book and looked again at the schematic map that decorated the fly-leaf.

As she studied both maps Pearl realised that something was missing. She could make out Cheung Chau and Peng Chau. It was the island between them that wasn't there. She felt an unbidden rush of excitement. She knew the missing island, a tiny volcanic outcrop about one and a half miles in area and shaped like a capital L. In the hinge of the "L" there is a cove. Hei Ling Chau is a very quiet, poorly known and rarely visited place, which supported a community of about ten farming families until the 1950s when it was taken over for government uses. There once was a ferry service but due to lack of demand in recent years that stopped.

The only way of getting there is by private means and even then an entry permit is required. The island has been a leprosarium for more than twenty years and these days it still has about 150 patients in varying stages of the illness, even though new cases of leprosy are becoming increasingly rare. Pearl remembered that there had once been talk about siting an official typhoon-shelter there but nearby Cheung Chau was considered a superior site. The decision about the typhoon-shelter was probably the last time Cheung Chau's smaller neighbour had come to any form of public attention, and that was more than fifteen years ago.

Pearl's five foot ten inch frame was now slumped over the desk. She straightened up and pushed her shoulders back to ease the tension that she felt settling into the muscles around her neck. She had found Kaz's wreck site. She'd be willing to put money on it.

Now, where was Kaz?

Thursday 11 August: 8.00am

BJ Cresswell picked up the phone. She was in bed. The phone was a muted ivory colour, and blended with the neutral theme of the master bedroom of the Robinson Road flat which she had rented upon arriving in Hong Kong two months earlier. On this particular morning she had company, Herbie Proust. Herbie was a member of the Hong Kong Police Force, a Detective Sergeant attached to the Narcotics Bureau and this morning, he was under the bed's grey and taupe-striped duvet cover when the phone rang, administering an unexpected – and as the phone continued to ring and she became agitated – possibly a rather inconvenient level of pleasure to BJ.

As she picked up the handpiece it flashed through her mind that she was about to come if he didn't stop.

"Herbie, Herbie." She wriggled her legs together but he pried open her slim white thighs with amazing ease and by the time BJ said "Hello?" Herbie had inserted himself firmly into her.

He relaxed for a second and exhaled. BJ forgot the call, squealed and pulled him in deeper. She dropped the phone. He thrust hard, head buried into her shoulder, shoulders arched, hands braced against the bedhead.

"Uhoooooo." She came again.

"Errrrrrrh." He slumped against her.

She picked the phone up. "Hello?"

"Cresswell Public Relations?" There was an element of shock evident in the man's voice.

"Private relations at the moment, darling. What can I do for you?" BJ recognised the voice. It was John Simons, one of her regulars.

"Bit of a problem, BJ. A client of mine has run into a difficulty. The situation requires – a female touch – as it were." His voice was pleasingly clipped but with a whiff of a background bark that suggested former military service.

"Mmh. Who is involved?"

"A woman. The fact is, I am about to take her back to her apartment but I don't quite know what to do after that. The matter needs careful handling. Needs a little PR, as I said, and I also want you to make quite sure she doesn't have anything on her that I may have – I'm sure you'll understand what I'm saying BJ – may have had difficulty locating. Regardless, make sure she doesn't remember the last twenty-four hours, will you?" He gave her an address. "I'll leave the key for you under a pot near the front door. OK?"

"Sounds do-able. I can take care of that for you." BJ was surprised. The address was in Upper Albert Road, one of Hong Kong's most posh residential areas outside of The Peak District. She looked at Herbie, aware that he was a cop. "Is the, er, tenant still out? Good. I'll bring extra resources just in case." She smiled at Herbie, who smoked, happily oblivious to the conversation, just as he now seemed oblivious to BJ. She offered him breakfast, but he wasn't interested, said he had to get to work, and they left the flat at the same time with a vague undertaking to meet up again some time.

BJ followed Herbie's taxi to a building in Hing Long Lane and she watched him enter the Bright Sparrow Building, which must be where he worked. It was a pretty sleazy end of town and BJ found it interesting that the Hong Kong Police Service would locate their Narcotics Bureau in such a place and she wrote down the address before directing the taxi-driver to take her back to Upper Albert Road. She was about to go in through the gate to No. 28 when John Simons and another man closed the door of the flat on the ground floor. She paused and admired the gardenia hedge and smoothly moved out of their range of sight.

John looked washed out but the other guy, a tall Asian man who carried a metal walking-stick, looked as though the sun was about to come up in his face. She wondered if he was the client John was always badgering her about – if it was him, he was a heavy user and there had even been times recently when BJ had sacrificed some of her personal stock to keep him happy. BJ didn't like the way he swung his walking-stick like a weapon. *Not a punter to get on the wrong side of.*

*

Kaz woke up. Was she in hospital? She remembered something that didn't seem to fit with where she was now. She had been lying on a bed and there was a window high up in the wall then. But this time was different. She was lying on a sofa in a sitting room and the sun streamed onto a nearby balcony on which there were tropical plants in beautiful, weathered stone pots. A pair of potted palms guarded the doorway and gently waved their clear green fronds at her. She lifted her head. It hurt.

She heard a domestic sort of noise, and tried to look as though she was asleep. It wasn't hard. A female voice said: "Wake up. You must wake up." Then someone smacked her face which made her eyes flick open almost reflexively. Her head hurt again. Some hairs on her head shifted with the movement. That hurt too.

"Wake up. You have an item belonging to a client of mine and he wants it back. It is a small pin in the shape of a circle, with some stones around the edge. It's like a lapel pin. He wants to know if you have it." Kaz registered that the woman was blonde and wore a white suit. She hit Kaz again, harder this time.

"Whaa ...."

"Exactly. The owner wants it back. No hard feelings."

"I don't ...."

"Have it. Of course not, but just give it back will you and stop mucking everyone about or things will become unpleasant for you." The voice was impatient. "My instructions are quite clear – take delivery of this item in any way I can. No-one will be any the wiser and my client will have his little treasure back safe and sound."

"Photograph ...."

"He doesn't want a photograph, he wants the item. Drink this coffee, that's the girl. Sit up first, and watch my suit won't you. It's just back from the cleaners." The first gulp of coffee was blissfully hot and it had a remarkable effect on Kaz. She sat up and looked the woman up and down. Her head was clear, her wits sharp, but it only lasted a second or two. The hallucinogen that BJ had put into the coffee kicked in almost instantly and its sharp edge dissolved and Kaz watched the blonde's face distort into a swollen orb, with the white suit sucked into it until finally the entire mass absorbed itself.

Some time later another face ballooned into her line of vision. This one looked familiar and worried and the foreshortened body to which it barely seemed attached rushed across the room to her and stroked her head and held her hand until a white van came. It was two days before Kaz surfaced from the dose of LSD that BJ had given her, which effectively topped up the injection of heroin that the taxi-driver had administered the previous evening. Kaz would only ever remember snippets of those hours. The memory of being watched, the closed room and a white suit was a different matter though. She would have trouble shaking those.

Clearly, she had briefly gone mad.

Tuesday 16 August: 9.30am

BJ's bottom went into an exaggerated wiggle again as she strained to maintain her balance. Six-inch heels did not encourage a graceful ascent of the steep sandstone steps that led to the entrance of The Peninsula Hotel. Jeremy Freeman was fascinated by the wallowing white pencil-skirted backside labouring ahead of him, as much as he was fascinated by the woman's head of hair, which was such a uniform shade of platinum blonde that it could have been natural.

He tried not to follow the sway of the white-clad buttocks. His old enemy, vertigo, could be invoked from sails far less gloriously slung, like those on the yacht in which he occasionally roamed Hong Kong Harbour. Jeremy sighed and puffed a little as he reached the top step. The trouble with being in one's mid-forties was that one started to puff a little now and then. He turned and looked at the view and gulped for breath as he lit a cigarette. He nodded pleasantly to the doorman and walked into the hotel.

Now where had his lovely "white witch" gone?

*

Emmie Franklin had one of Hong Kong's best views from her office, across the harbour, with enchanting Victoria Peak framed centrally in the window. The space was elegant and refined, much like Emmie herself.

"Come!"

Emmie was PR Manager for The Peninsula Hotel and at thirty-five was at the height of both her beauty and her career. She wore her habitual costume – a black embossed silk cheong-sam that was slashed to the thigh, even though the hem ended modestly at mid-calf. BJ opened the door and when Mrs Franklin indicated that they should both sit in the visitor's chairs, BJ stared at Emmie's creamy thighs for a second too long.

"Something wrong, Miss Cresswell?"

"Not at all, Mrs Franklin. I was just admiring your traditional dress."

"I never wear anything but the cheong-sam. It is not so much traditional, as a mark of respect to my culture." BJ looked around the office impassively while Emmie re-read her application for the job of PR assistant. Her work history was brief, to say the least.

"You have a considerable gap in your work history. How long have you been in Hong Kong, Miss Cresswell?"

"Just two months, Mrs Franklin. I've been travelling for the last two years and came here for a holiday. I like Hong Kong very much and would like to stay if I can get a job, but there doesn't seem to be much happening in PR here, which is surprising, given the level of activity in the film industry." BJ avoided mention of what she had been doing while out of PR.

"Imported, Miss Cresswell. All the offshore film-makers bring their own PR people and the local film-makers have their own contacts, mostly with expanding agencies, not established bodies such as we represent at The Peninsula. Most get on, due to friends and family contacts. You know the sort of thing."

BJ didn't know the sort of thing. She had no family, no friends and very few contacts.

"What happened to the previous assistant, if you don't mind me asking, Mrs Franklin?" BJ's voice changed tone with the question, her east London roots evident and very different to the London drawl she preferred to affect.

Anxious, darling? thought Emmie Franklin.

*

Emmie was having a moment. Dressed with elegant simplicity and wonderfully groomed and made up, she wandered through life drawing lust, admiration, love at first sight, envy, name it – she drew it all – without effort. She wore her jet hair coiled high above her beautiful and serene brow, which topped a face of classic oriental beauty. People would literally stop and stare at her. Even four years after their marriage, her husband – who was the Chief Executive of Hong Kong's International Sports Associaton – still stared at her over the breakfast table each morning, the dinner table each night, and from whatever sexual position he nominated for them at bedtime.

Emmie usually felt longings for no-one. But she did now. The woman who sat in the visitor's chair was walking sex, and according to her profile, was not even twenty-one. Emmie had a delirious surge of desire. Emmie was a lesbian but had not bedded a woman since she had married Mr Franklin, at which time she had stoically sworn off sex with women for good. Her liaisons with women had been without exception disastrous, personally and career-wise and

Hong Kong, liberated though it considered itself to be, was prudish about overt same-sex relationships.

*

"What duties does the job entail, Mrs Franklin? I have to be sure that the position can fulfil at least some of my career aspirations if I am to get on in PR." The clear London tones had returned and Emmie's eyes clouded a little with lust as she let them stroke her, reminiscing over the amorous early days of her affair with another Peninsula Hotel employee, Anneka Stone. Anneka had a very chiselled English expatriate accent that also drifted off into a wry London nasality at times. She paused and knitted her fingers together, willing herself to stop thinking about women and concentrate on the job at hand, that of finding a decent assistant.

"It will entail a lot of routine work as well as some extra-curricular duties, Miss Cresswell. Can you accommodate that?"

BJ smiled and nodded.

"Oh yes."

*

BJ knew that her time was coming. There had been a portent of it in America, she thought she had it by the balls in Tokyo, but it was going to happen here, in Hong Kong of all places. This was where she knew she was going to get her big break. This was where she was going to make her mark.

BJ had followed two of her classmates from school to America after they did their GCE "O" Levels, but all she found was a bunch of hippies threatening to change world dynamics with free love. BJ already knew better. She watched as her pals became mesmerised by the hippy men they took up with. BJ just thought they were like all men, they just wanted their own way but instead of beating their women up to get it, they gained control with a sing song, patronising dominance. BJ's American legacy was something different – she took away a drug habit and the realisation that sex could be put to better uses than free love.

BJ wanted money and sex was the only way she knew of to get it. She could read the expression in Emmie's eyes easily. BJ's armoury in her bid for world domination included a level of sexual experience way beyond her twenty years. She knew the look of lust. It was always the same.

This job is mine. Play it straight now and I'll bed the bitch later to keep her happy.

"I'm known as being very accommodating, Mrs Franklin. I'm young, I've got talent and I'm free. Life's out there and I want it."

Emmie sighed. She knew exactly what she meant.

Tuesday 16 August: 10.30am

Pearl unlocked the door to Flat 1, 28 Upper Albert Road. It was nearly a week since she had found Kaz there, unconscious on the couch, and she had only just been well enough for discharge from the Peak Hospital this morning. She had made a statement about what had happened as far as she knew and a copy of it was attached to her discharge papers. The original, as a matter of legal requirement, would be copied to the Hong Kong Police Drug Information Office and the resident Physician who had organised the paperwork warned her that the DIO were at liberty to hand information over to the Hong Kong Police Force's Narcotics Bureau if they thought a matter required further investigation.

She read it out to Pearl after they put their things down: "I remember feeling a little uneasy at the airport – I don't know why and the driver of the taxi I hired was willing to bring me over to Hong Kong side. I was tired and probably went to sleep. Then I remember being in a dark room with a high window and something white. The next thing I recall is waking up, and being told I was in hospital with a drug overdose."

Kaz folded up the paper and put it on a table. She looked around. "This apartment is beautiful." She didn't notice that Pearl was dabbing at her eyes with her fingers. Kaz had no recollection of having already been here, nor of Pearl finding her and calling for an ambulance. The two women looked around them. By any measure, the apartment was beautiful. The building, formerly a private home of stately proportions, was about 120 years old. It had a deep colonnaded southern balcony, complete with sandstone pillars, which gave it shelter from the heat and there was another, wider, open terrace on the north side, furnished with wrought iron furniture and hung with baskets of ferns and potted orchids.

The floor was carpeted in beige-grey wool on which rested a number of antique pieces. Nothing lightweight, just solid nineteenth-century rosewood Chinese furniture, made at a time when elaborate ornamentation was scorned in favour of highlighting the grain of the wine-coloured wood. Kaz sucked in her breath when she saw the bathroom. It was all cold grey and white marble and gleaming rosewood cabinetry.

"Benson has good taste," said Pearl. She looked around with pleasure. "He left everything here. I even had to get rid of his clothes and shaving stuff." She stroked the photograph of her mother that sat in a silver frame on the sideboard that dominated the living room. June Bowen's beautiful features regarded them sternly from under the brim of her Blue Cross Group hat. Her eyes were squinting as if in strong sunlight, and the detail of her dress had faded with time. For all that she was a beautiful woman and the likeness between her and Pearl was clearly evident.

"Peter Benson and mum were lovers once." Pearl picked up the photograph. "I'll take it away."

"No, Pearl, she belongs here with me. I adored your mother, you know that. She was so different to my poor old mum. I used to think of your mother as being a sort of upper-class bohemian, a trend-setter – not that I would ever have said anything like that to her. She would have been appalled. How trendy is that?"

Pearl put the picture back, still looking at it fondly. "Kaz, I'm worried about you. I really should stay here, you know. You don't seem to be popular in some quarters."

Kaz was sitting on the sofa where Pearl had found her and Pearl tried to not find it spooky that she had absolutely no recall of having been in the apartment before, no memory of waking up and sipping from the cup of LSD-laced coffee before her mind cast off its familiar anchors and she floated off into some entirely different space altogether.

"What happened to me last week is obvious. It's to do with my work, Pearl." Her voice sank: "It's simple. I've been attacked because of the promise of money." She frowned and picked at her fingers. "Lots of money. Lots."

Was Kaz right or was she being paranoid about her damned wrecks again? "If you really think so, why don't you just go public with the site's location and squash the mystery surrounding it? Isn't there some international body that can seal it off for preservation?" said Pearl.

"No, there isn't, and anyway, why should I go public?" Kaz was shocked. "Sales of my book are close to 23,000 copies now. That's all but 3,000 sales in the last two weeks. Has the academic story tickled people's imaginations? No way! There's a lottery out there that can be won, with a little daring, or a little kidnapping or a little drugging, perhaps.

"I'm bankable, Pearl. And don't forget that I did all the work myself –found the wrecks, did all the dives, everything. No-one wanted to be associated with a crummy Ph.D. student trying to prove all the pundits wrong by finding the wrecks of some early trading ships in the South China Sea. Why should I just give all that away?"

Not far under Kaz's defiance was anxiety, much anxiety. "As for the museum incident – I was certainly there at the wrong time, but the fact that my name appeared in the paper connected me with the robbery, and then the airport business last week is something else. Whoever picked me up knew what flight I was on and had a little dose lined up for me by a compliant taxi-driver. I can't remember anything much at all. Oh Pearl, I have to get over to Squid Cove. I *have* to see if everything is secure...."

"You're going nowhere for at least a day or two, Kaz. I'll go over and check it out for you."

"You will? Oh you are a jewel...."

"You must be getting better."

"I'll just tell you where it is."

"No, let me tell you where it is, Kazzy. Your site is at the south-west cove on Hei Ling Chau Island." She smiled slightly. "It's as obvious as the colour draining from your face that I'm right. Anyone who knows the islands and has the wit to compare a district map with the diagram on the flyleaf of your book could spot it. You left off Hei Ling Chau between Peng Chau and Cheung Chau. A tiny little L-shaped island? – Kaz?"

Kaz cried, with shock, relief or frustration, Pearl couldn't tell. "I thought I was so bloody clever just leaving it off the map. I left out a few islands. How – ?"

"Simple. I know Hei Ling Chau. I didn't necessarily know why your map looked odd but it was bloody obvious something was

Red Bird Summer 29

missing. Now all we have to do is hope that there isn't another smartarse like me out there. But that's not the biggest problem, of course."

"What do you mean?" Kaz was tired again, and seemed worried. "Is it that easy to find the site or does your old connection to the island make you more aware of its location than most other people are?"

"I don't know and it's hardly relevant because there are other complications attached to your site that you don't seem to be aware of. By the way, I've arranged for Dr Benson's former housekeeper to come and look after you. She's a bit of a grim piece but she's a terrific housekeeper and if she likes you, she'll look out for you. She's going to stay in the servants' wing" – Pearl nodded in the direction of a corridor that led off at an angle to the bathroom – "which is a rare treat for her. Dr Benson never let her in the place if he wasn't here and that arrangement stood for the fifteen years she worked for him."

The doorbell rang on cue – Pearl had asked Mrs Chan to arrive at 11.00am. Mrs Chan stepped into the apartment lobby as though preparing to be led to execution. With head bowed she carried a package of food tied up in a cloth, a small canvas bag of belongings and her shoes. Pearl sighed. This would take a while but it would work. She turned and kissed Kaz on the forehead. "We'll get over this, Kaz. Tomorrow we may be able to make some plans if you feel up to it. Mrs Chan will help you unpack and settle in."

Kaz looked panicky. "Pearl, what are you going to do now?" She ferreted around in her handbag, looking for a tissue. She felt teary again. Her fingers closed around a card.

"I run an organisation, remember, duffer?"

"What's this card do you think, Pearl? It says BJ Cresswell, Cresswell Public Relations." Pearl took the small white card from Kaz's hand. It was adorned with flowing pale grey script. She turned it over. No contact number, no address. Just the name and the company name.

"You've no idea? Not an appointment card, a press contact maybe?"

"No, I'm sure I've never seen it before. It's useless, look, there's no address, no telephone number, no contact details at all."

Pearl walked to the slim desk that stood behind the sofa on which Kaz sat and consulted the Hong Kong Telephone Directory. "Let's see ...." She lapsed into silence and flicked through page after page. Eventually she snapped it shut. "Nothing. No Cresswells, no BJs, nothing under the Public Relations listing in the business section. Do you mind if I keep it?" She smiled casually, dropped another peck on the top of Kaz's head and left. But the smile she had forced for Kaz went when she closed the front door behind her. She walked to her car which was parked in the visitors' area beside the Governor's residence, and accelerated into Upper Albert Road in front of a line of vehicles that had stopped at the pedestrian lights near the apartments.

BJ Cresswell indeed. Clearly, Kaz was caught up in something very odd. Was it really about her work or could it linked to the theft at the museum? She changed gear and changed her mind at the same time, swung right at the end of Garden Road and headed towards Causeway Bay instead of going back to the office. She would go to the museum and talk to the Director, Albert Ho. He might be able to shed some light on it all.

Tuesday 16 August: mid-day

Kaz was summoned to luncheon – there could be no other word – which was to be eaten on the southern verandah. *Ah*, thought Kaz: *the Empire Bites Back*. A square white linen cloth was spread at an angle across the heavy wrought iron table and on it was a bowl of steaming brown-coloured soup, a plate of rindless cheese and lettuce sandwiches and a small cut-glass bowl that contained a number of austere Scottish digestive biscuits. The setting was further embellished with a silver teapot, jug and sugar bowl and a blue and white willow-design cup and saucer. Mrs Chan indicated the spread to Kaz and said gruffly: "Dinner at six o'clock, missy. OK?"

Kaz dawdled over the meal until Mrs Chan returned. The housekeeper was clearly delighted when she saw the empty soup bowl and plate. "All right, missy?"

Kaz smiled broadly at her. "All right, Mrs Chan? It was bloody lovely. You've made my day. Thank you." The two women beamed at one another. Kaz went into the bedroom where the wooden shutters were drawn against the heat and where a fan gravely stirred the heavy air. She liked the masculinity of the rosewood bed with its splendidly panelled headboard and the carefully turned-back white as white topsheet. She went to sleep immediately. Mrs Chan cleared the table and tidied the kitchen and informed herself in her low pitched voice that Miss Kaz was OK and that she would make her a small chicken and rice dinner.

With tea.

*

"BJ Cresswell." BJ smiled as she spoke her name into the phone and tilted her voice up on the final syllable of her name. Perhaps it would be Mrs Franklin from The Peninsula.

"You remember that matter you sorted out for me last week?"

"Oh it's you, John. Thank you for the reminder. I haven't billed you yet – two hours of my time and the medication amount to one thousand five hundred Hong Kong dollars."

"I'm surprised you've got the cheek to ask for payment after the stuff-up you made of the job, BJ. But don't bill me yet. I have something else for you to do. My client is convinced that Dr Henderson has his lost property, even though it didn't appear to be on her. My client is of the opinion that if you hadn't overdosed the bitch to the point where she ended up in hospital, there may have been a chance to get it back."

"I did as you asked, John, even down to body-searching her. She did not have the object your client described anywhere on her, and I *mean* anywhere. What more do you want done?" BJ was on her guard. It was late afternoon and rather than having the conversation she had hoped for – thanking Mrs Franklin for selecting her to be her PR Assistant, assuring her of every attention in every way etc. etc. – she was sparring with John Simons again. BJ needed a job. An ordinary job. With a regular income she could pick and choose her own private PR gigs and if she worked at The Peninsula, well, she would have exposure to any amount of rich contacts. But it seemed that yet another day was about to go by with no firm prospect of getting secure work. It was still hand to mouth, or prick to mouth if things stayed as they currently were, just to make ends meet. BJ was getting edgy.

"My client wants Dr Henderson set up. Thoroughly. Busted in possession of drugs. A lot of drugs. Can you organise that? Good. And BJ?"

"Yes?"

"I need supplies. The usual."

"I'll see what I can do. As for your little project, I'll do my bit but I won't get involved if there's any fall-out. Is that clear?"

"It's clear. Get onto your contact, or down on your contact or whatever you have to do and I'll pay for the earlier stuff-up and this new job. It needs to be done quickly. My client is getting edgy about getting his property back and he has a particularly nasty temper when thwarted."

BJ hung up and looked at the telephone. She loved it. It was so elegant – a special purchase she made after seeing one like it in France last year. She looked dreamily out of the apartment window. Another job to keep her afloat. Good. The rent was paid for a year, the result of two spectacular months of work in Tokyo, before she wound up in Hong Kong with no prospects except the names of two men she had been advised to meet – both susceptible to blonde companions. One of them was Herbie Proust. She had got her hands on Herbie all right but now it was a matter of how useful, if at all, he could be to her. She needed a regular supplier instead of taking the risks she was currently forced to take to get her drugs, by trawling the bars around Wanchai. Perhaps Herbie knew of such people through his job. Everyone said there was a lot of drugs corruption in the Police Force. Perhaps if she saw him again she might be able to persuade something useful out of him. She had to be careful though. If he was an honest cop ....

"Herbie? It's BJ. BJ Cresswell. You know ... we, ah, met a week or so ago. I was thinking – are you free for lunch?" She waited for the knock-back or the brusque enquiry as to how she had come by his number. What attraction was there in lunch with her to someone like him? They hadn't exactly talked much. But he agreed readily enough and they set a time for the following day.

Tuesday 16 August: 9.30pm

Pearl neither liked nor disliked Jeremy Freeman. He bored her more than anything, but as a professional contact, he was indispensable. He knew everyone and he had a very impressive way of classifying people. For Pearl it was like having access to an automatic demographic sorting house. Thanks to Jeremy, she had achieved some large donations for the June Bowen Foundation simply by knowing when people of influence would visit Hong Kong. He was also able to judge, from the occupations of people who landed in the place, what was likely to happen. He might bump into a bevy of strange hair-dressers and make-up artists so he knew the arrival of some major film name was imminent. He'd chat them up and hey voila! it would be Jeremy who'd get the scoop for the dailies.

He and Pearl sat at a table in Stormy's, Jeremy's newest favourite "illegal" in Cameron Street, Kowloon. It was supposed to have a gambling room at the back.

"Saw an intriguing woman the other day. Hong Kong now has a 'white witch', Pearl. I know her from somewhere," he announced. "Can't place her though. She looks like an old-style movie-star, right down to the platinum blonde hair and big bum. She's completely pale, skin and hair, and she wears heavy eye-make-up and has blazingly red lips. She's an anti-fashion statement."

Pearl was curious enough to ask why Jeremy had singled the woman out. He paused in the process of eating a dish of lotus root poached in sesame stock and took stock of his dinner companion. Pearl was dressed in a pale mauve and silver threaded silk halter-topped evening dress, the hem of which skimmed the top of her thighs, and she wore knee-high mauve leather high-heeled boots. Her hair was a halo of golden brown. Her face. Well, that was another matter, Pearl's face. He smiled gently.

"You're right, why single her out?" Why single her out, indeed when a chap was sitting next to a woman like Pearl Green? "Try a little of this snake fillet. Squirt the gallbladder juices over it. No. Like that." He took the small oval organ from Pearl's fingers and directed a stream of straw coloured juice over the top of the creamy white snake meat. "Gives it a citrus flavour." Pearl ate without hesitation. Her mother had been one of Hong Kong's top gourmets in her time, and Pearl was very familiar with the subtle taste of butter-seared cobra fillets. The addition of the gall-bladder juices was a novelty and her mother would have appreciated the citrusy tang it added to the dish.

"Jeremy, it's not that I'm not interested in your 'white witch'. You know I find all your foundlings fascinating, but I'm more interested in gossip at the moment. Gossip about a theft from the Hong Kong Archaeological Museum, to be precise. A magnificent bestiary collection was just whisked from the first gallery in early August and there was little more than a paragraph about it in the papers; and most of that was about Karen Henderson. Oddly, one of the stolen artefacts has a slight connection to my family. Any rumbles around?"

*

Jeremy continued to look at her fondly as she spoke. Pearl Green was his stellar social connection in Hong Kong, even though he was the one with the A-rated social life, which informed the content of his gossip columns for the Chinese and English weeklies. He was invited everywhere but he still didn't have what Pearl had. She was a member of Hong Kong's rarified set, odd, mostly isolated people who were for all that somehow tribal.

She had dominated the social pages when she was younger. Hong Kong was a little late in embracing the sixties and perhaps it lacked the atmosphere of socio-cultural change that hallmarked that period as forever unique in Britain and America, but it had enough glamour and chutzpah to attract all the key players – the models, film stars, producers, directors, pop stars and rock stars – everyone who went with the whole crazy tour group.

Hong Kong had rocked and Pearl had contributed to the legend for a time. But her personal circumstances were such that she had been forced to grow up very quickly and now – could she be much more than thirty? – she seemed to have been part of the old social stratosphere forever. She was his living treasure and as the sixties ended and the 1970s became established as the decade of sex and drugs, Jeremy felt nostalgic for the old days.

What satisfaction was there in reporting nowadays that some young thing was sharing men and needles, compared to the bright casual joy with which the earlier generation of socialites whirled through the sixties? They weren't quite in the same class. He sighed quietly. He had, futilely as always, hoped that Pearl had invited him to dinner for his company, but all she wanted was information.

*

"I know nothing about this, Pearl. Most people find archaeology as boring as bat shit so it's hardly surprising that it didn't make page one."

"But people aren't bored with rare antiquities, Jeremy. Antiquities equal money in people's minds, especially antiquities with the provenance of this collection."

"Then it's a criminal matter and I can't help you. I'm social. I'm sure you have your own contacts to consult in that regard." Pearl shrugged off the familiar veiled reference to her criminal connections. Yip Yee Koon was the last person she would go to and ask about the thefts. He might feel obliged to tell her and that could be very embarrassing for both of them. Silence settled between them. Jeremy offered to escort her home.

"If you remember why your 'white witch' intrigues you so much Jeremy, let me know. I'm on the lookout for anything strange going on in Hong Kong at the moment. I've got the interests of the JB Foundation to look out for and I am worried about my best friend's well being." They had reached the marble foyer of her apartment building and she pressed the buzzer to summon the lift. She made no move to ask him up for a nightcap.

He saluted and smiled. "Sure thing! Goodnight, Pearl."

But she had already disappeared into the lift.

Wednesday 17 August: 8.00am

Kaz looked with delight at the potted rainforest orchid that thrived on the balcony. It shed a breathy halo of amethyst light from the damp, early sun. The bedroom doors were open and the air that streamed into the room was still cool, ravishingly cool. Mrs Chan brought in a breakfast tray. Kaz smiled at her carer and exclaimed, again to her amah's delight, "I swear Mrs Chan, you are spoiling me!"

Mrs Chan was radiant. In all the years she had worked for Dr Benson there had been little thanks for any services rendered; she had never had a key to the apartment, nor had she ever been permitted entry while he was away. True, he had always paid her whether she worked or not and so she had done well, as she was frequently able to work for others when the Doctor was absent. But now she had her own key, her own room and bathroom and a housekeeping budget. Mrs Chan was in heaven.

Kaz had ladled a second copious helping of jam onto a piece of toast from the tray of goodies that Mrs Chan delivered at precisely 7.45am before it occurred to her, between munches, that she felt normal, completely normal. She flung back the sheets and walked briskly across the room to the bathroom, showered and dressed in her favourite slacks, shirt, and walking boots. She packed her leather fieldwork bag and sought out Mrs Chan, who was in the kitchen. "Mrs Chan, I'm going out. I have a key, so if you need to go to the market, don't worry if I'm not here. I'll be back for dinner. OK? You make sure you eat too, please. Bye bye."

Mrs Chan beamed happily. She was also unused to being instructed to take care of herself.

*

Kaz walked to Queen's Road Central via Albert Path, one of the elegant curved pathways that connect Upper Albert Road to Hong Kong's lower urban levels. It had rained overnight and the streets gleamed with dampness; there was already a faint smell of tar in the humid air. She inhaled. She loved it. A taxi came by and tooted. She eyed it off carefully but decided to let it go by and instead jumped on a tram and rode south for a couple of miles and smiled and waved at a group of workers who found the *gwaipor*'s company on the antiquated transport system hysterically funny. Pearl was in the kitchen when she arrived at the Connaught Road flat, busy re-drafting the press announcement of Kaz's appointment as Director of what was now referred to on paper as the Bowen Foundation's Research & Scholarship Scheme. It was time to go public.

"Have a read and let me know what you think. It will be in tomorrow's *South China Morning Post.* You look amazing by the way, Kazza. How do you feel?" Pearl took off the tortoiseshell framed clear glass reading-glasses that she wore in the belief that it focussed her eyes more efficiently on the mounds of paperwork she waded through, day in, day out. It quietly amused Kaz how Pearl would re-focus her vision when she removed them. She would really have to speak to her about it – sometime. When it *stopped* being amusing, perhaps.

"I feel terrific. All the stuff must have finally left my system. I could run to the top of Victoria Peak if I wasn't so worried about Squid Cove. She helped herself to a cup of instant coffee and Pearl buttered two thick slices of fresh brioche and pushed them toward her. Kaz ate her second breakfast hungrily.

"Well let's go over there, now," said Pearl. "By the way, I had the most wonderful snake dish last night. We must go to Stormy's. You'll love it." She swallowed and gulped rather noisily. She was starving. Eating snake always had that effect on her. "Kaz," she said, licking buttery fingers, "We have to clear something up about Squid Cove. It's a quarantine zone – a restricted entry health site. You worked there unauthorised when you did your Ph.D.. That's not on, not now."

"I didn't know."

"I don't believe you. I think you knew exactly where you were. While we're there, check out your site and I'll talk with the Matron, Matron Cheung. She'll be pleased to see me after all these years. She doted on mum and they were good friends in their way. She is responsible for authorising visitor access. We don't have to give her chapter and verse about your work – we'll just tell her that you're doing some survey work around the beach area."

"What if she knows about my book?" Pearl grabbed her friend by the arm and marched her towards the lift.

"I doubt Matron Cheung reads much in English and unless it has already been translated I think that's one problem you can strike off your list. Pheww, Kaz. You do paranoia well." They crossed the lobby to the front door of the Fire Service HQ and pushed their way through the traffic that swarmed along Connaught Road. Kaz's walking pace forced the taller Pearl into a longer stride in order to keep up.

*

It was only eight o'clock on a regular Wednesday morning but Pearl felt like celebrating. Instead of taking the lift downstairs and unlocking the office, she had just walked out of the front door of the building and was now heading for the harbour. There was even a tossy little breeze that flattened the emerging hum of heat and threw the fine ends of her hair around like little mare's-tails.

"Isn't this great, Kaz?"

Kaz smiled at her. Pearl hadn't been in love yet. *That* was great. But this was OK.

Wednesday 17 August: 11.30am

BJ waited until half past eleven before she rang Herbie. When he came to the phone, she wailed at him: "Herbie, I'm downtown and I've broken the heel of my shoe."

"Ah, BJ. I'm glad you called. I can't come to lunch after all. You'll have to get yourself a cab. Sorry."

"Oh Herbie. I haven't got enough moneeeeeeeey ...." She cried pitifully into the phone in the public phone box. "Oh Herbie, come and get me?"

"Where are you, luv?"

"Just a minute, I'm near some lane. Hing Long Lane. It's off Des Voeux Road West."

"What are you doing there?"

"I'm looking for a location for a client of mine. He wants to film a scene from a movie in a rundown part of Hong Kong."

"Well, you're on the money there. Look, you're near my office. You can come here. Walk down Hing Long Lane until you come to a building called the Bright Sparrow and take the lift to the top floor. There's a buzzer." She hung up and smiled gently at the phone. *Of course there's a buzzer. It's the Narcotics Bureau isn't it? I'm also sure there's a couple of highly sensitive alarms and cameras too.* She left the phone booth and walked confidently to the building. Before getting into the lift, knocked the heel of her shoe against the door grill until it came loose. She dangled it in her hand and hummed under her breath as the lift took her to the seventh floor.

*

It was a forty minute trip by water-taxi to Hei Ling Chau and Sim Yun-Wing was happy to wait for his customers to make the return trip. He thought that Hei Ling Chau was a monastery for a minor order of monks. This was a popular misconception of many Hong Kong residents who had either forgotten that a leprosarium had been built on the tiny speck of volcanic rock back in the 1950s or chose to forget it. These days, the hospital had fewer and fewer patients. The disease was slowly becoming less prevalent and admissions of new cases decreased every year with the introduction of new treatment drugs.

While the craft bounced south across a slightly choppy South China Sea, Pearl thought about Kaz and her work. The reality was that the foundation would be a secondary interest to Kaz's post-doctoral interests. June Bowen, Pearl's mother, had done occasional volunteer work at the hospital and Pearl knew Hei Ling Chau well. There were two visitors' villas in the grounds of the hospital, which she thought Matron would probably agree to renting out to them for use during what was obviously going to be a long-haul excavation, especially if Kaz continued to refuse to trust anyone but the two of them to know the location of the wrecked ships.

Then there was the issue of being safe on the island at all, while the leprosarium remained there. Pearl's frown cleared. It was so bloody obvious. She would simply buy Hei Ling Chau, move the patients to a better location and convert the building into a general community hospital and outreach clinic for the many people who lived on the small outlying islands. It could start operating after Kaz's excavations were completed.

She smiled with delight. *Is this the effect of taking a day off? Or perhaps it is the effect of eating snake. They say it clears mists from the brain.* Pearl had long thought about doing something for the southern Hong Kong island communities. If the site of Kaz's discovery was even half as extensive as she was expecting it to be, the work could be done safely with proper security and buildings to store the contents of the ships. When the excavations were over and done with, the buildings could be re-assigned to other uses.

Pearl hummed and looked over the side of the little boat. She felt light-hearted, a bit as she had when she sat in the Archaeological Museum waiting-room the previous afternoon, after she had decided on the spur of the moment to visit the Director, Albert Ho. Albert had not even pretended to welcome her enquiry into the robbery, and rudely showed little interest in what he seemed to see as her supposed concern about the small pin artefact. No, her moment happened before she went into his office and waited in reception while Albert took a call. That was the remarkable part of the afternoon's events, for it came to her that it was time to think about doing something strictly for herself; to even take a different direction in life.

The thought was a one-off, a notion from the blue. Pearl had thought of nothing except the June Bowen Foundation for eleven years. It had been her total focus through her entire adult life so far. But the thought that came to her was pre-cast, solid and persistent, and she had let it travel through her mind where it had played out as if she were watching a short film. The meeting with Albert was brief and she found it hard to concentrate. He seemed angry about the thefts and if he knew anything, he wasn't about to tell her. They parted with their usual level of mild mutual hostility. Albert had been one of her mother's lovers and the only time her choice of companion had ever been of concern to Pearl. Fortunately, the affair was brief and her mother had backed off from him. She never spoke of him to Pearl.

And now here she was, bumping along in a boat and experiencing a strange throb of adolescent anticipation that was like fire in her veins and as brilliant as the golden lights that the morning sun lit up in her best friend's rich brown hair.

Wednesday 17 August: 11.45am

Detective Sergeant Herbie Proust had served with the Hong Kong Police Force for ten years, five of them with the Narcotics Bureau. The Force's Drugs Unit occupied premises in downtown Hong Kong, well away from Central Division HQ. The unit occupied the entire seventh floor of the Bright Sparrow Building, a former private primary school. Access to the seventh floor was monitored by an elaborate alarm system that started at the lift. As well as offices, remand and interrogation cells, the Narcotics Bureau acted as a storage site for quarantined illegal drugs.

Herbie was one of the contacts BJ's Tokyo mentor had given her –a straight cop but with a known weakness for blondes. When BJ met him at Simpson's Bar the previous week, his attraction to her was very obvious and she thought it sufficiently worthwhile to entice him into an encounter, to see if he could be useful to her in some other way. It was rarely difficult for BJ to entice men into an encounter. She came over as a casual lay, with no complicated agenda. Her equipment screamed availability, and Herbie had responded accordingly. After a couple of drinks, she took him to her flat for what she assumed would be the usual quickie.

Herbie was a surprise. There was the standard wham bam thank you ma'am dining-room-table exercise but then he stayed on and they moved into the bedroom where to her surprise, they made passionate love. It had been a long time since BJ had made love and the night that followed and the next morning were a rare treat for her. But it was during the night when he finally slept that her major interest in Herbie Proust arose.

Herbie talked in his sleep. And talked. He muttered about a wall of white. He moaned and tossed his head around while BJ watched him, sifting through the words, thinking of her own theme of white and where it had led her during the past two years. He was probably just dream-rambling but there could be something else behind it. She needed an opportunity to get ahead in Hong Kong. The money she had earned in Tokyo was running low. She had not intended to take in clients for paid sex here, but so far had had little choice but to do so. And BJ knew that was a risky business in a place like Hong Kong, which so expertly took the measure of all newcomers.

Herbie had been her one non-paying indulgence. With his connections, he could also be the key to her opportunity to get ahead.

*

"Thanks, Herbie. You're a love. May I come in?"

Herbie shut down the screening camera near a set of grills in a holding area outside the lift door. The lift was in its own little compound, separated from a second entrance by a reinforced wire cage. The lift was the only entry and exit to the entire floor. There was no fire escape up to the seventh floor and if there ever was a fire everyone would be cooked. He looked BJ over. She was a gorgeous piece of work. She wore a low-necked sheer grey blouse tucked into the waist of a tight, short, white skirt and her large pale breasts rose in two sumptuous curves from a row of frilly ruffles. Her platinum hair was drawn up into a high bun and she had a white leather handbag slung over her shoulder on a long gold chain. She held a pair of very high-heeled, white, patent-leather shoes in her other hand. The heel of one of them dangled at a tragic angle. He looked at her breasts speculatively but made no move toward her.

She followed his eyes and looked up at him invitingly. No reaction at all.

Cameras, she thought, *there must be more cameras*. She followed him across a no-man's land of bare linoleum floor and he unlocked a door. Beyond the door was another reception area. *Two layers of entry so far.* She noticed that the second foyer beyond the lift entrance was guarded by yet another grilled door which also had two cameras mounted in opposite corners, one trained on the lift and the other on the door through which they were about to walk. BJ wondered if they held suspects here. Perhaps all the equipment was about people-security, not anything else.

"We're not supposed to permit unauthorised personnel beyond the foyer, but today's your lucky day, luv. Apart from Mrs Latham, I'm the only one here. She's deaf as a post and everyone else is out doing fire training. I'm it. Hope there's not a big bust."

"Well, let's go out for lunch then if there's no-one else here. Who'd know?" She looked at him, clearly disappointed that their date was off.

"Sorry. I can't leave. I'll fix you up with a taxi back to your place if you're skint. I don't want you ever to come back here again though, got it? The Chief Inspector would have my guts for garters if he knew I'd let a punter in here."

He was clearly uncomfortable, so she took his arm and pressed her breasts against him. So far he hadn't seemed to bother about how she had managed to ring him at work. It had already been a big enough risk, pretending to be in that part of town on another assignment, when in reality she knew where he worked because she had followed him there on the morning he left her apartment a week ago. She had gone through his wallet while he was still asleep too and copied down the work number from his card. If he twigged anything, she intended to look hurt and say something like, didn't he remember that he'd given it to her?

She had to do something else, something that would let her get a bit of a look around the place. "I need to go to the loo, Herbie." She reached up and whispered into his ear and invited him to come with her. She felt his body stiffen, but not in sexual response. He looked worried, and instead of looking tempted, he frowned and looked at his watch.

"Can't it wait?"

"You know how it is with us girls sometimes ...."

"All right. Here's the key, I'll order a taxi for you. Don't be long." She opened a door and stepped into what was unmistakably a former school toilet block. There were a dozen booths and small lockers on the right hand side and a bench ran the length of the room's other side and there were shelves above it. But the room had one more remarkable feature. With a casualness of breathtaking proportions, the shelved wall was lined, in staggered rows like tiny dolls-house bricks, with thousand upon thousand of blocks of pure heroin, all clearly engraved "Red Bird '999'".

BJ exhaled loudly. *So, this is what he was muttering about in his sleep and this is what Tokyo George had heard about somewhere.* She had difficulty taking it in, but there they were, precisely stacked, each block roughly six inches long. She ran on her bare feet to the end toilet and banged the door, then whirled around and scanned the wall again. White bricks of compressed, purest heroin! She took a handkerchief and nail file out of her handbag. Holding a brick with her handkerchief, she eased it gently out of place with the nail file. She exhaled again, expecting the adjacent bricks to topple as the loosened brick edged forward, but nothing happened and she silently whooped with joy: there was another block behind it. A double brick veneered heroin wall. It was BJ's lucky day.

"Are you all right in there?" Herbie knocked on the door and she saw it begin to open, just a fraction. She sucked her breath in hard between her teeth to stop herself from shaking.

"Give a girl a break, will you? I'm having a heavy period. I'll be out in a minute." The door quickly closed again. She took out the second, neighbouring brick – *don't look at the door, he won't come in now* she told herself – there was another brick behind that, too. She reached her hand into the small cavity she had created and used the nail file to pull out two more bricks from the back row, ignoring the slight amount of damage she caused as she applied pressure to remove them. She wrapped them in the hanky, placed them carefully into her handbag and zipped it shut. She turned around and flushed the toilet then neatly replaced the first two bricks she had extracted. She dusted off a few crumbs of powder from the bench and washed her hands at the sink (but not before licking her thumb and forefinger) and opened the door.

Red Bird Summer 44

The whole operation had been completed in less than three minutes.

"Everything all right in there?"

"Thanks, yes. Shall we make another time now or would you like to come to my place for a bite to eat tonight?"

"I might make it another time, sweetheart."

"Thanks again, Herbie, thanks for bailing me out. You're a love." She gave him a demure peck on the cheek and without a qualm of nervousness passed through the layers of security screens and took the lift to the ground floor. A taxi was waiting for her and she stepped into it solemnly, as though she was stepping into a Rolls Royce.

BJ remained calm and composed even after she had let herself into her Robinson Road flat. She took out a set of scales from the kitchen cupboard and placed each block carefully in the little metal tray. The first block weighed sixteen ounces, as did the second and the third. She had just stolen three pounds of the purest heroin money could buy. She finally smiled a shaky smile. She had made her mark in Hong Kong all right. She was rich.

And she had done it with one magnificent stroke of sheer good fortune.

She laughed loudly and drew one of her long red fingernails across one of the blocks and sucked on the powder, then did the same thing again.

And again.

Wednesday 17 August: 1.30pm

Emmie interviewed the final job candidate and at 1.30pm took the pile of applications to the General Manager's office. "Steven, I will be engaging Miss Cresswell as my Assistant. Her details are all there, will you sign off on it?"

"Does she have the qualifications and qualities you are looking for, Emmie? Your last assistant was very efficient and I'm sure he will be hard to replace." There was a faint line of worry on Steven's handsomely curved forehead. He knew Emmie's sexual preferences very well and the selection of a male would have pleased Steven much more.

"I think Miss Cresswell will be an asset to the PR Department and to the hotel. Will you ask your secretary to make the offer on my behalf? I'm meeting Sir Douglas and Lady Breda Crowley at the airport, and they are due in at two fifteen." Steven nodded and took the folder from her.

"Oh and by the way, Steven, Miss Cresswell can start next Monday."

*

The skipper dropped Pearl and Kaz off at the Hei Ling Chau wharf at ten o'clock, and as Pearl made her way to the hospice to see Matron Cheung, Kaz sprinted off to her work-site. Matron Cheung wept at the sight of Pearl and when Billie the cook heard the unusual outburst of emotion from his boss he ran into Matron's office, all concern for her welfare. He carefully lowered the cleaver he had brought with him and he too beamed at Pearl. They all talked at once. Pearl felt tears start to her eyes. Everything they could have to say to one another framed a set of memories that were still so intense that she would never cope with revisiting them all at once, so she came straight to the point of the visit:

"Matron Cheung, I am here with my friend Dr Karen Henderson. We would like to rent the guest villas while we do some work here. Would you have any objection?" Matron still could not speak but nodded her head in vigorous agreement and wiped her cheeks with the hem of her apron. "We will pay the hospital well for our accommodation and food and general keep and I am sure we will not disrupt your daily routine. If you agree, we will move in this Friday. Karen will be here during the week and I'll come and go as I can. Karen is an archaeologist and she wants to look around the island for some evidence of past cultural activity and do some surveying work. She won't bother anyone."

Pearl's voice had unconsciously dropped. She didn't want to lie to her mother's old friend, but she was aware of the need for caution. People in Hong Kong loved to gossip. But Matron Cheung was so thrilled to see her former volunteer nurse's daughter that she waved everything Pearl said aside and wrapped her up in a great hug.

"Of course, anything you want. Oh Pearl, to see you again, it is so wonderful. Billie, have we some food to spare for Miss Pearl and Dr Karen?"

Kaz came back from her work site, heard the happy voices and smiled. It seemed they were in luck and that Pearl's decision to come here so openly might not be the fabulous blunder Kaz quietly considered it was – for even though she had worked on Hei Ling Chau off and on for five years, she had never sought permission to do so.

Kaz's friendship with Pearl included many things but never Pearl's experiences here on Hei Ling Chau when she and Lady Bowen helped out the illegal immigrant, Dr Lin Dei, back in the autumn of 1964. Pearl rarely spoke of that time. Kaz had never spoken to Pearl about the island, either. She had her own boat and made her frequent excavation trips early in the mornings, before the mists lifted from the harbour and before the curious tourist ferry and hire-boat crowds festooned the waters from Hong Kong south to Macau. She would conceal the boat in a small bay in the southeastern cove where she had discovered the sunken vessels and dive for as long as was possible, returning to Hong Kong well into dusk in summer, and as late in the short winter afternoons as she could safely manage. During those years she saw less and less of Pearl and for some time it seemed that their lives had taken irreversibly different paths.

Kaz stared out to the dark, grey-green waters of Squid Cove and thought about the next great block of work that was before her. She felt a familiar wobble-spin in her left middle ear, a feeling that came on when things overwhelmed her, a feeling that told her very quietly that perhaps she had made one dive too many. She shook it away. There were probably six or seven years more work in front of her and she had to be in shape to do it.

She left the beach at Squid Cove and walked back to join Pearl at the hospital.

*

"Kaz! Come and have some lunch." Kaz grasped her backpack and strode bravely towards the kitchen. In all the years she had worked on the site she had never set foot on any part of Hei Ling Chau, other than the narrow stretch of grey sand that fringed the cove of her site, the site she had dubbed Squid Cove. She dawdled, aware of people waiting for her. She fervently hoped that a tour of the hospital would not be obligatory and made a mental note to donate some of the proceeds from her book to the hospice patients.

This experience could put an end to her diving.

Thursday 18 August: morning

The *South China Morning Post*, Thursday 18th August:

EXCITING NEWS FOR HONG KONG'S ARCHAEOLOGICAL FRATERNITY

The Board of Directors of the June Bowen Foundation is pleased to announce an expansionary initiative for the Foundation, with the formation of an academic grants scheme to assist students from the Asian Region to achieve doctoral status. Students currently enrolled or about to commence a Ph.D. programme in Regional Archaeology will be eligible for assistance from the foundation.

Pearl Green, Bowen Foundation Executive Director said yesterday:

"Dr Karen Henderson's appointment of Director of the Bowen Foundations's Research & Grants Scheme follows publication of her major doctoral work that convincingly argues that there are suitable sites for marine archaeological studies in the south-east Asian region. The objective of this research and grants scheme is to create a flow of new academic talent into the discipline of archaeology generally and it will provide much needed support to archaeological projects in the region.

"The Board is confident that Dr Henderson's appointment will attract additional funds to the June Bowen Foundation. This will facilitate further research and enable more students to achieve their full academic potential."

A photograph of Pearl and one of Kaz accompanied the article. The snap of Pearl was four years old and was taken when the foundation had been presented with a cheque by the Hong Kong Jockey Club. She had been photographed standing between the Chairman of the Hong Kong and Shanghai Banking Corporation, Sir Hew Nuttingsall and the since-demised Secretary of the Hong Kong Turf Club, Johnnie Glover. She was holding a larger than life cheque and smiling broadly at the camera.

I looked so happy.
Somehow, the thrill of receiving big cheques had worn a bit thin.

*

"Have you seen this article, Toby?" Toby Blake nodded without looking at Lady Hurford, who had come into the governor's reception room, where Toby ran his office and many of the affairs of Hong Kong from a splendid teakwood desk. Lady Hurford had expertly folded the broadsheet *South China Morning Post* into a manageable oblong and peered at her article of interest through an ornate lorgnette.

"Well I'll be darned. Dr Henderson, indeed. I remember when she was a slip of a thing and sat in that chair" – she pointed to the antique courtier's chair that did duty as a visitor's chair – "and complained about wanting to be an archaeologist and being thwarted by that odious mother of hers. And now she is to head up a new scheme of some sort for the Bowen Foundation. Director of the newly initiated *Research & Grants Scheme*. I'll be blowed!"

Lady Hurford took absolutely no notice of Toby except to read at him and he reciprocated by methodically opening envelopes and smoothing thick sheets of correspondence into neat piles, to be recorded and presented for the Governor's attention where necessary and dealt with by himself where not.

"I'll invite her to take morning tea. I want to hear more about this. I'll get Miss Stone on to it immediately." Toby wished that Lady Hurford had not mentioned the Stone woman. The confidantes of two of the colony's most influential people could not even bear to look at one another, let alone work together.

"Right-o then Lady Hurford. May I ask when you are planning to have Miss, pardon, *Doctor* Henderson at the Residence?"

"Tomorrow would be convenient. I have no morning engagements. I want to find out what the Bowen Foundation is up to. Dr Henderson is quite famous these days, I believe. The woman's a published author. I wonder what her mother would make of it all if she had survived that dreadful train accident?" All Toby had to do to maintain engagement with Lady Hurford's one-sided conversation was to lightly nod his head and tch-tch a little. He had absolutely no interest in Dr Henderson even though he had once thought that he might quite like to marry her. *Totally unsuitable.* She had turned out

Red Bird Summer 49

to be wild and unpredictable for a time, until she settled on that young Ph.D. student for a husband. He clicked his tongue. Toby had been fated to marry badly. His wife Belinda had left him three years ago, for a rock star, of all people, and Karen Henderson's brief bout of wildness was very tame in comparison to the way the heavily tattooed Belinda lived these days. Toby placed a pile of letters on an oblong tray, made one last entry in a large leather-bound book, cleared his throat and scraped back his chair.

"Excuse me, Lady Hurford, but the Governor's mail is ready to present to him. There are one or two urgent matters for his attention and he is due at Stanley at mid-day to open a new primary school."

*

Albert Ho read the article as he sipped a cup of peppermint tea. He permitted himself a slight arch of a finely groomed brow as he finished reading, but the controlled gesture was overtaken by a quick burst of anger. To think that such an important professional development had happened right under his nose and without him being consulted! The encounter that he had had with Pearl Green on Tuesday had been slightly unpleasant too. He wished now that he had been less critical about Dr Henderson and the matter of the theft from the museum. He had deliberately led Pearl to believe that he thought Karen knew more than she was saying about it and now the damned June Bowen Foundation was about to provide funds for the most badly needed archaeological work in the South-east Asian region and he, the region's mostly highly respected archaeologist, was excluded from any involvement in the undertaking.

Albert picked up a small bronze owl that sat on his desk and regarded it carefully. That bitch Pearl Green had sat right here in his office just two days ago, knowing that this announcement was imminent and all arrangements were in place and had said nothing of it to him. All she seemed interested in was the exquisite little celestial orb pin that was stolen from the museum at the same time as the Tang Bestiary collection. Why should she be interested in that? Did she know something about it? Albert upbraided himself for taunting her about the connection it had to her mother's death and they parted, more like enemies than the casual acquaintances they should be.

If only he could implicate Karen Henderson in the antiquities theft. That would give him the ammunition he needed to discredit her and by association, the June Bowen Foundation. Was that all these two women were in cahoots about? Albert wanted his artefact back. It was valuable and he had been happy to know that it had been safely stored in the archive room for years, ignored, no provenance that anyone else had been able to determine. It was his emergency fund, his running away money, if things became so bad that he ever had to disappear quickly and quietly. He paced around the perimeter of the beautifully appointed circular tower office twice before giving in to his need for a hit. He rang John Simons.

*

Pearl and Kaz sat at the round iron table that occupied centre space on the apartment's verandah, overlooking Connaught Road. The verandah itself was as wide as a road and stretched the full length of the old Fire Services HQ building. They ate scrambled eggs and drank coffee and re-read the *South China Morning Post* story about Kaz's appointment. Kaz had already eaten one breakfast cooked by Mrs Chan but now, as she ate and read, she idly wondered if it was worthwhile keeping an apartment for herself when Pearl had this huge penthouse all to herself. You could have twenty people in here and never bump into them unless by appointment.

She was distracted as she read. Pearl had just finished telling her about the encounter she'd had with Albert Ho and Kaz had been less than thrilled that Pearl had convinced Albert that their only concern in relation to the museum theft and the subsequent attack on Kaz was related to the theft of the antique funerary pin. "I reminded him that it was associated with my mother's death and that I viewed the theft as being equivalent to a personal threat, especially when it was accompanied by an attack on my best friend who just happened to be in the museum at the time. You should have seen his face! He actually sneered at me. Chilling. That man has the most changeable face. I used to think he was handsome but now he just looks ..." Pearl thought about how Albert looked. "Really, he looked ill."

Kaz was far from entertained. "It doesn't do to try to trick the Albert Hos of the world, Pearl. Albert isn't a man to take humiliation lightly, believe me, and he'll be furious about being excluded from all this." She tapped the *South China Morning Post* article with a fingernail. "If you make an enemy of him, he will do what he can to smear your name. Don't give him any opportunities, is my advice. Some odd things have happened over the years, when

Albert Ho has been on the scene in some way ...." She waved her spoon in the air dismissively.

Pearl just said, "Albert is a prominent Hong Kong citizen, so of course there's dirt on him somewhere; that goes with the territory. He has always interested and revolted me in pretty much equal measure, but I do feel that he is convinced you stole that little pin. Why, I wonder?"

"I don't know."

"He hinted that the call he took while I was waiting to see him was from an anonymous caller who had impeccable sources about the theft. I don't think the caller existed. I think Albert was on a fishing expedition to see if I knew anything more about the theft. Anyway you are right that he will be furious when he realises that he's excluded from something new happening in his own field. Who wouldn't? But if we can keep him focussed on that artefact it may keep him from being too curious about our other activities."

"You realise, don't you, Pearl" – Kaz put her cup down – "that he already despises me for what he considers to be a sensational and cheaply attained academic reputation? Now that I'm going to be based in Hong Kong, well, it's going to be awkward. I'm already invited to speak at events where he used to be the preferred archaeological darling. I agree that he'll be furious that we haven't conferred with him about the grants scheme. Maybe he'll convince himself that we nicked some of his bits and pieces to fund it. I think he lives an odd life, does our Albert."

The phone rang. Annie Cheung, the young administrator who ran the day to day business of the Bowen Foundation, was on the line. "Pearl, Lady Hurford's social secretary wants you to call her immediately, here's the number...."

Thursday 18 August: later in the morning

Kaz considered the things Pearl had said about Albert, pictured Albert reading the article in the moring paper and decided that she owed him a visit and a conversation about her new role, face to face. She knew that she still wasn't on top of things, otherwise she would never have let the announcement go ahead without informing the likes of Albert Ho. There would undoubtedly be others in the regional archaeology community who would also have their noses put out of joint by the sudden, non-consultative nature of the grants scheme announcement. Kaz fretted and gave up on the criteria list she had started on to help select eligible students. *I really should have thought this through more. Pearl said they parted quite badly after she called on him on Tuesday and that could make things even worse....*

Kaz still could not bring herself to use taxis for transport so she caught a tram out to Wan Chai and then walked to the Archaeological Museum. She panted in the heat and when she opened the museum door and felt the coolness exuded by the sandstone walls and the dry, humidity-free atmosphere of the first gallery, she changed her usual custom of striding to the archive rooms at the end of the warehouse-like space, and instead, sank gratefully onto one of the visitor's benches in the lobby.

"Sad, isn't it, Dr Henderson? Sad, that those cabinets remain empty?" Albert walked toward her, gesticulating at an empty display cabinet and speaking in a hail-fellow-well-met way. But Kaz saw his eyes and her kind intentions evaporated under his chilling regard of her.

"Albert, how – usual – to see you here." She smiled. He grimaced. It was always so difficult to tell if this woman was serious. Was she offering him an insult? It *was* entirely usual for him to be here. This place was his. There would never be another Albert Ho, never another Director of Hong Kong's Archaeological Museum to come up to his measure. He was the museum.

Kaz rose from the wooden bench, careful to appear a little below par. She staggered very slightly and grasped Albert's arm. He looked gratified. She leant on him a little, too. He looked delighted. She looked at the smooth and slender hands and wondered if they became claws upon command. She was sure they could. She drew her own long-boned hand a little wearily across her forehead. *Forget the peace treaty, it's time to strike.*

"Pearl tells me that you think I stole your poxy little funerary artefact, Albert. Is that correct?" He frowned but made no comment and Kaz smiled with an undeniable touch of vindictiveness; "Ah, Albert. Your silence means that you do think I was involved somehow. How could you?"

"I *have* wondered if you had a role in the theft, Dr Henderson, apart from offering your cranium for target practice of course. Why did the thieves bother to come into the archive room after stealing in excess of twenty million Hong Kong dollars worth of antiquities – heavy objects at that – just to pocket a little antique pin, worth, mmmh, probably not much?" Kaz said nothing.

"You returned to the museum in what seemed like rude health after you were struck by the thieves and later that evening you attended a conference, only to fly back to England first thing next morning. All that activity hardly implies that your head injury was debilitating. Perhaps you took the opportunity to pocket something for yourself when you regained consciousness and before I found you in the archive room, on the morning of the theft, hmm? Kaz looked at his smooth hands again and wondered about the hand she had seen pick up the key to the archive room door, the last thing she remembered until Albert shook her back to consciousness when he unlocked the door and found Kaz dazed and bleeding. She looked at him closely. *Had he hit her? Was he the thief? Why would he do that?*

"Keep going, Albert, I'm listening."

"Perhaps you know something more about the pin than its most recent history? Before it became" – he paused, hunting for the word he needed – "*associated* – with the unfortunate death of June Bowen? And perhaps you know who has it now." His last sentence was a statement, not a question and his features were flushed by a livid line across the top of his sharp cheekbones. Kaz watched him carefully. He wasn't really talking to her, he was talking to someone else about her. He looked quite manic. "Yes. That's it. You know who has it." His brow cleared as though he had experienced a genuine flash of insight into the matter. He didn't seem quite in control.

"Are you quite mad, Albert? Have you any idea what happened to me when I got off the plane last week? There was a particular welcoming committee for me in the manner of a little drugging and kidnapping. Someone had it in for me, clearly. You, by any chance? Did you organise my kidnapping, Albert? See how much sense this nonsense makes, Albert?" He came back from wherever he had gone and looked at her almost kindly. Kaz wanted to shiver, to keep the look from reaching her. What she said had momentarily made

Red Bird Summer 54

some lunatic sense and she didn't want Albert Ho's gaze on her any more, for any reason. She wouldn't even try to talk to him about the June Bowen Foundation initiative now. "I'm here to do some work, Dr Ho."

"I'm afraid, Dr Henderson, that security in the museum has been stepped up since the theft and that unauthorised entry into the archive rooms is no longer possible without a Hong Kong Police Department Permit from the Criminal Screening Unit. If you come with me I'll have my Secretary give you the paperwork you need to submit. The waiting period is only about eight weeks, I believe."

"Or may I call you a taxi?" Albert smiled nastily. Kaz smiled in relief. Albert had just given her a leave pass. She could resume her work at Hei Ling Chau without anyone being curious as to why she was not following her accepted routine of working in the museum when she was in Hong Kong.

"You are so helpful, Albert. You'll never know how much." She looked into his face, which was calm and exquisitely smooth again and she smiled at him: "I'll catch the bus home, though, thanks."

Thursday 18 August: 6.00pm

"I'm not happy. My client didn't get his item back and you agreed to get me more stock. I haven't heard a thing from you for nearly a week."

BJ took a deep breath. "As far as I'm concerned, I carried out my side of the agreement and if your client wants further action, he'll have to negotiate a new deal. May I remind you that he was satisfied that Dr Henderson didn't have his item after I examined her. If it had been on her, I would have found it. Unless it was in her stomach." BJ winced at an unpleasant memory.

"I must also insist on full payment for my, um, materials. I'm not in Public Relations as a charity job, you know." There was no smile in her voice now.

"My party will be less than happy."

I'm sorry your party isn't happy. Is there some other way it can be rectified?" BJ's voice was very calm.

"Just one." She did not respond.

"I said, just one."

"I heard you."

"Be at my apartment by 8pm with the goods. That should rectify things a little." BJ remembered how she had once rectified a situation in Tokyo with a dissatisfied customer after going to his apartment. It entailed many unpleasant procedures and concluded with her carrying small bags of heroin in uncomfortable body spaces.

She drew in her breath and in what BJ thought of as her best professional voice said: "I'm terribly sorry but I'm not available this evening, I have a dinner engagement with the Governor's Personal Secretary. Perhaps another time?"

There was a gratifying pause on the line, even though it was brief: "The Governor's Personal Secretary?"

BJ nodded happily and said, "Quite. I expect to be in the social pages on the weekend. At least that is what the Governor's Secretary has intimated to me."

*

"She can't come round, Albert, she's going out with Toby Blake."

"Well that's no coup. Even I could go out with Toby Blake. They'll be going to the Restaurant Rendezvous, no doubt. He goes there so much that I think he probably owns it."

"Apparently Toby's addicted to Chicken à la King, the chef's special. He takes all of his girlfriends there. They say it's why his wife left him. She couldn't stand another dish of the stuff and ran away."

"Incorrect, John. She left him when her glue allergies cleared up and her looks returned. She cleared off with Smut Jones from The Froth, when they stopped off here on their World Domination Tour. Did you go to the concert? It was legendary."

"Sometimes you don't talk like a museum director, Albert."

"Not so. I *define* how museum directors talk, John." Albert was now in a relaxed mood. He had had a few drinks to give the marijuana John always had on tap a little kick along but he was after more heroin to top up the dose he had treated himself to earlier in the day. It was an addiction, sure, but one that Albert had well under control.

"I've got a good damned mind to go around to the bitch's flat and help myself, John. I know she's got the stuff. Let's go now, before she goes out." John Simons had spent most of the day drinking and was not as focussed as Albert. It didn't improve Albert's mood when it took John a moment to remember that he hadn't the faintest idea where BJ lived. When Albert suggested they go to the Rendevous Restaurant and waylay her there, John just snorted his disagreement but then had to change the subject hastily as Albert's mood almost instantly became dark and brooding.

"Whisky, Albert, have some of my very best Irish. The very thought of going to the Rendevous Restaurant and demanding heroin from BJ while she is out on a dinner date with the Governor's Private Secretary ... are you having a laugh, Albert?" Albert took the proferred glass of whisky and downed it in a gulp and silently handed it back for a refill. John sighed. This was not going to be one of their more fun nights.

*

BJ thought that the Toby Blake excuse was a flash of genius. She had met Toby briefly when she ordered a pot of tea in the The Lobby Café at The Peninsula Hotel after her interview with Mrs Franklin. BJ was impressed with Toby's title and Toby was impressed with BJ's breasts and it seemed that a date could be mutually pleasurable. But he left before she could wangle him into putting a time on the engagement.

She was going out tonight though, that part at least was true. She sat at her dressing table and finished off her make-up with a slash of red lipstick. She had to work fast to protect her investment. She had risked taking her lovely little haul to a passport photo booth and photographed it before parcelling the blocks up and hiding them in an abandoned cemetery. They would be fine where they were – at least for now. She could never keep that amount of drugs in her apartment. After that she had rung the man she thought of as her Hong Kong adviser. He was available and she was off to meet him at The Short Stay Bar in Wanchai. BJ needed to find out more about her product.

She hailed a taxi. BJ had built her success in Tokyo on hiring an adviser who knew the local traps and who had, for a fee, protected her from harm. The arrangement worked well and BJ cleaned up in Tokyo, with his help. He had referred her to his Hong Kong counterpart but so far, apart from being linked to John Simons as a reliable buyer, their connection had been minimal and unlike her Tokyo man, BJ felt intimidated by him. But maybe he would come into his own now. She just had to be able to put aside her instincts that told her not to trust him and trust that he could dispose of the drugs for her, without disposing of her too.

The bar was quiet when she arrived but he was there, seated at a small round table and with a gin and tonic well under way. It unfolded that he was very knowledgeable about how the heroin trade had developed in Hong Kong – not that she was interested – but he explained how Hong Kong's chiu chau chemists had a long tradition in the production of ultra high grade heroin and there were supposed to be hundreds of flourishing laboratories, to the extent that in the late 1960s, Hong Kong, along with the Golden Triangle region in Thailand/Burma, emerged as a global force in heroin production.

"Some even say that now it outranks the product sourced and sold by Marseille's Corsican drug syndicates. The Asian laboratories also produce substantial quantities of pure heroin for the American market but there is little awareness of Hong Kong's growing role in the international trafficking scene." There was no doubt he knew his stuff. BJ handed over the passport sized snapshot of her haul. He clutched his glass, slapped the photo face-down on the table and covered it with his cigarette packet.

"Have you any idea ...?"

"No, that's why I need your help. It's the real stuff ain't it?" In her excitement BJ's south London accent surfaced.

"I'll get us another drink." He came back with a double G&T and a vodka and orange for her.

"Well? What's it worth?"

"This product is famous. Currently, I'd say that it's worth about HK$9 million. When it's cut and the quantity of saleable product is increased, it will bring at least ten times that. The brand, Red Bird '999' is also known as Red Bird Rising and refers to a mythological Chinese bird, the Phoenix. Do you know the story of the phoenix?" BJ shook her head, impatient for him to get down to business. Why would she want to know about Chinese mythological birds?

"This batch was produced in the summer of 1964. It is famous, or infamous, depending on your point of view, and bears the mark of a group of Hong Kong chemists who are members of a powerful and well organised international processing and marketing syndicate that originated in Shanghai. The focus of the drug trade has shifted and now Hong Kong dominates the region. Most people who buy the stuff here and overseas don't realise that they are using a Hong Kong product, unless, unlike you, they are familiar with the Chinese mythology that surrounds the phoenix. BJ nodded her head but said nothing. She cared not a sod for these bloody Chinese myths and birds and wished he'd stop blathering about them.

"Where did you get it?" he asked. They looked at one another carefully. BJ had thought about what she would say when he asked her this very question, but her mind was reeling. She had to get sorted and leave Hong Kong fast, in case the theft was discovered. She would sell enough to John Simons to keep him quiet and pay this man well for his advice, but otherwise she should not be here.

She had waded out into deep waters. She thought about the gleaming white wall of heroin blocks and felt over-awed by what she had so effortlessly done on so slight a notion. She waited for the familiar pang of discontent, a yearning for more and more and more – but nothing happened. There would be no return visit. This score was a stroke of magic truly worthy of the "white witch". It would never happen like that again.

She ignored his question: "The problem is, if it's worth that much money, what the fuck am *I* going to do with it? How am I going to convert it for sale? How can I market it?"

Her adviser shifted in his seat and lit a cigarette. He looked at BJ, not unkindly. "That's not a problem. I can sell it in its current form and guarantee you HK$9 million right here and now – three million a block. My commission is a million. Your profit will be nearly one million pounds sterling. What you need to do is make up your mind if that is going to be enough, to make a nice little amount on the raw product, or do you want to go further with the transaction? By that, I mean have it processed and then sell it.

"That's where things might get interesting and for someone like you, I'd add, *dangerous*. No-one wants to do this sort of business with a woman, least of all a prostitute." BJ bridled but saw his face and decided not to challenge him. She'd get him for what he'd called her though. She regretted using him. He scared her.

"This product was one of the first major production runs in Hong Kong when the processing laboratories started to get really big back in the early 60s. These blocks are so pure that processing of this quality has never been replicated. When word gets out that the Red Bird is flying after all this time, there will be a great deal of interest in it. A very great deal. It's your call."

"Meaning?"

"See the carvings in each corner of the bevelled edge? They reveal its provenance and tell those in the know its origin, production date, number in the sequence of the overall quantity produced, even the alias of the chemist. If it is still in its original state after more than ten years, it has to have been quarantined, and what people will want to know is – where is the main stash? There was a lot more than these three blocks in that shipment, and there was only ever one shipment of Red Bird."

BJ sipped her drink and fluttered her eyelashes in what she trusted was a convincing gesture of incomprehension. It usually worked. He continued: "There is said to be a store room somewhere in Hong Kong that contains this product, as high as a white mountain, and many have tried to find out where it is. So you see, it isn't hard to understand that people will be very interested in you, because as the seller, they will assume you are able to get more, much much more and they will also assume that you know where the rest of it is. You are in a lot of danger, my dear."

"I don't know anything about all that." BJ cut him off before he asked her again how she came by it. She tried to keep the vision of the wall of heroin out of her mind. "I got it as payment for a job I did in Tokyo."

"Must have been some job."

"It was. And worth it by what you're saying. It was payment for some risky business I undertook for a client. Seems he didn't know what he had. And that's why I thought it could be anything too, even fake, like."

"The truth is more likely that your client wanted a courier. You've only been in Hong Kong for a short while. How do you know he won't turn up looking for it?" BJ adopted an expression of fear. It was one she could put on without much effort. He had to believe that she had imported the stuff, please god, otherwise her life was as good as over. Her luck to steal Asia's most famous heroin ... she took a long draw on her vodka and orange. He had to think that she was just another stupid cow, easily tricked, frightened, grateful to get a little money for her score. So be it.

"Well?"

"I didn't think about that. I accepted it at face value, though I had been expecting to be paid in cash. I thought I was safe, leaving Tokyo. No-one in Customs looks at girls like me. We are just holiday-makers. I put the blocks in lovely Japanese soap boxes, wrapped up in cellophane with a lovely golden seal. They looked like gift soaps. But now you've got me worried. I'll take the eight million if you can get it and I don't care who makes more from it, you included. I knew I'd be out of my league with this stuff if it was any good. And if someone else can make ten times that again, good luck to them. A million pounds will get me nicely settled somewhere."

He seemed satisfied with her answer. "I will have the money for you tomorrow, my dear, and of course, I will take delivery of the product at the same time. Don't mess me about. As they say in the chiu chau heroin-processing laboratories, the harbour in some places is very deep and holds its secrets well." He smiled benevolently. BJ let him have the pleasure of seeing her shudder. She didn't have to act much.

"I'll do it. It's still better than the only other alternatives I seem to have on the back burner at the moment."

"Nothing interesting around for a lovely-looking young woman like you? Surely not."

"Just the usual. I can meet you at 4pm if that's convenient. The stuff's not at my flat, mind. I'm not dumb you know. I have no choice but to trust you, have I? I have to think of myself, don't I? The Cameo Coffee Lounge, four o'clock. I'll have it. Make sure you've got the money."

She got up and made preparations to leave, aware of many male eyes on her as she straightened her fine white silk evening dress and smoothed the hem down over the pale silver tights she wore. Her adviser's face was flushed. Could be the G&T or maybe he was angry at her tone. Not cringing enough for him, maybe.

Careful, girl, don't be smart!

"Sorry. I hope I didn't offend you. Goodnight!" She waved him a cheery goodbye before she hit the pavement and signalled a taxi. Wanchai at night was a Hong Kong drawcard that kept the folks coming for the peep-show, but it had another side, and BJ didn't want to be part of that tonight.

The taxi whisked quickly through the traffic and the harbour twinkled with lights. There was no comfort for BJ in the beauty of it all. Nor would she have taken comfort from her adviser's expression as he watched her leave. He made a phone call from the front desk and then gestured to a bar girl for another drink. As she placed the glass on the table, he tucked a twenty dollar note into the band of her bracelet, murmuring as he did so, "Yes, thank you very much, quite insanely dangerous. Soap, eh? Wonder who the hell she thinks I am?" The bar girl smiled vaguely at him and agreed, although privately she asked herself, *Isn't that the* status quo *around here these days, living dangerously and wondering who the hell you are?*

*

In the taxi, BJ went back over everything he had said to her and decided that if the drugs she had stolen were as famous as he said and she really was in a shitload of danger, then the smartest thing she could do was disappear until the deal was done. Back at her flat, she packed a small bag. She was glad she had hidden the heroin away from home, even though it was a risky thing to do. The heroin would be safe where it was and she would be safer out of here.

She looked around the flat with some regret. Renting such a quality place had been a nice step up for her. But she had the keys to a new life now and a place like this was nothing compared to what lay ahead. She left the building by the fire escape and walked some way along Robinson Road before hailing another cab, which dropped her off at a small, spotless guesthouse in Kennedy Road. She took a room with a bath and relaxed in the big, old-fashioned, iron tub and blew a bubble of oily froth into the air. There was tomorrow to get through and after that she would leave Hong Kong as fast as she could book a seat. A first class seat of course.

Friday 19 August: 9.30am

Mrs Franklin was not happy with the Manager's Secretary. "You say you have left two messages for Miss Cresswell and there has been no reply? When?"

Jenny Brown was an asset to The Peninsula. A thorough administrator who was studying to advance her career, she just wished that someone would educate Emmie Franklin in the use of basic office manners. Mrs Franklin specialised in rages, rages that were never about anything important. She was luminescent now. *What is wrong with her?*

At that moment, Jenny's boss, Steven Wong, came to the door and thanks to glory be, Emmie reverted to the smiling Mrs Emmeline Franklin, beloved by all except subordinates and others vulnerable to her whims.

"Try the number again for me, now, will you Jenny?" she said brightly and she laughingly approached her cousin Steven with some news about a PR coup she was planning for the Marco Polo Lounge, The Peninsula's flagship venue for the local glitterati and international jet set favourites.

"No-one less than Franka Derova, Steven. The press will go wild. She is going to model for Chanel during Hong Kong Fashion Week and has agreed to have lunch here, at the Marco Polo. She will wear an outfit from the autumn couture collection. It will be wonderful fun."

*

Emmie's voice tilted upwards on the words *wonderful fun* but she had already had a run in with Franka's agent. The woman was a thin wisp of venom with a sallow complexion and there was no suggestion of anything wonderful, let alone fun, in the negotiations. The agent wanted payment other than lunch, and Emmie's offer of nothing less than a night in the Presidential Suite – usually charged at a premium HK$20,000 – barely raised an interested eyebrow.

Emmie was encouraged to throw in six bottles of Moët Chandon champagne and a tub of top quality grey pearl Russian caviar, valued at HK$15,000. HK$35,000 worth of goods and services – not a bad tip to add to a free lunch. But wait, there was more. The agent said that she wanted a genuine pearl spoon from which to eat the caviar and which she would keep as a memento.

Emmie agreed to the terms. She needed to make an impact. Things had not been going so well of late and she had failed to win several promising contracts for The Peninsula. After the deal was struck, she booked the suite for the evening in question and now just had to hope that her cousin didn't find out about her little sweetener. She could order the food and beverages through Catering – they would be able to put that against her function budget, thankfully. If Steven did get a whiff of what she had agreed to, Emmie would be looking for another job. Her family connection with him wouldn't save her this time and she knew it. Steven was a very fair man but he had a few too many principles for Emmie's liking.

*

"That's good news, Emmie, we need some favourable exposure. The Overton Group is dominating the celebrity pages lately and I'm concerned that we seem to be overlooked in the press more often than we used to be." He smiled and returned to his office without inviting a reply. Emmie turned to Jenny and spat at her, "Inform me the minute you make contact with Miss Cresswell." Jenny smiled kindly at Emmie and thought that it must be awful being in her head. *She seems to be her own worst enemy.*

*

Albert Ho was rarely seen arriving at the Archaeological Museum. Museum legend had it that he metamorphosed into an owl at night, leaving by the mullioned windows of his second-storey office for a quick snack, only to return and slumber at his desk. Even the museum guards who made their first round at 8am each morning rarely saw Albert arrive. He would materialise at an exhibit case or would emerge from behind a tall shelf, always with an affable, light smile on his handsome features.

Today was different. For the first time in anyone's memory, Albert was not present when the doors opened to the public at 9.30am. There was a faint stirring in the ranks. Even his annual absences were always taken at exactly the same time of year. He had no wife, children or other family, and no-one had any idea if he had a social life, or friends. Albert had the Hong Kong Archaeological Museum.

But not today.

*

BJ lay in bed and looked out of the window at the heavy summer sky. It would already be unbearingly humid outside. She visualised the scenario for the exchange of drugs and cash to take place that afternoon. She saw herself presenting the elegant black and gold wrapped parcel to her adviser, not unlike a daughter presenting a special present to a beloved parent. Once she had the money, she would disappear from sight. She would leave the few possessions she had brought with her at the guesthouse and give him the slip when she left the Cameo Coffee Lounge. BJ had no intention of him ending up with everything. *Including,* she thought grimly, *my life.*

She ordered breakfast and forced herself to eat something with the two cups of tea she consumed. She was way out of her depth now, and there was no-one who could help her. John Simons? She sighed. He was probably her only choice but what could she tell him? He'd be curious and he would know that whatever she was doing would almost certainly be about drugs and money and there was that client of his who seemed to have taken a set against her ... she wouldn't fancy running into him without notice.

But her adviser had said – hadn't he – with a perfectly straight face, that the next stage of the game was insanely dangerous if she chose to play it? Did he really think she believed today's transaction was excluded from that threat? She was in the arena already and he was about to get his hands on a potential one hundred million Hong Kong dollars worth of drugs from her in exchange for less than a tenth of that amount. How did she know if he really had or could get the money to pay her? Why bother paying her at all when there was the harbour?

Combined stress and excitement had unsettled BJ after booking into the guesthouse and she had celebrated too hard, using far more of the heroin she had set aside for her own use than she had intended. She felt ill as the tea and toast settled and she shivered as she thought of the day ahead. *I need some luck right now,* but all she seemed to be able to do at this hour of the morning was shake, not with withdrawals of course, but with fear. She turned the air-conditioning up and got back into bed.

*

Mrs Chan answered the telephone. Her voice was deep and a little gruff: "No, Miss Kaz is not here, Miss Pearl." Pearl hung up. Perhaps Kaz had forgotten they were supposed to be going to Government House for morning tea. Pearl refused to worry. Kaz loved shopping and could lose hours roaming the Hollywood Road area, scouring through all manner of shops, looking for pieces to add to her antique animal collection. She loved handbags too, and could spend days in Handbag Alley, examining everything on offer, from classic Schiaperelli brown leather knock-offs to classy Chanel copies. Kaz acquired and disposed of handbags with a speed that

Pearl found distressing. There was one exception, her old leather satchel that should have been pensioned off long ago.

Pearl put Kaz out of her mind and resumed her attack on a pile of paperwork. It was nine forty-five and they were due at the Governor's residence at a quarter to eleven, with morning tea set for eleven sharp. She had an appointment at the bank afterwards and there were the accounts to go through before she and Kaz could leave for Hei Ling Chau later that afternoon. Pearl would usually contemplate such a full day with relish but this morning she walked into the adjoining office and somewhat peevishly asked Danny and Annie if they could set aside some time for her at 3pm. "I've an announcement to make and you two are pivotal to it," she said somewhat more mysteriously and tersely than she needed to. Annie and Danny looked at one another. They were original Bowen Foundation employees and adored their beautiful, serious boss. They often found Pearl preoccupied, but never terse. There must be something wrong.

"I'm going upstairs to dress.... Tea with the Governor's wife!" The way she said *governor's wife* came out as *govnor's waif*. An ancient English accent had surfaced from somewhere and Danny and Annie wanted to giggle. They were careful to avoid looking at each other. Pearl had a very cool transatlantic Hong Kong accent composed of Posh London pollinated with a pinch of New York Intellectual, but occasionally her mother's plummy tones would emerge. June Bowen could have slain dragons with her accent if she had chosen to and sometimes it re-emerged through her daughter.

"Dr Henderson is accompanying me. If she arrives, send her on, will you? Smartly, if you will." The morning tea was about Kaz, not her. Theodora Hurford could see Pearl at any old cheque presentation, and Pearl had no qualms about Kaz hogging the tea tray, as it were.

*

Albert Ho was in a jam – a traffic jam – undecided whether to go to the museum and make a belated start to the day or head home and sleep off last night's spate of over-indulgence. His head was so clouded with the aftermath of too much whisky that he had difficulty remembering how he had spent the evening. But then he saw Kaz as she came out of the Hong Kong & Shanghai Bank and he asked the taxi-driver to stop. He had something to say to Dr

Henderson, didn't he? Hadn't she offended him? He got out of the vehicle and to Kaz's considerable discomfort, stood too close to her on the footpath and rambled on at length about the comparative histories of funeral pins in Asian and Aztec cultures.

Kaz stopped him in mid-sentence as he was reciting how iridium-rich pits in the Gulf of Mexico provided material, at the cost of lives, for funeral pins and other funerary ware for the upper classes: "And your point is, Albert? I'm going to be late for morning tea at Government House." He gave her a very dark look and got back into the cab. Kaz watched the vehicle weave back into the traffic and wondered why Albert, unusually, was so very drunk at this hour of the morning and what had been his real reason for apprehending her the way he had?

*

BJ was at the bank, making enquiries about opening a bank account. She peered at Albert and Kaz. They knew one another, it seemed. BJ had recognised Kaz in the bank, as the brunette bird she had drugged and body-searched the previous week, and kept Katz at a discreet distance as they left the bank at the same time. But she drew back quickly for cover behind one of the granite pillars that supported the roof of the bank's portico, when she recognised another familiar face, the man whom she had seen, some days ago, leave the flat in Upper Albert Road with John. He reeled out of a taxi and hailed Dr Henderson. BJ dipped her head and pretended to check her bank book until the man stumbled back into his cab. Dr Henderson made off up Garden Road.

BJ watched her swinging walk take her rapidly out of sight: *What was that about? That was the bloke who was with John and more likely than not the bloke who got me to do the number on this Dr Henderson, and here he is, greeting her like an old pal.* BJ also wondered if he was also the bloke John was acting for, the one who wanted a truckload of heroin to set someone up. BJ decided she'd follow the brunette. *You never know. I'm not rich yet.*

*

Around mid-morning, Emmie returned to the manager's suite and demanded to know if Jenny had been in contact with Miss Cresswell, and when the answer was no, she stamped out of the office without saying a word. Jenny sighed and looked at her

Red Bird Summer 67

endless work list with relief. Anything was better than having to deal with Mrs Franklin in one of her moods.

Friday 18 August: 11.28am

Kaz broke into a trot as she neared Government House. She reached the sentry's gatehouse at 11.28am, breathless.
"Tea! Tea!"
"I'm sorry madam, I can't help you. I do have some water if that will help."
"No! Tea! I'm expected for morning tea." The guard raised his eyebrows and asked for identification.
"Lady Hurford. Late." She flapped her Driver's Licence at him. He called the doorman, who whisked Kaz into Lady Hurford's sitting-room through the servant's corridor – the quickest route through the rambling residence – just as Lady Hurford was pouring Pearl a second cup.

The doorman announced her and Lady Hurford beamed at Kaz. Pearl recognised the look and smiled to herself. The prodigal had not so much returned, it seemed, but had stormed the parapets and was now in control of the castle.

"I am so very sorry, Lady Hurford, for my unpunctuality. No excuse will suffice."

"Rubbish, my dear. This is Hong Kong. The traffic is mad and people are madder. It is a miracle any appointment is ever kept at all, let alone kept on time. Do sit down. My, what a perfect little scarab brooch that is. Very very old, I expect, hmm?" Kaz, who had bought the perfect little object for next to nothing from a junk shop in Hollywood Road, had no idea about its provenance. For an archaeologist, she had very bad taste in jewellery. If it sparkled her way, she wore it.

"Just a small souvenir, your Ladyship."

"Oh please, my dear, call me Theodora. We have a lot to talk about and protocol in its various promulgations is so tiresome. I am sure Lady Green agrees. I have spent years talking to people who could possibly have had something interesting to say but never quite got there because they worried so about what bit of protocol-addled nonsense follows what. So I insist! Call me Theodora!"

Pearl smiled quietly again. Lady Hurford had never invited *her* to call her Theodora. With them, it was protocol all the way. Still, they usually stood on opposite sides of a big fat cheque and Pearl didn't care what people called one another or how they referred to one another if there was money in it for the Bowen Foundation. Lady Hurford was quizzing Kaz about her career and glowed as Kaz paid tribute to the encouragement Theodora had given her, leading Kaz to defy her mother's wishes and take up the study of Archaeology rather than make a suitable marriage. *If her mother had still been alive to say it,* Kaz thought, *she would have have opined that her daughter had made what turned out to be a most unsuitable marriage.*

"And a book as well, m'dear. –A book as well as a doctorate. – And you're still only a slip of a girl." Kaz beamed. At thirty-two, she might look like a slip of a girl but she was a woman of iron will and grit beneath the smooth shoulder-length auburn hair, short black jersey sleeveless dress and white linen jacket slung casually around her shoulders. Her dark brown eyes gleamed and her voice dipped a little as she took control of the room. Karen Henderson's greatest power was in her speaking voice. It was quite magnetic, silvered with happiness itself, some said.

"What a life adventure," said Theodora when Kaz finished a brief summary of her five year's work on the sunken ships. "And exactly where did you find your treasure ships m'dear?" Lady Hurford placed her well-bred cup back onto its saucer as she asked the question. There was no answer. She looked at Kaz, who had at least the good grace to blush.

"I can't say, Theodora. It is such a sensitive subject that to reveal the whereabouts at this stage would invite unparalleled attention. The whole study would be ruined by salvage operators."

"And just what are savage operators, m'dear?"

"Sal-vage, Theodora, although I fully expect them to be savages. Not," she hastily said, "that there is any indication that there is anything of value to salvage at the site but people are very curious about it and it is my responsibility that it be preserved for academic investigation."

Lady Hurford beamed afresh. She admired the intellectual and personal integrity that Kaz was trowelling into the conversation. Pearl was able to relax in the lovely room where she had been a guest so many times. She was happy to be an observer until she judged it time to intervene and mine Lady Hurford's contact list of people or organisations that might be willing to contribute to the foundation's newest project.... If she could steer the conversation back to that area.... Kaz was on to pottery now and once she started on that she could be pretty hard to shut up.

Pearl was not to have her turn. There was a discreet knock at the door and Anneka Stone entered the room. Anneka had not been aware of Karen's arrival and her features blanched unpleasantly at the sight of her. Anneka hated Karen Henderson. It was nine years since Kaz had been her assistant, her office slave. Now, Anneka's career in PR management had stalled while Kaz was basking in the glow of career success. Kaz had learned a couple of lessons at Anneka's nicely capped knees, one of which was that she was capable of giving no mercy, if that was how it had to be.

"Lady Hurford, I do apologise for the interruption, but I feel you should see this." Anneka proferred a small silver tray to the Governor's wife, on which lay a folded note.

"Really, Miss Stone, must I read this now? Can't you see ...?"

"I am sure you will be pleased you have done so, Lady Hurford." Theodora Hurford frowned, took the note from the tray, adjusted the lorgnette on her substantial Essex nose and read. Her attention was immediately captured. Kaz and Pearl glanced at one another. Anneka smirked.

"Thank you, Miss Stone, that will be all." Anneka turned abruptly on the heels of her beautiful, cream, high-heeled shoes and closed the door with a very definite snap. The older woman turned to Pearl and Kaz. "Do you know what this says?"

"Hardly," said Pearl, coming over all earl's great-granddaughterish:

"It says that the Bowen Foundation is supporting the hoax of Dr Henderson's alleged marine archaeological finds in Hong Kong waters in order to secure profits for the foundation. It says," she paused, "that you have fabricated your Ph.D. material, Dr Henderson, and that the site does not exist. It says," she paused again, "that your research and your book are based on spurious information and that you should be stripped of your higher degree unless you are prepared to reveal the whereabouts of the site you claim to have excavated."

Pearl felt a slight clicking sensation just below her ears. Her jaw must have dropped.

Kaz just laughed. "Who knew that we were invited for tea with you this morning, Theodora, hmm? These sorts of allegations follow me wherever I go. My work will ultimately be open knowledge, but until then, the more sensational aspects of it attract all the wrong types. They do this sort of thing to get me to cough up the information that *they* want.

"It goes with the job. I expect you get bored when people curtsy to you all the time when all you may really want from a garden party is a bit of decent conversation. It's part of your patch. Even my publisher receives several similar letters every week. It bores me, frankly."

Lady Hurford considered that what Kaz said seemed eminently sensible. She was right about the damned curtsying too. *Revolting custom.*

"Who is the note from?" Kaz's voice was deep and fluid. She was not fazed.

"Well, so now you mention it, it doesn't say."

"Doesn't Miss Stone screen your mail? What value is there in passing on anonymous correspondence? And who, Pearl," Kaz turned and winked at Pearl, "knew we were coming to morning tea with Lady Hurford this morning? Apart from Miss Stone, of course." Kaz let the last sentence hang in the air. Lady Hurford threw the note into the waste basket and morning tea proceeded amiably.

Friday 19 August: 12.10pm

BJ waited outside Government House and it was just after mid-day when her target, Dr Henderson, left the grounds in the company of a tall, slight woman with long brown hair that escaped in streams from under a knitted cap. They stopped and chatted outside the great iron gates of the Governor's residence for a minute or two before the hatted one waved at the security guard, hailed a taxi and headed off along Upper Albert Road towards Garden Road.

Kaz walked along Upper Albert Road for a few minutes in the opposite direction and then took the connecting path to the level below. BJ followed her. Her brief from John was to set this woman up, and even though she was about to become a millionairess, BJ was still of a mind to take out some insurance by keeping her current contacts happy.

Just in case things didn't work out this afternoon.

*

Pearl just made it to the bank in time for her 12.30pm appointment. She did not notice Yip Yee Koon, who watched her being ushered into Allan Martin's office with undisguised curiosity. Soon afterwards, he watched as Allan escorted her to the door where they paused, laughed, and shook hands. Pearl clacked across the marble tiles of the central hall in her leather boots until she reached the great vaulted portico of the Hong Kong and Shanghai Bank at Number One, Queen's Road Central.

She spotted Yip as they seemed to pass one another accidentally and nodded a mutual, silent greeting. Pearl gave him a radiant smile. Unusual, thought Yip, to see Pearl Green smile so brightly. *Was she in love?*

When they were at school, Pearl had once been good friends with Yip's daughter Annie. She often accompanied the family to their holiday home in the New Territories or was a guest at the family's private box at the Happy Valley Race Track. But after her mother's death, Pearl's interests and associations changed. By the time Annie married and became the rich young wife of a powerful Hong Kong businessman, the two women were poles apart in interests and sympathies. Yip sighed and thought it such a shame the connection had gone. Pearl was a little older than Annie and had been a good influence on her once. But each day now, Annie became more of a spoiled, pouting, money-squandering woman who had acquired little wisdom and showed absolutely no common sense in living her highly privileged life, seeking the thrill of instant gratification in all things.

Yip Yee Koon presented his card to the receptionist at the great teak desk in the bank's central lobby and spoke with scrupulous politeness. "I have an appointment with Sir Hew Nuttingsall."

The receptionist made a discreet telephone call and five minutes later Yip was seated in a deep armchair in the private sitting-room of the Bank's Chairman. He stated to Sir Hew that before they got to the reason for his appointment, he wanted to know the exact nature of Lady Pearl Green's current business with the bank. There was no hesitation on the part of the great banking chief in following the order. He summoned his personal assistant and handed her a note. "Quick as you can, Miss Simmons."

*

Pearl returned to the office. The laughing handshake she exchanged with Allan Martin had just sealed the approval of a bank loan of HK$18 million which gave her a ninety-nine-year lease on Hei Ling Chau Island and a fifty-year lease on an abandoned monastery on Lantau Island. All Pearl had to hope for now was that those involved would be delighted to close down the leprosarium and would welcome the relocation of the remaining patients to the beauty and serenity of the former monastery on Lantau.

Even better, the transaction had not been hampered by any legal problems. The hospital on Hei Ling Chau had been built by the Hong Kong Government and ownership would remain with the Government. She could do whatever she liked with the infrastructure of the place. That was the good news. Pearl fretted over the next step – breaking the news to Kaz and Matron Cheung. Maybe she should tell them both at once. They both had strong vested interests in Hei Ling Chau, with Kaz paranoid about protecting her site and Matron – well she had worked there for most of her adult life and had buried her only son on the island. Her roots were there.

Pearl dropped into the office and went through some figures with Danny and cleared a list of requests and messages from Annie before she took the lift to her penthouse apartment. She packed two overnight bags, one for herself and one for Kaz and stocked another case with items for Matron's use – some craft materials for the patients; two packets of dried mushrooms and a quantity of dried spiced pork, some salted plums, a bag of small dried fish and a box of lychees. The fish smelt and Pearl wrinkled her nose as she tried to eliminate the odour by wrapping it in two layers of plastic. She had just finished when Kaz appeared.

"I'm starving Pearl, how about lunch? Those wafer biscuits that Lady Hurford calls morning tea didn't go far."

"Sure, grab one of those bags."

They talked as they left the building and crossed the road to the covered food market. Pearl waved her hand towards the water-taxi depot. "I have some news to take with us for Matron Cheung that will also affect you. It's related to what we were talking about on Wednesday, you know, the difficulties with continuing work on Hei Ling Chau. I've had a bright idea that has just come off."

Kaz laughed: "What? Have you organised to shut down the leprosarium or something like that, Pearl? Have you?"

"When we get there, Kazza. I need to speak to you both at the same time. Matron has a lot of history vested in Hei Ling Chau." And besides, you might push me out of the boat if I tell you now." Kaz felt a little uncomfortable but stoically spooned away at a bowl of congee. Whatever Pearl had done, it would be for the greater good. But she felt a small, threatening tilt in her inner sense of calm, knowing that at its core was her increasing worry that this arrangement between them might not work out in the long term. If they ever came to real logger-heads over anything ....

*

From the other side of Connaught Road, a pair of black-outlined pale blue-grey eyes in a very pale complexioned face watched the two women eat. BJ peered into the entrance lobby of the Fire Services HQ, from which Pearl and Kaz had emerged, carrying some luggage. BJ looked at the discreet brass plaque attached to one of the sandstone pillars which supported two solid teak doors that must be twenty feet high. *The June Bowen Foundation. So this is where the tall one must work. I wonder what the bags are for? Where is this Hei Ling Chau? The tall one said, "Just the afternoon for a trip to Hei Ling Chau"*. BJ inspected a bolt of fabric on display at the entrance to the shopping alley adjacent to the building. She decided to keep her eye on them for a bit longer and strolled casually between the nearby alleys full of cheap household goods, clothing and kids' toys.

"Buy a handbag, Missy?" She shook her head and brushed angrily at her arm as she felt a tug on the sleeve of her white silk blouse. "Nice handbag, hold lots of good things. Plenty of room for presents to take home, Missy." She recognized the voice. It was her adviser. He waggled a cheap red plastic handbag in her face and laughed. "Just the right size to hold a couple of bars of lovely soap, don't you think? Tell you what, I'll buy this and then you can contribute the soap. I know you haven't got any at home, so shall we go to the shop where you buy it and get a couple of bars?"

BJ smiled weakly and nodded. He *had* set her up after all. She thought quickly. She could dart off into the alley and try to escape, but where? Or, she could take a different risk, play him at his own game. "Lovely. I know just the soap you mean. I can take you there now but it's a water-taxi ride away. Are you up for that?" His mouth twitched, but not with what appeared to be humour.

"Interesting. Where, exactly?"

"Cheung Chau." The man looked at her carefully. Had the stupid little cow not remembered what he had said to her last evening about the dangers of the harbour? Or was she planning a surprise of her own? "My friends over there" – she gestured towards Pearl and Kaz as they finished their meals and gathered up their bags – "are about to go and we can share their taxi if you like. Yoo hoo! Halloo! Wait for me, girls."

Pearl and Karen turned as they were hailed by a white-suited, pale-complexioned young woman. Kaz felt dread crawl up her back. A man the woman was with dropped a handbag to the ground and retreated into the alley. BJ continued waving at the two women and hurried across Connaught Road, dodging traffic as she did so but never for a second dropping eye contact with them.

Friday 19 August: 1.00pm

Yip Yee Koon said, "I see. So exactly why has Miss Green purchased Hei Ling Chau Island, may I ask?" Hew Nuttingsall looked uncomfortable. It was bad enough hosting this man in his private suite, a man reputed to be the criminal overlord of Kowloon Walled City, whose main source of wealth was said to rest with his power over Kowloon's Walled City triads. But to have to answer the damned chap's questions about one of his clients was – "need I repeat myself, Sir Hew?" – just dreadful. Dam and blast his greed in going to the chap for loans. Dam and blast it.

"I believe, Mr Yip, that Lady Green intends Hei Ling Chau to be an acquisition that will lead to further development of her foundation's philanthropic activities. There are now only about 150 patients in the hospice and the time will come when leprosy will be officially wiped from the books, in Hong Kong at any rate. Lady Green intends to develop the leprosarium into a community hospital and day clinic for the people in the group of southern outlying islands. I consider the acquisition to be financially judicious and there are many who say that people who purchase outlying islands now will be the wealthiest people in Hong Kong in the future, if we continue to develop at the rates we have experienced during the past decade."

Yip Yee Koon rested his chin on his interlocked, arched fingers. *So. She has bought an island.* Hew shifted in his seat and bit his thumbnail. Yip drifted back nine years, to the last time he and Pearl had talked: that conversation had taken place on a small island. It had taken place over the body of the man who had shot and killed her mother.

"She has come far, that young woman. I wish her well and apologise for being so curious, but I make a substantial annual contribution to the work of the Bowen Foundation and would not like to think that those funds are being poorly managed. Now, Sir Hew, my real business today is this...." The two men bent over the notebook that Yee Koon had drawn from his pocket and Hew Nuttingsall scratched his forehead tensely as he was taken through a list of figures, some ticked off, most not.

"The reason for my visit today is to inform you that I intend to waive the remainder of your debt, Sir Hew. Our association is at an end." Yip rose easily from the armchair and walked from the room and left Hew slumped in his chair, wiping his forehead as ferociously as though he was out on the golf-course in the heat and sweating like a pig. He was seized by the need to know why Yip had so casually erased a debt that would have earned him several million dollars in income and he ran clumsily to the door. Yee Koon was still in view, walking along the carpeted corridor towards the executive lift.

"Why, Yip?"

"I simply thought, why not, Sir Hew. Goodbye."

*

Pearl challenged BJ as she halted squarely in front of them. Kaz kept on walking.

Pearl said, "Who are you and what do you want?"

"I'm, ah, Barbara." Kaz's face was writ loud with mistrust. Pearl's glance rested coldly on the arresting, pale-featured face that remained completely composed and colourless, even though its owner had just laboured through Connaught Road's eternal howl of traffic and the afternoon heat blast.

"Your full name."

Pearl remembered Jeremy's description of a very pale woman he had seen at The Peninsula, dressed in white, the one he referred to as a white witch. Was this her?

"Just Barbara. Look, I just heard you say to your friend that you're going to Hei Ling Chau. I need to go there too. I thought I did, that is." She stopped talking, uncomfortably aware of the haughty expression of the tall one, the one whose hair was trying to escape from under that awful beanie thing. Pearl towered over BJ and made her feel like a naughty kid. The other one, also above average height, paused. She was hostile and edgy and didn't try to hide it. "That is, I thought maybe we could share the fare. Sorry," she said as Pearl took a step towards her with her jaw set and her eyes very cold, "I mean no harm. Sorry."

"Have you got leprosy?" Pearl barked at her imperiously. "Have you a relative with leprosy perhaps? Or is it simply that you want to get leprosy? Hei Ling Chau offers little but leprosy, but I suppose there is the odd sick-o who wants to go there and look at lepers. Is that what you want to do? Look at lepers? The worst cases of course. What's your name again?"

"Barbara."

"Barbara who?"

"Just Barbara. And no I don't want to look at lepers. I just want to go to Hei Ling Chau with you. Please. I'm in a bit of a spot here. Let me come with you. Please."

"Barbara is obviously not aware of the implications of what she is asking." The tall one spoke to her friend without taking her eyes from BJ's face.

The other one – the one she had dosed with LSD – ignored both of them and started walking towards the water-taxi depot again. The tall one called out to her, "Kaz, wait!"

BJ begged. "In the taxi – please, in the water-taxi. I'll tell you everything. I'm being...being stalked by a man who wants to harm me and I'm terrified."

If time had been on her side, would it have occurred to BJ to ponder the various ironies of her predicament? She had caused Kaz harm by drugging her and had further assaulted her by inspecting various bodily crevices for a small object wanted by one of her buyer's clients. BJ had done these things while fully aware that Kaz had already been given a vein-full of heroin; and she had done it simply for a fee. It had been just another job. Here she now was in the position of begging her victim for help and that help came with the price tag of having to go to an outlying island which, apparently, was full of lepers. BJ's face remained impassive but her pointed fingernails dug into the palms of her hands and the white lace handkerchief she carried was now soaked with anxious sweat.

"Kaz?"

"Pearl, don't even consider it." Kaz's lovely voice dripped with anxiety. She had a visceral distrust of this woman but Pearl didn't seem to notice and just winked at her.

She said to BJ, "Right-o, we'll drop you off there but after that you can look after yourself. And be advised, there is no public transport to and from Hei Ling Chau so I have no idea how you will get back. But never mind, get in." They had reached the water-taxi depot and the sunny-faced skipper was delighted with being offered such a good fare – and in his own language – by a very commanding-looking young woman.

The temperature of the water was an even 23 degrees Celsius and the boat bounced through the swell that kicked up a cooling spray of water. Not too far behind them another water-taxi, with a solitary *gwailo*, also bumped along with an equal and pleasant measure of afternoon ease ….

*

"Well? What's the story?" Pearl's voice was ice.

"I met a man…he's a lot older than me…this was several weeks ago. I was with my boyfriend at the time but he didn't seem to care about that and he went for me, really hard. It was very embarrassing and my boyfriend didn't like it. I've not seen him since. Then this afternoon, I was browsing through the alleys and came out at the Connaught Road end, and I was looking at the harbour when you two walked out of that big building across the road from it, and I heard you say you were going to Hei Ling Chau." She paused and looked at them to see how her story was going down. Clear hostility still dominated their features so she contemplated her handbag instead. "He turned up beside me and grabbed me and frightened me. He said I had to go with him immediately. I said I was going to

Cheung Chau with a couple of chums and was just on my way to meet them. He went away when I called out to you."

"You said *what* to him?" Kaz cut in, cold and sharp.

"I told him I was going to Cheung Chau."

"But you said you heard us say we are going to Hei Ling Chau. Please explain. And who the hell is he?"

"He's, um, look, I really don't know. I told him Cheung Chau in case he decided to follow me." BJ was a little surprised. *Was this woman dense or something? Did she really think she'd tell any guy the truth, let alone this particular one?* "He told me that he would be my mentor, my adviser. He said he would help me settle in here and help me find a job and so on. I knew what he meant, of course, I'm not dumb." But the ploy of the dumb blonde who didn't realise she was dumb and so elicited sympathy, didn't work on this occasion. There was silence. BJ said, "He's quite old, at least fifty I suppose, smart, English. I've only seen him twice – when he made a pass at me at the restaurant and then today. He scares me. Sorry." BJ was rarely sorry but she did a good impression when she needed to. These two were out of her league, somehow she couldn't seem to get them to focus on her. Now if one of them had been Mrs Franklin ....

"Well, Barbara, the news for you is that you are not going to Hei Ling Chau Island. You are in fact going to Cheung Chau, where you will be quite safe, unless your *adviser* follows you there of course. There is a couple by the name of Mr and Mrs Tung on Cheung Chau – ask for them and they'll put you up for the night. There are two ferry services each day. You have money I suppose?" BJ nodded. She couldn't have spoken if she'd wanted to. She was terrified. She had told him she was going to Cheung Chau. What if he followed her? The tall icy one was still talking: "And then after that, good luck. If this man is as dangerous as you seem to think, go to the police with your complaint. They are there to help people when they get into strife. Otherwise, you know," Pearl glowered at her, "people will think it's you who are up to no good, got me?"

Kaz spoke to the skipper, giving him new instructions. Move from above? He was to go one way to Cheung Chau where the very pale *gweipor* would be dropped off, then one way to Hei Ling Chau, with a pick-up from Hei Ling Chau only on Sunday for the two other dark-haired *gweipors*.

The skipper thought it strange that these ladies should be going to such isolated islands when they looked such city-types, but he also believed the popular myth that Hei Ling Chau was a spiritual place, and young ladies of these times increasingly pursued spirituality. This could be an important future income source and the skipper decided to note the time and date in his diary and keep an eye open to see if this was a new trend he could somehow cash in on. Spiritual day trips perhaps....

The little boat arrived at the Cheung Chau wharf and the skipper prepared to secure it with ropes so that the *gwaipor* could get out safely, but one of them blocked the exit. It was Kaz: "Your name and address? Or I'll get the skipper to take you back to the Hong Kong Water Police Wharf." BJ looked over the side of the boat into the hard grey water. This was, after all, much too easy. "You win. I'm Barbara Jane Collins and I'm staying at the Frangipani Guesthouse on Nathan Road."

She climbed out of the boat without another word and walked along the wharf that serviced Cheung Chau's fishing fleet and led to the village. She looked incongruous in the rural-cum-marine setting in her short white skirt, white fishnet stockings, white high heeled shoes and white silk blouse. All she had with her was a handbag, her last three housand Hong Kong dollars, a powder compact, lipstick and her small flick-knife in its pearl-handled case. It seemed a very long forty-eight hours since she had so easily stolen the three blocks of heroin.

Two days ago she was exulting over her prospects of a wealthy future as she wrapped up the three blocks of Red Bird "999", but everything had gone wrong since. BJ had half expected her mentor to do some dirty dealing; and while his intercepting her in public had played out to her advantage, she was now without means of getting rid of her haul.

He had been quick to have her followed, even though she had left her flat almost immediately after returning from their meeting in Wanchai. But he underestimated her street cunning. She was no closer to consolidating her millions, but she was still in one piece; she had the drugs; and she would set up another deal, even if it didn't net as much as he had promised. Behind her, she heard the motor of the water-taxi splutter as it fired up and Kaz and Pearl, relieved to be rid of the spooky young woman, grinned at one another as the craft manoeuvred back into deeper waters.

"Barbara!" Kaz shouted but BJ was no longer interested in her rescuers and she ignored them and kept on walking. "We're not going to Hei Ling Chau by the way. Don't you know that leprosy is highly contagious and the island is closed to the public? Hei Ling Chau is just code we use when we go to Macau for the weekend. We both play poker. Wish us luck!" The skipper beamed. Macau. Double good luck for him! But his joy at doubling the trip price was short-lived when Pearl said, "Please head south towards Macau, Skipper, and then turn back to Hei Ling Chau. We will go there after all. Thank you."

BJ smiled grimly. She bet they didn't play poker as well as she did.

Her whole life was a poker game.

Friday 19 August: 2.30pm

Kaz and Pearl discussed Barbara Collins. "Nothing she said is true. The only thing that caught my attention," said Kaz, "was when she said her name is Barbara Jane – BJ. Remember that card I found in my handbag? – 'BJ Cresswell'." Pearl nodded. There was the spectre of something white that hung in Kaz's memory from the morning Pearl found her unconscious in the Upper Albert Road apartment, but she could never capture it enough to describe it. Could it have been this woman who administered the drug to her? Pearl fretted over and over it. Damn. They'd let her off too lightly. They should have made her show them some ID, at least.

Pearl still had the task of breaking her news to Matron and Kaz to look forward to. She thanked Nurse Mae Lim, who took their baggage to the two guest villas when they arrived in the grounds of the leprosarium; then Pearl and Kaz went to the Matron's office immediately.

"I'm going to come straight to the point," said Pearl. "I've bought the lease on Hei Ling Chau. A 99-year lease from the government."

Kaz whooped and smacked the air and Matron sat down hard on her office chair.

"I've done this for some very good reasons. This building will be remodelled into a fine community hospital in a few year' time. It will have a small operating facility as well as a day clinic and all sorts of other health services."

Still not a word from Matron, who fanned her face with the hem of the apron she customarily wore.

Kaz's eyes gleamed. "What about the patients?"

"I have also made a second acquisition. The 99-year lease for the former monastery on Lantau Island became available and I managed to secure it for a very good price. The monks moved to a smaller island north of Hong Kong late last year and the buildings have been lying vacant ever since. They require a lot of upkeep and the monks needed tourist income if they were going to remain there and they didn't want that. So, I have also acquired that lease for fifty years, and the June Bowen Foundation will put the buildings there at the disposal of the leprosarium for as long as the last patient needs to be looked after. The leprosarium administrators have agreed, the deal is financially secured and Matron Cheung, it is now only your blessing I need. What do you think?"

Matron Cheung pressed the hem of her apron into her large face and cried loudly.

"I guess that's a 'yes' all round then, is it?"

"I'm all for you being President," said Kaz. "And I think Matron Cheung is impressed too, yes Matron? What a purler you are, Green. I should have known you would solve our little problem with style."

"Well, I do like a challenge. And I've secured a nice little piece of real estate for the future *and* have expanded the foundation's future operating capacity overnight. Grant money will roll in for this project, but even so, the hospital re-development will have to be managed judiciously. I estimate it will be at least five years before it can be opened to a public who are confident that the spectre of leprosy has departed from Hei Ling Chau." She smiled broadly at Kaz.

"Matron Cheung, now for a tougher piece of news. Now that the legal and financial matters are finalized, the patients can be moved and that can happen very quickly. The patients will love their new home. They will have beautiful grounds and views all around them and seclusion will be a privilege, not a punishment. There are the most wonderful gardens and fountains. It's magic. And there is a very special, private wing for you and excellent accommodation for your live-in staff. Billie will have to be supervised with that cleaver he waves around when he sees the kitchen and he will be in heaven when he sees the size of the vegetable gardens. You are all going to love it."

They looked at one another, faces beaming. Kaz said: "I guess you could have sorted this out in other ways Pearl, but never so spectacularly. How can I ever ...."

"No debt, Kaz. Not between us. This is just good business. I'll get on with the plans for the hospital redevelopment, while you run the foundation's scholarship scheme and do your post-doc work. We'll end up with some stories to tell our grandchildren, I reckon. We are going to make a big difference in our own fields, Kazza. *We are going to make our marks.*"

Kaz looked at her. Pearl's voice had dropped away to a whisper and Kaz again felt tears threaten. All she seemed to do lately was fight off tears. For all Pearl's triumphs, the basic validation of hope that love brings with it had been absent through many long and lonely years for her, despite all the successful business deals she had pulled off.

I wonder how long it will be until Pearl realises all this and lets her guard down? She hugged her friend and blinked back more tears while Matron Cheung blew her nose loudly and cried all over again.

*

"I would like to speak to Mrs Franklin please. Miss Cresswell speaking." Jenny Brown made a clicking noise with her tongue. Friday afternoons were always busy and Jenny was racing to get through the list of jobs she had to complete before she could leave the office.

"At last! I've been trying to reach you since Wednesday afternoon. Just one moment, I'll put you through to Mrs Franklin."

"Ah, the elusive Miss Cresswell!" BJ heard the smooth sarcasm in Emmie Franklin's voice and automatically lied about her recent unavailability:

"The tap in the bathroom exploded and the entire flat was flooded. I had to move out and haven't been able to make calls. I do hope it has not been an inconvenience, Mrs Franklin."

"Of course not. I am prepared to offer you a six month probationary period as my assistant, starting on Monday, at a rate of HK$3,750 per month. Usual discounts for Pensinsula Hotel staff will apply to meals and so on and for this job there is a small clothing allowance, as appearance for PR staff is of paramount importance. That allowance is HK$700 per month. I'll see you at 8.30am sharp. We work a 45-hour week."

"That's wonderful news, Mrs Franklin. Thank you so much. See you Monday then."

BJ was in the solitary phone box on Cheung Chau Island. It was now just after 3.00pm and rather than being stuck out here at the end of the earth, she should have been about to make the biggest deal of her life. Instead, she had been forced to accept a job that would cover the monthly rent on the flat she had abandoned, but not much more. Her problems were far from over.

BJ made up her mind. She had to get off this island and back to Hong Kong and fast. Surely one of the locals would take her there for a fee and then she would retrieve the heroin and take a sample around to John Simons. He'd be able to sell a little high grade pure powder for sure and that would give her enough money and time to find another punter and get a good price for the whole consignment. She tottered back to the jetty. She would have to forfeit her flat for good, no question of retrieving all her stuff now. It occurred to her that she shouldn't even go back to the guest house in Kennedy Road, what with her adviser on the loose. BJ rarely thought amusing thoughts, but she did now, felt the unfamiliar curve of her lips as a smile rose. *Maybe I'll even stay at the Frangipani Guest House on Nathan Road, ha ha.*

"You want boat, missy?" She did. An old man smiled toothlessly at her and gestured her to come on board the little sampan on which he obviously lived.

"Hong Kong!"

He closed his eyes and nodded happily: "Twenty dollar?" She nodded happily. The boat was filthy and BJ gave up trying to find a clean space on which to park her impressive backside. She'd be able to afford to buy plenty of white sharkskin skirts in another couple of days. She put her sunglasses on and sat bolt upright as the boat pulled away from the wharf and headed south. She waved her arms at the man and said repeatedly, "Hong Kong, Hong Kong. You go

Hong Kong that way." He smiled his toothless smile and maintained a southerly course. At last BJ cried. She was under threat from someone who was supposed to help her and now here she was apparently being kidnapped by a toothless old man.

She laughed between burping sobs, exclaiming aloud, "Why didn't I stay in south-east London and marry Larry Dunn? I could have had two or three kids by now and we'd have Friday night fish and chips and a few beers to look forward to at the end of each week and scratch along like everyone else in the neighbourhood for the rest of the time. They were happy, weren't they?"

"They probably were, but you would never have been." Her adviser emerged from the covered living area of the sampan. "As I was saying a little earlier, how about we sort out that matter of ours?" He gestured at the boat owner to turn around and the engine of the small craft, surprisingly powerful for its size, revved hard, and the vessel swerved sharply east.

"Perhaps your friends will help you out. Now, tell me where you have hidden the stuff or I will personally see to it that you never get back to Hong Kong."

BJ tried to shrug her shoulders; but the gesture, more of a terrified jerk, was a dead giveaway. He took a step towards her and she said: "Okay, I'll take you to it. You can have it but just let me go. Please let me go." Her hands were cold; the middle of her stomach hurt; and the pain ran in hot lines down each leg. He ignored her and spoke to the boat owner in Cantonese. BJ's stomach descended into further turmoil as the boat turned around and the three uneasy travelling companions headed not for Hong Kong but to Hei Ling Chau.

"Sure. After you learn a lesson."

*

Emmie replaced the receiver and smiled. At last something had gone her way this week. As of Monday she would again have an assistant who could take over the humdrum everyday tasks of the PR office. Not that Emmie bothered too much with routine matters but there was a lot of paperwork in the filing cabinet which needed attention. God knows what was in it all. She wandered into the administration office and instructed Jenny Brown to organise an orientation session for Miss Cresswell, after which Emmie would put her to work. She thought of the luscious skin of the young woman and how her white cleavage shadowed to blue as it plunged to intriguing depths. She reminded herself of her undertaking to be professional at all times, and she would be.

She really would try to be.

20 August: Saturday morning, Hei Ling Chau Island

On Saturday morning, Kaz came out of her villa eating a peach and waved to Pearl. "Want to come and look at my little secret? It's this way." Pearl put down the notebook she had been scribbling lists in and followed her. "Peach?" Kaz hurled the fruit and Pearl's long arm arched into the air and neatly caught it. "There's a tree in the courtyard of the villa and it's loaded with them."

Pearl had the odd sensation, just for a second, of losing all the air around her. Her mother was here. She stood in the courtyard of the same villa that Kaz now occupied, eating one of the last of the season's peaches and she saw too, the look of pure delight on the face of Dr Lin Dei – the man June had tried to help out – when he too had eaten from the little tree, relishing the late season fuzzy-skinned fruit.

The place was full of memories and she shook them away. The reality, when she looked around in the morning light, was that of a small bare island already promising to bake in another hot August day. Hei Ling Chau was ugly and Pearl wanted to change that. Why? For her philanthropic purposes or was this just another monument to her past? She could visualise the long slope from the hospital to the wharf landscaped, with a tree-lined road and a planted woodland alive with grazing geese and ducks. She would re-invigorate the enchanting kitchen garden, its stone wall still standing at the rear of the building, and she would landscape the two guest villas so that they would attract people to stay here again and fill the island with the buzz of human activity.

She sighed. Kaz turned and looked at her. "Feeling a bit rough, old pal?" Kaz put her arm around Pearl's shoulders and Pearl hugged her gratefully. "It's odd, Kaz. When we were here on Wednesday the place didn't have this effect on me, but now...." She looked around her, "I can see ghosts everywhere."

"Let's go to Squid Cove, Pearl! There aren't any ghosts there, just lovely lovely sunken ships."

They walked to the island's most easterly point and Kaz talked about how she had found the second layer of ships.

"It was in the middle of the fifth year of work here that I found the evidence I needed. I moved a pile of ballast stones from a trench at the base of the top layer of ships and found some remnant rotten wood underneath. I knew, Pearl, just knew, that I had hit the deck of another ship. Sure enough, when I excavated it very very carefully, it revealed an intact layer of blue and white pottery. It was fourteenth-century Ming Dynasty at least two hundred years older than the fragmented earthernware specimens I'd previously excavated, which directly overlaid the other. Stratigraphically, it was like winning the lottery.

"I took samples of the blue and white pottery but made no mention of the find in the thesis. I focused that work on the sixteenth century as you know. The whole thing's exhausted me, Pearl; the thesis, the book, knowing that there's years and years more work to do and today with what you've done, well...oh look, we're nearly there!" Kaz looked around her fondly. The cove where she had spent five years excavating the two ships lay in the hinge of the L-shaped island. They turned a corner. "This is it. Isn't it wonderful?"

Pearl took in the landscape of some scraggly shrubs and a few rocks protruding from gritty, grey-coloured sand near the edge of the waterline. It was bleak.

"It's depressing," said Pearl, "How could you have spent so much time here on your own?"

Kaz's raised an eyebrow in surprise. Not once during the five years she had spent working here had she ever had such a thought. She stopped. They were near the rocks and she pointed out to sea. "Just there. See where the water goes from grey-green to very deep grey-green? That's the ledge."

Pearl peered and tried to look impressed. As she did so the water in that exact spot was roiled by the smooth seal-like head of a black-helmeted diver emerging not fifty feet from where they stood; and the figure started swimming towards them.

Kaz yelled and the swimmer stopped in mid-stroke, turned briefly to look at them and swam quickly seawards. Kaz ran into the water after him. Pearl laughed at the sight of her lunging through the water in her twill work-slacks, a long-sleeved shirt and field boots, and wondered if every day at Squid Cove was this exciting.

II

RED BIRD'S FEATHERS RUFFLE IN WINDS OF CHANGE

6 September

Monday 6 Sepember: 6.00am

John Simons opened the door of his flat in response to some furious knocking. Albert Ho stood on the doorstep looking vibrantly, glitteringly alive. "That's fantastic dope, John. Strongest I've ever had. I feel as though I'm nineteen years old."

John looked for Albert's walking-stick but he didn't have it with him. John didn't like the look in Albert's eyes. They glistened supernaturally. Maybe he really was the owl that people only half jokingly whispered he was. Maybe he had flown from the museum on the previous evening and was on his way back in a state of only partial metamorphosis. John surreptitiously looked at Albert's hands. No feathers, definitely, no trace of feathers.

"Come in, Albert. Coffee?"

"No thanks. I want more of that stuff, John. I need more and I have to have it right away."

"Steady on, Albert." John had seen a little of what Albert was capable of when he let himself off the leash, and some of the stories John had heard whispered about him were frightening.

Albert said, "I'm going to do the job that you tried to get that precious little PR type to do for me, so I need a lot of heroin. I'm going to make sure Karen Henderson's reputation is dead in the water. Can you get me twelve packets? That's a nice round dealing quantity and will leave me with a little to celebrate the bitch's professional demise."

"Ah, you intend using what, exactly, for money, at this hour of the morning? If I can get my hands on that much stuff, that is." Simons was nervous. He had easily enough to fill Albert's order stashed in his kitchen in food containers and this early morning visit was almost as though Albert could smell it. "My dealer says the market is down. A packet is $150,000 so ten will set you back HK$1.5 million, enough drugs to set up a franchise. Are you sure about this?"

"I have the money and I want the goods as soon as you can arrange it."

"OK. But not here. I'll meet you at the coffee-shop near the entrance to Star Ferry – eight o'clock." John closed the door and leaned on it. He had just enough time to halve the quantities in the fourteen bags BJ had sold him the previous day. He opened the door again. Albert was still waiting for the lift. John smiled weakly. Something had changed between them. Maybe it was having so many drugs around that was making him feel paranoid or was it the look in Albert's eye? It really almost wasn't human.

*

"Hew? Albert. I need money. Now. The conversation was brief. Hew Nuttingsall replaced the receiver. When would that man ever leave him in peace? And Albert had just laughed when Hew suggested that they have dinner that night. "Why, Hew?" he had said, "Let's just stick to business shall we? I'll be at your place in fifteen minutes. You know I'm good for the transaction, it's just that with an estate like the one I inherited, it takes a while to convert assets into cash. You know the sort of thing I mean."

*

There were no hitches with the transaction and for John Simons it was the deal of a lifetime. He took a suite at the Hilton Hotel to celebrate and watched one and a half million lovely crisp Hong Kong dollars float through the air and sprinkle themselves over the bed and the carpet. All he needed now was to stay on good terms with BJ so she would keep feeding him more ....

Monday 6 September: 9.00am

"Pearl, Chief Superintendent Smythe to see you." Pearl was intent on a column of figures as Annie showed the senior Hong Kong police-officer into the room.

"Thanks, Annie. Good morning, Chief Superintendent Smythe."

"Morning to you, your, um." He seemed to recall something about the woman having a title.

"Please call me Pearl. I don't use my title, Chief Superintendent if that's what you're contemplating. It's hardly relevant."

The reedy Hong Kong senior police-officer thought it an odd comment for someone to make. Everyone was interested in having a title, in his universe at least. He closed the door and walked with rather jerky, self-conscious steps into Pearl's shabby office. He was immaculate in khaki drabs and mirror-shiny black leather lace-ups. His knee-length shorts, starched to extremes to combat the assault of late summer heat, stood out from his bony, hairy knees. Pearl allowed herself the luxury of an inward shudder. He wore long khaki socks and Pearl wished that they covered his knees so that she didn't have to have that forest of hair in her line of sight.

"Tea, Chief Superintendent?"

"No. Thank you, your ... Miss Green." He seemed happily settled on calling her Miss Green, so Pearl left him to it. "I'm here about some information we have received from a reliable informant. It has been reported that you and Dr Henderson both have a connection to one of the items stolen from the Archaeological Museum early in August."

He raised his hand to stop Pearl as she opened her mouth to speak.

"Let me clarify for you first, please. I have spoken to Dr Henderson about this matter and am satisfied with her account that she merely recognised one of the stolen artefacts as that found at the scene of the, er, death, of your mother, several years ago. Is that correct?"

As he finished speaking and looked up at Pearl, the irises of his china-blue eyes were almost totally lost in a descending tumble of bushy red eyebrows.

"That is correct, Chief Superintendent." *What is this about?* "Karen was involved in the museum theft as you must be only too aware, as she was a witness. After the theft, she looked at the notes relating to the stolen artefacts. Kaz didn't know until then that one of them was associated with my mother's case, nor was there any reason she should. The artefact itself had absolutely nothing to do with my mother's death." She paused. "When my mother's case was closed, the pin went to the archaeological museum. I've never had any interest in it. – Have you solved the museum thefts yet?"

"Not exactly. My informant also mentioned that Dr Henderson was kidnapped when she returned to Hong Kong from England on August the tenth, and that you are aware of this incident. This is also a very serious matter."

"Kidnapped is a strong word, Chief Superintendent."

"We have a copy of the hospital record of Dr Henderson's admission after she experienced a severe drug overdose. She required hospitalisation for a week. The records also confirm that she had both heroin and a large amount of Lysergic Acid in her system."

"Surely it was the hospital's responsibility to report the matter to the Police if they thought it was warranted? It wasn't up to Karen or me to report it, surely? We never gave that a thought."

He ignored the question. "The medical records also indicate that Dr Henderson was probably attacked rather than having self-administered the drug doses."

Pearl looked puzzled. "Of course that's so. But how can you tell?"

"She was physically assaulted."

Pearl was visibly shocked and he dropped his gaze.

"My apologies, Miss Green. I thought Dr Henderson may have discussed the matter with you." He changed the subject. "Someone wanted her out of action, that's plain enough. Can you think of a reason why?"

"No. Certainly not. Have you asked her?"

"Dr Henderson is of the opinion that her work is somehow involved in the attack. Apart from the usual drugs notification by the hospital to the Drugs Information Bureau, the police were not informed of the matter, which is regrettable. Kidnap is a very serious crime Miss Green. With all due respect to you and Dr Henderson, your casual treatment of the matter is, shall I say, unusual. Are you sure that you can't shed any further light on any of this, Miss Green?"

Pearl looked at Smythe. She wished she could turn her back on him but she couldn't, of course. She was becoming unhealthily absorbed in the man's unnatural amount of body hair. It oozed out of his nose and ears and escaped in fronds from his starched collar.

*

The whole world is out there and here I am, locked up in this great sandstone box with its cast-off furniture, with an unnaturally hairly man. What am I doing here?

*

"No, except for one small thing, perhaps. Kaz found a business card in her handbag on the day she was discharged from hospital. She has no recall of being given it. Who has made these allegations, Superintendent?" Smythe shook his head. "Well, they are right about Karen being given a good dose. She's a strong woman but even so it took her nearly a week to recover and she still won't get into a taxi by herself. Does she, er, realise that she was ... assaulted?"

"I presume so." He picked up his cap, rotated it in his hairy hands and studied the badge that adorned the crest. "Whose card is it by the way?"

"B J Cresswell is the name, Chief Superintendent. BJ Cresswell, Cresswell Public Relations."

*

Until that moment Superintendent Tommy Smythe had little interest in this matter. One of his officers had picked up on the report when doing a routine scan of drugs-related cases admitted to Hong Kong's hospitals. It was referred to him when the officer recognized the high profile names of Lady Pearl Green and Dr Karen Henderson. Superintendent Smythe decided that he would follow it up personally as a matter of routine and file it away as quickly as possible. A case-related referral from the Drugs Information Office (DIO) would help that bureau out – its role in helping with drugs clean-up was remarkably poor.

But when the faintly toffee-nosed Miss Green stated very clearly that the name on the business card was BJ Cresswell of Cresswell Public Relations, things changed.

"By any chance would you still have the card, Miss Green?"

"Come with me, Chief Superintendent Smythe."

They left the office and walked across the ballroom-sized foyer to the lift-well. Smythe lived very well in The Peak district of Hong Kong, but he had never seen anything quite like Pearl's penthouse apartment with its austere cream sandstone-block walls covered in art. The height and detailed work in the ceilings, the sheer scale of everything came as a shock after the shabbiness of the downstairs office.

"Take a seat!"

She went to a desk behind one of the many lounge chairs that were dotted around the living-room and extracted a small white oblong card from a drawer. She handed it to him. Hand-written in flowing charcoal grey script were the words: "BJ Cresswell. Cresswell Public Relations."

"Tell me about this again, would you mind?"

"Dr Henderson found it in her handbag after she was discharged from hospital. When I found her at her apartment the morning after she'd been kidnapped, she was completely off her face and raving about a white orb. When this card turned up, I looked up the phone directory for anything to do with either a Cresswell or a BJ but there was nothing.

"The other thing you possibly should know is that Dr Henderson and I were accosted – no, that's too strong a word – were singled out –by a woman at the Connaught Road water-taxi depot two weeks ago or more. She said her name was Barbara Jane Collins and that she was staying at the Frangipani Guest House in Kowloon. She had a very pale complexion and was dressed entirely in white. Could she be connected to this BJ Cresswell?"

"Who knows? What happened exactly?"

Pearl recounted the story of how BJ had pressured herself and Kaz on the afternoon they had caught a water-taxi to Hei Ling Chau, Pearl to see Matron, Kaz to check out her site.

Tommy Smythe smiled cheerlessly. "I don't know about your Miss BJ Collins but the name BJ Cresswell has come up in relation to another matter and this may be the beginning of some progress in that at least, Miss Green. Thank you very much for your time. Mind if I keep this?" He waved the card at Pearl who nodded and saw him to the door, not without some relief.

Monday 6 September: 9.30am

The intercom crackled, making BJ lose her place in some interesting calculations she was doing. "Miss Cresswell, my office, now!"

Emmie's office looked more like a house. Pale pewter-coloured curtains trailed over a silver-grey carpet and the room was full of bone grey Empire-style furniture. The cabinet that, in a house, would have held drinks and glasses contained stacks of magazines. The coffee-table sported a forest of exotic tropical orchids, all in glorious bloom.

"Yes, Mrs Franklin?"

"Have you finished typing up the Fleetwood contract yet and have you started on the filing backlog and are you aware that the poster for the 'Marco Polo Lunch of the Month' promo has to be at the printers by close of business today?"

BJ nodded and, uninvited, sat down opposite Emmie, notebook and pen at the ready. "Yes, Mrs Franklin, everything's under control and will be finalized by close of business." She dropped her gaze to the notebook in which, Emmie assumed, the girl made notes about her day's work.

*

Today was the beginning of BJ's third week in the PR Department at The Peninsula Hotel. For the past fortnight, Emmie had seen her assistant's appearance steadily deteriorate. Her snowy skin became duller by the day and she plodded through her work with a lack of interest that was so obvious that Emmie was surprised when she showed up each morning. But she did, looking more and more haggard and unkempt as the days went by. Emmie's attitude towards BJ had changed from being initially helpful – it was after all quite a responsible role she had taken on – to that of open irritation at her lack of energy and her shabby appearance.

What is wrong with her? Is she homeless?

*

BJ was no more homeless than she had been for the past five years, but she hadn't been having much of a time of it at the Bright Flower Mansions in Greater Kowloon either. Each night was a blur of noise and heat and the room she had taken for a month overlooked a busy night-market. It was on the outer edge of Kowloon City and it was cheap. She had risked one visit to her stash on Hong Kong side but only to move the package of drugs to an empty crypt in a largely deserted cemetery near North Point. She had given in to a moment of impulsive longing for a hit and had brought one of the blocks back with her. Empty crypts were supposed to be bad luck symbols but not for her. It was as safe a hiding place as she could think of.

She spent each day worried that her mentor would find her and really do for her this time. She really needed another good contact so she could get rid of the stuff. But each night, instead of going out, looking, she stayed in her room. Time and again she would draw the blade of her flick-knife across the block of Red Bird "999" and scoop up small amounts of pure powder that added up and up and up until she would lose consciousness and only gradually come back to awareness through layers of uneasy, dream-sodden slumbers.

Her skin was covered with raised red bites from what BJ was convinced were fleas in the bed. She felt more ground down by the squalour of her living conditions each day. When she finally complained, the housekeeper just laughed at her. The shared bathroom was rarely cleaned and the water pressure from the shower-rose released not much more than a trickle of dirty brown water. The pipes must be creakingly ancient and the water was barely lukewarm.

She had only two sets of clothes to her name, the white outfit she had worn on the day she was supposed to make her millions and a cheap black cotton suit that she had bought at the markets. It was difficult to get them laundered properly and the garments hung off her as she rapidly lost weight. When the roots of her hair starting growing out to its natural brown, she dyed it dark brown. The colour change was too hard and combined with her dingy complexion to make her inconspicuous. For the first time in her life BJ was pleased to be so.

Each day was torment for her. She relived again and again the beating she had taken from her mentor, when he ambushed her in the boat she had hired to take her back to Hong Kong island after those two snooty pieces had abandoned her on Cheung Chau. He and the old boatman had held her down and tied her hands and when the sampan reached a small beach on what seemed to be a deserted island, he dragged her onto the sand and beat her savagely. When blood started to appear through the fabric of her white suit, he shoved her back onto the craft and headed for Hong Kong where, he told her, there would be another instalment after she handed over the drugs.

BJ knew what the second instalment would be. She begged for her life but all he did was laugh and then kick her contemptuously until she fell from the seat and lay on the floor of the boat all but unconscious. The sampan finally merged with hundreds of others near Kowloon. Desperate, BJ wriggled into a sitting position. With one huge effort she stood up and threw herself over the side into a congestion of boats in the heart of the marine community off Tsim Tsa Tsui. Her mentor had little chance of following her among the tangle of craft and she had literally got away with her life. BJ shuddered as she remembered surfacing beside another boat with the feeling of something pressing on her head. Her relief at finding a plastic bag draped over her head was almost too much for her and she felt herself start to slide into hysteria as, still bound at the wrists, she manoeuvred from boat to boat. As she reached the harbour's edge, an old woman half-hauled her to the shore, muttering disapproval at the sight of the stranger who had arrived uninvited and half dead on her patch.

*

Each morning BJ faced again the terror that he might find her. She got out of bed, washed as best she could, dressed, and put her nose gingerly out of the grubby lobby of the Bright Flower Mansions. She made her way to work along the back streets which she came to know quite well. When she arrived at The Peninsula she would apply her make-up in one of the public powder-rooms and straighten her hair and clothes as best she could. She didn't leave her desk all day unless absolutely necessary. Her money was running dangerously low and there were still two weeks before pay day. Yet she feasted on every junkie's dream of pure heroin every night.

Each day after work she would hurry back to her room. The food she bought along the way invariably lay uneaten beside the sofa, to be thrown out next morning. On some of the few nights when she remained conscious after eight o'clock, she would go out for a walk. One night she saw Toby Blake, arm in arm with a good looking brunette, strolling along Nathan Road. She hurried to avoid being seen and dived into a small arcade with a variety of sex aid shops. A man leered at her and she cried.

For the first time in her opportunity-driven existence, BJ did not know what to do next. Could she trust John Simons to sell her Red Bird for her? He kept dangerous company and she was terrified of giving her adviser any way of knowing that she might be back in business. He had introduced her to John in the first place and maybe they were friends.

But yesterday was Sunday and desperation had finally moved BJ from her inertia. As the endless morning wore on and she sweltered in her squalid room, she sobered up enough to realise that she simply had to change her circumstances. She bought a dog-eared chemistry book from a second-hand shop and by midafternoon felt confident that, if she could get her hands on the simple ingredients she needed to convert her "999" into cut, marketable heroin, she would be in business for herself. By late afternoon she had done exactly that and had coaxed thirteen pyramid-shaped piles of cut heroin into existence. She sealed each pile into thick plastic bags and packed them carefully into wax-lined white envelopes. These she placed into a sturdy zipped plastic carry-bag. She tucked the parcel under the bed and went out to make a phone call. If John Simons was her only contact then the reality was that she had to use him. She walked to the nearest pay phone.

"I'll call him now."

"You'll do what?" She hadn't noticed the man walking close by her and she jumped, but it was only a stranger who thought she had spoken to him.

"Sorry, love! Talking to myself again. Bonkers, I am." BJ felt her stomach grind with fear. It was time to move her life along. She couldn't spend the rest of it like this, muttering to herself and jumping with terror when anyone spoke to her.

*

Emmie noticed another change in her assistant this morning. Her complexion and eyes were clearer than they had been for some time and her hair was well groomed even though that shade of brown didn't particularly suit her. She also seemed more interested in the work so perhaps she might yet shape up.

Emmie was right about BJ feeling better. Something had finally gone her way and she was more clear-headed than she had been for the last two weeks. Before Mrs Franklin summoned her, she had spent the first hour at her desk estimating what her income from last night's sale would buy her and how far it would bail her out of her current situation.

*

When she met John Simons on Sunday afternoon at the Merline Coffee Shoppe, he was surprised by her appearance but positively gob-smacked into silence when he tasted a pinch of the product she offered him. They met again at a noodle restaurant in Kowloon that evening and he bought a dozen bags of heroin for HK$1.5 million cash from her on the spot. BJ was staggered in turn to learn that he could get his hands on that sort of money, and on a Sunday. He must have cash reserves put by somewhere or have access to money, which was odd. He usually looked as though he was down to his last can of beer. She priced each bag at HK$125,000.00.

"I knew you'd come good, BJ. I can sell some of this tonight." Albert would be his first customer for sure.

"My supply lines have been slow but you'll do well out of this little lot when you sell it on, John", she had said generously, "and by the way, for the sake of future business, make sure I remain anonymous to your clients or I'll find another buyer. Got it?" A hint of the old BJ was in her voice.

"As for that spooky client of yours, don't ever, ever ring me and demand I come around to your place to keep his vile little requirements satisfied again. Got that too? BJ Cresswell Public Relations is out of business. No more one-off jobs. It's strictly a sell-buy arrangement between us from now on." John nodded again. He was about to make $300K profit out of this transaction. He would do – and gladly – whatever she wanted.

*

"Miss Cresswell, am I addressing the air? I repeat. Did you make a note of that?"

"I have made many notes this morning, Mrs Franklin. Excuse me."

BJ rose from her chair, ignoring Emmie's impatient look. She left without a word. She had finished her calculations while Emmie ranted on about work. Yesterday's sale was based on using less than a third of one block of the Red Bird "999". By processing the drugs herself, she should be able to generate at least $HK20 million in sales, providing she became better at it and got a higher yield from each batch. She still didn't have a good feel for how much of the actual pure stuff she should use in proportion to the cutting agents of quinine and milk products. The book she had found was old and the article on processing heroin was said to be for historical interest – whatever that was – and most of the ingredients were too obscure for her to bother about trying to source. Never mind, it had worked. All she needed was buyers to shift the stuff, and quickly.

When BJ had returned to the Bright Flower Mansions the previous evening with the roll of money in her handbag, she had worked out a new plan. She would move from one serviced apartment to another until she disposed of all the drugs. Then she would leave Hong Kong and live safely and luxuriously somewhere else. She rather fancied Spain. In the meantime, with HK$1.5 million cash in her handbag – more than one hundred and twenty thousand pounds sterling – BJ rather fancied a preview of what it would be like to take the rest of her life off from the boredom of work. Her career in PR – other people's PR at any rate – was over.

In the reception office of The Peninsula Hotel's PR Department, BJ carefully covered her typewriter and tidied her desk. She didn't need this gig. It was time to celebrate her affluence with some new outfits and a new hairdo. Her two year affair with white was over as well. White had served her when she needed attention.

Her time had indeed come, here, in Hong Kong, just as she had thought it would. Now it was time to let loose her dark side.

*

At ten-thirty, Emmie closed the latest edition of *New York Interiors* and went to the outer office. There was no sign of BJ. Her desk was neat and even the cover had been put over the typewriter. The Freeman contract lay untouched beside the machine and the filing cabinet was in the same jumbled mess as it had been for months. Emmie wasn't altogether surprised. She phoned Jenny Brown and demanded that dismissal papers be actioned for Miss B J Cresswell, effective 10.00am, Monday 6th September. No outstanding payments due. Except one, thought Emmie. If I get my hands on the little bitch....

Monday 6 September: 10.30am

Pearl made a cup of tea and went back over some of the things CS Smythe had said to her. Since she and Kaz had seen the diver who surfaced exactly above Kaz's archaeological site two weeks earlier, Pearl's plans had started to fragment. Kaz had refused to leave the island since. Pearl and Matron worried about the risk of infection. Pearl's work piled up and the plans to transfer the patients from Hei Ling Chau stalled. For Kaz, everything was tainted by the memory of that smooth black head and goggled face that had stared at them momentarily before turning and swimming vigorously out to sea.

They had assumed that the diver would make for the south-westerly edge of the island but when they made their way across the small rocky headland and through a miniature wilderness of coastal heath, all they saw was a small motorised dinghy going south, hell for leather.

*

Kaz did as much Bowen Foundation work as she could manage, using the island's one telephone as her only means of communication. Apart from her daily visit to Matron's office to use the phone, she stuck to her worksite and the guest villa.

Pearl had a constant barrage of calls from Matron demanding that Miss Doctor Karen leave. Both Matron and Pearl knew that leprosy could infect individuals differently and incubate over different time spans but Kaz was immune to any suggestion that she could be at risk of infection and refused to budge. After two weeks, when Kaz still stubbornly refused to return to Hong Kong, Pearl made it her number one priority to hire a Project Manager to organise the move of the patients to Lantau as soon as she could.

Annie persuaded Pearl not to hire someone from outside and offered to take on the extra workload herself; but as she went through what had to be done, she quietly regretted what she had inflicted on herself. Then there was the horror of moving in at the other end. That needed a fleet of ten topline buses, suitably modified for patient transport, which could manage the steep ascent to the monastery.

Pearl was so relieved to be able to delegate the work and get back to her own backlog that she seemed to lose interest in it and left Annie to consult or construct an increasingly endless stream of lists.

The weather had seemed to get hotter if anything and everyone was out of sorts.

*

Pearl felt oppressed by the thought of having to go back downstairs to the office and sat on in her apartment as Monday morning wore on, ignoring the piles of work that awaited her. She extracted a box from her desk, which she put on the coffee-table and unlocked with a key attached to a chain she wore around her neck. She took a small book out of the box, lifted the phone, spoke to an overseas access operator and gave her a number. "Pick it up," she muttered, and dutifully, someone did.

"Gates."
"Pearl."

"Pearl! Lovely to hear your voice. What's up?" Pearl smiled. Any other father would ask how she was getting on; was she well; was she in love – not 'what's up'! However there was nothing unusual about the greeting and Pearl got on with telling James what had been happening in Hong Kong since the beginning of August.

"None of it makes sense and that bothers me, James. If there's criminal activity going on, which has accidentally involved Kaz – and that would fit, when you think about the museum theft in early August – it would be understandable. But this is a series of incidents, unrelated, but all having the same result. – They impact on Kaz. – I have had a feeling for some time that something unusual is going on in Hong Kong. Something – I don't know – I'd like to say evil but I know how that sounds."

James was surprised. His daughter rarely made rash statements.

*

Kaz checked the regulator by blowing a few short, sharp breaths through it, made sure the tap was completely open, straightened her mask and slid into the water, trying not to think that she now looked much like the diver whose head had popped up, seal-like, in exactly the same spot two weeks earlier. Today was the first time she felt confident enough to get back in the water and she slid easily into its cool depths. At last, after more than nine months, she was back in her medium, back at work, her real work. Late morning dives were always best at the cove. The water was still and the tide, at its brief still stand, created hardly a stir of sediment movement.

Kaz swam with the sure confidence of one who knows her stuff and made her way down the southern flank of the first submerged boat. It was a wooden planked vessel and she counted thirty-five barnacle-encrusted boards before reaching the base. It sat on what looked like a rock shelf. But if scraped, a further tier of planking, narrower than those of the vessels that overlaid it, could be seen. This "rock shelf" was Kaz's second layer of boats, the ones she was convinced were crowded with antiquarian treasures from China.

She was near what she hoped was a good entry point into the hold of one of the vessels in the lower layer. She had spent months working out if she could gain access through the bottom of the first layer of boats or if she should just go in directly through the ship's flank. Eventually, as she realised that she would probably continue to have to work by herself, it was easiest to cut a hole in the side.

She had cleaned down the intended access point on her final dive last year, before her book was published and she became caught up in what had become an academic and personal whirlwind of success.

She dived with a short tow-line that had her tool bag attached to it. From this she drew a hand drill and started to make a small hole in the timber. It would probably take her a few dives to drill enough holes until she could insert the sharp snout of a saw and laboriously cut an entry point.

Thirty minutes. Better go up and lay off for awhile. Although the water was only twenty metres deep, she rose carefully through its brown-yellow column and broke the surface smoothly near shore. She took off the mask, slipped the air tanks off her shoulders and made her way to the beach. It was hot and she was beautifully cool after the dive. She lay on the sand and flung an arm over her eyes for shade and it was there, lulled by the heat and tired from nights of worried sleeplessness, that she fell asleep.

She didn't see the man who walked up to where she lay and certainly didn't see him take a long metal syringe from the backpack that he carried. He stopped and studied her sleeping form. The syringe had been a touch of genius. Planting the drugs on Dr Henderson was one thing but if he could leave her zonked out on a good dose, she'd be dead in the water. And here she was, an easy target. A swift jab would be a fine accompaniment to the packets of heroin he had strewn over the floor of her room and photographed.

He pushed the syringe into her arm with a vicious jab. She jerked awake and looked him in the face. Before he could complete the injection, she rolled onto her side and tugged out the needle. She tried to stand but got no further than a shaking crouch. She tried to speak but her voice was already slurring and thick. She continued to look at him as she slewed into unconsciousness and collapsed back on the sand. He waited but she didn't move again. He kicked her gently in the ribs. She was unconscious. He kicked her again, a heavy blow, fed by a swift spurt of rage.

He took in her diving gear and looked speculatively out to sea. He smiled. He had paid a lot of money for the drugs John scored for him this morning and it now seemed as though he might just have scored himself an unexpected bonus. Even if she remembered their encounter, it would only ever be her word against his. No-one would ever go near her again. She was ruined, professionally and personally, and it served the bitch right for trying to cut him out of his own circle of influence and respect in his own discipline. In addition, he now knew the location of her famous study site. If he was right, he was not only vindicated in levelling the score with her, but was also potentially a very very rich man.

Albert was pleased with himself. Even locating her had been a gift. All he'd done was to ring her place of work and say that he wanted to speak to Dr Henderson about the new scholarship scheme. What fools those people at the June Bowen Foundation are. Innocent fools. Yes indeed, he had told the pleasant young woman who spoke with him, he had heard about the new scholarship scheme and had an interested student. Yes, he did need to speak to Dr Henderson about it urgently and where did you say she is? They had obviously been so excited at the prospect of some interest in their new project that they even forgot to ask him who he was or what university he was from.

He jabbed at Kaz's prone form with his toe. Not a whimper out of her. He left the syringe beside her and disappeared into the small wilderness at Hei Ling Chau's most south-east point. A minute or two later there was the sound of a boat engine firing up.

Kaz didn't hear it.

*

"Miss Kaz, lunchtime Miss Kaz." Mae Lim was grumpy. Didn't she have enough to do without having to look for Miss Kaz? She went over to Kaz's villa at a neat trot. The small combined living and sleeping room was clean and tidy, with everything stowed neatly – except for some clear plastic pouches lying on the floor. Mae Lim looked at them quizzically. Anyone would. They were quite large pouches of white powder and she counted ten. She blanched. She had an idea what might be in them. Miss Kaz had drugs here. She found Matron, who accompanied her to the villa and confirmed Mae Lim's suspicion that what they were looking at was, almost certainly, a great deal of some sort of illegal drugs.

Matron picked up the edges of her apron and thoughtfully cupped her chin in its folds. What should she do? She despatched Mae Lim to the hospital to help with the patients' lunches and puffingly made her way towards the cove where she knew Dr Karen liked to go. Yes, there she was, sound asleep on the sand, and next to her was a very large syringe. Matron Cheung spoke to Kaz shaking her arm, but as nothing approaching consciousness was evident, the elderly nurse groaningly picked up the slender form and staggered back to the villa. Kaz's face was sunburnt to the point of blistering. Before she left the beach, Matron glanced at the syringe and carefully pushed it under the sand. Dr Karen was in enough trouble.

Matron called for help from the head nurse, Lily Wong, and together they got Kaz out of her wetsuit and into bed. Still again Matron tried without success to rouse her to consciousness. She made no attempt to hide the pouches of powder from Nurse Wong. If Dr Kaz had brought drugs here, Matron was of the opinion that she should pay for it by whatever means the legal system levied. Matron wasn't going to touch them. To her they were far more infectious than the worst case of leprosy she had ever encountered.

She called the helicopter ambulance, the great medical emergency system that Hong Kong has in place to respond to disasters on the outlying islands, and by the end of the lunch break, Kaz was in the Peak Hospital for the second time in a month – and again with a large amount of heroin in her system.

On this occasion the police were informed, but Dr Sanders, the attending physician, didn't fancy Kaz's chances of being arrested. He was sure she'd be dead first. Not only did she have a truckload of heroin in her system but his guess was that most of the damage was coming from the chemicals used to cut the product. It didn't take long for them to be confirmed as being old-fashioned, toxic and present in crazy quantities. Either an amateur or a psychopath had produced what amounted to a lethal weapon.

He told Pearl this when she bounded into the hospital at 1.30pm. Pearl studied Dr Sander's face intently. Kaz had not regained consciousness, her blood pressure was so low that she was in danger of having a stroke, and her major organs were under incredible stress. Strong and resilient in mind and body though she was, Kaz was facing death. Her breathing was laboured, she had broken ribs and a punctured lung, and her lovely skin was sunburnt red raw and blistered from lying in the sun, unconsciousness, until Matron Cheung had found her.

"The police intend to post a guard on this room, Miss Green."

Pearl became aware that he was talking to her again. She nodded her head jerkily in response.

"If your friend makes it, there will be a major investigation, so be prepared. I think you too should have police protection and until that can be organised, I suggest that you stay here. You can have the room next door."

At this, Pearl left off staring at Kaz's poor burnt face and looked at him disbelievingly. "Police protection? Me? Why?"

"This is the third recorded attack on Dr Henderson resulting in hospitalisation in slightly more than a month. *If* Dr Henderson is an innocent victim of a series of targeted attacks, *if* this is another planned attack, why not you too? You are closely allied personally and professionally. If this is a vendetta against her, it is connected to either her personal or professional life, so I ask you again, why not you?"

Pearl was astonished. This medico was thinking like a policeman, not like a doctor. "I have to make a phone call."

"Go ahead. I'll organise the room next door for you."

"Thanks," said Pearl. She used the telephone in the hospital lobby. She didn't see Ben Sander's face as he watched her stride along the corridor and she was out of his sight by the time she halted, trembling, and dropped her head into her hands and cried aloud, "Please, no, not again!" The sight of her best friend lying close to death and the memory of finding her mother's body collided in Pearl's mind in a flash of emotion so strong that it felt like the crushing onset of a migraine headache.

Monday 6 September: 2.00pm Hong Kong time

James Gates was very surprised to hear from his daughter twice in one day. "You must stay with Karen, of course, Pearl. Does her husband know?" That was when Pearl realised that she hadn't had a proper conversation with her father for a long, long time. If she had, he would know that Kaz and Drew Pierson had divorced two years ago so there were no longer any living family members to notify about Karen's condition.

"In the whole world, James, not one. Isn't that too sad?" Pearl never called James "Dad" or even the more formal "Father". "She's so alive, so well known, so wanted everywhere, but she's really only got me at the moment."

There was much talk on the other end of the line.

"They died. Both of them. Her mother was killed in a train accident about six years ago and her father died the following year, some said from guilt. He'd left Karen's mum, effectively, when he went to live in England and made it clear he didn't want her to join him. Karen was their only child."

"James, Dr Sanders says I can stay at the hospital and a police guard is being organised for Kaz." She didn't mention to James that Dr Sanders thought it wouldn't be a bad idea for Pearl to have some police protection too, nor that the police presence was to keep Kaz in, as well as keep undesirables out.

"Dr Sanders is the attending physician. Dr Ben Sanders. He's very efficient. Very frank. He said Kaz isn't going to just cruise through this. He also said she may be arrested. They found heaps of drugs in her room over at Hei Ling Chau. Oh, would you come over Dad, would you?"

James Gates held the hand piece away from his ear and looked at it. *Was that his beautiful but hard as nails daughter on the other end of the line saying, Would you Dad, would you? Well well, there was hope for them yet.*

"I'll see you tomorrow, then. Thanks, Dad! Thanks so much." Pearl hung up. James Gates was on his way. She frowned. Their relationship had improved, no doubt about it, as they dealt with the legacy they had both inherited from Pearl's mother, June Bowen.

June had always steadfastly refused to name Pearl's father, and both James and Pearl found out only after her mother's death that James was her biological father. Long before Pearl made the discovery, Pearl and James seemed destined to be natural enemies, but in the years that followed her mother's death, their relationship mellowed into civility and mutual respect, but never included filial love.

Perhaps there was room for something more.

*

James buzzed his secretary. "Peggy, get me Tokyo, will you please?"

"Certainly, Sir!"

"Bob?"

"Sir?"

"Peter Benson. Still about on your patch, is he?"

"Afraid I don't know, Sir. He's not operational, of course."

"Find out what you can about his movements, will you Bob? Let me know, or let Peggy know if I'm not here. I'm going to Hong Kong. I'll call you from the usual number if I don't hear from you through Peggy first."

"Right, Sir." James lolled at his desk, chewing a pencil. He hadn't seen Pearl for nearly two years and she seemed to be in some sort of trouble. But Peter Benson hadn't been heard of for more than six months and this had been brought to James's attention when Peter's work watch had turned up in a pawn shop in Hong Kong a week or so back. The pawn-shop owner had checked the Special Operations Branch engraving on the back against a list of notifiable codings and had rung the Hong Kong Police Service. It had been handed in.

And now here's Pearl on the phone saying something odd is going on in Honkers. Well, well, well. What do those Zen Bhuddists, that old Pete is so fond of, say? Ah yes: If you understand, things are just as they are; if you do not understand, things are just as they are. Sounds just the right sort of belief system for a chap like Peter to take up. He understands everything and nothing.

*

Pearl returned to Kaz's room and took up a vigil at her bedside as the afternoon gradually began its long softening into late summer twilight. Dr Sanders popped in from time to time and a nursing aide kindly brought her some soup, sandwiches and a pot of tea. At 10pm Ben Sanders returned with news for her.

"You can move in next door any time you're ready." He stood at the door, looking at her. "You should get some sleep if you can. I'll organise pyjamas for you and will wake you if there are developments. Try to rest, Miss Green. Your friend will need a lot of comforting when she wakes up and you'll need your strength as much as Dr Henderson does." Pearl swallowed. Even given the circumstances, these few words were the kindest she had heard from a man in years. She felt her cheeks warm with colour.

"How is she?"

"Breathing more easily and her blood pressure's up a little, but not enough to send me home just yet."

Red Bird Summer 109

So, he had overstayed his shift and didn't seem to have any intention of leaving. "You are not going to hand over to someone else?"

"No. She's my patient and until there's a change for the better...."

"Or worse?"

"Yes, that too. I don't believe your friend took a life-threatening dose of heroin. I've lived with someone who did and she doesn't fit the mould, believe me. I'm going to see her through this."

"You *lived* with a drug addict?"

"My brother. He died three years ago. Big overdose."

"I'm so sorry. This must be so horrible for you to have to deal with, to know what's happening in Kaz's system when to the rest of us she just looks as though she's out of it ...." She changed tack. "My father will be here tomorrow. Kaz doesn't have any family of her own."

"It must be good to have a father who can be around like that. You're very lucky."

Pearl was taken by surprise at the remark. "I suppose I am. Funny, I never thought about my father in that light before. My mother would have disagreed, let me tell you." Pearl smiled.

He looked at her: *She's one of a kind, I think. And she's so beautiful when that face lights up.* She felt his eyes on her and she looked back at him. They held the gaze, saying nothing. There was a noise from the bed.

"Christ, I'm thirsty! What does a woman have to do to get a beer around here?"

It was years since the silver-voiced Karen Henderson's Australian accent had surfaced so clearly and it was a splendid example of the very best when it did. Pearl and Ben laughed. Ben said she certainly deserved a beer and Pearl gave her a drink of cold water. Pearl advised Kaz not to smile in case her lips split and bled again and Ben urged her to have a laugh, seeing that she was alive against all the odds.

Kaz sank back into unconsciousness.

Tuesday 7 September: 11.30am

Detective Sergeant Herbert Proust and his three colleagues were waiting for the resumption of their daily briefing from Michael Ferguson, Chief Inspector of the Hong Kong Police Force's Narcotics Bureau. Ferguson was trying to deal with the usual panic button response from Central Division to a break-out of highly lethal heroin on the streets. A woman was in the Peak Hospital hovering on the brink of death, after what appeared to be a self-administered overdose. Nearly a kilogram of heroin had been found in her possession at the outlying island where she had been staying.

She had come around once but was basically in a coma. If she survived, she would be arrested for possession of a contraband drug in quantities that suggested she was a dealer. The police laboratory was in the process of analysing it right now and the Narcotics Bureau had the opportunity to clear the case up quickly and notch up a much-needed win in the unceasing war that waged between the inadequately resourced drugs unit and the relentless inflow of illegal drugs into Hong Kong.

Michael was summoned to the phone for the second time in just a few minutes by his secretary, Pam Walsh. He returned, scratching his head of thick black hair. "This briefing is cancelled. Regular duties. Dismissed."

The four men who left the room glanced uneasily at one another. Ferguson's briefings characteristically went on until lunch time, after which he disappeared to the Hong Kong Yacht Club or the Hong Kong Jockey Club for a lavish luncheon followed by a drinking session that lasted until early cocktails. Pam Walsh stoutly guarded his whereabouts and was always able to call him if an emergency cropped up. His presence at the unit during the first two or three hours in the morning, when he was on the ball and relatively free from his longing for the first beer of the day, was usually sufficient to keep the unit ticking over smoothly.

He returned to his office, closed the door and took the phone call from his senior officer at Division Central. From the news that had just come through from the chemists, Ferguson now knew, that not only was there a glut of high grade heroin on the streets, but that it had been cut by someone who clearly didn't have a clue about the chemistry of processing. Two of the major ingredients used had turned the stuff into a toxic brew. Added to this, the Chief Chemist said he hadn't seen such pure base product since the haul of '64. That haul was Red Bird "999", sometimes called Red Bird Rising or Phoenix. The stuff that showed up in analysis was indistinguishable from the Red Bird which had never, to anyone's knowledge, been seen on the streets before.

Ferguson was sure of his facts. The closure of the laboratory in which the Phoenix had been manufactured was the highlight of his career as head of the Hong Kong Narcotics Bureau. – He had seized the entire shipment and it was quarantined right here at the office, in total safety in the ladies' toilet block. – Ferguson had never thought to remove the stuff to another site. There were only two females on the staff and the toilet block was located within the effective security core of the Bureau's offices in Hing Long Lane.

He was restless now and walked to the door of the office, changed his mind and returned to his desk. His head hurt. It was nearly lunchtime and he could murder a beer. He took a fountain pen from his desk drawer, and after contemplating the empty pages of his notebook for a minute or two, wrote:

1. Has a new chiu chau heroin-processing laboratory opened with a new product equivalent to "999"?
2. Was more of the 1964 vintage made than accounted for, which has surfaced in the hands of an amateur?

He looked at options 1 and 2, wrote another sentence and underlined it: <u>Or, did the "999" on the street come from these offices?</u>

Michael sighed. The unit worked on the honour system. Drugs were confiscated all the time and storage space was at a premium. Any officer who wished to steal confiscated drugs could do it just like that. But Ferguson's officers were all career policemen with perfect records and he had perfect confidence in them all. Even the second interrogation cell had been taken over for drugs storage. There was no disposal system in place but drugs were moved to other storage areas from time to time and there was a good inventory system. Pam maintained it assiduously.

Ferguson rang through to her and asked to view the records, satisfied himself that no outward movements had taken place and then called her back to his office. "Everyone in the briefing-room in five minutes please, Pam!"

Baffled, his staff re-assembled, including Mrs Latham, the unit's filing clerk.

"I want a stocktake done. We have to eliminate a certain risk. DS Proust, you take Pam with you. DS Wong, you work with Detectives Crabb and Lee. Mrs Latham will mind the phones. Proust, your job is to check the toilet block. Wong, your team can do the interrogation cell. I want it finished today. Chop chop! Proust, Wong, get Pam to ring me if necessary!"

He glanced menacingly at her, mouthed "usual place" and left them to it. It was nearly one o'clock and the first course at the Jockey Club restaurant would have already been served. Best to stop off at The Press Club for a swift pint or two and some fish and chips. He would catch up with the others later on, at the Yacht Club.

He stalked from the building in Hing Long Lane and waited for his driver. "What a morning! Press Club, please, Eddie!" Eddie Ng was surprised at the change in routine but didn't query his boss.

Michael Ferguson set off for what was to be his last afternoon as Chief Inspector of the Hong Kong Police Narcotics Bureau.

*

There was no talk among the Bureau staff. If the women had been absent, Detectives Wong, Crabb, Lee and Proust might have speculated on the orders they had just received. It was obvious to them that the boss's decision to do a stocktake was linked to what was happening on the street. Each man folded in to himself. There was never any casual talk around the office about the drugs that surrounded them during the course of their working day. – The storage of them on site was just the way things were and the security in the building was tight.

Pam followed Detective Sergeant Proust into the ladies' toilets with the inventory of the drugs held in there and a checklist she had quickly drawn up. "What do you think DS, if we count the rows and numbers of blocks in each row, we should be able to do this in no time at all. You can see that the blocks are intact all the way from the benches to the ceiling.

Red Bird Summer 113

"Herbie nodded. She was right of course, all they had to do was estimate the total number by simple arithmetic and then count each block to verify it. They started. The blocks were stacked in forty-five rows from the base to the ceiling in a total of eight wooden shelves and seventy-five blocks ran the length of the wall, so there should be 3,375 blocks of pure grade heroin there, but Pam's records showed double that amount.

"It says there are 6,750 blocks," she said, puzzled.

"Oh god, Pammie! That means there must be two rows of them." Herbie Proust had a quick and sensible mind. They looked at each other and groaned.

"That means we have to count both rows", wailed Pam.

Herbie considered. It would be a ridiculous exercise to prise each brick out to check that there was another one behind it. They were laid with the precision of tiles and extracting them would create havoc. He wasn't about to take it on himself to do that. "Let's first off count that we have our 3,375 blocks here and worry about the other bit later."

They took it in turns to touch and count each brick and record each row and it wasn't until the fifteenth row near the end of the wall, that Pam noticed something a bit odd.

"These two aren't straight and there's a chink out of each corner and a bit gouged out of each base. See? They're not sitting uniformly."

"Let's see! You're right. Got a nail file?"

She had; and returned with it. Herbie gently inserted it into each irregularity in the blocks and the first one he applied pressure to came out easily enough but a piece of powder crumbled off it in the process. He placed the block on the bench and pried out the second brick. "We'll call these 15A and 15B.

"Look at that." He flattened his hand and poked it into the crevice. "Nothing behind it!" He moved his hand to the right. "Nothing here either!" He paused and twisted his hand in the confined space. "The one beside the one on the right is missing too." He wiggled his hand in further until he could feel the edge of the brick that lay beside the missing one. "I can feel that there are other bricks sitting behind the front row so I think that means that three blocks of this stuff are missing from this part of the wall."

They looked at one another and Pam said, "I'd better ring the Chief Inspector. What are you going to do with those two?" She nodded at the damaged blocks that Herbie had pried out of the wall.

"I think there's going to be a bit more poking around in here today but not by us. Let's leave them here and lock the room up."

*

As he was on his way to the Press Club, Chief Inspector Ferguson spotted old Charlie Lawson walking along Queen Street North. "Eddie, drop me off here, will you?" The startled driver did as bid and was dismissed for the day. Old Charlie Lawson was one of Hong Kong's oldest and best. He could drink a fellow under the table and was happy to do so at any time of the day or night. Ferguson now had a thirst on him that outweighed his desire for food and Charlie, always happy to see an old pal, particularly a generous old pal like ol' Mikey Ferguson, was delighted to be his drinking companion for the afternoon.

Thus, as Pam Walsh tried to track her boss down through his usual haunts and as it became obvious that he had broken with his daily rituals, she came under more and more pressure from the Unit Detectives to get someone in authority over to the Bureau to investigate what they had found in the ladies' toilets. They agreed that none of them were prepared to go home that night unless the discovery was reported to a higher authority. Pam finally telephoned the personal secretary of the Hong Kong Police Service Chief and confided her concern about being unable to locate her boss. Mrs Charlton, a woman of great influence, frowned. Did poor little Pam Walsh think that Chief Inspector Ferguson's habits would have escaped her notice?

It was not Michael Ferguson's lucky day. The Chief of Police himself hurried around to the Narcotics Bureau, sealed the unit off and stood down all personnel for re-assignment. Five senior officers from Central HQ were despatched to Ferguson's known watering holes to enquire into his whereabouts and when he was finally located at Sumo's Bar in one of the less salubrious parts of the Wan Chai District at 5pm, slurring over a young Chinese waitress and drunk as an owl on an empty stomach, it was not only the end of his day, but the end of his Hong Kong policing career.

Thanks to a reminder from the invaluable Mrs Charlton, the Chief of Police remembered that he had been anticipating that Ferguson would push his luck too far, and today was the day. He installed Chief Inspector Harry Burton into the job, seconded the Narcotics Bureau Detectives to Central Division and put in four Detectives from Traffic to take up the work of the Narcotics Bureau while it underwent a restructure.

Herbie Proust watched as the gleaming white wall of Red Bird "999" was dismantled and moved to Central Division's security lock-ups with all the other mixed bags of seized drugs that had been stored in the interrogation cells for so long. He felt distressed by the sight of it but couldn't have said why. Although it turned out that only three blocks were missing, the systems in place at the Hing Long Lane premises had clearly broken down.

The early day of a new dawn of responsible police management was on its way.

*

Pam Walsh sighed as she finished clearing out her desk and packed up Chief Inspector Ferguson's papers and personal possessions. She was to be seconded to assist the Chief's Personal Secretary, Mrs Charlton. Pam had the feeling that life was about to become a lot more ordered and a lot less fun than it had been when working for her cheerful, alcoholic boss. When she had, under some duress, divulged Michael Ferguson's daily routine to the Chief of Police, rather than being reprimanded, she had been congratulated on maintaining loyalty under difficult conditions. Pam had an inkling of how it must feel to receive a battlefield commendation. It had been a bit like that sometimes. She took a last look around the office and went home.

Herbie Proust received his secondment orders with relief. After the disquiet caused by the discovery of the missing drugs, he spent a lot of time considering how easily Pam's nail-file had fitted into Blocks 15A and 15B and he also recalled the day, quite recently, when he had admitted BJ – was her name Crookwell? No, Cresswell – into the offices and gave her the keys to the ladies' toilet. Herbie decided it was best to say nothing. There was no evidence to implicate him in anything, mainly because he'd been careful to turn off the security camera when she came into the office and it was a long shot that she'd taken the stuff anyway. He strained to remember. He was sure she had only been in the toilet for a couple of minutes. The stuff could have been removed years ago.

Let's face it, he thought, three of those blocks'd be enough to set a chap up for life. Then he felt uncomfortable again. Maybe that had occurred to BJ too, if she'd realised what she was looking at. He put her from his mind, pleasant enough memory though she was, and with the eyes of one of Central Division's security specialists on him, cleared his desk and left the building.

Wednesday 8 September: 9.00am

Despite the events of the previous day, the Hong Kong Chief of Police, Gerry Gallop, was persuaded to change his mind about sending an officer to the Peak Hospital to arrest Dr K Henderson in Ward 11, for possession of a criminal amount of illegal drugs. He hadn't been happy about it, but the call from the Chief of Staff of the British Home Office was more of an order than a request. The Hong Kong Police Chief had no idea what it was all about; but, with the current situation in Narcotics, he had to be satisfied with authorising a twenty-four police presence on Dr Henderson's floor instead of arresting her.

Kaz regained consciousness fitfully until late on Tuesday night, when she woke up, feeling calmer this time, the sensation of sand-papered thirst absent from her throat, the pain mostly gone from her head, and with her sun-mortified flesh a little cooler. She had turned her head on the pillow and saw Pearl and a man standing close together in the corridor outside her room. They were looking out of the window and she saw Pearl turn her face to him and kiss him gently on the lips.

Kaz thought she must be hallucinating and closed her eyes and it wasn't until the next morning that she woke again. Pearl was beside the bed, smiling at her.

"That's more like it," said Kaz. "I had an odd dream about you."

James Gates came into the room and he also beamed at her.

Kaz had met Pearl's father only once or twice years earlier; but she cried when he told her that he had some business he could do in Hong Kong and decided to come over and help out in some way after her ordeal. James's type of help was not so much of a domestic order, more a matter of using his considerable influence to do a little wheeling and dealing around the traps, see what's going on perhaps. Kaz needn't know about that.

There was some awful rumpus going on with the Narcotics Bureau bunch but he had managed to get ghastly old Gerry Gallop on the phone just after he arrived and spoke to him about Kaz. Gallop could be an all-round nuisance of a man when he got his crooked teeth into something. Whatever had set him off yesterday had done a good job of stretching his mental faculties and James had little difficulty in persuading him that, in his position of Head of the British Government's Home Office, he would take responsibility for Dr Henderson while she remained in the Peak Hospital, even if it happened that she was arrested for the possession of the heroin found on Hei Ling Chau.

Now James looked at Kaz, a small flush of returning colour already draining from her face as she slumped back on the pillows after only a few minutes of chat with Pearl. He cleared his throat and said, "Karen, will you answer some questions for me? It will be very useful if you can." She looked at him and nodded. "I'll keep it short. Can you remember anything at all about Monday?"

She nodded and swallowed with difficulty before she spoke again. "Diving. Went diving."

"Good, and what about after the diving?"

"Beach."

"Right. Anything after that?"

Kaz's eyes had closed again but scrunched up at a memory. "A man. Thought it was a knife. Screamed. I screamed."

"What man?"

"Albert Ho." Kaz's eyes flew open and she sat up. "Albert Ho. Get the police. Get my clothes. I want the police." She threw herself with a horrible weak determination out of the high bed and tried to crawl to the bathroom. Pearl and James tried awkwardly to help her to her feet. Dr Sanders came into the small turmoil-filled room and took in the situation at a glance:

"Everybody stay very still and that means you too, Dr Henderson."

James noticed how Pearl looked at him. Kaz slumped to the floor and cried. James patted her head and he and Dr Sanders helped her up. Pearl smoothed down the bed sheets and fluffed up the pillows.

"Right! What is going on here and why is my patient crawling around on the floor screaming?"

"Dr Sanders," said James, "Karen has just had a very strong recall about what happened to her on Monday. She is as you can see a most determined woman, and has unilaterally decided not only personally to apprehend the man who attacked her, but to summon up the entire resources of the Hong Kong Police Service to assist her. I expect nothing less of her, naturally.

"But I do agree that we should summon the police. Dr Henderson has identified her assailant. I'll telephone old Gerry Gallop. Time to make this official."

But Pearl surprised him. "If Kazis right, Dad, and it is Albert who did this to her, we may be close to sorting out why she has been the subject of these attacks. Having someone she knows in the picture makes it less of a random puzzle, don't you think? Brings in the notion of motive, wouldn't you say? Bringing the police in could be a mistake at this stage. They'll only see the drugs stuff and not what's going on behind it. With Albert in the frame we've now got a different perspective on what's been happening to Kaz.

"All the police want is perpetrators and victims and although Kaz is certainly the victim in this case, they'll pounce on the opportunity for a sensational drug case clean-up story; and on the face of it, she does look like the guilty party." She finally stopped and drew breath.

James noted how she had recited very intimate details in front of the good doctor while still sounding like the level, calm and very much business-as-usual Pearl. Ben Sanders listened as she spoke with the rapt face of one at an orchestral concert, about to hear a favourite piece. James did not miss this. Nor did Kaz, and she recalled the scene at the window last night. It was him with Pearl. Hallelujah, Pearl was in love at last. She smiled.

"Fine", said James.

"You agree?" This was too easy.

"Yep. I like the way you think, Pearl. What are you going to do?"

"I dunno, James. What *are* we going to do?" James noticed that he had ceased to be "Dad" and had reverted to being "James" again. So much for progress.

James shrugged. "I have to phone home. I promised to check in with Peggy about something. I'm going to the, um, office, to put the call over security lines, and so it will take an hour or so. Then I think I'll go back to my hotel and get a bit of rest. I'll see you all tomorrow. Good to see you on the mend, Karen."

Pearl smiled as James left. *He's either getting careless about his precious Special Operations in Hong Kong needing to remain covert or he trusts us. I wonder which?*

*

Peggy had some news for him. "It seems it may be as you thought, Sir. Dr Benson left the Maromji Monastery nearly six months ago now. He planned to go south in a simple fishing vessel. He is meditating upon the teachings of the Zen Master, who was said to have travelled the sea route south from Taicang, in the fifteenth century, on one of the boats in the great exploration fleet of Zheng He. Dr Benson is looking for insight by travelling the same route. He hasn't been heard from since."

"Thanks, Peggy! Let me know if you hear anything else. You can get me at the Mandarin. Room 417."

"By the way, Sir, big bust-up at Hong Kong Narcotics Bureau yesterday. Chief Inspector Ferguson has been stood down and the staff seconded to Division Central. The Chief has put in replacement staff from Traffic while a review goes on. Gossip says it's something to do with the drugs quarantined in the Division but no-one really knows."

James wondered if he did.

*

James made the call to Peggy from Dr Peter Benson's old office in what was these days the South East Regional Information Bureau, a semi non-government organization that monitored mainland radio broadcasts and provided translations to various Hong Kong media outlets. It had been re-structured eleven years earlier and the office was located in the Political Science Faculty of an external arm of the University of Loweth. Peter Benson's position, originally directly attached to the university, had never been replaced after he left suddenly in the autumn of 1964. The Faculty Head these days was a bona fide faculty head but James retained an office, locked to everyone but himself, for use when various projects brought him to and from Hong Kong on some of his occasional covert HO business.

James was tired of the deception of doing government business under the aegis of a QANGO (quasi non government organization). It seemed these days to be a little passé. A little too Spy Versus Spy. He locked Benson's room, which was still stuffed with specialist communication equipment – now out of date but so loved by the man who had worked there, before he discovered that Bhuddism had more fascination than gadgets. He left, nodding pleasantly in response to the curious gazes of the Ph.D. students who provided him with occasional translation services, as he did so.

In Upper Albert Road, he hailed a taxi for his hotel. Tomorrow he intended to check out Dr Albert Ho in earnest. It was important but not urgent. If Albert Ho was the man who set up Kaz with the drug haul, he obviously thought he'd done a good enough job to leave no evidence of his involvement. He'd be getting on with business as usual in James's estimation, and if he was, that suited James entirely.

Thursday 9 September: 9.30am

After walking out of the Peninsula on Monday morning, BJ set about transforming her appearance so that on Tuesday, when she arranged to inspect serviced apartments, she was no longer BJ Cresswell. She was now Belinda Jean Cook. BJ Cook proved to be very efficient and she found a good furnished apartment at North Point, handy to her stash and well away from central Hong Kong. By Tuesday afternoon, with a new look, a new name and somewhere pleasant to live for a time, poor old BJ Cresswell was erased, without even getting to celebrate her 21st birthday.

The weight BJ had lost during her two week ordeal at the Bright Flower Mansions had transformed her appearance. Now, she could have comfortably blended in with London's fashion and music set rather than looking like a minor actress from a 1950s movie. Her hair was cropped into a black shiny bob, her pale skin was highlighted and brushed into sculptured sharpness around the cheekbones and her mouth was pale beige, the old red lipstick consigned to the rubbish bin along with the white suit and high heeled shoes. Belinda wore a crisp cotton shirt and a slim black skirt. She was smart rather than sexy and was unrecognizable as the woman who had left Emmie Franklin's office without a backward glance on Monday morning.

*

The North Point apartment BJ found was expensive but the security was top-grade and she moved in on Wednesday afternoon. On Thursday morning she set off to buy more clothes to match her new style. After that, she would retrieve her stash. She had to get busy processing it, and rather than risk being seen coming and going from the abandoned cemetery, she was going to keep it in the apartment. If her new cover was good enough, it would do. If not, BJ doubted she would be around to lament the loss of her goods. Her major worry was still that of having only one client. If John knew that, he would almost certainly start to argue price. But if she had another client or two, that would make a difference. She chewed on a tendril of her newly darkened hair and thought about John's friend, the tall intimidating Asian man. Perhaps he could be useful to BJ Cook, somehow? If he was kept sweet. She'd mention him next time she phoned John and see what he would tell her about him.

BJ had the feeling that keeping that man sweet meant keeping him full of drugs. And she was just the babe to do that.

In the meantime, there was always night life in Wanchai, with ships still arriving each week with military personnel on Rest and Recreation leave. They were all busting for as much as they could cram into their week's break and BJ, who had plied her wares around the district during her incarnation as the "white witch", knew it could be a dangerous place to deal. Then there was BJ Cresswell's adviser to consider. He frequented Wanchai for his activities too, whatever they were, but he would never recognize her as BJ Cook. She was safe from him at last.

As BJ thought about how easily she had transformed her appearance, it occurred to her that perhaps another BJ, a young upper-crust Hong Kong type, could attract attention from a better class of customer so that BJ Cook could stay away from the bar scene altogether. It would have to be someone without BJ Cresswell's innate talent for invoking instant lust and violence. This one could stroll the bars, the well-lit bars, the ones that had visible Military Police on duty. But discreetly. With a few little packets in her ladylike handbag.

*

BJ took the lift to the basement and waited to speak to the building supervisor while he sorted out a problem for another resident. She was off-guard, staring off into middle space as the man finished his business and turned to leave. In doing so, the walking-stick looped over his arm swung out and smacked her hard across her ribs.

BJ dipped her head with the reaction of one who has learned to respond to pain with the downward gaze of the dominated. She willed herself to play the new role of Belinda Jean Cook, a hard-nosed modern woman, no longer BJ Cresswell, sex for hire. BJ would have cringed as she had just reflexively done, and she would have said or done anything until she found an advantage over the bastard. Belinda Jean was made of plainer, more fractious stuff.

"Watch it you silly old bugger. Are you trying to put me in hospital with that stupid stick? I'll have your guts for garters if you do that again. Got it?"

"I'm very sorry," the man said. "Please. Sit down. That was stupid of me. I'm running late and wasn't thinking...."

Although he seemed genuinely solicitous, BJ shook with superstitious fear. *It was him. Talk about summoning the Devil. John's mate, the scary one.*

She thought quickly. She needed to get his name or find out where he worked. Most importantly, she had to find out if he lived here. If he did, she didn't. It was that simple. BJ knew trouble when she saw it.

"I'm sorry too, sorry you're such a dimwit, Mister." He smiled, coldly. BJ was not used to being ignored by men. Belinda had to have a few tricks up her sleeve, surely. "Cat got your tongue?" He flinched. "Well? One minute you're apologizing for whacking me

Red Bird Summer 123

with that bloody weapon and the next, thin air ... so, cat got your tongue?"

"I'm Albert."

"Live here, do you, Albert?"

"No, actually, I have been visiting friends." Albert was very sober in all respects. Since Monday evening, after returning from his task on Hei Ling Chau, he had been staying with his sister who lived in these apartments. He decided to defer the celebration he deserved for ruining Karen Henderson's reputation until there was something in the press about her arrest. He had a room in Veronica's apartment which he rented to be available for his own use at times when he wanted to have a dry spell. This morning when he woke up his head was clear, and he decided that he could confidently return to his own house in Sheung Wan.

"Where do you live then?"

He had already dismissed the mouthy young woman he'd accidentally struck. Albert wanted her to shut up. She was annoying him. He wished he had hit the bitch harder. "Where I live is entirely my business. Now if you will excuse me ...."

Two taxis arrived. BJ stood up, wobbled and delicately fell over. The building supervisor was concerned and wanted to call an ambulance. Albert was now out of temper with the bitch. He got into the first taxi without a backward glance.

BJ, who assured the concierge that she would seek some medical advice, jumped into the second cab, saying, "Follow that taxi!" The taxi-driver spoke no English, the line was completely lost on him and BJ resorted to pantomime to get her message across.

When Albert's taxi pulled up outside the museum, BJ quickly waved the driver on to Central. "Got him!" She clapped her hands in her new excitable BJ Cook style and laughed out loud.

*

The early morning bustle of Hong Kong citizens off to their day's work also brought James to the museum as Albert's cab delivered him to the door. *Chap has to be Albert Ho*, he thought, as he watched Albert alight and pay off the driver. He fitted the description Kaz and Pearl had given him of an impeccably suited man about six feet two inches in height, of slender build, who sometimes used a walking-stick for no apparent reason. Good looking, about fifty-five years old, patrician features. James noted the excitable reaction of a young woman whose taxi swerved towards the kerb behind the other cab, as if also about to stop, but which instead she waved on, laughing and clapping her hands at Albert's retreating back as he walked towards the museum's side door, apparently oblivious to her existence.

James acted on an impulse. "Follow that taxi please." The driver shrugged and fell into the traffic behind the yellow cab and stayed with it as it snaked through thick traffic to Central, before stopping outside the Lane Crawford Department Store. "Stop here! Thank you, driver." James paid and kept an eye on the young woman who emerged from her taxi and took stock of her surroundings as though it was perfectly usual to conduct a 360 degree street scan before making another move. James made an appreciative audience. In his profession, this type of thing was often an advised line of action.

He followed her at some distance into the department store where he put himself through the immense tedium of looking at rack after rack of clothing while the young woman selected an armful of dresses and laboured into the changing rooms with them. This initiated a flurry of comings and goings by two shop-assistants. At last she emerged with several garments draped over her arms. If James had been less confused by the caravan of textiles that were whisked in and out of the changing-room, he may have noticed that the young woman had changed from the simple black shift she wore when she entered the store into a different outfit altogether. She paid and left her purchases at the desk. He watched her go into the next department, unencumbered by parcels.

In Shoes, the same ritual was followed as in Dresses and James's quarry floated from Shoes in a wonderful pair of beige heeled classics rather than the flat black courts she had arrived in. A similar operation went on with Handbags and a superb gold-chained beige number appeared over her shoulder as she left, no sign of her previous handbag in sight.

The ultimate revelation, for James at any rate, was Hair Products. He examined a range of men's hair grooming aids and discovered that not only could the hair regenerate after follicle death, but it could regain its original colour as well. He was so interested in this that he failed to recognize the luxuriantly coiffed red-head who walked out of Hair Products and strolled by him with a sly sideways glance. James was so taken by the thought of taming his fading head of hair into silky compliance simply by the application of a rare oil used until recent times only by members of the aristocracy, that he completely missed the young woman's hair transformation from raven haired bob to lustrous auburn locks. When he realised that she had expertly lost him, he wandered back to Dresses and spoke with one of the sales assistants.

"My daughter ordered some new frocks this morning and has arranged for them to be delivered, I believe. I'd like to surprise her by taking them home before she arrives if that can be organized. It is her birthday today and she can have some fun trying things on before the party."

The assistant made noises about what a lovely father the young lady was lucky enough to have and James left Dresses – or was it Frocks? – with the parcel, addressed to Miss BJ Cook, Flat 7, 14 Tin Hau Temple Road, North Point.

*

BJ thought it was a pity that the bloke who'd been trailing her had been so easily diverted in Men's Hair Products. If he had stayed on her case she would have given him an even better run for his money at Marks & Spencers, where she stocked up on underwear before walking north to The Hilton where she had a coffee before visiting a jewellery shop on the ground floor. BJ fingered the diamond earclips she had purchased which went very well with a discreet diamond and gold pendant she had also fancied. She was very pleased with her morning's work so far. Her new persona had emerged very easily and now all she needed was a name.

James also was satisfied with the results of his morning's foray into fashion and he took a cab back to his quarry's apartment in Tin Hau Temple Road. The building supervisor was absent from the front office. James left the parcel on the desk and wandered down to the basement and the residents' carpark, from where he had a view of all the taxis that disgorged their passengers at the front court of the apartment block. He did not have long to wait. He did not recognize the red-head but he did recognize the handbag and the shoes. He was impressed.

She leapt nimbly from the cab, ignored the concierge – who didn't recognize her – and walked briskly into the lobby of Block A. Within five minutes she was back, and left in the same cab she had arrived in.

Several taxis waited for fares at the front of the building and once again James found himself giving directions to a driver to follow the taxi in front, which this time headed for the urban maelstrom of North Point. The lead taxi turned right at the major intersection at North Point Road and headed east before looping up Flower Road, where two abandoned cemeteries kept a few decaying old mansions company. James became concerned. This was a rare, under-developed area of Hong Kong Island, where there was hardly any traffic and no-one at all on the street, and he felt conspicuous.

"Stop here please, driver!" Miss Cook's taxi had stopped another five hundred yards in front of him, at the base of what was a very steep hill. James paid his fare and walked leisurely through the derelict gate of one of the abandoned mansions – just another property developer perhaps, looking for an opportunity to cash in on some other family's past glory. He peered carefully through the gate. Miss Cook had paid off her cab too, and she watched it retreat while looking about with those watchful, pale eyes. He felt a prickle of unease. With observational powers like hers, surely she must have noticed his taxi, at least.

He was relieved to see a gate in the brick wall at the back of the derelict house, near the kitchen garden. From that vantage point he could walk up the hill through the abandoned cemetery next door, reach the second mansion on the other side, from where he would probably be able to observe Miss Cook without being seen. He was puffing after the uneven uphill walk. Fortunately, he didn't even need to open the side gate of the house that stood adjacent to the abandoned cemetery on the highest part of Flower Road. Several palings had come adrift and James had an excellent front row view of BJ as she crouched in front of one of the old crypts.

These old burial grounds were a clear reminder that the tradition of looking after the graves of ancestors was on the way out in modern Hong Kong. How long since these ancients had been laid to rest? For the most part, the tomb's circular seals were broken and the ground was sprinkled with worn and broken funerary items. Very few people came to this quiet end of the island – it may be full of ghosts to frighten the living – but the truly frightening message was from the living to the dead, telling them that those left behind were now clearly forgotten.

BJ extracted an oblong parcel from the second crypt in the fourth row on the left and put it carefully into her beautiful new handbag. James thought that the handbag could have been made to accommodate the parcel. She looked around nervously. James was interested. It looked quite heavy. Money, perhaps? And what was she about to do now? Hike back down Flower Road in her pretty high heels? Or had she something else lined up?

BJ left the cemetery and started the downhill walk. James could not see the road but he heard a vehicle draw over to the kerb and from his vantage point in the garden heard her voice – well-modulated, pleasant – and the slam of a car door. He hurried along the side garden to the front of the derelict house and caught a glimpse of the yellow taxi as it turned and headed off down Flower Road. There was another taxi making its way up the hill too. It was empty and he wondered about an empty taxi looking for a fare in this deserted area and decided not to hail it. Perhaps its appearance was not a coincidence. He waited until the driver turned around and gamely walked the two miles back to North Point Road.

It had been an interesting diversion. Without doubt Miss Cook was up to something, but for James, it was time to visit Chief Gerry Gallop and keep him sweet before Gerry remembered poor old Karen doing the hard yards in hospital and decided to arrest her after all. He didn't like Gerry's chances.

*

Pam Walsh smiled at the man who strolled into the office she shared with Mrs Charlton and so casually asked to see Gerry.

Mrs Charlton bristled. "The Police Chief is unavailable, Sir. May I take your details?"

James thought that a perfectly reasonable request and gave his name as James Gates (Sir), Chief of Staff, British Government Home Office, London.

Mrs Charlton coughed and Pam smiled a little more widely. Mrs Charlton at least had the good sense not to apologise and merely asked him to take a seat while she went in to advise Chief Gallop of his presence.

"Gerry, long time! Thank you for organizing that little matter yesterday. Short notice, I know. Much appreciated."

Gerry Gallop did not like Gates, or "Sir James" as he had been for the past few years. He was a flippant sort of fellow and in the past had been known to visit Hong Kong from time to time – either incognito or pretending to be a journalist – stirring up trouble and generally embarrassing the Police Service, always slinging off about the atrocious drugs clean-up record. – "Sir James."

James waved the reference to his title away. "Information, Gerry, I both have and need information. I believe there's been a bit of a to-do with your Narcotics Bureau lot this week. Anything connected with some very high grade heroin, by any chance? Stuff that has been cut either by a total ignoramus or a psychopath?" James knew he shouldn't enjoy himself at Gerry's expense but Gerry's face was a picture. "You remember Dr Henderson, the woman who was overdosed, found full of the stuff with ten packets strewn around in her room on Hei Ling Chau Island, taken to hospital in a critical state, under police guard, hmm?"

Gallop's expression settled but he paled. He'd completely forgotten about the damned woman who'd been admitted to the Peak Hospital more than half dead. With all the drama going on over at Hing Long Lane she had escaped his mind. He hurriedly made a note for Mrs Charlton to follow up on her condition.

"The woman in question is my daughter's best friend, Gerry! She is Karen Henderson, post-doctoral research archaeologist. Excellent credentials, far from being a drug addict. She is conscious now and has identified the man who filled her left arm up with that particularly savage concoction. I just thought you may be interested in knowing a bit more about it, particularly in view of what has been happening over at Hing Long Lane." James took care to emphasize the words Hing Long Lane.

Gallop gulped. He is a cautious man and that is not a bad thing for a Chief of Police to be. He never makes nor issues impulsive statements and most of his policing philosophy is shaped by the background papers and policy scripts he is fed, which is all fair and good. But he is painfully slow and that is why Chief Inspector Michael Ferguson enjoyed fifteen years of the good life before being sprung, largely, it must be confessed, by Mrs Charlton's observations rather than Gerry's.

"Come along, Gerry, what's going on?"

"Who did you say is your daughter, old man?"

"Pearl Green, June Bowen's girl. June and I were married once." James was deliberately vague.

"The old Earl of Towney's grand-daughter?" That was exactly the sort of thing Gerry would know. "The drugged woman is the best friend of an earl's grand-daughter?"

"Well yes, put like that, I suppose that's quite correct."

"Damned scandalous. I'll have her released immediately."

"She's not in prison, Gerry. She's in hospital. There's a guard. I think that's a good thing, don't you? Particularly if she was attacked rather than going doolally and innoculating herself with a thumping great hit of heroin. No. The problem requires subtlety. She knows the man who did this dreadful thing to her and that is why I have come to see you."

Gerry Gallop settled back in his chair, lulled by the comfortable and predictable votive offerings to his power. "What should we do, do you think James? Home Office business is it?"

"Could be, in one respect, can't swear to it of course." James pressed his index finger to the side of his nose in the universal gesture of complicity and Gerry nodded solemnly. "Chap in your position has the capacity to do some really clever policing, I expect?"

Gerry nodded solemnly again, although he did wonder what the deuce the fellow had skipped to now.

"So rather than hove in and arrest this fellow on the say-so of Dr Henderson, you could initiate a much more clever operation, I imagine?"

Third nod.

"... along the lines of putting a twenty-four hour watch on the man? Plain-clothes of course," James added hurriedly, having a sudden vision of smartly turned out uniformed Hong Kong Police Officers clipping along the streets of Hong Kong hot on Albert Ho's heels.

"Wouldn't be a problem, old man. But why bother? We can just pick him up and clean up the whole operation in one hit, surely."

"Of course, Gerry, but there is the matter of the drugs stolen from the Hing Long Lane quarantine storage."

Gallop felt a twinge of something like anxiety. How had Gates known about that?

"What if he is the chap who master-minded that op? If your chaps tail him they may find out any number of helpful things to do with cleaning up your case."

Gerry Gallop's fourth and final nod was so slow that James realised he had reached information overload.

"Let's put it all on the table then, shall we? You organise a plain-clothes tail of the man – has to be day and night – he's probably a dangerous cove. – He attacked an innocent woman, don't forget! And I'll drop in here daily for a written report of his movements. Of course, if he commits a crime you'll want to deal with it. Quite realise that. Now, you need his details."

James wrote out Albert's details and handed the slip of paper over.   Gerry's brow cleared a little as he realised that James had considerably set out the operational plan in writing. He thought: *Always much better to be quite clear about things. Especially about Mrs Charlton giving James a typed report each day. Dashed good idea.* Then he looked at Albert's title: *Sort of chap digs up old pots and pans and trinkets of one sort or another.* Gerry always thought that sort of thing an unsavoury carry-on. "Do you think the past can teach us anything, James?"

"Apropos of what, hmm? Bit of a baffling question to spring on a chap."

Gerry coughed. "Sorry. Well to put it simply, things that have happened before – buildings, all that sort of thing. Do you think digging them up does any good? Find it annoying myself, thinking of all these pots and pans types running around digging things up just so they can say that people from that particular time had bowls with paintings on them whereas at that particular time they had bowls with something else on them." He furrowed his brow in concentration. "Or nothing on them at all. Always struck me as the most remarkable waste of time. Then other coves write books about the real past – wars, for example."

James was impressed. Gallop was rarely heard to utter entire sentences, but clearly he had given the subject of archaeology considerable thought. Had it mixed up with history, but still .... "In answer to your question, Gerry, and apropos particularly of bowls, it can't teach us a bloody thing, in my opinion."

Gerry Gallop was pleased. He beamed at James and extended his hand as he walked him to the door. "Great privilege to meet you again! We'll consider ourselves in operational mode, The Home Office and The Hong Kong Police, as of this moment, shall we?"

James nodded. Such inter-departmental liaisons were necessary, but he felt sure that if Gerry knew the half of what he'd got up to in Hong Kong over the years, he'd rather be put out to pasture than be associated with the British Home Office. They shook hands and James left, feeling a little sickly.

Thursday 9 September: 1.00pm

The concierge didn't recognise BJ as she arrived dressed and coiffed as the refined, red-haired friend of Miss Cook, Flat 7, Apartment Block A. They would have to meet sooner or later, so she went to his little office that doubled as the apartment's car-park check point.

"Hello. I'm Sally, Miss Cook's friend. Flat Seven, Apartment Block A. Is she at home, do you know? She should be expecting me."

The man shrugged and smiled at her and handed her a square parcel. It was a big parcel, addressed to Miss BJ Cook, the purchases she had made from the clothing department at Lane Crawfords. "Nothing to sign? No? Thanks, then! No delivery charge to pay?" The man shook his head. Sally balanced her smaller parcels on top of it and walked carefully to the lobby of Apartment Block A. She felt deliriously happy. She had a new wardrobe and yet another new identity. It was time to sit down and sort it all out. She had bought a couple of trinkets to amuse herself – nothing showy – and the blissful designer handbag which held the two intact blocks of Red Bird "999" product perfectly.

Barbara Cook would have laughed out loud while waiting for the lift to take her to the seventh floor but Sally Walters was very ladylike and used the time instead to admire her beautiful new Balenciaga heels.

The diminishing BJ Cresswell, ascendant Barbara Cook, and embryonic Sally Walters sat together on the rug in the middle of the sitting-room floor of Apartment 7. Sally cried a little from the stresses and strains that the day had imposed, but the two BJs were made of different stuff and took an inventory of the day's achievements. They had food, clothes, jewellery and a pleasant, safe – if temporary – place to live. Most importantly, the drugs were secure.

Sally had a lot to do. New dresses to hang, four pairs of new shoes and a tote bag to put away in the big built-in wardrobe. There were scented French soaps and bath oils to place on the marble vanity top in the bathroom, seven pairs of silk knickers and the same number of matching brassieres to stash into the dressing table drawers, accompanied by stockings, a raft of cosmetics and two bottles of concentrated perfume – patchouli back notes for Barbara and citrus with a touch of amber for Sally. Nothing for BJ Cresswell of course. Sally was not even aware of BJ Cresswell's presence. The groceries BJ Collins ordered had been left at the back door to the flat and in the guest bathroom there were different sorts of bottles to examine and line up in order of use for the processing operation that would begin later in the day, after she had made a salad, perhaps. Bathroom two was to be the laboratory. Sally thought that perhaps she should have bought a laboratory coat so that she could really look the part of the chiu chau chemist she felt she had become.

She was exhausted. She ate an apple and walked around the apartment, looking at the expensive purchases, particularly the new designer handbag and its sister tote bag. One, a fitting coffret for the wonderful Red Bird; the other, a good place to store money and other necessities. But the best was yet to come. She drew a white box from the handbag. Seeing the whiteness of the box reminded her of something – or was it someone? – She felt uncomfortable. The box would have to go. She opened the lid and looked at her stash, two solid oblongs of heroin wrapped in cellophane and sealed with a gold stamp. They were beautiful. She carried the box into the second bathroom, fetched two blue-and-white china fish-print bowls she had bought with the grocery order. Then she prised open the seal, peeled back the cellophane and placed the blocks beside the partially used one she had already taken from the crypt when she moved into Bright Flower Mansions.

Damn. That's what I didn't do properly on Sunday. I couldn't weigh the bloody ingredients. There was probably too much pure stuff in each of those bags I sold John. I have to have scales. There was nothing for it but to go out again. But should she go out as Barbara Cook, or stay dressed as Sally Walters?

The remains of an aggravated BJ Cresswell had an answer. *Does it matter? Just get out there and get what you need. Do the work!* BJ was impressed with the way that Barbara Cook had dealt with that punter in Lane Crawfords but she wasn't too sure about this latest addition to the menagerie. The red-head. She tended to fluff around. When you are about to process a shit-load of heroin to sell on the streets of Hong Kong, the persona you are going to adopt just to go to the shops is irrelevant.

BJ lurked uneasily on the perimeter of BJ Cook's quick and calculating mind but barely clipped the outer edge of Sally Walter's more domestically included mental universe:

The blonde wouldn't have fluffed around like this. The blonde, the "white witch", would have thought ahead and had half the stuff processed by now. What is even more annoying is that neither of them will touch it, not so much as a drag of the finger across one of the blocks ....

Thursday 9 September: 1.30pm

Kaz ate a bowl of soup and drank two cups of tea. Her drip lines had been disconnected but she was still very weak and confined to bed. Even so, Pearl felt confident enough about her friend's state of health to leave the hospital for the first time since Monday evening. Ben Sanders went with her. They hailed a cab and went to the Fire Services HQ. Danny Tsiu and Annie Cheung saw Pearl get out of the cab in front of the building and were about to go to the door to greet her when they were met by the sight of a very tall man kissing their boss – passionately – in full view of all Hong Kong. They looked at one another. "Did we just see that?" said Annie.

"I don't think so," said Danny. "I've never seen anyone kiss Pearl, even her father. Are you sure it's her, Annie?" They were sure.

Pearl put her head around the door and smiled brilliantly at the two of them. "Karen is getting better and we've – I mean I've – come home to change and then go back to sit with her again. Everything okay here?"

With the patient transfer from Hei Ling Chau to Lantau Island less than twenty-four hours away, Annie could have commented that given they were organizing an operation of roughly the same scale as building a four storey wooden horse and then squeezing it through the gates of Troy, yes, everything was fine thanks, but she didn't have the heart.

But Danny did. "Pearl. Of course everything is under control here, but the transfer of the patients from Hei Ling Chau to Lantau Island is still scheduled for tomorrow. Will you be there to help?"

"We sure will, Danny. Ben is going to help too. Oh. I'm sorry. Annie Cheung, JBF Administrator, and Danny Tsiu, Finance Officer, please, both of you, meet Ben Sanders. Dr Sanders has been looking after Karen."

The two staffers nodded stiffly at Ben although Annie felt inclined to giggle. The sight of him and Pearl kissing had genuinely shocked Annie. Her boss just didn't go around kissing men in public. Or in private as far as she knew.

"Anything I need to know, apart from the broad plan? Everyone confident about what they have to do? No problems on Lantau?"

Annie loved the way Pearl could summarise enormous detail in one broad verbal sweep. It was a gift, her ability to look at the big picture. For Annie's part, all she had done for days was worry over lists and when they became too challenging she would simply start a new one.

"It will work out, Pearl. The transport is organised, there is a staff complement on Lantau cleaning and stocking up with food and getting the medical supply inventories established. Billie is already there dancing about the vegetable gardens in delight, from what we hear. The first patients will go out tomorrow morning and we should have the last ones settled in by about 5pm."

"Dr Sanders is going to help."

It was the second time Pearl had said that and Annie wondered just what Dr Sanders planned to do, but she didn't feel it was her place to ask. She looked sideways at Danny but Danny was already glancing back at rows of figures, his interest in the conversation limited, as this project had nothing at all to do with the foundation's finances. But he privately thought that Pearl's personal expenditure of funds on what hardly seemed to be a project of great urgency, was ill advised.

"We'll see you later."

Danny looked up at Pearl, this time clearly not happy. "But Pearl, there are accounts for you to approve and cheques that need signing. When will you be back at work?"

"I'll be back on Monday, Danny, don't worry." She looked at Ben Sanders, squeezed his hand and drifted out of the office towards the lift to her apartment. Pearl had things on her mind that did not include signing cheques.

*

Sally Walters strolled around the Kitchen Department of the Sun Wah Emporium in North Point. She was looking at kitchen scales. She chose a sturdy model and a dainty brass set for measuring out the pure product itself. Sally had read through the chemistry book that BJ had picked up last week and realised that the correct proportion of the cutting agents for the product should be around 80% of the overall finished product, not 50% as had been estimated by that other person. She also bought some dextrose and a quantity of lactose to replace most of the quinine that BJ had used. Sally couldn't resist a set of stylish measuring spoons and also found a set of very elegant black and gold screw-top jars, about the size of the complimentary pots of jam that come with hotel room-service breakfasts. She thought they could be very elegant containers for packaging the product for more discerning buyers and looked forward to the cosy domesticity of filling them and displaying them on the kitchen bench. Perhaps she should also buy gloves and that lovely apron?

She hummed as she left the emporium. She would return to the apartment, make something to eat, and then get on with cooking up the next batch of Red Bird.

*

After he left Gerry's office, James again made his way to Miss Cook's apartment block in Tin Hau Temple Road for another explorative look around. He had in his mind the story about the young blonde woman who intercepted Pearl and Karen when they went to Hei Ling Chau a couple of weeks earlier. Barbara Jane Collins was the name she had given them. There was also the card that Kaz found in her handbag after the second attack on her, the night she arrived back in Hong Kong in early August. *BJ Cresswell.* The topper was the parcel of clothes he picked up from the Clothing Department in Lane Crawfords and delivered to the owner's address in Tin Hau Temple Road – a purchase made by one Barbara Jane Cook. Three young women, all very different in appearance but all with the same initials in common – BJC.

James was about to pay off the taxi when he saw the redhead as she left Apartment Block A and once again got into a cab. This time he followed her to North Point where she headed into the huge Sun Wah Emporium. James was very careful as he watched her browse her way through the Kitchen Department. It was the third time today he had followed her and he had already noted the careful way she had of scanning her environment, not to mention how easily she had given him the slip in Lane Crawfords. Had she twigged his presence here? He felt a little uncomfortable. Clearly his field expertise was not as it had been in the old days. She had run rings around him in Lane Crawfords.

James became intent on trying to choose between a stainless steel and a copper skillet. He rather liked the copper model and was becoming absorbed in the process of selection, even tempted to match it with a small copper braising pan, when he noticed that his quarry was leaving. The Kitchen Department was very busy at this time of day with many Hong Kong housewives intent on purchasing new woks, bundles of bamboo chopsticks, specialty teas and packets of dried cooking ingredients.

He didn't follow her this time. He had seen what she had purchased. One set of scales was a hint, but the little brass mock-antique ones were a dead give-away – drug dealers loved fancy scales. He thought the gloves, apron and jars just frivolous. He waited a little while and left the store as she slipped into yet another cab. He then hailed a taxi but took no further notice of his quarry.

"Central Police Station please, driver! Quick as you like!"

*

Sally watched James before her cab turned left into Tin Hau Temple Road and she twisted around in the seat in time to see his vehicle head towards Central. She frowned. She hadn't noticed him in the store. Was it a coincidence? She didn't think so. Where was he going now? Sally felt an unfamiliar pain in her lower belly and legs.

It seemed to take forever to reach the apartment and she scurried into Block A, feeling as though she was under fire. Letting herself into Apartment 7, she called out, "Trouble!" She sat on the rug with Barbara Cook and they discussed what Sally had just seen. BJ Cresswell hovered in the background, an apparition now, unseen and unheard by the other two.

"How many times have we seen him?"

"Twice. We both saw him in Crawfords and then I saw him in North Point Road just now. And he might have been in Flower Road, except I couldn't make out who was in the taxi behind me and the taxi-driver I sent up to look for a fare didn't score. I know because I waited my cab for him to come back down the hill. So I can't be sure about that. Who is he?"

BJ Cresswell struggled to make herself heard but her voice was now just a whisper of a memory to these other two. They had not only thrown away her stuff, they had thrown away her voice, memory, her entire persona. This bloke that the red head had seen following her was obviously her adviser. Why wouldn't they listen? He had found her. He knew what she had. He had come for her. He would kill her – or would he? Would he realise that this black haired bint and this red headed piece were her? BJ Cresswell had transformed herself into two people. How could he possibly know that? But he must. And she could feel the discomfort of it in her guts.

"What will we do? What if he's filth?"

"We can hardly run away. There are all of my clothes for a start..."

"Not to mention MY heroin."

Barbara and Sally stopped their chat. With enormous effort BJ Cresswell asserted herself. Clearly these two creations of hers were idiots – the red-haired one going on about her clothes. Who did she think had paid for that wardrobe? Santa Claus? And why did they think there was a different set of clothes, accessories and a bottle of hair dye stored in the second bedroom? For Halloween? These two were going to have to go. Clearly her adviser knew about Sally and she wasn't prepared to risk Barbara Cook back on the streets.

She was too loud.

*

DC Lee had been seconded to Central Division with DS Proust and their other colleagues, DS Wong, DC Crabb, Mrs Latham and Pam Walsh. The men and Mrs Latham were all now in Traffic. But on Thursday afternoon Detectives Lee and Proust were pulled off their regular duties and summoned to a briefing about a surveillance operation, initiated by The Chief of Police. DS Proust was impressed. He had never heard much that was positive about the Chief and some people said he couldn't tie his own shoelaces, but the briefing notes were concisely written, even if Gallop didn't speak to the two police officers directly. He had delegated that task to his Personal Secretary, Mrs Charlton.

"If you have any questions, gentlemen, please leave them with me immediately for clarification. Otherwise Chief Gallop considers you operational." They read the brief instructions, which were to maintain full surveillance on the Director of the Hong Kong Archaeological Museum, Dr Albert Ho.

"Yes, Mrs Charlton, there is one thing." Herbie Proust resented clarifying operational orders with a civilian, but this woman clearly had some power. "How much of a watching brief? Day and night?"

"Central Division considers a full watching brief to be twenty-four hour surveillance, Detective Sergeant, unless specifically stated otherwise."

"Just how are we supposed to get any sleep...?" He had nearly called her "ma'am" but managed to stop just in time.

"Ah yes, of course. There needs to be a relief shift organised and I will ask Chief Gallop to authorise that as soon as possible. Can you manage to go through until later this evening? Shall we say your shift change will take place outside of the target's home at 11.00pm?" She made a note and picked up the phone.

"Is she the Chief of Police, DS Proust?"

"I reckon that's the idea, DC Lee. Let's go over to this museum and see if we can find our bloke."

*

Albert enjoyed lingering in his office after the last of the staff left for the day. As they popped in to say goodnight between five and six o'clock, he saw clear signs of relief on their faces that the boss was back in his eyrie. It was Albert's long habit to be the first to arrive at the museum and the last to leave. It added to the myth he lived there in the form of some sort of nocturnal animal after closing hours and either roamed around or flew home... a myth that he rather enjoyed fostering. Today, he had done a good day's work, his head was clear and he deserved a drink.

He took his walking-stick from the coat hook and left the archive tower by the side door, carefully testing the lock as he did so. He hesitated when he reached the street. The day's heat was a little softer now and the light on the harbour was changing from burnished copper to the purple of ripe eggplant. It was a brilliant afternoon for being on the water. He walked a little way along the harbour front and hailed a water-taxi.

"Hei Ling Chau Island, please!" He sat back in the passenger seat and lit a cigarette. The day's achievements hadn't shut out the one thing that had been on his mind all week – the two packets of heroin he had hidden on the island for his own use. He had also thought more and more about the syringe he'd left behind. It would have his fingerprints on it and he should have thought of that earlier. There was still nothing in the press about the drug haul, and the calls he had made to the Peak Hospital yielded no information either – literally none – as to whether Karen Henderson was dead, alive or even a patient. She had vanished off the radar. Albert didn't want anything that might look like evidence against him left lying around in case something went wrong with his little scheme. The bulk of the heroin would be quarantined by now and surely the police were viewing it as an active case. He would slip around to the beach where he had found her and the syringe would probably just be there, lying on the sand. Then he could retrieve the packets he had hidden and be back in Hong Kong by 8.00pm for that drink.

Or perhaps something a little more exciting.

*

They hadn't been on the watch for more than an hour when DC Lee and DS Proust saw Albert lock the museum door. To their surprise he hailed a water-taxi and the ten minute wait until another one came along in that relatively quiet part of the harbour made both officers edgy. Only an hour into the operation and it looked like they had lost their man at his first move. But they eventually caught sight of his boat heading south and were within a reasonable distance of him by the time they cleared the southern tip of Hong Kong Island. The bigger worry came when Albert's water-taxi veered into the deserted waters west of Cheung Chau and Peng Chau.

"Where is the bugger going?" The two former narcotics officers knew the harbour well, nooks and crannies, good spots for drug drop-off points and suitable locations for chiu chau heroin-processing laboratories. "He's never going to Hei Ling Chau," said Herbie. "It's quarantined."

"Perhaps he has a relative there, DS?"

Herbie saw sense in that. Why else would anyone go willingly to Hei Ling Chau? Why were they following this geezer anyway? He pulled out the briefing notes: they didn't say, of course. Herbie had been in Drugs for so long that he had automatically considered the surveillance to be drug-related, but with him and Tony Lee now attached to Central Division, the bloke could be up to anything.

"Tony, get the driver to veer south and crawl into the south-west end of Hei Ling Chau, quietly as he can, will you? We don't want this bloke to cop us. It's a wilderness there and the island ain't too big. It's only a quick walk to get around the whole place."

*

Albert's boat approached the island from the north-west. The hospital was already lit up. He said to the skipper: "I'm here to see a relative. I wo'n't be long. Please wait." The skipper, like every other water-taxi operator in Hong Kong, shared the belief that Hei Ling Chau was a monastery, so this man's relative must be a monk. He bowed respectfully and said that of course he would wait.

*

The skipper of Tony and Herbie's water-taxi threw a rope around a knobbly tree root sticking out from the shallow rock face which protruded from the most southerly point of the island. He cut the engine and the two detectives got out and stretched. Tony asked him to wait and not to start the engine unless he said so. The skipper shrugged – he had a good return fare and of course he'd keep the engine quiet if that's what they wanted. Tony put a cigarette between his lips and was scratching around for a light when Herbie whispered, "Don't! – Look!" From their vantage point behind some scrabbly trees, DS Proust and DC Lee could clearly see Albert Ho walking towards the beach. He scanned the upper littoral zone carefully and then fell to his knees. He snaked his head from side to side, peering at the grey sand as he crawled towards the edge of the cove, prodding at the sand carefully as he went.

"Is he praying, DS?"

"He must be, DC. I don't know for what though, in this god-forsaken place."

If Albert was praying, the response from on high was rapid. He stopped, pushed his splayed fingers into the sand and extracted an object. He had the syringe. DS Proust and DC Lee watched him draw the long steel object – more commonly associated with veterinary work – out of the sand. He stood up and dusted sand from his shirt, lifted the needle high into the air and spoke to the early gathering dusk. "I've got you now bitch. Finger-prints? Not any more."

DS Proust quickly considered the brief he and DC Lee had been given. It was no more than to observe the movements of this man and make a report to The Chief of Police – aka Mrs Charlton – by close of business each day. It wasn't detailed enough to cover the situation that had now developed.

It had been a tough week for the two detectives, but they were being handed something on a plate here. Herbie Proust hadn't spent ten years in Drugs to knock back an opportunity to arrest a punter. *One more off the street.* He stifled the urge to move forward, but it was the wrong time to wait, because Albert – who had waited too long – plunged the syringe into his arm. The two detectives winced. Albert cried out, much as Kaz had cried out earlier that week when he stabbed the cruel steel point deep into her arm.

Kaz had cried out in a combination of pain and surprised fear at being attacked in a place where she had long felt secure.

Albert's cry was different, exultant, hungry, animal. But the result was the same. He fell and was unconscious before his body hit the grey sands of Squid Cove.

Thursday 9 September: 6.00pm

Mrs Charlton was not at all happy to see Sir James, but her new and somewhat flippant assistant, Pam Walsh, grinned at him like a fool.

"Ladies, I'm so sorry to interrupt you again. I fully appreciate that you need to finalise your duties for the day."

Sure, thought Pam, *aligning the blinds on the eastern windows with those on the northern side is a chore. And as for putting the covers over the typewriters – well....*

"Problem. I've encountered a problem since leaving here and I think it is linked to something quite important. I need to see the Chief again, rather urgently. Drug-related, don't want to cause any waves given events at Hing Long Lane this week ...."

Mrs Charlton did not acknowledge Pam's enquiring look. Chief Gallop had left the office for the day almost as soon as James had, earlier in the afternoon. His daily afternoon tiffin was taken at his home on Victoria Peak, followed by a nap at about 4.30pm and dinner at 7.30 with his wife. The Chief of Police limited evening engagements to one per week, preferably to be honoured during the weekend break when the stresses of running the Hong Kong Police Service could be kept at a decent distance for an hour or two.

Mrs Charlton instead contacted Chief Inspector Harry Burton as a manoeuvre to keep her boss's routine undisturbed and the CI, newly ensconsed as head of the Hong Kong Police Narcotics Bureau, was very happy to talk to Sir James Gates. Even so, Harry felt the conversation a bit garbled, with Gates making repeated references to some cross-dressing female, who had been stalking around the island recently – and more particularly this afternoon at North Point – taking things out of abandoned crypts and afterwards buying a variety of suspicious looking scales, gloves, aprons, etc.

"Has to be drugs, don't you think, Chief Inspector?"

"What if she's just cooking a lot, Sir James?" Harry Burton was ill at ease. He had been in Central Division for fifteen years – in Traffic – a challenging, thankless role and one he'd been glad to shed. But, hells bells, he had been I/C of the Narcotics Bureau only for two days and had a lot to think about. There hadn't been any time to develop an operational perspective, and his first job was to work out how a team of sixteen personnel could run an effective anti-narcotics presence without a whisper of drugs experience between any of them, with the suspected exception of the Unit Typist who had confessed to smoking a marijuana joint, as she called it, at a school break-up party.

"One of the sets of scales she purchased is very suspicious, Inspector – it's a favourite of drug dealers who like to weigh out the pure material on a small, hand-balanced device rather than those used to brew up the additive mixtures. Herbalists and chemists are generally the only other people who use such scales."

Chief Inspector Burton grunted. He remained puzzled.

James soldiered on. "People aren't idiots. As for the apron and the gloves – well – Australians have an annual event called a "Bake Off" where people glove and apron up and cook en masse across the continent. But in Hong Kong? No-one is that interested in home-cooking to dress up for it. There's something odd going on and I've got a rock-solid commitment from the Chief of Police to get to the

Red Bird Summer 143

bottom of what's going on around the traps this week, right down to having a surveillance operation put in place, and an open-handed offer of any other assistance I may need. Are you with me? I'm calling you in my official capacity, I'm afraid, Chief Inspector." James waited for Harry to challenge his authority, but poor Harry was well beyond thinking on the hop.

"What shall we do, Sir James?"

"A quick raid is in order, I feel. Very quick. How, er, quickly can you get a carload of your very best officers to North Point?" Without any idea of who his very best officers were, Harry nominated three of his new team to be at the apartment block on Tin Hau Temple Road within an hour. James twitched.

"What is your plan, then, Chief Inspector? And by the way, half an hour would be much better, if you can manage it."

"We'll ... go to the apartment, I imagine. Break down the door if necessary."

"I think you'll find the apartments have two entrances. There is lift access to the front door and a rear staircase adjacent to the kitchen. You'll need to cover both exits. Tell you what, Inspector, I've had a go at this sort of thing before. I'll meet you there. Give your – let's say, 'less-experienced' – officers a bit of encouragement. Think they'll mind a bit of outside interference?"

At heart, Harry was offended by the offer but a superficial relief removed any tinge of sarcasm from his voice: "Jolly well better not, Sir James, we're grateful for every bit of assistance we can get, coming up against something like this when we are barely operational."

"Wonderful, Harry, and by the way, please call me James. Now..." – he decided to keep it simple – "...there could be two of them and happily, I can give you good descriptions of each of the young women...."

*

Chief Inspector Burton and four officers made it to North Point in less than half an hour as it happened, while James was held up in a traffic snarl-up at the five-ways intersection in the centre of town. As they arrived at 14, Tin Hau Temple Road, they observed a woman leaving Apartment Block A. The Chief Inspector tipped his cap to her and she returned the gesture with a tight smile. She had short brown hair, brown tortoiseshell-framed glasses and she wore a smart little beige suit and low-heeled court shoes. She carried a small suitcase, a beauty case and a fabulously smart beige handbag with a long shoulder chain. She nodded pleasantly to the building supervisor, who smiled at her vaguely. She climbed into a taxi and was whisked away.

*

"Now, men, there are two entrances to each apartment in this building, by lift at the front and there is also a rear staircase. Ng, Drake – Apartment Block A, go to level 7 and keep watch on the rear door. Anyone comes out or tries to go in, apprehend 'em. Chiu and Teo, take the lift to the seventh level and keep the front door of 7A under surveillance. Same thing, come or go, if anyone tries anything, apprehend 'em. Got it?"

Inspector Burton's team was impressed. The Chief Inspector seemed to be on top of his stuff all right. "Sir, where will you be, Sir?"

"I'll be right here. I'm going to go to the front door and get into the bally place. Could be trouble. This is Drugs, remember, not Traffic." As one, they patted their gun-holstered hips. DC Chiu was already having fun. Directing traffic at the five ways in the CBD had nothing on this for excitement. But the door to Apartment 7A proved extraordinarily strong. It was a security door with the added feature that the barrel lock had three thick steel shafts, each of which could be operated independently of the others. DS Chiu quietly went downstairs and left DC Teo to struggle with it. He showed his ID to the building supervisor and acquired a master key, glided back up to level 7, quietly excused himself and opened the door.

The Chief Inspector gave him a sour look but Teo massaged his shoulder in relief. The door swung open and the three officers stood on the threshold of Apartment 7A. All was quiet. They admitted DC Drake and DS Ng through the back-stair door and began to search the roomy flat.

"Sir!" DS Ng was in the second bathroom. Unlike the first bathroom, the second bathroom was filthy. There were splatterings of brown stains in the sink and up the tiled wall. It was if someone had shot brown gravy from a water pistol. There was a stained towel in the bath and another one on the vanity counter. DS Ng lifted up the hand towel on the bench top and felt his eyes widen. There was a large white tablet of fine grained material sitting in a very smart marble soap dish. Clearly, it was not soap. It had bevelled edges and was inscribed "Red Bird '999'". The block had been cut down so that half of the last "9" was obliterated.

Jubilation revealed Harry Burton to be a generous man. "We've done it, men! Two days operational in Narcotics and we have completed a successful raid! You are all to be commended and I shall see to it that you are! DC Chiu and DC Drake, secure the doors after us and wait here! I'll have Fingerprints here directly. When they've finished, make an inventory of everything you find, then tape the doors. No entry except by police officers. – Make sure the building supervisor understands that very clearly will you? – DS Ng, you will accompany me back to Unit, access this contraband into the inventory system and start cross-checking it with the drugs register. I've a suspicion that you will find it in the list of missing blocks from Hing Long Lane."

James arrived, somewhat flustered. He had already assumed that the raid would be too late to apprehend Miss Cook but even so he was generous in his congratulations to Chief Inspector Burton and his team. He took a look around. Most of the clothes Miss Cook had purchased yesterday had been abandoned and from the cuttings of hair strewn in the hand basin and the brown stains, he acknowledged that his red bird had not only flown, but had risen from the ashes of her former personas in yet another form.

Who was he to look for now? And where?

*

BJ checked into The Peninsula Hotel, closed the door of room 129 and pulled off the glasses that she found so annoying to wear. She felt faint. *I must be losin' it. I forgot me bloody moniker din't I? Who'd I register as again?* She felt her pulse race then remembered the wallet that held the room-key. She opened it and read: Miss Christine Barbara James, Room 129. Christine James. It would do. Christine James was her most self-effacing make-over yet. Christine was going to sell the rest of the stuff in one swoop if she could, over at Wanchai most likely, and then leave Hong Kong next week regardless of what she got for it. She still had money, enough to set up modestly somewhere else.

She threw her suitcase on the bed and unpacked. Christine had few possessions. The room had a safe and she set the combination, unzipped the beauty case and extracted the carefully wrapped soap box. It felt lighter than it had and she realised what had happened before she even opened it. She had left one block behind at the apartment, the partially used one that she had planned to process when she returned from the Sun Wah Emporium, before she realised she'd been sprung and had to get out of North Point as quickly as she could move.

*

Christine sat on the side of the bed and briefly sobbed and wiped at her nose and eyes. No ranting for Miss James. She had gone to all the trouble of getting rid of those other two cows and now she had left nearly a third of her lovely Red Bird behind at the Tin Hau Temple Road flat.

I'll give it an hour and go back. I can't leave it there, not after all I've gone through.

What do you mean, after all you've gone through? You've only been around for a couple of hours and you've already lost one of my "999" blocks and can't even remember your own name. Stupid bitch. BJ Cresswell was clearly furious with her latest invention. She opened the soap box and scratched her nail across the back of one of the blocks and sucked on the powder greedily, laughing and taunting the brown haired Christine James as she did so. She had to get some strength back. Not only did this latest piece not remember her own name but she couldn't even remember why she was afraid and why she intended to go back to North Point! What a fool! There was nothing else for it. The third block of heroin might be lost but it was now clear that the "white witch" was going to have to return to safeguard the rest of it. This bitch was a liability too.

She picked up the telephone. "Room service? Do you have in-house hair and clothing services? Good. Send someone up with some samples will you? Dressy. White. All white. Size Six. Oh, yes, and a blonde wig. I'm going to a fancy-dress party. Thank you."

It was time for BJ Cresswell to take control of this situation. What was left of Sally Walters frowned and BJ Cook decided to ignore the stupid cow. Only Christine James seemed impressed.

Red Bird Summer 147

Thursday 9 September: 7.30pm

Herbie Proust and Tony Lee broke cover and ran across the beach.

Herbie had made up his mind what to do. "I am arresting you for the possession and use of suspected unlawful drugs," said Herbie, before he realised that Albert was out of it, couldn't hear a thing. He took his pulse, watched his chest rise and fall weakly and only a faint haze of expelled air appear on the glass face of the watch he held to the man's face. "I don't know what he just poked into his vein, Tony, but I don't like this. Let's get him back to Hong Kong!"

He forestalled the driver's mild burst of complaint as they struggled back through the scrub to the water-taxi, with Albert a dead weight between them. "Detective Sergeant Proust, Hong Kong Police Force, Division Central. – Hong Kong Island, Central Police jetty! – Quick as you can!"

Tony added a few extra hurry-ups in Cantonese and the boat took off at such speed that they could almost instantly see phosphorescence strike the sides of the craft in showers.

There was now a sliver of pale moon. Herbie thought how very good it would be to go cruising on a night such as this promised to be, with good company, a few beers, lovely women. They laid Albert on the floor of the boat and covered him with a small tarpaulin. During the rest of the journey, Herbie measured Albert's pulse and checked his breathing every couple of minutes.

*

Kaz ate her first solid meal since the attack on Monday. The texture of the food felt odd in her mouth and the dominant flavour, even through its blandness, was that of bitter salt. It burned her throat as she swallowed. She noticed a police officer on duty outside her room and felt comforted by his presence, unaware that she was still under threat of arrest. Kaz was at the end of her rope in ways other than physically. There had been three attempts to harm her during the past month. A sob came to her throat. She had to admit it. It wasn't a case of someone knocking her out and drugging her as part of some scheme to get at her work site – someone wanted her dead.

"D-E-A-D," she said, spelling it out.

"Not you, Kaz. You're much too much alive," said a voice. Drew Pierson walked into the room. Kaz didn't take her eyes off him as she rang the nurse call bell.

"Yes, Dr Henderson?" Sister Simmonds came into the room.

"I'm hallucinating again, Sister."

"You seem quite lucid."

"I thought I saw my former husband walk into the room."

"You mean this gentleman?" The nursing sister gestured towards Drew, winked at him and left.

"Kaz, it *is* me. Pearl said there was a point at which they thought you wouldn't make it. That you really would die. She rang me and I came as quickly as I could." Kaz's body was still striving hard for recovery – bits would come good and then other bits and pieces would fail her. She was doing well to stay awake for half an hour at a time. Her rich brown hair was unkempt and there were spooky little grey strands fingering through it and her skin was pasty and there were dull red spots on her cheeks. She had lost more than a stone in weight and Dr Sanders also thought that she might have lost the hearing in her left ear. She smiled at Drew and went back to sleep.

Drew sat in the chair beside the bed, held his ex-wife's hand and wept awkwardly. And that is where Pearl and Ben Sanders found him. – Dr Drew Pierson, the man with everything: position, unlimited career prospects, a wonderful house with mullioned windows and climbing roses at the front door, a delightful wife. – Found him weeping over his first wife's wasted, bandless hand as she slept; sleep being her only weapon against the battering that death continued to make on her system as she struggled to emerge from what the hospital's chief chemist described as the most toxic dose of cut heroin he had ever encountered in the human bloodstream.

*

Pearl looked at Drew with a bleak and unsmiling face. "You're a fucking bastard, Drew. You should have left her alone. She was getting over you."

Ben Sanders looked at the woman he loved. "You swear!"

"You better believe it."

"I still love her, Pearl. When you called and said she may die, I felt my life collapse. I love her. She's stubborn and I am a bastard, but there you go, I love her.

"Are you the Doctor?" Drew's tone was peremptory as he spoke to Ben, his face devoid of humour.

Ben's face was stone: "I am The Doc-tor. Nurse! My brain hurts. Nurse…!" Pearl looked at the man she had fallen in love with so carelessly. She thought his name was Ben Sanders, but there you go, apparently he was John Cleese.

"OK. I can see you really are a doctor," said Drew. "Flippant bastard. What is your prognosis?"

"What business is it of yours? I believe that you are Dr Henderson's *ex-husband*. No relation to the person in this bed – my patient as it happens – no shared offspring, no shared estates, nor shared table, cutlery, dirty washing, old pot plants and so forth? You are merely a hospital visitor and visitors are requested to remain for no longer than fifteen minutes. When Dr Henderson regains consciousness and thinks that you may be something other than a hallucination brought on by a bad case of indigestion, I'll contact you. In the meantime I suggest you piss off."

*

"Why don't you like him, Ben?"

"He's a pompous twit. She's too good for him."

"But he's always been a pompous sort of twit, he's quite lovable though. It beats me how he and Kaz ever lived together," Pearl said. She leant over the stainless steel table in the clinician's room where Ben was sorting out some things that looked hideously medical to her. She kissed him.

"Well sod him just breezing back into her life when she's half dead. Kaz is in a very fragile physical state and shouldn't have to deal with anything other than staying alive. If she makes a full recovery, there will be enough emotional fallout for her to deal with without having her ex hanging around too. If she becomes well enough to be discharged – and Pearl, it is still touch and go for her – her lungs and heart are really struggling with this – she won't be able to cope by herself in her apartment, and she won't be able even to contemplate working. You realise all this, don't you?"

"It won't be my concern. Drew won't let anything happen to her, Ben. Drew's back. He's not the type to make this trip just for old time's sake. It will be a matter of whether Kaz will take him back. And Kaz loves Drew. She always has. She blamed herself when their marriage deteriorated and when she saw he was infatuated with that red-headed piece in the UK, she loved him enough to stand back. I think that Drew has grown up enough for Kaz at long last. We won't have to worry about her." Ben heard Pearl say *we* without seeming to give it any particular thought and the word sung to him.

"You'd better scoot, Pearl, before I'm tempted to break hospital rules."

*

Albert remained quite still and tried to work out where the water-taxi had berthed. There were bright lights. Then he saw the sign: Hong Kong Water Police Wharf, Central Division. He also saw a man get out of the boat and speak in urgent tones with the officer on duty. Then a second man left the taxi and the first man called out to him: "There's an ambulance on its way, Tony, and Constable Louw is phoning ahead to the hospital." This man came back and took Albert's pulse again, frowned and gently lifted an eyelid. There was a tweak of resistance. *This bastard is conscious.* "Can you hear me? What's your name? Can you tell me your name? Can you hear me?" He started the familiar refrain of arousal, but while Albert's eyes remained shut, Herbie noted that his breathing pattern had changed, probably because he was conscious and nervous. *At least the bastard isn't dead on my beat.*

Herbie and Tony Lee heard the howl of the ambulance siren and so did Albert. Albert weighed up his options. How long had he been unconscious? He had no recall of being carried to the water-taxi. He had come to during a trip which seemed to go on forever, as clenching pain ripped at his head. He had to get out of this somehow.

I can't go to hospital. It's over. I'll be ruined. His right arm was covered by some sort of canvass sheeting and he could feel the coldness of something against his right hand. He stretched his fingers and felt the outline of a wrench or a pair of pliers – something metal, stout. The ambulance siren sounded closer. The men were back on the wharf and – Albert was almost sure – unseen by them, the skipper of the water-taxi had also left the boat and was smoking and staring off into the gathering night.

The boat was secured to a bollard with a simple knot. Albert made a movement and the taller of the two men on the wharf turned and looked his way. Albert froze. He seemed to have eyes like lamps. He began to walk towards the boat. Albert had only seconds to act. He leapt to his feet, unlooped the rope and dived into the skipper's seat. The engine fired up easily but he accelerated too hard and the craft bucked and arched into the air. He was aware of shouting and movement behind him but he didn't look, just concentrated on the boat, smoothed out the clutch and acceleration until the engine revs stabilized. He went at full throttle north until he was well clear of the Central Wharf. As he hadn't thought to put the boat's lights on, he was inducted into a whole new world of marine navigation when a cargo boat loomed up in front of him. He veered sharply within spitting distance of the hull and, sheltered by the vessel's flank as it pummelled through the harbour waters, found the lights, turned them on and swerved the boat in an arc of phosphoresence to head for Kowloon.

With a bit of luck he could get to Tsim Tsa Tsiu and shelter in the sampan community. Albert felt elation for a minute or two before it occurred to him that, however successful his manoeuvres, he had just made a fugitive of himself. He laughed into the night sky, the heroin he had taken now pouring strength and power through his veins. He had been a fugitive all his life.

He might as well make it official.

Thursday 9 September: 8.10pm

Emmie Franklin took the key to the Presidential Suite from the desk clerk and escorted Franka Derova's agent into the suite of rooms that offer the Peninsula's premiere accommodation. Her cousin Steven seemed to think that successful public relations relied on building mutual good will and trust with clients. He had no idea how grasping people could be, and it seemed that the more they were in the public eye, the more vociferous their demands. Emmie had quietly organised the fulfilment of her obligation to the letter and left the woman lying on a velvet upholstered sofa, loudly swigging Moët Chandon from a crystal flute and shovelling down caviar with a pearl spoon that Emmie had purchased. The spoon cost an astonishing HK$5,000. Emmie further tweaked the extravagance by having a hole drilled in the handle and a silver chain attached to it. The woman had been enchanted with the gift and it clinched the deal.

For all the risk of Steven finding out, and the potential for unpleasantness, Emmie was pleased with the day's work. The lunch that the agent attended in the Marco Polo Lounge with her internationally famous client in tow would be all over the weekend papers. Franka Derova had looked spectacular dressed in the latest Chanel couture, and Dewi Lo from Hong Kong's most popular chinese-language fashion magazine was going to produce a six-page segment to publicise the event. The Marco Polo Lounge was always a dream venue and Dewi had taken swags of photos. Emmie would appear sitting next to Franka, even though she only did so for the duration of the photographs, but that would be enough to get her name into all the fashion-related press in Hong Kong, and maybe even elsewhere, for at least the next week.

She was smiling a little as she congratulated herself on a job well done and so felt her mouth sag significantly when she saw BJ Cresswell standing near the entry of the Lobby Coffee Shop. *Damn girl. I wonder what she's doing here? How dare she?* She also became aware that the pulse in her neck took a quick leap and her hands felt moist. Miss Cresswell looked almost like the Miss Cresswell who had walked in to her office to be interviewed for the job of PR Assistant three weeks earlier. Emmie fought off a sudden beat of desire and thought instead about how the little upstart had come so close to humiliating her by walking out of the job on Monday morning.

"Miss Cresswell!" BJ turned and looked Emmie up and down. She let Emmie walk right up to her without uttering a word. "Miss Cresswell, what are you doing here?"

"What's it to you? Am I still in your employ, Mrs Franklin?"

"Hardly."

"Then get fucked! – Preferably not by me!"

Emmie grabbed BJ by the arm as she started to walk away and swung her around hard. She was very close to Emmie's face but didn't back off an eyelash when Emmie said, "I demand an apology. For the disgusting remark you just made and for walking out on me." A passing couple, dressed in evening wear and heading towards Reception, looked pointedly at the two women.

"You heard what I said. I said, 'Get fucked and preferably not by me.'" BJ's voice had become a hoarse shout. Emmie was as shocked by it, as were those in earshot. People dived behind their newspapers or pointedly looked at their shoes or watches – everyone in the coffee-shop must have heard. Two women sitting together said something behind their hands and spluttered with laughter.

Emmie had to salvage something from this. Her face would be all over the social pages in another day or two, and when they saw her, people wouldn't associate her with the world-famous Franka Derova, they would associate her with this little tart. So she said in a firm, loud voice, that BJ could consider herself dismissed for wilful misconduct and that Emmie would initiate a defamation of character law-suit against her at the first available opportunity.

The coffee-shop went very quiet, so Emmie knew they had all heard. BJ laughed, disengaged her arm from Emmie's and strolled off. But a little further along the lobby she turned and called out to Emmie's stiff, retreating back, "Does this mean our date in the Eros Suite tonight is off, darling? Or are you just being a tease?" Emmie had the good sense to keep on walking, her slender frame the very picture of graceful dignity. But she seethed with anger. *I'll get you, bitch.*

She meant it. She was going to do for that piece of blonde flotsam. She returned to her office and picked up the phone. She would ring Mr Yip. Emmie had known Yip Yee Koon since her early rise to prominence in Hong Kong as an interior decorator. The commission she had carried out for the Yip family home was her first major job. She had found that the family lived in virtual isolation – unwelcome guests in an expatriate-dominated neighbourhood – and when Mr and Mrs Yip had given her the brief to style the interior of their traditional Chinese home in up-to-the-minute western décor, Emmie got the joke. From that time on she had been on pleasant terms with the family and she knew that she could always ask Mr Yip for assistance.

Perhaps he could refer her to someone who would teach that little tart a good lesson in manners. A beating perhaps....

*

At nine o'clock Albert abandoned the water-taxi on the fringe of the city of sampans at the northern end of Tsim Tsa Tsui and caught a cab to Dentist Street in Greater Kowloon. He would disappear into Kowloon's old Walled City for a while and he would stay at the *Emperor Inn*. Albert had been lost in his own way in the Walled City many times – mostly lost to care in one of the salons at the *Emperor*. Sometimes he would spend days there, feeling like a character from a nineteenth-century novel, as he reclined in a salon shrouded in smoke, his memory adrift somewhere on mare's tales of expelled drug-laden air. But the habit that had crept up on him so insidiously eventually made him tire of the threads of opium smoke. He wanted stronger hits and that meant injecting but then he found he needed both to inject and drink alcohol as well as take other substances, until increasingly he lost control of what happened next, so his life became more introverted and secretive – but he always knew where he could go and be safe from discovery and the law, for a few days, weeks or – now – maybe years.

The barman at the *Emperor Inn* was never surprised to see an old customer show up. They usually did, sooner or later. In one of the two small salons above the bar, Albert considered his situation and acknowledged that it was grim. He had borrowed one and a half million dollars from Hew to set Karen Henderson up with the drugs he'd bought from John Simons last Sunday. But for all its impact, he may as well have thrown the money into the harbour. There was nothing about her arrest in the papers, no information at all, and for such a major drug bust – what was going on? Why weren't the Police shouting their successful recovery operation to the skies?

And who were the two men who took him away from Hei Ling Chau this evening? What a fool he had been. He should have waited until he was at home to take a hit and not only that, his main stash was still there. The stuff he had bought from John was the strongest he had ever experienced. The two men at Hei Ling Chau were probably police, keeping the area under surveillance after Monday's haul. He should have thought of that too. But they were in a private water-taxi, so what if they weren't cops? What if they were just a couple of day-trippers who had stopped off for a look around? He may have put himself out on the edge for nothing.

At last he was calm and he acknowledged that he wouldn't have done this once. *I would have taken better stock of the situation before I merely reacted.* The drugs had him. He was on his way down now. He smiled slowly. If he was going to go down he'd take as many people with him as possible. Karen Henderson was his original target but there would be more, now. He'd take Pearl Green down too and her whole foundation. – She was part of the plot against him as well, he just knew it. – And if he could get his hands on that Cresswell bitch who had started all this by stuffing up Henderson's first overdose, he'd carve her into little pieces. If she had delivered as instructed in the first place and he had recovered the funerary pin, things would never have got to this point. He smoked a pipe and felt the comfort of the fragrant, heavy smoke drifting in and out of his nostrils, thinking about it moving around his system.

Albert counted his immediate assets. – He had only ten thousand Hong Kong dollars in his wallet. That would buy him some time if he stayed here, where accommodation, as well as life, was very cheap. He took another puff of the pipe and sighed in satisfaction on the exhale. There was the site of Karen Henderson's archaeological work. He would have that at his disposal now and could mine it. There could be limitless wealth buried under the waters of that small unprepossessing cove. It came to Albert as a sudden and very good solution that he could remain on that island once his immediate affairs were sorted out. No-one would ever think he'd hide out there. But first, he needed more money. Hew would have to help him out again.

Hew could buy some of Albert's assets this time. He'd find more value in that than just handing over wads of cash. Albert would have to risk going home to get them but there should be no problem in doing that, surely. While he was there, he could also pick up a few more small portable assets which he could trade on later. If only he had the funerary pin that had gone missing during the museum theft – that would buy him an island – but it had disappeared, another thing that the Henderson bitch could pay for. – How would he ever find it again – it, so precious – his future wealth snatched from under his nose in his own domain?

He thought about his old friend. Hew would not be on his hit list of course, he was too valuable to Albert, but he did occasionally wonder if he was on Hew's. Albert stood up. He needed a quick word with the barman. Fang knew the ropes for issuing a death contract. The little matter of being on the run wasn't going to ruin Albert's plans.

He had a few scores to settle, and in the Walled City doing so was as easy as One, Two, Three.

III

RED BIRD FLIES HIGH

Thursday 9 September to Friday 10 September

Thursday 9 September
9.00pm

Herbie Proust was still thinking like a Narcotics Bureau detective when he realised there was no back-up for him and DC Lee and no-one to debrief to about the incident with the surveillance target. He and DC Lee were due to go off shift at 11.00pm, so all they could do was send the ambulance away and leave the distraught water-taxi skipper with the officer on duty at the Central Division Water Police Kiosk, to sort out the report about the theft of his craft. DC Lee spoke to the officer on duty in rapid-fire Cantonese.

"What did you say to 'im, Tone?"

"Just that he was to report the theft as being by a surveillance target who was being brought in for questioning about a drug-related matter. Is that OK?" Herbie was impressed. In Drugs, DC Lee had always been a very timid, by-the-book type of chap and would never have dared sum up a situation with such confidence, but here he was now, using his initiative.

"Excellent work, Tone. We'd better go to the bloke's house for the shift change. He might even go back there." Tony glowed at the praise from his DS and the two men made time to go to the food market on south-side and eat before taking a taxi to Albert's house in Sheung Wan. Tony wasn't happy being there at that hour of night.

"Only down and outs live in this part of Sheung Wan, DS." They heard a low whistle come out of the dark as they got out of their taxi. There was a black car parked near the corner between two street lights. Herbie and Tony walked cautiously towards it. They both recognized DS Fraser but not his offsider.

"Sandy", said Herbie, "We've had problems with the first shift, big problems."

DS Fraser introduced his colleagues to his offsider. "DS Proust, DC Lee, meet Sir James Gates. He's going to do most of the graveyard shift with me. Sir James had this operation authorized by

Red Bird Summer 159

the Chief – it's some sort of special clearance thing between departments, as I understand."

"Thanks, DS Fraser. How d'you do, Sir James! Sandy! We've got a problem. The target has bolted on us." James got out of the car and walked up and down while Herbie told them about the events of their shift.

"Have you got the syringe?"

"Right here, Sir." Herbie pulled the syringe from his trouser pocket. He had bagged it up. "Should be OK. For prints I mean."

James said, "You followed Albert Ho to Hei Ling Chau Island. That is where Dr Henderson was found on Monday by the staff from the leprosarium. What condition was he in?" Herbie gave a quick briefing on what he and DC Lee had seen.

"He must have come around quick, Sir James. He hardly had a breath in him by the time DC Lee and me got him into the boat but then 'e bounded off like something possessed."

"I think this could be the syringe that was used on Dr Henderson earlier this week, DS, and she has been close to death these past few days. Analysis of its contents will shed more light of course and there is always the possibility that they have become degraded from lying out in the elements and have lost some potency.... You saw him pick it out of the sand, you said?"

"Yes, Sir, and then he jabbed himself with it and wailed. It was 'orrible."

"DS Fraser, can you organise an all-alert? OK by you, DS Proust?"

"We could break into his place." Tony Lee could hardly believe he'd said that. In the presence of this Sir Someone Or Other.

"Splendid thinking, DC Lee. And happily, I can authorise such an action. Wish I'd thought of it myself." James almost felt the heat of the DC's flushed cheeks as they walked the short distance to Albert's house in Ong Hing Terrace, a slice of Hong Kong island property so encircled by dispiriting poverty that only a very few real estate visionaries and a handful of bohemians lived there from choice. DC Lee juggled the small living-room window and found that the lock just fell away at the movement. A minute later the men moved quietly in through the front door by torchlight.

*

Albert's house was beautiful. An old two-storey shop house, it blended into the poverty-degraded terrace without any indication of what was inside. Inside was the treasure trove of a man whose circumstances provided him with opportunities to collect, which he had done with an exquisitely fine eye. Art and objects were housed in an interior of such stark antiquity that only the brave or unhygienic would ever dare to live with such surfaces and finishes. It was a little one up, one down abode. There was no kitchen and the bath and toilet were at the back of the house in a separate pavilion. There was a rear courtyard garden, paved, pooled, planted and set with statuary whose forms sang in exact harmony with the scale of the place. James looked at it in awe. It was perfect.

"This is a rich house. Rich indeed. Those with particular vision can live in a way that most people with just money never even dream exists. Our man has the capacity to do this. What an entirely tragic waste."

DS Proust did not sympathise with James's grief for Albert's lost sensibilities. He felt as though he was in just another lair and that somewhere in this gaffe they would find a shit-load of drugs. But they didn't. There were a few bottles of wine in a cupboard, but only one glass. There were no plates, no cups and saucers, no saucepans or cooking implements of any kind. The man who lived here obviously never ate at home, never so much as had a cup of tea at home.

The sitting-room was over-stuffed with furniture and objects. A zoo's worth of stuffed birds and animals shared shelf space with books and objects. There was only one couch, a well-worn, small, brown and gold upholstered, cedar-framed, ornately carved thing. There was a vast globe, set in a dark timber frame which sat on the floor, and near it, a revolving cedar bookcase. Not surprisingly, the books were all on the subject of archaeology. The place was all Albert; yet of Albert, there were no signs to read. No hint of a presence. There may have been no hint of his presence here for many ages.

Or perhaps Albert *was* here, browsing in another of those ages, not present at present. He lived in a museum after all.

DC Lee was spooked. "I don't like it, DS. The bedroom. Have you seen it?"

"Nope. What about it?"

"There's no bed in it." They both went up the narrow staircase and DC Lee opened the narrow door. Indeed, there was no bed. He flashed his torch beam on a hinged screen, a desk, a wardrobe and a chest of drawers. No bed.

"Sir James? By the way, DC, it's not a bedroom. You can only have a bedroom when there's a bed in it." Tony frowned.

James was not aware of Albert's reputation for being a night-prowling, flying creature who would perch somewhere or other before returning to his true roost, The Hong Kong Archaeological Museum, each morning. Not one of his staff would have been surprised to learn that Albert Ho did not have a bed to sleep in.

"Ah, the screen!" He pointed to the faded timber-framed silk screen, the detail of which was highly erotic and which, if DC Lee had studied it closely, would have quite embarrassed him. "Just move it and you should see a lever in the centre of that wall. Give it a tug and see what happens. Tony was impressed when a double bed dropped noiselessly from a cavity in the wall. It was the only piece of modern furniture in the house and was made up, covered with heavy linen sheets tightly tucked into place. Four pillows were strapped to the mattress with leather belts.

"Take those off while you're at it, please, DC." Tony Lee was well impressed. Albert Ho must have an iron constitution. Each pillow weighed a ton, but then it became clear that each pillow was in fact two, strapped together. They sandwiched objects of some weight. James extracted a bronze animal of fantastical shape and sat it on the bed. It was a dragon. There were three others, exquisitely made and intricately carved to the point of pain; a tiger, a turtle and a bird.

"Now that *is* interesting" said Sir James. "There was a theft of a pre-Tang Dynasty bestiary collection from the museum last month. I think we have recovered the stolen goods, gentlemen. Put it all back. Let's get out of here. Thank you, gentlemen, you have done a fine job, and I will personally ensure that the Chief of Police is made aware of it. Goodnight to you."

Friday 10 September: 4.00am

The apartment buzzer rang. Pearl sat up in bed, struggling to drag herself out of a deep sleep. It rang again. How long had someone been in the lobby, standing on the bell?

"Wha ...?

Her shoulders relaxed. Ben was beside her.

"Someone's at the door." She leant over and switched on the bedside lamp. – Just on 4am. – Ben struggled to his elbows and then shot out of bed, naked.

"I'll get it."

"You'll frighten them. Where are your clothes?" He looked around vaguely.

"In the kitchen I think." She threw him her dressing-gown and he managed to wrap it sparingly around his torso.

"What about you?"

"Oh." She grabbed her nightie, threw a tee shirt over it, pulled on a pair of light wool tights and went out to the lobby. The bell went again. Someone was almost leaning on it.

She spoke into the intercom speaker. "Yes?"

"Yip Yee Koon. We must talk."

"Mr Yip. We only talk when times are bad."

"You continue to observe life well, Pearl. Times are bad."

*

"Mr Yip, this is Dr Sanders."

"How d'you do, Mr Yip! Please call me Ben." Ben gripped Pearl's cotton dressing-gown as tightly about him as he could but was unable to avoid showing quite a lot of leg. "I'll change." Yip Yee Koon nodded gravely. *So, the much speculated upon love life of the locally famous Pearl Green was not so different from everyone else's after all. Poor quality night attire and an obvious lack of decorum.*

*

"I will be blunt. There is something ugly going on in Hong Kong at the moment and it seems to be due to an unusual situation with drugs. I do not know exactly what is happening, but I do know that when there is a steady supply of good drugs on the streets, life is stable. When there are no drugs, there is violence because people mix the wrong substances, which unleashes bad elements from the brain – anger and violence and rage. Good drugs keep people calm and happy. They are flawed souls before they become addicted, so being calm and happy is not necessarily all bad." Ben didn't look convinced.

Yip looked at Pearl and said, "Have you ever taken drugs, Pearl?"

"May be once or twice, Mr Yip. You know my story. I had other things to deal with in my life, as you well know. How would drugs have helped that amount of pain?"

His eyes bored into Pearl and she looked back hard at him.

"We have not spoken together for years, Mr Yip, and here you are telling me about how things are on the streets as though I will understand exactly what is going on. I know nothing about drugs. If there is something ugly, as you say, going on in Hong Kong at the present time, I do not see what it can have to do with me. However, my best friend has been the target of three violent attacks during the last month and two of those attacks were drug-associated. Are you saying that the attacks on Karen are connected with some sort of drug war?"

"Drugs are certainly involved. I do not understand how at present, but your friend Dr Henderson is in danger again. No!" He held up his hand. "Let me finish. Tonight, there have been three death contracts issued."

Ben was shocked. He pushed himself back deep into the sofa and his legs sweated behind each knee. Pearl had not heard hard words like this for a long time but she had heard their like before. Mr Yip was not being dramatic. The extraordinary thing was that he was in her apartment, picking up their history as though there was no gap in time since they had faced one another on Sharp Island eleven years earlier, with equally hard words to say to one another over the body of her mother's murderer.

He said it all so calmly. He could have been confirming her grocery order.

"Are you going to tell us who is targeted?"

Yip nodded and said, "Dr Karen Henderson and a woman by the name of BJ Cresswell comprise two of the contracts."

Pearl felt a flutter of nerves ripple around her navel. She was un-nerved, de-centred. "BJ Cresswell. That name. Somehow that name is at the heart of all this. She's trouble. The third?"

"Pearl Green," said Mr Yip.

"NO!" Ben hurled the word at Yip, dived from the settee and grabbed his shirt. "Why don't you go to the Police if you know who these people are?"

Yip Yee Koon calmly removed Ben's hand and smoothed his collar back into shape.

"Pearl and Sir James and I will deal with this matter, Dr Sanders. The police have power only. We have influence. We also have knowledge and only that will prevent these deaths, or at any rate – he looked Ben in the eye – most of them."

"What *is* this?"

"Hong Kong, Ben", Pearl said. *This* is Hong Kong. Live here long enough – I mean really live here – and you'll understand. Hong Kong is not a children's playground. Its dirty side is very dirty."

Yip nodded agreement. "I see you haven't changed so much after all, Pearl. I have the power to stop the contract on Miss Cresswell but the contract on Dr Henderson and you was issued from within the Walled City."

Pearl's healthy complexion drained of colour and she shuddered. *The Walled City.* It was a long time since she had heard anyone refer to it.

"These contracts mean business. The terms are very generous and will be taken up. There is no judicial or police authority in the Walled City to stop such things happening. I of course have no more power there than anyone else."

Pearl suspected that he was not being strictly truthful. "Then what are Kaz and I to do? Stay hidden, here perhaps? We must have protection, Mr Yip, protection so that we can fight this, in the press. We must publicise it as widely as we can. We must turn a media lamp on us so strong that no-one will come near us for the blaze of publicity."

"And that will just drive it underground for a time. No. As I said, I can control the contract on BJ Cresswell and it is my intention to appear as though I have actioned it to see where that leads us, particularly, Pearl, if you are right and this Miss Cresswell is somehow at the heart of what is happening."

Pearl nodded.

"Are you in this too, Dr Sanders, or will you leave the room?"

Red Bird Summer 165

"I'm not leaving Pearl's side Mr Yip, if that answers your question."

Friday 10 September: 6.00am

When the patient transport – the *Jiang Li* – tied up at the Hei Ling Chau Island wharf, it was still dark. The skipper, a Mr Tan, pulled hard on his cigarette. It would be an hour before the first passengers arrived, so there was plenty of time to make up a brew and eat the thermos of congee his wife had prepared for him. He finished the cigarette and as he threw the butt into the water he saw a flicker of light to the south-east. *Night fishermen or perhaps early morning fishermen.* But the light was moving around too much to be on the water. *Someone is walking around over there.* Mr Tan thought about the disease that the poor people on this island suffered from and, wondering guiltily if some of them went for early morning walks, he withdrew into the cabin to eat his morning repast.

*

Annie Cheung had excelled herself in finding the *Jiang Li*. As was her habit in so many things, Annie often worked from a simple conclusion. On this occasion it had occurred to her that a ferry would be the perfect transport ship for the patients to be transferred from Hei Ling Chau to their new home on Lantau Island. Hong Kong's biggest and most successful shipyard operated on Lantau and that is how she came across the de-commissioned Star Ferry Company vessel. It was sea-worthy and in the early stages of a luxury refurbishment for its new role as a tour boat. It was perfect for the patients' transport to Lantau.

The Manager of the Choy Kee Company shipyard was fascinated by the story about the conversion of one of Lantau's monasteries into a hospice and it wasn't too long before a deal was done. The *Jiang Li* would transfer the patients and the remaining staff. More than half of the staff complement had been at the monastery since the beginning of the week, working to get things into order for the arrival of the patients.

As Mr Tan ate his steaming bowl of eel congee, Annie slept soundly. She had worried over and anticipated the problems that Friday would bring for two weeks and had expected to find little respite from it all in her dreams. The last thing she ever expected was to sleep in. But she did.

*

At 5.30am Pearl rose from the settee and announced, "I'll make coffee.... Mr Yip?"

He declined and asked, "Does your father know anything about this BJ Cresswell?"

"I wouldn't think so, Mr Yip. The only thing that connects her to the attack on Kaz is the white card that turned up in Kaz's handbag. Kaz has no memory of acquiring it. I made some enquiries but found no trace of anyone with the name Cresswell. Two days after Kaz was discharged from hospital, we shared a water-taxi with a woman who singled us out in the street and asked for help in getting away from some guy who was following her, so she said. We put her off at Cheung Chau. She had the initials BJ too – but she said her name was Barbara Jane Collins.

"I didn't think of her again until Chief Superintendent Smythe came to see me about Kaz's kidnapping, two weeks after it happened. I told him about the incident with the woman near the taxi depot and he asked me if I'd heard of a BJ Cresswell, after I had given him the name and a description of this Barbara Jane Collins woman. I showed him the card and he said something like, 'At last we may make some progress'. He took the card away with him. No explanation of course."

"What does Miss Collins look like?"

"She's about five feet four or five – she was wearing white stilettos so she looked taller. Ummm, platinum blonde hair – long, pinned up – she is very curvaceous and on the day that Kaz and I met her she was dressed totally in shades of white. She's pale, almost too pale. Red lipstick and lots of eye make-up. That's about it."

"The 'white witch'!"

Pearl waited for Mr Yip to add something else but he didn't.

"I've heard that name somewhere else. How do you know her?"

"I don't; but the reference to a "white witch" is about. Nothing very detailed, but the "white witch" is for hire. She is new to Hong Kong."

Pearl smacked her forehead. "The 'white witch'! God I'm stupid. Jeremy's 'white witch'. Jeremy noticed her. He saw her at the

Peninsula. You know Jeremy. Every new person who comes here is indexed by him in socio-economic order. He said she looked like walking sex."

Yip gave Pearl a sly look. "I told you we could solve this with our knowledge of Hong Kong. We are on the way already, Pearl. The Peninsula will be my next stop this morning. I feel the need for English tea and toast. Or I may take the buffet lunch in the Marco Polo Lounge." Pearl looked at him. They had both been pesent in the Marco Polo Lounge on the day when Pearl's mother was killed.

"I'll buy you dinner in The Marco Polo Lounge when this is sorted, Mr Yip!... Deal?"

Yip Yee Koon rarely smiled and he did not do so now. He stood up and gravely took his leave of them, turning to Pearl to say, "You should use your title, Pearl. You really are a lady."

*

Ben said, "I feel like a goldfish."

"Shut up, Ben! I'll make that coffee. I can't help it if my mother was an aristocrat."

*

James phoned. "Dad? I'm so relieved you've called. Mr Yip has been here. There are contracts out on Kaz and um, me. And on another woman, BJ Cresswell. But I've got to go. I'll explain later. I'm meeting Annie at the water-taxi depot at seven fifteen and I haven't had a shower yet...."

"Are you serious, Pearl?" James was appalled.

Pearl said: "Serious about what? Oh, I see. Well, how can I not go? What about Annie? You will? I guess I could stay at home." She turned and looked at Ben speculatively. "There's a lot to do. When will I see you? OK. Thanks, Dad." She hung up.

"I've been ordered to stay put. James seems to have taken control of the Hong Kong Police Force. He's going to organise increased security for Kaz and have a plainclothes officer put on duty in the downstairs foyer, as well. He's going to meet Annie and he'll come back here in a few hours time. He's probably got to squeeze in a visit somewhere along the line to Government House to make sure that the Governor knows what his orders are for the day." She stopped talking. Ben was quiet and not looking at her. In Pearl's experience with men, not looking at you when you were talking was rarely an encouraging sign.

"Ben?"

"Pearl, I think it's time we talked."

"Already? We have to talk already? We've only just met one another."

"Don't be funny. Your life. It's so complicated. Hong Kong philanthropist, who incidentally it seems also has a title, is moving the patients from Hong Kong's leprosarium to another island hospital today. That's before lunch. Then in the afternoon she expects to spend time ducking and diving a bit, because there's a death contract out on her and on her best friend, incidentally. In the meantime she's in cahoots with a man who seems to have immense power within a square mile or so of land that has no political or applicable legal jurisdictions, who is going to try to stop her being bumped off, while she waits for her father to arrive, who in his own way also seems to be running Hong Kong.

"It's like being on the set of a movie. In spare moments they will all pursue a 'white witch' who seems to be at the heart of the problem. For all their expertise, nobody seems to know exactly what the problem is. I think I'm out of my depth Pearl. And really, I just want to kiss you."

"The only way you're going to manage that is to stop talking."

There was silence in the big room.

Friday 10 September: 7.30am

When James left DS Fraser in Sheung Wan it had just gone 4.00am The DS radioed in for shift-relief and DC Brodie would be along directly. James walked for a few blocks until a taxi cruised by this deserted end of town, which he caught and took to the Peak Hospital to check on Kaz. She was sleeping peacefully enough, although her breathing was still laboured. He sank onto the bed in the room next door, exhausted, and slept for a while. When he woke, he phoned Pearl to give her a report on Kaz. It was then that Pearl dropped her bombshell about the visit from Mr Yip.

James got busy, contacted the Police Chief at home through Division Central and organised additional security for Kaz and a guard to be placed in the lift lobby of the Fire Services HQ. He explained to Gerry *that it is literally life and death, old man. Explain later. May need to call on some more of your resources.*

Gerry was glad to help. Being called upon at that hour and asked for immediate action was quite a novel experience and he felt quite jollied up and useful.

James arrived at the Connaught Road water-taxi depot at 7.45am but there was no sign of Annie Cheung. Pearl said they were to meet at 7.15am, but Annie would have waited for Pearl surely, and it was unlikely that Annie would be late. James scratched his forehead. A boat approached the jetty. "Where have you been?" asked James in his indifferent Cantonese. "I think I have missed my friend – we are supposed to be going to Hei Ling Chau together."

"Too late, your friend is there already." The skipper was having a very good morning. After dropping the Hong Kong fare at Hei Ling Chau he had cruised over to Peng Chau and picked up a passenger who wanted to go to Cheung Chau. Now he smelt another good fare coming up. "Want to go over there now?"

"I will soon but I have to see someone first. What time did you take her there, again?"

"We left here at about 5.15am By the way, not *she, he.*"

"Thank you."

The driver shrugged. James hurried away. DS Fraser and DC Brodie would still be on duty at Albert's house in Sheung Wan and they would be relieved soon by DS Proust and DC Lee. James had a feeling that they'd be interested in knowing about the early fare to Hei Ling Chau. Odds on, it was Albert Ho returning to complete his business that the two officers had interrupted the previous evening. What was his business there? Did he plan on hiding out there for a bit now, perhaps?

"Taxi! Sheung Wan please. Ong Hing Terrace." The driver looked curiously at the *gwailo*. Very few *gwais* went to that part of Sheung Wan. It wasn't even a good-time district. The morning light was gloomier in that part of town, if it was possible to imagine that a lack of money and a lack of hope could affect the quality of light in a place. He asked the taxi-driver to wait for him and scanned the street for a sign of DS Fraser. The vehicle was parked around the corner but it was empty and, as James quickly realized, locked.

Damn, thought James. He noticed that the door to Albert's house was ajar. James had closed it himself after the inspection during the previous evening in company with DS Proust, DS Fraser and DC Lee.

*

Annie reached the Connaught Road water-taxi depot just after eight o'clock. She was so frazzled by her unpunctuality that she was taking gulping breaths to calm down. "I must go to Hei Ling Chau. Can you take me there immediately? I am very, very, late."

The driver was interested. "You are coming back?"

"No."

You have to pay return fare, no passengers coming back from there."

"That is fair. OK."

"You are going to the same place that I took your friend?"

"Yes." He nodded and gestured her into the boat.

*

James pushed the door open. It was dark in the house. "Ha-llo?" There was no reply. He felt his way along the wall, groping for a light switch, but there was none. Of course. He should have realised last night. No kitchen and an outside bathroom added up to no electricity. Albert would live by candlelight and portable gas. James struck his Dunhill lighter. He had given up smoking several years earlier but remained attached to the expensive gold lighter, a gift from his former wife. Its flame showed him what he was looking for. On a high table next to the sofa was a candle sitting in a pewter dish, and there were matches. He waited until the flame climbed steadily and walked up the narrow flight of stairs.

He knew it would be bad. He had already caught the cold whiff of congealing blood from downstairs. DS Fraser's throat had been very thoroughly cut. Had there been any real need to place a stuffed tiger's foot next to the wound? Was that an artistic touch, or an ironic touch perhaps? Or was it for the benefit of someone else?

James leaned gingerly over the blood-soaked bed and detached one of the pillows from its moorings. It was much lighter than it had been last night when he and the three Hong Kong Police officers were here. All of the statues had been removed. Otherwise the house seemed just as it was eight hours earlier. Full, but empty. He was about to get back into the taxi and head for Central Division when another car quietly approached and pulled into the kerb behind DS Fraser's vehicle.

DC Lee, dead on time. James sighed, paid off the taxi and braced himself to give the young officer the news. "DC Lee. Bad news, I'm afraid."

"Nothing's happened to DS Proust, has it, Sir? He wasn't at our arranged pick-up point."

"Not that I'm aware of, Tony. But something has happened to DS Fraser and there is no sign of DC Brodie. I need to use your radio immediately, please."

Friday 10 September: 8.40am

Confusion reigned on Hei Ling Chau. Matron and Lily Wong had left and were at Lantau Island, preparing for the arrival of the patients, so that they would experience as little disruption to routine as possible. Mae Lim remained behind, to help Annie oversee the planned evacuation of the hospital. Annie was in charge of the whole thing. She had lists, check lists, counter check lists, everything she could think of to make sure that by the end of today, Hei Ling Chau would be Hong Kong's *former* leprosarium.

Mr Tan walked up the slope to the hospital on his gnarled old sea-legs. He had expected the first patients to be on board by 7.00am but there was no sign of any movement at the hospice. Mr Tan was fearful about approaching the building. He was one of relatively few people who knew what the disease of leprosy was really like. He had an uncle who had died badly, abandoned by his family in a makeshift hospice in Kowloon, before this hospital was built to care for Hong Kong's lepers in the early 1950s. Mr Tan saw that the place was in chaos. A woman holding a clipboard came to the door.

"Please, you will have to wait, Captain. We have not had the help we are expecting." Mr Tan was a kind man and had no intention of sailing away on the *Jiang Li* and leaving all these poor people floundering, but no thanks he wouldn't come in for a cup of tea, he'd go back to the boat and wait. On his way, he heard the sound of an engine. *Ah. This will be the help they are waiting for.* He boarded the *Jiang Li* and smoked another two cigarettes before he realised that the engine noise had stopped. *Perhaps I am just imagining this. People say this island is haunted,* he thought, but nonetheless remained uncomfortable.

The water-taxi skipper cut the engine as the boat made its way into the cove where Kaz's sunken ships lay. Annie said: "Are you sure this is the right place?"

"Very sure, miss. This is where I dropped your friend off." Annie looked at the beach. It was bleak, with a few scrabbly shrubs at the border between the grey sand and the exposed rock that was Hei Ling Chau. Annie hadn't been to the island before, but she had thought the approach would have had more form to it, somehow.

"I thought there was a wharf."

"That is further to the north-west."

"Then why have you brought me here?"

"Because this is where your friend wanted to be dropped off."

She shrugged, paid and jumped out awkwardly when the boat scraped the sand. *Pearl must have had a good reason to get out here. Maybe the walk to the hospital is shorter.*

Annie waited politely until the skipper manœuvred out of the cove. She sighed. She really did feel very out of sorts this morning. She picked up her heavy overnight bag – she was to stay on Lantau tonight – and walked up the long slope.

Eventually, two small mudbrick villas came into sight. Ah! These must be the guest villas she had heard about. The hospital was not too far from them, according to Pearl.

Annie reached the first villa and put her bag down. There was a stone in her shoe. She leant against the wall near the door, removed the shoe and was about to shake the stone loose when she heard a movement inside.

*

Annie was very nervous about the day's work. Unlike many people in Hong Kong who believe that Hei Ling Chau is a monastery, built for an order of reclusive monks, Annie knew better. She was a clever young woman but woefully superstitious. There were ghosts around every corner of Annie's life and as she peered cautiously through the door, she fully expected to come face to face with one here.

*

The villa seemed to be just one room which opened out onto a small walled courtyard and Annie's ghost was out there, prising up bricks from beneath the iron fire pot, used to boil up water for guest's baths. She bit her lip in relief. This was no ghost; this was just a man digging something up. He held up two clear plastic bags of white powder, examined them and carefully replaced the bricks. He stood up and started to walk towards the door. Annie reasoned that this man was most unlikely to be digging up his talcum powder. She thought it would be a good idea that he didn't suspect she had seen him.

She backed away. He'd be at the door in a trice so she called out: "Ha-llo, is anyone there?" and clumped her feet noisily as though she was in mid-stride up the hill and had glimpsed the man only as she passed by. "Oh. Hello. I'm Annie. I'm looking for the hospital."

"It's a little further on, over that rise."

Annie nodded her thanks and resumed her brisk walking pace.

The man looked at her speculatively. She walked a little faster.

"Thanks. I'm running late and they'll be worried."

Albert smiled benignly before he strode up behind her, grasped her around the neck and shook her violently. He dragged her into the courtyard of the villa and threw her hard to the ground. "Let's give them something to worry about, then."

But Annie didn't hear him. Her head had hit the bricks hard and she bled profusely, no longer conscious.

*

At 9.30am Mae Lim telephoned the Bowen Foundation and spoke to Mr Chiu, the Finance Officer. Annie had not yet arrived.

Danny was aware that Annie and Pearl had planned to go to the island first thing this morning. "Refer the matter to Miss Green please, Miss Lim. I cannot help you. Good day."

He poked at the side of his head with a pencil as Mae Lim went into a diatribe about how she would speak to Miss Pearl if she could but she wasn't there either, and things were going to go hopelessly wrong, and she had known it all along.

Danny listened. It was completely unlike Annie or Pearl not to keep an appointment. He considered the situation – the trip to Lantau and offloading the patients at the other end would be a lengthy process from what he remembered of conversations around the office as the project plan had developed. He gave Miss Lim instructions to start loading the boat, and, much relieved by his easy air of authority, she hung up. At last the day could get going properly.

Danny gave Annie a call at home. She must be ill. If that was the case he would go to Hei Ling Chau and help sort things out. There was no reply from Annie's apartment and Pearl's line was engaged. Danny frowned as he shut the daily ledger. His dissection of the month-to-date figures would have to wait. He locked the office and walked across the football-field-sized foyer to the lift that gave access to Pearl's apartment. A uniformed police officer stood guard near it. Danny bade him good morning, excused himself and reached for the lift button but the officer stopped him.

"You cannot use the lift. The upper floors of this building are off limits." Constable Mok Wai-Keung had his orders. He flashed his identity card. No-one had said anything about Miss Green's friends or employees being permitted access.

Danny's face flushed with annoyance. "I must see Miss Green, if she is at home. I am her employee and there is a problem that only she can deal with." He shook his head. "Today does not seem like a normal day."

Constable Mok disagreed. So far, today was very much like most of his normal days.

"Please ring the bell and you can listen to me speak to Miss Green. Really, Sir, it is very urgent."

The officer shrugged. Couldn't be any harm in that. His orders were clear. No-one to enter the lift.

"Pearl. It's Danny. Thank goodness you are there! Pearl, Annie has not arrived at Hei Ling Chau and Miss Lim is very concerned about the movement of the patients. It seems there is some chaos happening there. Where is Annie? I thought you were to meet her at 7.15am and go there together. Pearl? Pearl, are you there?"

"Danny, what did you say to Miss Lim?"

"I instructed her to start loading the patients, Pearl. I hope that was the right thing to do. She said the transport vessel has been at the jetty since about 6am and the skipper is becoming impatient with the wait."

Pearl forced herself to be calm, but wondered where the hell was Annie Cheung. "That's excellent, Danny. Now listen. I don't want you to go anywhere but home. I'll explain everything later. I will organise some assistance on Hei Ling Chau. Don't worry about

Red Bird Summer 175

anything, just go home. Don't go out until I telephone you. I promise I will explain everything later on. Will you do as I ask?"

Danny Tsiu customarily did as Pearl asked. Except she usually asked him for breakdowns, analyses or balance sheets. She did not usually ask him to go home and lock himself in his fifth floor apartment in Causeway Bay.

He looked at the guard. "What is going on?"

Constable Mok shrugged. "Who knows? People get into trouble all the time. Do as your employer says. That is the simplest solution." Danny nodded and left but he suddenly felt anchorless.

*

Pearl's face was now bleak with anxiety and Ben could read the trail of her thoughts as she wound through the maze of events that were strung out but not yet strung together by any logic or purpose, striving to think how and if Annie could fit into what was happening. Then the lobby buzzer went again.

"It's James."

"Hurry." James showed his Home Office identity badge to Officer Mok, who scratched his head and looked worried. This certainly was a very big badge, solid silver by the look of it, and heavily embossed. Should that override his instructions to block all access to the penthouse apartment?"

"Pearl, tell the Constable that I'm your father and that you want me to come up. OK?" James was allowed into the lift but only under Constable Mok's armed escort.

*

Pearl pounced on her father. "Annie hasn't arrived at Hei Ling Chau!" Annie Cheung was very dear to Pearl. Over the years she had blossomed from being the shy office junior into a brilliant organiser and administrator. And through the years Pearl became more and more fond of her, as well as being increasingly reliant on her administrative talents as the size and scope of June Bowen Foundation business increased. The thought of her dear Annie getting caught up in this mess was more than Pearl could bear.

James said, "I'll go to Hei Ling Chau immediately. I really want you to stay here though, Pearl. If the word about these contracts is right and if they have come out of the Walled City, whoever picks

Red Bird Summer 176

them up will mean business and as they are death contracts, death is all they will be paid on."

Once again Ben shuddered at the hard words they seemed able to exchange so easily.

The Hong Kong that Ben moved around in, conducting his well-ordered and very pleasant life, was far different from the Hong Kong these people spoke of. James saw this. "Stay with her, Ben! Don't leave her for a moment. No matter what happens. Kaz is quite safe. The other patient on her ward has been shifted and the floor has been isolated and is under double guard."

"I'll go to Hei Ling Chau first... Annie ...." Pearl walked him to the lift and put her arms around James's neck and wept.

"Pearl, this isn't like you."

"I'm not like me anymore, Dad. I never will be again." She wiped her eyes and walked back into the apartment and into Ben's arms, where she cried again.

Friday 10 September: 10.00am

Emmie didn't hear Yip Yee Koon open the door to her office and he spoke before she had any idea that he was in the room.

"I have come to talk to you about our conversation last night, Mrs. Franklin."

Emmie jumped and closed the newspaper. It was only Friday and the major social columns would not appear until the weekend, but she had hoped for some early coverage of the previous day's luncheon. There was nothing. That hideous little rock and roll star on tour from America dominated the papers – Froth From The Filth or some equally inglorious title and his dreadful wife, Belinda, another former Hong Kong socialite made good.

"Mr Yip! I was very angry when I called you last night. Miss Cresswell abused my goodwill and guidance badly enough by walking out on her job here, but to speak to me in the manner which she did – in such a public place – I...."

"But she was not altogether incorrect in what she said, is that not so? You are a lesbian, Mrs Franklin. Is your memory so short? Do I not clearly remember a day some years ago when you made a very misguided public display of your affection for another woman? Your appetites clearly outweigh your judgement."

Emmie's even, ivory skin flushed around the temples. He was right. It was said Yip Yee Koon knew everything about everybody in Hong Kong, while remaining himself a complete unknown.

"You are correct, Mr Yip. But I have been faithful to my husband since our marriage. – Miss Cresswell, well, she was the first woman I have been attracted to since then. It was just a bit of harmless dreaming, really, and when I engaged her I did so after much deliberation and a commitment that I would remain faithful to my husband and resist my ... urges. I intended to remain professional and help her with her career in PR. She has repaid me very poorly."

"But she saw your lust and interpreted this as a weakness in your character and treated you accordingly. Now you seek revenge. What do you have in mind? A small beating? Perhaps a little scar to mark the occasion – on the face perhaps. Or would a small breakage satisfy you, a finger, a nose, something to induce some pain for a time?" Emmie was very uncomfortable. It all sounded so sordid, the way he put it. She just wanted to pay the bitch back without having to think about the details.

"Or of course, there is death. How about death, Mrs Franklin? I can contact a man who will broker a contract for Miss Cresswell's death. That will get rid of the embarrassment of running into her again and will get rid of your – urges – for a time, at least." Emmie cowered in her grey, suede-covered chair that faced the walnut desk she used as part desk, part props department.

"Death?"

"Why hesitate? You don't have to implement the contract. You just have to pay. $10,000 HK for a beating or a breakage of a small bone. $30,000 HK for strangulation. It's a matter of tailoring the contract to your needs. No further obligation involved. What do you say?"

There was a moment when Emmie thought that Mr Yip was joking but he rarely smiled, let alone cracked jokes.

"It's as easy as that? ... I can have her killed?"

"Yes. I simply leave here with your instructions and pass them on. You pay the money at the completion of the contract. In cash. That's it." Yee Koon was fascinated to see how easily she was swinging from a state of being almost apologetic for being angry with Miss Cresswell – cringing at the thought of a broken finger – to the point of justifying herself that a death sentence was the only appropriate punishment for Miss Cresswell's social transgressions in the Peninsula Hotel the previous evening. He smiled inwardly. The dark side of human nature was always so predictable.

"What happens to ... the body?"

"The usual, I expect, Mrs Franklin. Bottom of the harbour. A convenient and popular Hong Kong burial site. Well, what's it to be? Thumbs up she lives, thumbs down she dies."

Emmie gave the thumb's down without hesitation. Yip paused for only the slightest of moments before he nodded. "It will happen very soon. You will know that the job is complete when you are asked for payment. You need have no other concerns."

He left her quaking. He had seen this many times. Would she call it off? Would his gamble that she must, prevail? Or would she eagerly wait for the request for payment? Yip rarely smiled even to himself but he knew the attraction of the word *gamble* and how it could occasionally result in a smile. When the gamble paid off, of course.

Friday 10 September: 10.30am

BJ came to at 10.30am. Or rather, she was at last able to open her eyes at that time. The man with the weird hair saw that she was awake and he stood up and came towards her. She flinched and closed her eyes again. He wore dark glasses, usually a bad sign. He would hit her next. She went into her act: *flinch and crush your eyes closed and then when they do whatever they are going to do, bite your lip so hard that you draw blood. It amuses them so much that sometimes they stop. Never cry. Crying brings out the ugly in the ugly, whereas a little writhing and retching gives them some easy jollies.* She kept her eyes closed but there was nothing. No striking, no plunging, no pinching, twisting – nothing.

"Get up!" She opened one eye. He had sat down again. "I want more heroin. I want you to get me more magic powder. I want a lot more."

"You'll have to pay for it. I don't get it for nuffing."

"I paid last night, din't I? And now I want more."

"OK. I'll get you more." This was dodgy. He sat with his head slumped in his hands, brooding. Was he weighing up if she'd come back with the drugs or just scarper? She waited. If she said anything he'd most likely slap her down – or worse – for being a smart-arse, to think she could wriggle out from under. She dropped her eyes and bit her lip again, getting ready to draw her own blood.

*

It was during the hour before midnight that BJ finally got the break she needed. Nothing like this bloke's crummy twenty grand. This bloke had happened along in the early hours, after she had sold off nearly an entire block of Red Bird "999" to an American she met in a bar. She sold it to him for HK$4 million, just like that, and it was still a good deal for him. It had been so easy. He was a gentleman, businesslike and pleasant. There had been no sex involved as part of the transaction either and now the money was in her tote bag, rolled up in one hundred thousand dollar lots.

She felt a dull thud at the bottom of her stomach. *This bloke wouldn't have robbed me while I was out of it, would he?* She'd met him long, long after midnight, after she'd finally taken a big hit of some of the stuff she'd held back, a hit she had longed for, the hit to be taken when she was rich and about to become richer. She had floated in ecstatic happiness along Spring Lane in Wanchai, laughing and playing hopscotch on the broken pavement slabs, just like a kid. Then this bloke with the funny hair was there beside her and in a minute she had sold him the rest of her own packet. Why not? She had plenty more.

It was a generous bagful – "Pure 1964 Red Bird", she remembered saying – and gave it to him for $HK20,000. The problem was, she could not remember anything else.

*

She slowly eased off the bed and took stock of herself. She was still fully dressed. Her shoes and bag were neatly arranged by the bed. She patted her jacket pocket. He hadn't laid a finger on her. The little flick-knife in its pearl lipstick case that she carried for protection was there. They were in a small room and it was dark, but only because the blinds were pulled down. It was crowded with furniture and there were clothes and other things everywhere, draped over the backs of chairs, stacked on a small table near the window and piled in boxes on top of a wardrobe that took up most of one wall. There was only one exit and the punter sat in a cane chair within grabbing distance of it. She would have to bluff her way out and after she'd done so, it would positively be the last appearance of BJ Cresswell. BJ was no longer to be trusted, passing out like that with four million stashed in her handbag. But it was still BJ Cresswell's passport and BJ who had to get out of Hong Kong and BJ who always wanted more and more and more:

"How much stuff do you want?"

"How much you got?"

She laughed. "OK, I've got lots more. How much money can you come up with? Whatever you can pay, I can get. Half now, half on delivery."

He laughed right back at her. "Really? Well, let's say half now and half on delivery, at your convenience of course. What do you take me for you stupid bint? We'll go and get the nice drugs together." He got up and walked to the window, raised the blind and threw the wig he was wearing onto the bed. BJ recognized him. Herbie Proust.

He spat the words at her. "I'm arresting you for the possession and sale of illegal narcotics. I am Detective Sergeant Proust of the Hong Kong Police Force and you are under arrest for the possession and sale of a quantity of illegal drugs. You have the right to remain silent, but anything you do say may be taken down as evidence and may be used in the courts of law."

BJ closed her eyes. It was like hearing the chanting of an old hymn, the family favourite. It was her turn to step up to the microphone, to be the lead singer: "My old dad would have been proud. I 'ad to be set up though, din' I? And what about when I tell them that you gave me the shit in the first place?"

She had her hand in her jacket pocket.

"Shut-up, street filth."

He instructed her to hold out her hands, wrists together. She made a fist of both, extended her right hand and made a show of jerking it free. In the brief flash of confusion, she sprang the blade on the knife and went for his chest with it. She pushed it in hard and after the initial resistance, which made her want to faint, she felt it slide in between his ribs.

"Bingo! Target, I'd say!" She laughed delightedly.

He recoiled and fell to the floor and watched her, but it was as though he was seeing a movie play out in slow motion. He fell on a pile of old linen and BJ was upon him, and with great concentration she lunged at his heart again and again with the knife. After a little while she could hear a noise and she stopped, panting, and realised that it was her own air being jerked in and out of her lungs, on a high wheezing note, with each fall of her arm.

She climbed off him. He felt spongy somehow. He still looked right at her, though, except now there was blood starting to ooze out of his mouth and his nose. She walked to the sink near the window and calmly washed and dried the blade, retracted it into its pearl-cased handle, wrapped it in a hanky and calmly placed it in her tote bag. Then she saw her clothes. Her white suit was spattered with blood. She looked in the mirror over the washbasin. It was on her face and all through the blonde wig she wore. She felt panic rise but forced herself to gather up the drugs she had sold him and put them into her bag. She looked around the room, opened the doors of the big wardrobe and expelled a long sigh of relief when she saw that it was full of women's clothing.

She pulled off the white suit, washed as well as she could and put the bloodied clothes into a striped shopping bag. She pulled on a skirt and top and checked her appearance. Then she checked Herbie. His eyes were still open but they were sort of glazed now and she thought he was probably dead. *Pity really. He was a good lay.*

She walked carefully downstairs to the main door, which opened directly into Spring Lane. She looked right and left but saw no-one, not a flicker of interest in her from any direction. Perhaps he really had been by himself and may be bumping into her was an accident. May be he often put on stupid wigs and went off to buy drugs. BJ hurried towards the more open Hennessy Road end of Wanchai. Within five minutes she was in a taxi. Half an hour later she arrived back at the Peninsula.

The hotel staff looked at her curiously but politely handed over the key to room 129. Her blonde hair was gone and her mousey brown hair was flattened against her head. She was dressed in a long cheap-quality green silk skirt and a magenta and orange mandarin-collared top. On her feet were elegant beige mid-heeled shoes and she carried a beautiful chain-handled leather bag, sadly mis-matched to the outfit.

BJ was oblivious to her appearance. After the night she'd had, anyone would look at a girl oddly, wouldn't they? She let herself into her room and threw the rolls of money she'd made onto the bed. She laughed, stripped off the clothes she had taken from the room in Spring Lane and stuffed them, along with her bloodied white suit, into her suitcase. She'd take that for a walk later and buy a whole new wardrobe as well as a new suitcase. When she left Hong Kong tomorrow, she'd be BJ Cresswell on her passport but she would be someone else entirely in her head. And that person was the one who was going to retire to a rich life on the Spanish coast.

She spent the next half hour restoring her appearance to that of Miss Christine James, the rightful occupant of room 129. She unlocked the room safe – the soap box was still there, with its one remaining block of heroin. Christine James had something in common with Sally Walters in that she did not use heroin, and the box was firmly replaced. Christine James wasn't a murderess either and she took the flick-knife out of the handbag where she found it, wrapped it in a hanky and added it to the contents of the suitcase. It could go into the harbour this evening along with the rest of the kit left over from that unsavoury blonde woman.

After taking care of the essentials, Christine felt strangely fatigued. She would go out and buy new clothes, including some more suitable night clothes and undergarments, and then rest up for the remainder of the day in preparation for what had to be done tonight. Somehow, tonight, she had to get rid of the last block of "999". She crimped her generous mouth into a tight line. The voice was faint, but it was there. *Perhaps,* the "white witch" whispered to her, *you will need me again after all.*

Friday 6 September: 11.00am

There was chaos on Hei Ling Chau when James arrived by water-taxi late in the morning. Only twenty of the one hundred and fifty patients had been transferred and they were the most seriously ill who had been ferried to Lantau in a smaller vessel. There had been much debate about whether it was wise to move patients at the extreme end of the disease but the consensus between hospital administration and the more pragmatic nursing end of the hospice was that to segregate the patients, some of whom had lived side by side for many years, was much worse than the temporary trauma of being moved.

Mr Tan's wife had not considered that her husband would require lunch and when Miss Lim arrived at the boat with a covered bowl of chicken and rice, he ate it gratefully. He would not tell his wife he had eaten here. She had odd ideas about infection.

The arrival of Sir James Gates, Pearl's father, was very comforting to Miss Lim after such a stressful morning. True, Sir James had only come to the island to find Miss Cheung but Mae Lim was confident he would be able to help them. He seemed to know instinctively what was required and seemed to understand exactly how to go about things.

"Miss Lim," he said – "Did you hear a boat approach the wharf? Any engine noises? – Apart from the ferry and the smaller transport vessels, of course." James had already questioned Mr Tan and was not surprised when Miss Lim replied that all she had been aware of that day were the needs of her patients.

Mr Tan's boat had been tied up to the Hei Ling Chau wharf since 6.00am and he was very bored. There had been other engine noises further away than those at the jetty but he had paid scant attention.

"Ah, yes. There were the fishermen, just on light," said Mr Tan.

Sir James was interested. "Fishermen, Mr Tan? At what time, exactly?"

"A bit after six o'clock I suppose. I had a smoke after tying the boat up and saw a light. I thought it was someone fishing, but the torch was wavering around too much and I decided it must be someone on the beach."

"What did you do?"

He shrugged. "Why would I do anything?"

James nodded. *He probably thought they were ghosts.* He looked at some of the patients being wheeled by. *Or some of the more mobile patients out for an early morning walk.* James took in the scene. Why had Pearl gone into this project at such speed? Why was this move such an imperative with her that it had all been conceived and executed in less than a month? "A whole new initiative for the Bowen Foundation", she had told him. "The realization of a dream to build a community hospital. What better location to serve the southern islands and their scattered and highly disadvantaged communities"? All very fine sentiments, but what was her real reason?

*

People had largely forgotten about the epidemic-rated outbreak of leprosy that flooded through Hong Kong during the 1950s and 60s. Building a leprosarium on Hei Ling Chau had served to keep the disease largely invisible. The prevalence of leprosy was waning and today, here they were, the last of the poor souls to contract leprosy, some of the last to have to endure its pathology – both social and medical – and all going to a new superb and serene location in which to live out their days. *Rather than dying on this piece of godforsaken rock.*

*

James caught himself out, sighing. He could see the sense in the relocation, or rather, could understand the humanitarian sense of it. He thought about Annie Cheung. He knew Annie only slightly but if she had arrived here as planned this morning, she was hardly the sort of woman to be sitting quietly in the hospital somewhere checking some list or other. Clearly, she hadn't turned up. But before he could assume that she had passed up the day's work for some other more pressing reason, he would have a look around.

The water-taxi operator said that the passenger who had made the journey from the Connaught Road depot left Hong Kong at about 5.15am. Mr Tan had seen someone on the beach with a torch at about 6.00am. James talked to the same taxi skipper at about eight when the man corrected James's assumption that Annie had already left for Hei Ling Chau – because his fare was a man. By 8.00am Annie Cheung had still not appeared at the taxi fleet depot.

*

James's other interest in taking a look around was to satisfy himself that Albert Ho had not returned to the island. The murder of DS Fraser in Albert's house, followed by a male passenger hiring a boat to Hei Ling Chau at about 5.15am that morning, could be a coincidence, but the timings fitted. Ho could have murdered DS Fraser just after four o'clock that morning and then returned here to finish off whatever it was that DS Proust and DC Lee had interrupted, during their surveillance of him early last evening.

James strolled away from the jetty where Miss Lim now seemed well in control of operations.

He called out to her, "I'll start with the out-buildings."

Friday 10 September: 11.30am

DC Lee stood guard in Ong Hing Terrace while the scene of crime team did their stuff and after this he returned to Central Division HQ. By then it was later in the morning and DS Proust had still not phoned in sick nor was there any other explanation for his absence from duty. The station was buzzing with the news of DS Fraser's murder and the more recent news that DC Brodie had been involved in a car accident on his way to join DS Fraser on the remaining part of the night shift. He broke his left leg in the collision and was now a patient in Queen Mary Hospital.

By 11.30am there was still no word from DS Proust, officially or unofficially. Tony Lee knew Herbie Proust well enough to know that Herbie would never fail to make sure his colleagues were covered at all times. DS Fraser had been let down by that very omission this morning, when DC Brodie had been injured. DS Fraser was now in the morgue.

Central Division was in a state of controlled chaos. The Chief of Police was seeing no-one and Chief Superintendent Smythe had been assigned as senior officer to the case of DS Fraser. Ong Hing Terrace was now cordoned off and there was only police-supervised resident access to and from the row of ancient terraced shophouses.

The immediate information about the cause of DS Fraser's death was that he had sustained a massive blow to the back of his head early that morning – the time was not yet established – which, if not responsible for killing him outright, certainly rendered him unconscious. – Then just to be thorough, the murderer had slit the Detective Sergeant's throat.

DC Lee gave a statement. Sir James Gates would give a statement later in the day. – CS Smythe knew verbally from James what it would contain. – DC Lee and DS Fraser's fingerprints had been found in the house and Sir James prints were being processed. Other prints in the house were being run for matches.

As the morning wore on, Chief Superintendent Smythe became more and more concerned about the whereabouts of DS Proust. The phone at his apartment remained unanswered and a car was eventually despatched there. The door was forced but of DS Proust there was no sign. An officer from Special Branch was assigned to the premises to conduct a routine search of DS Proust's possessions to try to get an inkling of anything he may have been involved in that would lead to his absence from duty without leave.

For in police parlance, DS Proust was now absent without leave.

*

But DS Proust had not gone AWOL. He had been fascinated to see the luscious BJ Cresswell in a Wanchai bar after he knocked off work late on Thursday night and had decided to hang around to see what she was up to. He still had vague suspicions about her. He saw enough to convince himself that she was either on the game or selling drugs, or both. He followed her, and by the early hours of Friday morning, he watched her change from the head-turning woman he was familiar with to a laughing, drugged out kid who played hopscotch along the footpath, taking care not to step on the broken paving but only on the magic bricks. Herbie still had his surveillance kit with him, which, among other things, included a wig, sunglasses and money. He laughingly approached her and joined in the game. The wig was bad – Herbie knew it, and the sunglasses were worse, but although she was wary, she was also off her face and he got away with his bad Roy Orbison impersonation.

She turned out to be a pushover. Money entranced her.

When he recognized her in the bar, she was very much the woman he had bedded, seductive almost beyond thought of possession, in company with a smartly dressed guy. They were drinking in the Happy Spring Bar. She had obviously taken her share on board and he easily saw that it was money – a lot of money – that she tucked into a big white leather tote bag. What vindication it would be for him if he could get her for dealing drugs. If she was dealing here that openly, in Wanchai, she was either good or stupid.

Herbie had become convinced that it was BJ who had removed the three blocks of the purest heroin ever to be produced in Hong Kong, the famous 1964 haul of Red Bird "999", right from under his nose at the Narcotics Bureau offices in August. If he could arrest her, it would clear his conscience as well as get the stuff off the

Red Bird Summer   187

streets. Each block in street value was worth about HK$20 million and she had got away with three of them. Here she was, walking the streets of Hong Kong with more than sixty million bucks worth of drugs to cash in on, because she had fooled him with her alluring tits and a broken shoe. And as for the processed value – he couldn't even compute it.

As he trailed BJ throughout the fag end of Thursday and the early hours of Friday morning, he saw that the "white witch" of his nightmares was nothing more than a tart. Was that all of it though? Did she somehow know that the Narcotics Unit had operated for years with a hugely flawed system of confiscated drug storage and did she plan her little heist? Or, when she came to his office that day a few weeks back, did she just have a stroke of luck?

How would she have known otherwise? Had he told her? During the night they spent together, had he told her about the drugs laid like house bricks along the wall of the ladies' toilet in the Narcotics Bureau offices? He couldn't remember. That's what he couldn't stand thinking about. And that's what he thought he might yet be able to vindicate.

And so in the early hours, he had stopped following her and picked her up. But not for sex this time. He paid her for a packet of drugs. She was well gone on them herself when he took her to a room that he had the occasional need to use in Spring Lane, in the heart of the Wanchai District. He pretended to snort the powder just before she passed out. He only had to wait until she came to, talk her into admitting that she had access to much more and then he'd arrest her for possession and dealing. If she had more, it would show up. She was a pushover compared to some of the individuals he had dealt with in his policing career in Hong Kong.

But Herbie was wrong about BJ being a pushover. She killed him without hesitation and as she stabbed him time and again, she also remembered the feeling of deep satisfaction it had given her to kill once before. The rhythmic stabbing of her knife into the flesh of Herbie Proust's chest gave BJ Cresswell the best orgasm she had experienced since she had jabbed another punter off into heaven on the last night of her Tokyo stint, just as he had ejaculated.

*

Friday wore on and the patients from Hei Ling Chau Leprosarium were slowly loaded onto the *Jiang Li*. Annie Cheung's head-wound still bled – but slowly now – into the bricks of the guest villa's small courtyard, where, eleven years ago, Pearl's mother had lied to protect Pearl from knowing too much about her colleagues' more dangerous activities. It was in that villa and under these same bricks that a man called Dr Lin Dei had concealed the secrets of China's nuclear research programme. It was under these same bricks that Albert Ho had hidden the heroin which he had used to set up Karen Henderson. He had acquired the heroin from John Simons, who had in turn acquired it from BJ Cresswell.

Friday wore on. As the temperature rose, the only thing that slowed the news of DS Proust's demise from sifting through the other odours abroad in the heat and humidity in Spring Lane was the presence of the Lucky Meat Butchery Company two doors down from where Herbie's spilt blood hardened in the pile of linen that lay on the floor of room eleven, at No. 15 Spring Lane.

Friday 10 September: 11.45 am

Kaz woke up again. Three faces looked at her this time. They belonged to Pearl, her nice doctor whom Pearl seemed to have latched on to, and Drew. She let herself swim out of sleep as she had done so many times during the past four days, no longer fighting when she sank again without making sense of much. But this time the sheer effort required to keep her eyes open was gone, and the awareness of what a strong physical sensation extreme weakness is was also muted. She lifted herself up on an elbow and said, "Drink!"

"Never changes!" said Drew, and Pearl laughed.

Pearl looked at Ben, but his attention was on the two police guards outside the ward where Kaz resided in solitary splendour, the only patient on the entire floor.

When Pearl and Ben wanted to return to the hospital, they had had a job of it to convince the officer on duty at the old Fire Service HQ that all they needed to do was take a taxi to the Peak Hospital where more police surveillance was in place and where Pearl would be quite safe. But Constable Mok had his orders and wouldn't let them leave until he had talked to Central Division who had sent a police car around as transport.

Red Bird Summer

Ben went off to find the Senior Physician. Pearl sat beside Kaz and gave her sips of water while Drew sat on the other side of the bed and just looked at her. Kaz put her head back on the pillow and they waited for her eyelids to flutter shut again as had happened so many times, but this time she turned to Pearl and said in a whisper: "Pearl, who *is* that man?" And when she saw their faces, she laughed, without making a sound.

Kaz was back. Just a little bit.

*

"She has sustained a solid assault on her organs but stroke was our major concern as you know, Dr Sanders. She had a massive amount of quinine in her system and some assorted dextrose products mixed in with a good shot of heroin. She's got a very sound constitution and should recover quite well. There could be some other fall-out that we can't button-hole quite yet. She also has a damaged left ear-drum, broken ribs and a punctured lung and all of those things will compromise her career as a marine archaeologist. Still, there's plenty of other scope for someone of her talents in her discipline, I imagine, outside of diving." Ben was talking with Cleeve Robinson, the Senior Consulting Physician at the Peak Hospital.

"Seriously. She won't be able to dive? Never?"

"She'd be ill-advised to try. I'm pretty sure the hearing loss in her left ear will be permanent as well. Oh and by the way she also mentioned that she frequently suffers from some sort of vertigo that interferes randomly with the functioning of the auditory nerve and is related to the state of the middle vesicle of her inner ear. A convoluted one, you might say." Dr Robinson laughed lightly.

Ben smiled at the little medical joke.

"I think she had already made one dive too many, before all this other business."

"When will she be discharged?"

"If she can be adequately cared for at home, I see no reason why she can't leave tomorrow. I want her back here twice a week for a check-up for the next month, but she may as well get on with things as far as her strength permits. She'll be weak for a time, obviously. Has she plenty of personal supports?"

"She has enough supports to fight over her at the moment. Thank you Dr Robinson. I'm happy to give the patient the news unless you wish to speak to her in particular. Oh and by the way, can she have a drink? She's hankering for a beer."

"Her liver has recovered remarkably well as have her kidneys. I'd imagine a San Mig or a Tiger Beer wouldn't hurt. Now, about the police surveillance. Obviously the hospital relinquishes all responsibility for her when she's discharged, you do understand that?"

Ben listened to the senior physician with respectful attention. Indeed, what would happen about security when Kaz left hospital?

Kaz had been admitted to Emergency on Monday and now, four days later, there were death contracts out on her and Pearl and the dynamics of their lives had changed. Ben didn't know who would look after Kaz – Pearl or Drew. That would determine where Kaz went, to her own flat in Upper Albert Road or to Pearl's place. There was a lot to work out. If the police surveillance continued, perhaps she would be more secure at Pearl's place.

Ben acknowledged a sense of unreality, a disconnection from his familiar self. What the hell had he done, falling in love like this, so suddenly, with Pearl? Pearl would speak passionately about how she and Kaz were two women living in an age of liberation for women, free from the need to depend on men for their life's work and well being. And in the next breath – if she wasn't telling Ben how much she loved him – she was adamant that Kaz would have Drew back because she had always loved him. Ben felt his head spin a little.

Not vertigo.

Confusion.

*

Annie had lost a lot of blood. James touched her arm gently and said, "Who are you?"

"Annie ...." She was alive. He ran to the hospital and fetched Nurse Lim. She in turn ran back to the guest cottage where Annie lay, still hanging on to a mere thread of life, while James rang for the emergency services helicopter and also rang Division Central, to request immediate police support. James returned with two blankets and a hopeful flask of water. They covered her and moistened her mouth. James felt like whooping with joy when her eyelids flickered a little.

"We simply have to find this bloke, Nurse Lim. This is the second attack that has taken place on Hei Ling Chau this week. Chances are it's the same man." Nurse Lim looked fearful and he urged her to remain calm, return to her duties and ensure that no-one was left alone. James felt immensely sad. He had not been to Hei Ling Chau since 1964 and even now he would shudder at his own part in the drama of that time if he ever permitted himself the luxury of such introspection. *Has there ever been happiness here?*

He thought about Pearl. Their personal history started in this place and was woeful. Now, Pearl would be heart-broken. Worse, she would blame herself for what had happened to Annie. He walked firmly back to the wharf. He couldn't think about all that now. There was a madman to find, one who may have murdered two people already today.

And it was only just approaching lunch time.

Friday 10 September: 12.30pm

Chief Superintendent Smythe attended a rare one-to-one briefing with Police Chief Gallop, who coolly informed him that three death contracts had come to his attention, two of them on the lives of prominent Hong Kong citizens. When he heard that Karen Henderson and Pearl Green were the latter two targets and that the wraith-like BJ Cresswell was the third, Smythe sat back in his chair, exhaled loudly and exclaimed, "Well I'll be blowed, Sir. What the devil is going on?" Gerry Gallop was very pleased with Smythe's reaction – hard chap to impress usually – very efficient and whatnot but rather a cold fish. "Seems a god-awful mess to me, Chief Superintendent. I've authorised police protection for Dr Henderson and Lady Green." – Tommy pricked up his ears at Gallop's use of Pearl's title. – "But we can't do that indefinitely. Then there's the Cresswell female. Never heard of her until now. Any ideas?"

"Just the one, Sir, which I'll get onto as soon as I can brief Inspector Chung to take over the investigation into the death of DS Fraser."

If there had been any doubt that there was a bloody great barney going on in Hong Kong, this latest news dispelled it. The attacks on Dr Henderson and now Miss Green's involvement seemed to herald the outbreak of some sort of internecine warfare. Smythe was confident that BJ Cresswell was the catalyst for whatever was going on, but how did that explain a contract being out on her? Smythe became aware that the glassy left eye of the Chief of Police was upon him.

"It's very convoluted, Sir. I'll put a team of four undercover officers out there to see what we can pick up from the streets. You should also be aware, Sir, that these three people have already come under police notice during the past month."

Gerry Gallop looked surprised. "I knew about the Henderson woman but, really, you don't say!"

"Karen Henderson was kidnapped and Pearl Green found the card of one BJ Cresswell of Cresswell Public Relations in Dr Henderson's handbag after the attack on her in early August. Dr Henderson has no idea how it got there. Miss Green and Dr Henderson had an encounter with Miss Cresswell after that, we think, although she gave a different name at the time.

"Miss Green was very clear that this woman – a Miss Collins I believe she gave her name as – appeared to target them as they were about to make a journey by water-taxi.

"I've been unable to find any trace of this BJ Cresswell, except to verify that she legally entered Hong Kong three months ago and gave her address as the Frangipani Guesthouse in Nathan Road. That guesthouse – not a very savoury sort of place – has no record of her on their books. The woman arrived here and just evaporated.

"Incidentally, Sir, the woman who targeted Miss Green and Dr Henderson also said she was staying at the Frangipani Guesthouse. –Coincidence? I wonder."

"Should we put out an all-points for her, Chief Superintendent Smythe?"

"Not yet, Sir, with respect. I will assign an officer to examine all of the camera footage of movements in and out of the Narcotics Bureau offices during the three months before the stock inventory showed that some of the confiscated drugs were missing. I want to know the identity of every single person who came and went into that building by date and time if possible – and if there is someone who can't be identified, they will be followed up."

"But what use is that? The drugs that went missing could have been removed any time from 1964 onwards, Chief Superintendent.

No physical inventory has been taken since they were initially lodged there." Gerry Gallop was becoming annoyed.

"Sir, you are quite right, of course. But Forensics say that the indentations on the blocks that concealed the missing ones are quite recent. Perhaps, Sir, this whole situation is just to do with drugs, and drugs that have recently come onto the scene, Sir."

"Frankly, Smythe, I'd welcome that. At the moment it's so bally complicated that any familiar solution at all would be welcome. You've my permission for any resources you need to get on top of it."

"Thank you, Sir." Smythe stood and saluted, ready to leave, while Gerry Gallop scribbled on a note pad.

"Here. Just give this to Mrs Charlton. She'll see to it."

Chief Superintendent Smythe allowed himself a very small smile. So it was true, after all. Mrs Charlton really did run the Hong Kong Police Service.

*

Amy was leaving the Jasmine Garden Bar when the *gwailo* stopped her. "Good time?" Amy was tired. She had worked the midnight to morning shift, washed, changed, and taken her young son to school, before going back to the bar to start her day job of cleaning the rooms. He looked like a nice man so she said, "$150 one hour," expecting him to laugh at her and walk on, but he didn't.

He just said, "Hong Kong or US Dollars"?

"Hong Kong dollars OK." They were near Spring Lane. She could use one of the rooms at No.15. All she had to do was pay $10 to the concierge. She laughed. This was her lucky day. $150. She would buy her little son Sean some good quality meat and vegetables for dinner and a present as well. And perhaps she would buy herself a new pair of shoes.

She took the *gwailo* by the arm and looked into his eyes. "You come with me. Nice room."

*

The police siren stirred up attention in Spring Lane but rather than attracting people out of their houses and shops, it all but emptied the street. Spring Lane is at the heart of the red light district in Wanchai and many who frequent the place would prefer not to have contact with the law. Chief Superintendent Smythe went to Room 11, leaving DC Lee to make enquiries about who found the body and when.

*

"I have not seen the woman before," the concierge lied, easily. "She was slim and wore a dark blue cheongsam."

She looked very respectable according to Madam Bao, who had a much better description of the male *gwailo* to offer, a tall man with fair hair, dressed in bone-coloured trousers and a white shirt. They paid for the use of Room 11 for an hour. When she heard the woman scream, she ran upstairs to see what the racket was about and the man almost knocked her down as he rushed past her.

"His face was red and his eyes bulged out of his head," she told DC Lee. "He looked like he had eaten too many raw chillis." The woman had also melted away and probably used the rear staircase that led into a laneway through a small, shabby back yard.

*

Chief Superintendent Smythe took off his cap and wiped his forehead. The smell of dried blood in the room was beginning to mingle with the smell of fresh blood from the nearby butchery. Herbie's body lay on a pile of blood-soaked bed-linen. Smythe closed the door and went downstairs. "DC Lee, I want you to stand guard at the second door on the right up the stairs. – Do not go into the room. I repeat, do not go into the room. – I'm going to radio for assistance."

Tommy Smythe was a kind man and he didn't feel it necessary that DC Lee should have to see DS Proust's body, if it could be avoided. The Detective Sergeant had died hard. The walls of the room were splattered with blood and his chest was a bloodied crust. Whoever killed him had done so in a frenzy.

Smythe waited until he heard the police siren approach before he informed DC Lee that DS Proust had been murdered. He relieved the Detective Constable of further duties and seconded him to the General Duties Pool until further notice. "Take the car, Lee. I'll hitch back with the SOCO crew. If you want to go off duty, you have my permission to do so."

Tony, who had attended the scene of DS Fraser's murder earlier that morning, managed to leave the building with dignity and even managed to get into the car before he broke down. He saw the scene of crime team pulling up in Spring Lane, sirens howling for the benefit of the locals, but pulled away before he was obliged to return their chirpy greetings for the second time that day.

*

Chief Superintendent Smythe's day was subsumed by the mountain of work that he was suddenly confronted with, all associated with the violent deaths of two of his officers. By 5pm he had all of the notification processes in place and DS Fraser and DS Proust lay side by side in the Police Morgue – in some sort of peace, Tommy hoped – awaiting autopsy. Their notebooks were in his desk drawer, along with their badges and formal records. All relatives had been notified, or were in the process of being notified, and Dr Bates, the Police Pathologist, had given Tommy the informal nod that the weapons used in each attack were different and that he was probably dealing with two different killers.

"Off the record, Chief Superintendent, I think one is left-handed. More tomorrow after the autopsies."

Friday 10 September: 2.00pm

The helicopter had gone. Annie was stabilized as far as possible and was on her way to the Queen Mary Hospital. The Water Police and a Crime Investigation Team arrived at Hei Ling Chau and sealed off the guest villa. When he heard the news at Central Division, Gerry Gallop's head started to spin, but he bucked up when James phoned and congratulated him on his efficient policing. A police presence would remain on the island and a thorough search was underway for Annie's attacker.

James accompanied Annie. He rang around until he found Pearl at the Peak Hospital. Pearl was distraught, but there was no easy way to cover up the gravity of what had happened to her young colleague. Pearl was devoted to Annie but like so many of the people in Pearl's life, Annie was only marginally aware of Pearl's attachment to her. James waited for his daughter to arrive – under police escort – by which time Annie had been taken into surgery. Pearl sat in the ante-room to the operating wing and rocked to and fro with unabated anxiety and James, surprised again by the explicit display of vulnerability from his usually stoic offspring, advised her to get on to Annie's family and anyone else she knew who should be told and if she couldn't do that, to go away until Annie was back on the ward. Pearl looked at her father in some surprise, but glad of something tangible to do, she left for home, again under police escort.

Friday 10 September: 4.00pm

Mae Lim checked the last patient on board the *Jiang Li*, took a fond last look around the hospital, confirmed that it was satisfactorily vacated and returned to the boat. She scanned the rows of patients and nodded to Mr Tan. "We are ready to leave Captain. All present and accounted for."

The patients were comfortable. Some had been on board for several hours and the more mobile had been able to walk around the decks. Although it had been just another day, this one had been spent out in the open, on the water, a rare treat. And now they were going to their wonderful new home on Lantau Island where there were magnificent gardens and sheltered pavilions. They would watch the geese, ducks and chickens frolic, would help with the vegetables and flower gardening and witness glorious sunrises and sunsets instead of seeing little but the grim little rhyolitic hump of Hei Ling Chau. There was a good spirit abroad on the *Jiang Li* and Mae Lim smiled, even though the day had been blighted with what had befallen poor Miss Cheung.

Que sera sera, she thought. *What will be, will be.* This boat represented hope for a better life for her patients, and that is what drove Nurse Lim's existence. She looked at her clipboard, and at last put it down. Matron Cheung would organise the patients at the Lantau end and Mae Lim could start to think about what her own life would be in this new place. – Matron Cheung had said that the quarters for staff were beautiful, with a private, walled garden and that she, Mae Lim and Lily Wong, both Senior Nurses, each had their own bedroom and sitting-room and small bathroom, furnished with simple and lovely wooden furniture. Mae Lim started to dream of embroidered bedcovers and soft towels and wall hangings and other things that were probably beyond her modest means....

*

Mr Tan puffed on the fourth cigarette from his second packet of the day. Even though these people had had bad luck with an unpropitious event, overall the day had been a good one. Mr Tan felt peaceful as he manoeuvred the *Jiang Li* away from the wharf and headed north towards Lantau Island. It was a quick run – they would be there in about twenty minutes but he would have another long wait while the patients were off-loaded into the fleet of buses that would take them to their new home. He would tell Mrs Tan of this feeling, how it made the memory of his uncle less painful somehow when he saw how well-cared-for people with this terrible disease were these days. It would make her sad all over again to think about that time – how families abandoned family members who contracted leprosy and literally sent them to die in squalour for fear of contracting what was understood to be a vengeful scourge. – But would she understand what he meant when he told her that the day's events had been a reminder that there are worse diseases to fight?

He thought sadly about the young woman who had been attacked so violently while they were all going about their business of loading the boat for departure.

He directed his thoughts back to Mrs Tan. *And what if, husband,* she would say, *in about five years time, you start to get strange rashes? Will you still feel as philosophical as you do tonight?* Mr Tan smiled. He was very fond of Mrs Tan, and who knows, perhaps she might be right. He looked at the water. Today, the heat was much as it had been all summer, but the water was beginning to get that deeper purple afternoon colour earlier than it had for many months. It could be a sign that the seasons were changing, but as Mr Tan also knew very well, it could also be that a big storm was on the way.

*

Sergeant Hanson watched the *Jiang Li* depart. Six police officers had been despatched to the island and a thorough search was conducted for the offender who had so seriously injured the young Bowen Foundation employee. Three of his men were making a final search of the heathy-scrub to the south east and now that the hospital was finally empty, a final inspection would be conducted of the entire facility.

Dick Hanson was without a solitary clue about how to proceed. Unless the bloke had smuggled himself onto the *Jiang Li*, somehow he very much doubted that he was still on the island. Of course they had inspected the vessel and had kept a vigil over it ever since that head wallah from the Home Office had found the victim. There was no way the perpetrator could have left the island, Hanson reasoned, unless he used a rowboat. Not so much as a splutter from another engine had disrupted the quiet of Hei Ling Chau since the Water Police contingent arrived and the *Jiang Li* had departed. He had a thought. "Junk."

"Sir?"

"Junk, Constable Wong. He probably left by junk. Damn me for not thinking of it earlier. Round up the men immediately." Hanson saw it all clearly. By whatever means this bloke had arrived on Hei Ling Chau – by a brass-band escorted flotilla of Royal yachts for all he cared – he probably left on a passing junk, just like everyone else who knows the ways of the outlying islands. Junks are the alternative ferry services for those who like the rather romantic and errant nature of the routes they follow or for those who just want cheap transport.

Sergeant Hanson and Constable Wong set off in the second police launch to see if it were possible to catch up with a junk or two and ask after any passenger pick-ups from Hei Ling Chau during the day. It was one of Sergeant Hanson's better ideas, but as Constable Wong well knew, it was too late. Any junk that had cruised by Hei Ling Chau and picked up the alleged perpetrator would be at Macau by now. Or close to Kwangtung Province. It would not be floating around between Cheung Chau and Peng Chau waiting for the Sarge to have his bright idea.

*

It was just on 6pm when BJ woke up. Her mouth was dry and the work she had done to restore Christine James – all pallid brown hair and dull skin – looked back at her from the mirror with disgust. Christine didn't do drugs and BJ's mouth would have to remain dry, her hands shaky and her eyes road-mapped with small red veins. Christine James had no vanity. She was not much to look at and had things on her mind other than her appearance. Being organised for the trip tomorrow was her priority and there was a lot to deal with, getting rid of the suitcase of undesirable clothes and other objects, for a start.

Christine was increasingly anxious that she be the only persona left in the theatre of characters that BJ's addicted and increasingly addled mind had created during the past few days. – Barbara Jane Cook was gone forever, big-mouthed bitch; smart little Sally Walters, too. – Too much concerned with playing house, that one. – There might have to be one last deal for BJ Cresswell to negotiate but Christine was confident that she could control BJ now. The remaining block of heroin had to go before she left Hong Kong tomorrow and she may as well try to sell it, otherwise she'd have to bin it in the harbour along with the incriminating clothes, not to mention that wicked little flick-knife.

There was no choice but for BJ to be let out one last time. BJ's hunger for heroin resonated deeply in Christine and she felt it, actually felt it reach her hands. The stuff was in the safe. BJ would croon as she touched it, would wet a finger and wipe it across the surface of the beautifully honed block, a work of art in itself, bevelled, engraved, coded, but most of all in perfect condition after years in storage, just waiting for the right person to come along who could pay for it. In the process, she, Christine, would be made rich.

There was another voice in the room. *Just have one for me and then I'll never touch it again. I promise.* It was BJ. Christine felt panic hit her stomach again. *Shopping! I'll go shopping again.* Christine viewed shopping as a chore but with the groping hunger eating at her so relentlessly that she readily understood the meaning of "visceral need", it seemed the only thing to do. She had bought only two new sets of clothes, hardly enough to get her by while she settled down in Spain. She left the room quickly and slammed the door. When she handed in her room-key, the desk staff turned to one another with worried frowns and mute, shoulder-shrugging looks that asked each other as clearly as though they had spoken: what is going on with that woman?

Christine walked through the Lobby Café to the ground floor powder-room. She had to see for herself what they had so obviously been staring at. She studied herself in the mirror. She was plain. No make-up. It must have been the wide slashes of powdered heroin white-washed across her cheeks, one of which terminated in a big lump of dried and bloodied flesh, stuck to her skin just under her ear. She shuddered, washed her face and ran out of the room, banging the door as she did so, and she hit Emmie Franklin squarely in the shoulder. Emmie flinched in pain.

"I'm sorry, Mrs Franklin. I didn't mean it."

Emmie rubbed her shoulder. "Do I know you?"

"No. Sorry. My mistake." BJ curled out of Christine's mouth, the cringing BJ who would do or say anything to cover a blunder while Christine James had enough tenacity to ignore blunders. People were not interested in holding her accountable for them, which was an advantageous by-product of being plain and therefore, invisible.

"Just a moment. Don't go." Emmie blocked the door. "I do know you. You're Barbara Cresswell, aren't you?"

Christine recovered quickly. "I'm sorry, Mrs Franklin. I owe you a proper apology for my behaviour. Can we talk?" They were in the ladies' sitting-room adjacent to the Peninsula's ground floor toilets, a spacious room that offered comfortable chairs, vanity tables stocked with powders, tissues, eau de colognes and best of all, solitude.

It was some time later, after cocktails in fact, when a Mrs Helena Hobsworth from North Carolina in the United States of America came in to powder her nose before heading off to the Marco Polo Lounge for drinks, that the delicate hand and wrist of a woman slumped into the booth Mrs Hobsworth occupied, accompanied by a heavy slipping noise as the body of Emmie Franklin slid from the adjacent toilet seat onto the floor.

Mrs Hobsworth screamed heartily.

*

It had been careless of Emmie to tell Christine James, especially so stridently, that BJ Cresswell was identifiable, despite all the efforts Christine had made to render her inconspicuous. It was the matter of the scar on the left side of BJ's neck. Mrs Franklin must have taken a good look at her at some stage. She paid dearly for the observation. Emmie's last sensation was of being dragged across the floor of the powder-room before she heard a door bang.

It was the last sound Emmie Franklin ever heard.

Red Bird Summer

Friday 10 September: 6.30pm

The September light was deepening as the last of the patients were loaded onto a fleet of buses which had been especially modified to transport the hospital stretchers safely. Matron Cheung did the section count – there were twenty patients in each one – ticked off the left hand column and added it to the sub-totals of the other trips that had already been made.

"One hundred and fifty-one. There are one hundred and fifty-one patients on this list. Nurse Lim!" Nurse Lim was still working, now helping two of the hospital orderlies secure the last of the stretchers into the makeshift transport. She poked her head out of the door of the bus:

"Yes Matron Cheung?"

"There are one hundred and fifty-one patients on this list."

"That is correct, Matron. That is the number of patients who left Hei Ling Chau."

"We only have one hundred and fifty patients, Nurse. Where did you find the extra one?" Matron Cheung felt quite jaunty even though she was exhausted. That would give bossy little Nurse Lim something to think about.

She totted up the columns of figures again and scanned the patient lists for names. Ah. There it was. Patient one hundred and forty-one did not have a name against the number. When she went back on board the *Jiang Li* to double check that everyone was disembarked, Matron Cheung saw the articles – a narrow plastic covered mattress, a pillow and an Aertex blanket – all in process of sinking. Matron's eyes bulged. "Captain Tan, man overboard!"

Mr Tan looked and saw what she saw. He looked at her. "You want me to jump in the water and find this person?"

She nodded vigorously.

"But Madam, they have sunk and I cannot swim."

Matron Cheung had to content herself with letting forth an almighty and convoluted scream. People in the nearby village, who had dreaded the arrival of their new neighbours and who cowered in their houses, fearful of instant infection, quaked over their rice bowls. Not only was the disease said to be terrifying to look at, it was terrifying to listen to.

Red Bird Summer

The horrors of the coming night were not over for the See family, who sat at their dining-table, huddled rather more closely together than usual, and who took frequent and nervous glimpses at the windows and doors of their small house, unenhanced by either glass or locks. The man who came to the window and leant in to their living space and asked for help was more frightening than anything they could have prepared themselves for. He was the materialization of a thousand ghosts. His head and arms were bandaged and he wore a white shroud that was wet and clung to him. When he leant deeper into the room and smiled at them, the two daughters of the house screamed loudly before clapping their hands to their mouths. This obviously distressed him and he commenced to unbind his wrappings.

At this, the lady of the house had enough. She stood up and yelled at him: "Go away, ghost, dreadful thing, whatever you are. Leave us in peace."

The ghost, dreadful thing, paused. A cunning look appeared in the one visible eye it cast upon the gathering. "Surrender unto me your vessel and I shall depart," it said, in high Cantonese. And so it was that patient number one hundred and forty-one escaped from care on the very night the old monastery on Lantau Island was first occupied as a hospital.

*

The story passed into village mythology for all time how one of the patients escaped into the night, taking the See family's boat, their only means of livelihood, ruining them in a moment. But several weeks later a giant of a *gwaipor* woman came to them and handed them ten thousand dollars to replace their craft and it followed that on many nights from then on, the Lantau Island fisher-folk half wished for the return of the ghostly dreadful thing that had so strangely brought luck to the See family's fortunes.

*

Matron Cheung rationalized to herself that if she had one hundred and fifty patients in the hospital and one hundred and fifty patients had boarded the buses, then the extra one, patient number one hundred and forty-one, was either a ring-in or a wraith, or a simple arithmetical error.

She took her leave of Mr Tan. "Mr Tan. I do not think there was anyone on that mattress. All the patients are accounted for. I cannot explain it but I do not think anyone has drowned."

Mr Tan felt better for the kind words, even though if someone had drowned he would still not have felt for a second that he should have jumped in and drowned as well, merely to keep them company.   Matron Cheung and Mr Tan shook hands and parted cordially.

The lights of the *Jiang Li* brightened and Mr Tan gently eased the old ferry away from the wharf to make his way north around Silvermine Bay, back to the shipyard. The *Jiang Li* would be an elegant boat when its refurbishment was completed. It would take many tourists on special trips and there would be piano music, the chink of glasses and the dancing of lights on the faces of the men and women who could afford to pay for such luxuries, rather than the sweat and fret of the thousands of people who had used the old ferry each day as it had plied across Victoria Harbour for so many years.

Mr Tan was happy to think that he had been able to skipper it one last time in its old role of serving the people.

*

Lights appeared on many fishing craft in the waters of Silvermine Bay and one boat with a small outboard motor navigated between them, using the last of the light for guidance, until it bobbed beyond the ring of boats and reached the strong south-flowing currents of the main channel, where she steered a struggling course north-east towards Kowloon. The wind was strong and the south-moving swell was beginning to break into small foaming waves.

The boatman steered the craft with difficulty and shouted above the noise of the engine, "Two nights now I have fought to cross these seas in a strange boat. What omens are out there, oh owl?"

But the only response was the brisk slap of waves against the hull of the See family's craft.

Friday 10 September: 9.30pm

The telephone in Pearl's apartment rang and James picked it up.
"James? Yee Koon. I believe Pearl is unavailable?"
James nursed a whisky. Ben was with Pearl. "She collapsed when Annie didn't make it through surgery, Yee Koon. They took her to the Peak Hospital and admitted her into the room next door to Karen Henderson. It was a security decision to take her there, of course. The ward is under police guard."
"And poor Miss Cheung?"
"Was Annie part of all this, Yip, old man, or just caught up in it somehow?"
"I don't know, James. I'm doing everything in my power to find out what's happening, and that's why I'm calling you now. There's been another death tonight. I must talk to you. This is one that I do know something about. "You have heard of a Miss BJ Cresswell?"

*

Christine had returned to her room after the nasty business of having to take care of the odious Mrs Franklin, a slow and difficult process, which Christine enjoyed not one bit.

When she collected her room-key, the desk staff had looked at her oddly, again. She had washed her face, so what now? What else could possibly interest them about her now? The point of Christine James's existence was that she was all but invisible in this glamorous location.

She paced and thought. There were still BJ's clothes to dispose of. She could not take them out of the hotel in her suitcase now. – It would arouse suspicion. – She might be just one very ordinary guest in this glamorous place, but she seemed to be drawing attention to herself and that was the last thing she wanted. Being taken for a room-hopper could be disastrous, given the contents of her suitcase.

Then she remembered the shopping bags in which she had brought back her afternoon's purchases, and stuffed BJ's clothes into one of them. She would go out for a walk and take that with her, then return and remove the remainder of the stuff in another bag later on.

Christine worked hard and it wasn't long before she had eliminated BJ, except for a slightly distressing twitch in her left hand. She purchased a thick foundation cream and covered the scar on her neck. BJ was all but gone. She opened the wall-safe and removed the soap-box. She remembered doing so this time, not like earlier in the evening, when there must have been enough of BJ left in the room to make Christine take some of the damned stuff. She looked at the single remaining block. It looked damaged. There were chips off it and the corners were rounded off – she thought that must have happened through being shifted so much. She lifted the block out of its coffret, wrapped it in one of the hotel's hand towels and stowed it away in the very ordinary tan leather handbag she had also acquired. There it kept company with the large amount of money she now had – all neatly rolled into bundles of one hundred thousand Hong Kong dollars.

Christine James didn't do designer handbags. – People noticed things like that. – This bag was in a satchel style, a little bit fashionable but made of indifferent leather and barely notable. Its contents though were sensational – about twenty million Hong Kong dollars worth of drugs, if sold at optimal value, sitting alongside more than four million in cash.

Somehow she had to get rid of the rest of the stuff. She knew BJ would head to Wanchai to offload it but Christine wasn't about to attract any attention of any sort there tonight. There had been those two miserable weeks at the Bright Flower Mansions in the back streets of Kowloon. At night sometimes, BJ had walked beyond the market precincts into some of the darker areas at the fringe where the older, very poor residential part of Kowloon intersected with an industrial zone.

Sandwiched inbetween these two areas was the Walled City of Kowloon. The entry into the walled city was no secret but it wasn't much frequented. Few people were drawn there by the attractions of the neighbourhood. BJ had found some of the stories about it fascinating, although she hadn't ventured in. Once you did, so they said, you might not get out and no-one would care. No guarantees. Christine thought that the place had possibilities, especially for someone like her. Even so, it was risky, but one thing was clear – tonight was for risk-taking and the Walled City was loaded with drug parlours. She might have some luck selling the drugs there and tomorrow, well, tomorrow she could resume the relatively dull existence that someone of her style could expect life to offer.

But before she did anything, she would find out if John Simons could take some more stock from her. She picked up the phone and called him. "John? I'm a friend of BJ Cresswell. My name is Christine James. BJ said you are interested in quality products."

The voice on the other end of the line was very cautious, but did acknowledge a fondness for a well-known brand of leather shoes; yes, that was true.

"Expensive leather shoes, I imagine?"

John agreed, tentatively. What had BJ put this bird up to?

"I've got a lot of very fine leather to sell, HK$10,000 per bag, an absolute steal, rare, white leather...."

"Now hang on, who are you again?"

"I'm BJ's friend. Why don't we meet? I'll see you at the Rendezvous Restaurant in Nathan Road. In an hour?" Christine put the phone down and considered the options. Surely it would be better for BJ to keep the appointment. BJ could do the business easily but if Christine showed up, she would have to win this bloke's trust before she could close the deal. It was easier to be BJ.

Just one last time. Luckily she had taken some precautions. Christine went to the hotel closet and grabbed one of her shopping bags. On her last night in Hong Kong, BJ had to get this right. No mucking about. Her future – Christine's – depended on it. And that future was a good straight life in Spain.

Christine had shopped for BJ but not quite to the true BJ style. She took out a white silk chiffon frock, a little more demure than BJ would really have liked, but it had a low neckline and was lined with pure silk. It was a smooth, curve-skimming sheath. She made up her face with pale foundation, applied smoky-grey eye make-up and red lipstick, and put on the undergarments she'd bought to go with the outfit, a lacy French bra, knickers and matching eggshell-coloured tights. She pulled the dress carefully over her head and finally put the blonde wig in place.

The wig did it. Christine reeled as BJ powered back at her from the mirror. Christine cowered. BJ looked at the brown satchel handbag that Christine had bought and laughed derisively. She took a white leather Dior handbag and large matching tote from another shopping bag concealed in the closet, opened it and carefully placed the wrapped drugs inside the larger bag. Then she added her cosmetics, all of her cash and a change of underwear.

BJ felt very strong, considering what she'd been through today. It would be fun to go out with John. – She'd never been to the Rendezvous Restaurant and it had a certain reputation in Hong Kong. – That punter who'd promised to phone her – who was he? – Toby Someone or Other? – had mentioned taking her there once. He had never done so, of course. He'd probably been afraid his wife would find out that he'd squired the beautiful BJ Cresswell on a dinner date – and now tonight was her last chance. Her last night in Hong Kong, a night to celebrate the success of her business venture here.

She twirled in front of the mirror. On the third twirl she stopped. Best not to do four. Somewhere in her mind she remembered that the number four meant death.

Friday 10 September: 7.30am

BJ baulked as the lift door opened. There were police everywhere. She made her way to the main door. The Lobby Café was cordoned off and the door of the ladies' room at the far end of the lobby was completely taped up. BJ felt good, in her element in fact, as she walked across the lobby, attracting admiring glances. Hell, she'd even worked here for a couple of weeks and now she was back as a guest. That said something about how well she'd done in Hong Kong didn't it? *Shit.* But what if someone recognized her? Well. What if? All she'd done was walk out of a job she was unhappy in.

She relaxed into her practiced, sensuous walk. She had lost weight. The clothes she'd bought that afternoon were American size 5 – which meant that she had gone down four dress sizes during the past three weeks. A few paellas, lots of tapas and Spanish wine would soon take care of that. She smiled dreamily. It was only a few hours and two flights away – Hong Kong to London and then London to Madrid. From Madrid she'd find transport to the coast, book into a hotel and start to look around at places to buy.

A portly man opened the door for her. "Let me get that for you." He looked at her rather intently, she thought. She smiled in acknowledgement of his admiring glance. "New to Hong Kong? Not with a film crew, by any chance?"

"New-ish. No. And I'm not with a film crew, but thank you for the compliment." She smiled again. She *felt* like a movie star.

"I'm Jeremy! – Ah, you wouldn't care for a drink in the Marco Polo by any chance, would you? I can assure you I'm a respectable sort of chap. I like to meet new chums – fodder for my newspaper column – and you seem as though you could be quite an addition to the Hong Kong scene. It needs a little bit of cheering up at present. Seems to be some sort of hoo-hah going on here tonight, I shall have to find out what's up, I suppose."

If BJ hadn't been running late for her appointment with John she would have jumped at the chance of having a drink with this puffy, pleasant sort of young-old colonial type. A rare opportunity. And if she had kept up with the BJ Cresswell Public Relations Consultancy she had come to Hong Kong to set up, he was exactly the sort of contact she'd have chased – someone who wrote a newspaper column.

"Thank you, but I'm due at the Rendezvous Restaurant. I don't have a card with me ...." Her voice was throaty and compelling. BJ was really back. "I'm in public relations. Did you really say you're a columnist ...?"

Jeremy looked at her with a vague sort of chumminess that concealed a most observant eye. She was a little different in overall appearance from the woman he'd seen three or so weeks back, sashaying up the steps of the hotel; but for sure it was her. His "white witch". Walking sex. Or at least she had been then. Now, she was something else. She was luminous, with a beauty that verged on transparency, in which sat red lips and smoky black eyes. Her hair, skin and clothes were all the same colour. If she had been even one lighter shade of pale, she would disappear.

"Perhaps another time then? Where are you staying? Kowloon or Hong Kong side?"

"Well, here of course." It was a full ten seconds before BJ realised what she had said and by then Jeremy had given her a farewell salute and was on his way downstairs to the Marco Polo Lounge where he was due to meet Emmie Franklin. Emmie had had a bit of a coup in entertaining a very famous international model in the Marco Polo Lounge during the week and Jeremy was going to do a full column on it.

*

The maître d' of the Marco Polo Lounge was a man expertly observant of guests' needs. When Jeremy came to the desk and paused, he was on to him like a shot. Mr Freeman wrote one of Hong Kong's most widely read social columns and was a regular visitor to the lounge.

"Good evening Marcus. I have an appointment with Mrs Franklin but I don't seem to see her. D'you know if she's about?"

Marcus Choy took Jeremy aside and spoke in low tones to him. Jeremy reached for a cigarette and struggled to keep his facial expression under control but there wasn't much he could do about his colouring. He went deathy pale and sat blank-faced until Marcus returned with a large brandy.

"The Lobby Café – the ladies' powder-room and all those police. No. You mean it happened, here?" Jeremy spoke quietly and Marcus nodded.

"Mr Freeman, perhaps you should talk with Mr Wong. Naturally this story is going to break in tomorrow's press, but..."

"I think you're absolutely right, Marcus. Please call him for me if you would be so kind."

Steven gave him a run-down on Emmie's life and career. Jeremy called Emmie's husband to offer his condolences and ask permission to run the story. The new widower referred to himself as Mr Franklin and approved the piece from the grief puzzled corner he was in. And so Jeremy's article on Emmie Franklin in the Saturday edition of the *South China Morning Post* did not hit the social pages, as Emmie had so longed for, but was a very well done page one tribute that accompanied the Hong Kong Police Media Release about her murder.

Jeremy wondered what the real story was. This was no random killing, surely. Not here. Emmie Franklin had crossed someone's bows sufficiently to pay for it with her life. The sheer immensity of someone coming into this hotel and killing an employee in the ladies' toilet could barely be considered. It was continents away from the character of the place.

He finally tucked his notebook into his inside pocket and left. As he walked through the lobby, he waved to the two staff on duty at the reception desk. They had worked at The Peninsula for years and were as familiar to Jeremy as his morning tea and toast. They waved him over. *The woman he spoke to as he came into the hotel, did he know her? No, he didn't know her. She's very attractive though, isn't she? Oh yes, indeed. Mr Freeman have you seen her before? Yes, here. And she told me she's staying here.*

Miss Fong and Mr Lee looked at one another. David Lee said, "She worked for Mrs Franklin, Mr Freeman, and now she's back here as a guest. She's been behaving very oddly, let me tell you ...." Jeremy listened. What to do with a bundle of information like that?

"Did you tell the police about this?"

"No, Sir. We're too nervous to mention it to anyone else. We're convinced she is up to no good and staff at the reception desk have been keeping watch on her in case she tries to leave without paying her bill. It's very odd how she goes out looking like one woman and comes back with a completely different appearance. Do *you* think we should talk to the Police?"

"Miss James, you say? If she has a connection with Mrs Franklin, the police will certainly be interested. Why don't we talk to your boss about this? He's on his way over."

Steven was emphatic. "Mrs Franklin did not hire anyone by the name of Miss James." He glanced at the guest register. "Miss Christine James. No. The woman Emmie hired was a Miss BJ Cresswell – I can't remember what the initials stand for."

Jeremy had occasionally wondered what a eureka moment would feel like when all the lights went on and clarification was writ large and logically in the brain. In a flash, he knew. His mind played back the conversation he had had with Pearl about the "white witch" when they went out to dinner at Stormy's a few weeks back. He'd dubbed his discovery the "white witch", but he also knew he had seen her somewhere before and now the name BJ Cresswell brought it all together in his mind, including why he had dubbed her the "white witch" so easily.

BJ Cresswell is the "white witch" was a briefly famous headline, accompanied by a photo of BJ, which had appeared in Tokyo's underground porn magazines early in the year. Fresh from London, she had made a series of porn films shot before a live audience, each one culminating in selected members of the audience taking part in the action. She was sensational. The Tokyo bars and night spots ran hot with stories about her.

There was one night, however, when things changed for the "white witch". At the end of her performance and after she quit the stage, her last client remained on the bed. When the audience finished clapping and cheering and started to boo and slow-clap instead, a stage hand investigated and found him dead. The "white witch" had disappeared and the man's death was put down to heart failure, but the subsequent autopsy found that he had died of a heroin overdose. There was no sign of the syringe used to kill him. It disappeared with Miss Cresswell.

Miss Cresswell's last performance in Tokyo was indeed sensational. She had committed a murder, live, on stage.

*

"Steven, may I suggest that you talk to the police about this Miss Cresswell, possibly a.k.a. Miss James, and have your security people keep her room under observation, unless the police do so immediately. I have to see someone. I think I can shed a little light on this business."

The group broke up and Jeremy left the hotel. As he reached the bottom of the great sandstone steps, a taxi pulled into the forecourt. Jeremy saw with delight the rare sight of Mr Yip Yee Koon alighting from a taxi in company with Sir James Gates, a high-ranking public service luminary from the UK but more familiar to Jeremy as Pearl Green's father. Jeremy was starting to enjoy himself. *What an incredible string of events! And now Pearl's underworld connections are surfacing again*, Jeremy thought, but not unkindly. There had always been a whiff of something other-worldly about Pearl's mother, Lady June Bowen and it seemed to have rubbed off on Pearl. Perhaps after all it was all down to the father ....

"Mr Yip! What luck! I need your assistance!"

Yip eyed Jeremy off with an obvious lack of interest. "You are going to tell me, Mr Freeman, that Mrs Franklin has been murdered here, at the Peninsula Hotel, are you not?"

"Ah. Yes."

"What else have you learned?" James nodded at Jeremy. They had a passing acquaintance and James knew he was some sort of vague chum of Pearl's, someone who shared her appreciation of fine dining, apparently. At the thought of food, James felt a stirring of interest. He could barely remember when he had last eaten. Yesterday?

Jeremy said, "I've had a revelation, actually. Have you ever heard of a woman by the name of BJ Cresswell?" The three men turned in unison and started to climb the stairs to the hotel lobby. Jeremy stopped. "By Jove, she said she was going to The Rendezvous, just around the hotel, in Nathan Road."

Part IV

END OF THE RED BIRD SUMMER

*Friday 10 September to
Saturday 10 October*

Friday 10 September: 9.00pm

She woke. He was there. Ben took her hand and looked at the fine blue veins and wondered what that hand would look like when it was old – would it be gnarled and arthritic or long and slender, if large-veined, the hand of a woman of ease? He lifted it and kissed it and held it to his cheek.

"We had to sedate you." Women like Pearl didn't like being involuntarily deprived of their faculties. He waited for her disapproval.

"I don't remember. It doesn't matter. My Annie really is dead, isn't she? What are the police doing? If only I'd gone to meet her when we arranged ...." He kissed her cheek and smoothed her hair and gave her water. She was remarkably alert given the strength of the sedative she had been administered.

"When you are feeling up to it, Chief Superintendent Smythe is here and wants a word." But Tommy Smythe was clear that he wanted more than a word. He wanted the beginnings of a full statement.

"Just to put things in perspective Miss Green: You said that if you had kept your appointment with Miss Cheung this morning, her death might have been avoided. But Miss Cheung did not arrive at the Connaught Street Wharf at the appointed time. She did not arrive until well after 8.00am and the boat taxi operator said that she was very flustered. Does that sound like Miss Cheung to you?"

Pearl said firmly that it did not. Annie Cheung was rarely flustered, as he put it. She could be excitable and occasionally disorganised but she could get on top of just about any problem that came up. "It must have been something unusual if Annie was flustered, as you say, Chief Superintendent. But what is more out of character is for her to be late. I'm sorry, but I have to go. Danny has to be told. He will be absolutely heartbroken, but he must be told."

Ben jumped in. "Pearl, I'll go to see Danny." He had observed how she took responsibility for every little thing. *Does she always do that?* "I'll organise anything for him that he needs. He'll understand." Ben was despatched to Causeway Bay in a police car driven by DC Lee, who had remained on duty rather than return to his Causeway Bay apartment to spend the long night thinking about his colleagues and how they had both met death so violently, simply for doing their jobs.

CS Smythe suspended the interview and had a coffee when Pearl showed signs of flagging, but when he returned an hour later she had obviously not rested and in fact was now feverishly awake. "Are you able to go on with this, Miss Green?" She nodded impatiently. He said, "The other thing we did not understand until a short time ago is why Miss Cheung did not have the water-taxi operator drop her at the Hei Ling Chau wharf, the obvious place for her to go, one would think. Then we found that the skipper had taken a fare to Hei Ling Chau earlier and dropped that passenger off at the cove to the south-east of the wharf.

"Clearly, Miss Cheung assumed that you were the earlier passenger, and she also assumed you had gone on ahead of her at the original, agreed time. The operator assumed, when Miss Cheung said she was following her friend, that his earlier passenger was that friend. So that's what he did. Except his earlier passenger wasn't you, Miss Green ...."

"Did you just say that he dropped her off at the cove?" Karen Henderson stood at the door. She had struggled out of bed when she heard that Pearl was in the room next to hers. She hung onto the door jamb for support, weak, her body weight down by a third, hair streaked with grey and her skin ashen with red wheels of peeling sunburnt flesh flushing her gaunt cheeks like a sickly omen of health. Kaz looked twice her age and also looked as though she had done a few extra hard rounds into the bargain.

"HE DROPPED HER OFF AT THE COVE?" The voice wasn't that of a sixty-year-old, however. It was the full Henderson real deal of silver and depth with a dash of sunshine, even at full shout. "I'm off-colour for a few days and every bastard in the place is BEING DROPPED OFF AT THE COVE?"

Pearl ignored Kaz. If Kaz couldn't dissemble about her damned site, she would have to. "The cove is where Kaz was attacked on Monday, Chief Superintendent. That's why she's so upset, isn't it Kaz?"

Kaz looked confused. "Annie was helping me plan the transfer of the patients to Lantau. If I'd left it to the hospital staff to organise their own way out of there – kept Annie away..."

"Rounded up a few stray galaxies, discovered a cure for cancer and conducted various other miracles ...." Ben walked into the room, hanging out the sun and the moon for Pearl as he did so.

"Chief Superintendent Smythe, have you finished interviewing my lover? I need to talk to her. Privately."

Smythe carefully rotated his cap, which rested on his right knee, which thankfully, from Pearl's perspective in the hospital bed at least, concealed some of his forest of hairs. His right foot jerked. *Damned younger generation. Always on about sex.*

"HE DROPPED HER OFF AT THE COVE?" They had forgotten Kaz. Drew appeared and led her gently away. Something had to be done about Kaz and her bloody cove.

Chief Superintendent Smythe left. *Most unsatisfactory interview. They're all barking mad.*

Friday 10 September: 10.00pm

BJ smiled at John Simons coquettishly, as though they really were out on a date. She still felt wonderful. She rested her crossed arms on the table and nodded her head in time to the wistful strain of Elton John's "Your Song". "I love that song, John, don't you – it's a little bit funny, this feeling inside? That's how I feel tonight, all brand-new, re-born, cleansed." John took a hefty swig of his beer and nodded good-naturedly.

"Well that's good, BJ. Things going well, then? Your friend who rang. She said she was going to meet me."

"She couldn't make it. And thanks for asking, but no thanks to you, things couldn't be better. I've got rid of all sorts of problems today. Now, are you interested in doing some business?"

Since the previous Sunday, John had grown the profit from the drugs BJ had sold him from $300,000 to three quarters of a million. He had it with him, in cash.

"How much will that buy me?"

BJ was feeling generous. Another three quarters of a million, so easily done. She would have more than six million dollars now, and she still had more powder to shift. She would give him a generous helping of her precious white stuff. She extracted six packages and placed them between them on the banquette.

When he looked doubtful she explained, "Two for the price of one, almost. It's pure, John, not cut at all. That's why the bags look so much smaller than they did the other day. Got room to stow them?" John almost purred with pleasure and he placed a comfortably plump envelope on the seat. She put it in her tote bag and finished her drink. "I must go. It's been a pleasure doing business with you, Sir. See you again?" There was no need for this punter to know she was about to leave Hong Kong, otherwise he might want to get his hands on some more of her goods, for free this time, or he would try to take advantage of her in some other way, or ....

"Well, by Jove, Miss, Ah ...."

BJ jumped. BJ, during the many demands of her long day, had forgotten about her mentor, but Toby's voice, cutting in so close and unexpectedly behind her, brought the memory of him back in full strength. *Who else knew her in here? Couldn't she go anywhere ...?* She rounded on him and grabbed him by the lapels. Toby recoiled and tugged his suit back into shape. "Well I really don't think ...."

"No you don't, you repellant piece of filth. Get out of my way."

She stormed to the ladies' room and shut herself in. People were recognizing her and she'd only been back out for an hour or so. She had to get away. There was a window above the wash-basins in the toilet and she opened it and peered out into the night. It was dark enough but she could see that she was only a few feet above what appeared to be a service lane behind the restaurant. She jumped.

*

John ignored the incident between BJ and Toby Blake and didn't bother to wait for BJ to emerge from the ladies' room. She would have done a bunk for sure and he didn't want to be around any longer than necessary, not with his pockets stuffed with packets of heroin.

Toby Blake was expostulating to three men who'd just entered the restaurant about the behaviour he'd been subjected to by some floozy he'd met briefly at the Peninsula, and who had berated him, when all he had done was wish her a very polite good evening. A

Chinese geezer stood slightly away from the other two men, who both listened attentively to Toby.

John had the uneasy sensation of being covertly studied by the tall Chinese man and as he rose from the table, he found that he was hemmed in. "Pardon me. I'd love to stay and chat but I must dash."

But it wasn't from Yip Yee Koon that the intervention happened. James stepped smoothly into John's path and gripped him by the arm. "And you are?"

"John Simons – just having a quiet drink and don't want to get involved in any of this. 'Scuse me. Last time I pick up anyone in this dump."

"But you had an appointment with Miss Cresswell, so we believe, Mr Simons."

John froze as he thought, *the cow has set me up*. He shook James off and made for the door. He didn't see Yip arch an eyebrow at the head waiter who neatly tripped John and sprawled him across the gorgeous Nepalese carpet that defined the restaurant's entry area. A packet of drugs slipped out of his jacket pocket. Another waiter appeared from the kitchen and deftly assisted the head waiter as he helped him to his feet.

James and Yip waited for him to straighten up. James presented his identification. "I have authority in my position as a senior officer of the Crown to have you held under reasonable restraint until the arrival of the Hong Kong Police. I am …."

John heard the words in a blur. *It was a set-up. She'd got all his money and scarpered. But why?*

Then he realised. Albert. She was paying him back for Albert. *That bastard*. John stayed silent but remembered what she had said to him when she sold him the drugs last Sunday, the drugs Albert wanted so urgently. Something about her teaching him a lesson for trying to involve her with his clients. *And I thought all that was settled when we did that deal and I paid her. She was just revving up, the bitch.*

"Okay, guv. Any chance of an information trade-off? I can tell you a lot. Like, it was her friend who rang and made the appointment. Christine James. You know her?" He nodded his head at the packet James held by its edges. "I've got more of those, you'll find." James ignored him. Yip gestured to the head waiter and pointed decorously at BJ's glass. The man nodded and disappeared into the kitchen before returning with a plastic bag. He delicately bagged up the glass and handed it to James with a small bow. James was impressed.

"Do you own this place, Yee Koon?"

"I do, James. I'm very fond of chicken à la king."

*

The lane at the rear of the the Rendezvous Restaurant connects to other laneways that eventually feed into Observatory Hill Road. As BJ laboured up the steep slope she saw the lights of a small hotel at the top. She had everything she needed with her, including her passport and money. Even a change of underwear and cosmetics. And of course, her drugs. BJ did not intend going back to Room 129 at the Peninsula. With police all over the place, it was too risky. That Christine twit may also have left fingerprints in the toilet.

This little hotel looked clean. Best of all, it was secluded. She only had to find one more punter tonight, then she could sleep and rest until tomorrow's flight. She'd be less likely to bump into people she knew around here, located away from the centre of the action. If she didn't offload the other fifteen packets, then so be it. She'd flush the stuff down the toilet.

She straightened her lovely white dress, patted at her wig and pushed open the doors of the Observatory Hill Hotel. "Hello. I'm Emma Jones and I need a room for the night, please. I'm so tired but I've agreed to meet my cousin Alex at the Indiana." She pulled a face. "I'd love just to have a sleep. I've had such a busy time in Macau."

She took the keys to room 8 and placed her possessions in the dressing-table drawer, left half of the cash in her tote bag and put the other half in the room safe. If something happened and she couldn't get back here, she still had half her money with her and if she was robbed while she was out – BJ smoothed over the thought of how that could happen – well she had half here in reserve. She repaired her make-up and left, waving happily to the desk staff as she made her way back out into the Hong Kong night. She spoke to herself, sternly: *This Emma Jones is a name only, got it? No funny stuff. BJ is in control. It's down to BJ to do the business tonight.*

*

BJ's translucence had dulled to a shade of dirty grey. She walked down the hill, back into the glare and hiss of a maturing Hong Kong evening. The streets were still pumping with activity and the disparate shades of neon lights blended, at a distance, into a blue-yellow pink-framed haze. She looked right and left, waiting for inspiration. Wanchai? Too dangerous now. Temple Street? She didn't know the ropes enough to get around Temple Street and it had a very dark reputation. That Old City place? If she could get out real quick, she still thought that was a best bet and it was only a quick taxi ride from where she was. She could be back at the hotel in a couple of hours.

She made up her mind. "Taxi!" The sense of elation she had experienced earlier in the evening returned. The night was hers. She opened one of her packets of drugs and started a new feast.

Friday 10 September: 11.00pm

Tommy Smythe rang his wife, apologized in business-like tones for his non-appearance at home for the second night in succession, replaced the receiver and looked levelly at James. James felt uncomfortable. This was not the first time he had made a report of something he had witnessed in the company of Yip Yee Koon, when Yip had disappeared into the background when the law materialized.

When the police had arrived at the restaurant and arrested John Simons for possession of trafficking quantities of heroin, Yip simply melted away and James and Jeremy Freeman were left to explain what had happened. That soon became a minor matter of interest to the Police, however, when Simons stated with considerable pleasure that he had purchased the drugs found on him from a Miss BJ Cresswell. He did not know where she lived except that he was sure it was on Hong Kong side, mid-levels somewhere.

CS Smythe did not look unhappy. "Our Miss Cresswell is materializing, Sir James. We have her fingerprints now, from Room 129 at the Peninsula. They will be further confirmed by the test on the glass she drank from at the restaurant. The crime scene at the Peninsula is also being fingerprinted, although the results of that have not come through yet. Understandably there is a lot of material to sift through there in such a public area. I have an officer going through the records for a match, using the first set. There are some clothes in the hotel room and some basic toiletries. The clothes are very utilitarian, as are the cosmetics. Miss Cresswell checked in as Miss Christine James and we now know that she was a very short-term former employee of the Peninsula. She worked for Mrs Franklin." CS Smythe looked perplexed and upset as he wondered what had happened to result in such a violent death for the beautiful Emmie Franklin.

"We also know she changes her name and appearance, seemingly at will." James added what Jeremy Freeman knew about her and Smythe made more notes, turning his mouth down in disdain as James related Miss Cresswell's known activities during her stint in Tokyo. "Charming. This matches our Interpol information. Anything else?"

"I think you will find that if you talk with Chief Inspector Burton about a Miss BJ Cook who took out a week by week lease on Flat 7 Block A, 14 Tin Hau Temple Road, North Point on Tuesday afternoon, you will also find that Miss Cresswell's fingerprints match those of Miss Cook. I was in Lane Crawfords when Miss Cook went shopping. She changed her appearance as she shopped. She was very good. Had me fooled for a time. I believe that Miss Cresswell became Miss Cook and then for one reason or another also took up the guise of a red-head, before her final appearance as the mousey Miss Christine James. I don't know why she went to such trouble, but it would be reasonable to think she was trying to put someone off her trail."

Smythe scribbled. This was all very illuminating. There was a knock at the door and Pam Walsh, who had volunteered to remain late at the office, entered the room. "Sir, Chief Inspector Burton has forwarded the report on the examination of the camera footage from the Hing Long Lane offices."

Smythe read quickly. There were no interruptions to the surveillance film with the exception of Thursday 18th August when there was no footage available between 11.30am and 2.30pm. On that day, the entire Narcotics Unit staff had been absent at fire training at Central Division with the exception of DS Proust and Mrs Latham, the filing clerk.

"Pam, see if you can contact Harry Burton for me, please."

He read the report and summarised it for James. "DS Proust and Mrs Latham are both shown entering and leaving the building in the morning and in the late afternoon. Mrs Latham can provide no useful information, and DS Proust, of course, is dead." Smythe scraped at his moustache thoughtfully.

The phone rang. "Chief Superintendent!" It was Chief Inspector Burton. "The chemist's report came through late this afternoon and the heroin from the flat at North Point is confirmed as being part of the Red Bird "999" vintage that went missing from the Narcotics Unit last month. It is known as Red Bird Summer or Phoenix around the traps because it was produced in the summer of 1964 by the first big local chiu chau heroin-processing laboratory and of course the phoenix is a symbol for the coming of good times."

CS Smythe's mouth had opened until it was very slightly agape. "Just a moment, Chief Inspector." He covered the mouthpiece of the phone and said to James: "Confirmed. Flat 7, Block A, 14 Tin Hau Temple Road, North Point – the block of heroin that Harry's lot found is one of those missing from the NB."

Speaking again into the phone, "Did you get good fingerprints Harry?" he asked. "Any chance someone could rush that through first thing in the morning? Well done, by the way, first full operational day on the job with a new team and pulling off a coup like that – commendation due, I would think."

James and CS Smythe continued to document BJ's movements. Somehow, she knew that to remain in the North Point apartment yesterday afternoon was unsafe, so she was either on to James following her and alarmed enough about that to clear out, or there was danger from some other source. They also knew that she booked into the Peninsula early yesterday evening, when she had the name and appearance of Christine James. She had left the North Point apartment so quickly that she had either abandoned or forgotten to take one of the blocks of heroin with her. Clearly she considered that to return was too risky. The street value of the heroin was about twenty million Hong Kong dollars, so she must have known that she was in extreme danger to abandon it.

"And now she's out on the streets shifting pure heroin," said James. "At least she won't be killing her customers this time, not directly at any rate. It's likely that the heroin planted on Dr Henderson was Miss Cresswell's first attempt at processing. It's the most toxic processed material that has ever been known to hit the streets of Hong Kong. She's either a psychopath or simply doesn't know what she's doing. The amount of quinine in the batch that poisoned Kaz is enough to stop a train. God knows how she survived it. We also have to find out if it's the same base material as our Mr Simons's little purchase of this evening. I hope all her processed product was in the haul planted on Kaz. At least we have that. I dread to think what impact that sort of mix could have out on the street."

Tommy Smythe continued to nod and scribble. He paused to look at James, and said, "The Police Chemist was called in after Mr Simons's arrest and is assaying the six packets he was arrested with. I wonder ...." He picked up the phone and dialled.

Dr Liu was chirpy enough, considering he had been recalled to work and the time of night: "Piece of cake, Chief Superintendent! Not much to analyse really. The stuff is as pure as it gets – "999". Someone has just chopped it off the original block, powdered it and bagged it up. It matches the profile of the 1964 Red Bird haul exactly. Should make the chaps in the chiu chau processing laboratories sit up and take a bit of notice. They'll be wondering where the rest of the vintage is stashed."

There was a knock at the door. Pam Walsh came in, now looking very animated. "Sir, the surveillance camera! They've captured a faint image just before it was shut-down. Just after 11.30am." She placed a blurry black and white photograph on the desk and James and Tommy Smythe leaned over it. They could make out a very high heeled shoe with the heel dangling loose and a handbag, a long pale oblong of leather supported by a chain. James smiled at the sight. He had seen its designer original – the bag BJ bought in Lane Crawford's – several times in the past two days. The shoes and the bag nestled against the discernible close-up curve of a woman's body. Further detail was impossible to determine, except for the face looking at the woman. It was faint and somewhat distorted but it was unmistakably Detective Sergeant Herbert Proust.

"The shoe," said James, tapping the photograph. "Look at the way the heel is dangling. I can almost hear it, can't you, Chief Superintendent? She sucked him in." Chief Superintendent Smythe didn't touch the photo. He opened his desk drawer and drew out a notebook.

"Proust's notes, Sir James. A bit of necessary reading before I can finish up for the day."

Friday 10 September: 11.00pm

Pearl woke up again. The Peak Hospital had become so familiar to her during the past month that she had not a moment's hesitation in realizing where she was and she rang the nurse call bell straight away. Ben hurried into the room.

"I want to go home, Ben. I'm lying around in a hospital bed for no good reason. I need privacy."

Ben heard the words *need privacy* and felt disappointment attack him with its drab, jealous little claws.

"All right, sweetheart. I'll organise a police escort for you."

"Pearl will not require a police escort, Dr Sanders. I will escort you home, Pearl. You are safe with me." Yip Yee Koon stood at the door and Pearl felt her brow relax, felt relief, felt safe.

She half smiled at him: "But Mr Yip, I intended for Ben to come with me, if you are free, that is?" She looked at Ben and he saw in her face what was missing from her voice. Beaming love.

Yee Koon made a small coughing noise. "Pearl. Your father and I now know a lot about the woman who has created all of this misery, Miss Cresswell as she calls herself, and we are getting closer to her. We know of her movements up until two hours ago. Your father is at Police HQ and I think by tomorrow this matter will be clearer. So let me have the pleasure of taking you home. I have my car waiting for you both outside reception." He was gone as smoothly as he had appeared.

Ben kissed Pearl and helped her out of bed.

"We're going home, Ben." Then she said it again, slowly. "We're going home. That sounds good to me." They walked along the quiet hospital corridor and looked in on Kaz. Kaz asleep now had something of the energy of Kaz awake. She was tensed on the mattress, her breathing still a little laboured, her forehead creased with the effort of resting. Drew slept soundly in the visitor's chair.

They reached the lift and Ben put his arms around her. "I love you Pearl."

The lift door opened and a man stepped out. Ben saw the man raise his arm and with his own arms around the woman he had fallen so deeply in love with, he used all his strength to swing her out of the way. There was noise and a short blast of light. The man retreated into the lift and by the time Ben hit the floor and the police

Red Bird Summer

guard started to turn his head to the sound, the doors had closed and he was gone.

*

James walked out of Central Division into a night where a slightly cool breeze drifted off the harbour – *what a change to be cooled naturally, instead of by the eternal air-conditioning the place runs on.* He stretched and flexed his shoulder blades. He would take a taxi to the hotel. Chief Superintendent Smythe had organised some dinner for them both, but James hadn't put his head down for more than twenty-four hours or even had time to change his suit.

*

Yip Yee Koon was waiting in his car when he heard the gunshot, followed by the sight of a man running out of the hospital, a jacket pulled up over his head. Yip watched him get into a vehicle which accelerated sharply away from the kerb. "Did you see that man go into the hospital?" he asked his driver, who shook his head perplexedly. Hua Leung had kept the front entrance of the hospital under close observation ever since the boss went inside, and had seen nothing.

"Hurry, before the police guard comes out of the building. Take me home, Hua. I have calls to make." Hua Leung was accustomed to responding without query to whatever orders the boss gave but he was curious about this one.

Yip saw it coming. "I know where that car is going and I know what has happened. Hurry now. I will need you later tonight so get some rest while you can."

*

BJ paced outside the northern entrance into the Walled City, the Dentist Street entry. The whole area seemed deserted. She peered through the arch made by the two shops, full of sets of dentures, that framed the entrance, unable to summon the will to go further. It all looked harmless, quiet, and that was the problem. Just around the corner in Spring Festival Lane the Kowloon night throbbed with neon energy. She couldn't go in here where the silence almost reached out to grab passers-by. It would be like voluntarily walking into hell.

She corrected herself. *Walking into hell had been her last night in Tokyo when she killed that punter as the finale to her spectacular Tokyo season. She rewarded him for his performance by giving him* an overloaded, spiteful jab of heroin. It had been a fitting finale to two months of inspired work. But afterwards, the guy her mentor "arranged" to look after her introduced her to hell. It turned out he was not only her mentor's brother but also a well-known Tokyo sadist. Her escape from police notice came with a price tag, a price tag straight from hell. When she boarded her flight to Hong Kong the next day, she was only just able to walk. That was hell. This was an opportunity to get away forever. She had to believe it.

At nearly midnight, what other options did she have? She took yet another scoop of heroin from one of the packets in her bag. She had a small torch with her and forced herself to walk into the Walled City's confined alleys. She kept the beam on the paving of the narrow alley. There were a few lights – a few candles or kerosene lamps – but it was so dark that any light was sucked away almost at its source and the quiet gave off as much energy as the hyped-up streets outside. There was an overpowering sense of concentration in the place. Walking the main alley was a test of holding on to sanity, every turn and twist new with threat and potential for harm. The pathway narrowed as she walked further in until she finally reached a junction that branched off to the left. The entrance was so narrow that she felt that it squeezed the actual breath out of her. For another ten minutes she walked in the watchful silence, but then she saw a sign. It simply said "*Emperor Inn*", and the small yellow lamp that illuminated the old sign, hand-painted and in English, looked almost rustically welcoming.

She pushed open the door of the inn. The multiple hits of Red Bird she had taken were beginning to work a treat.

Many of the bar's customers had heard stories of *gwaipor* who had entered the Walled City, but few had actually seen one within its confines. As BJ stepped into the bar she created a sensation. A good half of the room scattered to the alleys. *Ayah! It is a ghost! Run away!* Those who remained retreated to the walls and looked at the floor. The only person who seemed unafraid of her was the barman, Fang Li, a slothful, thin-haired, fat-bellied man, originally from Shanghai, who had entered Hong Kong illegally twenty-five years earlier. He had never left the Walled City. He squinted at her over a waft of smoke from the cigarette clamped between his lips, and assuming she had come for opium, jerked his head in the direction of a small door behind the bar that led to the upstairs salons.

BJ scanned the room. *The men.* She couldn't believe how scared they seemed to be of her. She executed an operatic dash across the room and made a growling noise. Four more customers slammed their glasses on the bar and ran. BJ giggled. This Walled City place was supposed to be Crime Capital – completely notorious – and here she was, a mere slip of a twenty-year-old girl, scaring the hell out of the locals. She took a bow and announced to no-one in particular, "Another sensational performance by The 'white witch'. Thank you, ladies and gentlemen. Or rather, gentlemen. Forget the ladies. If there are ladies in the audience, you ain't no ladies."

At this, the barman removed the cigarette from between his lips and looked at her sourly. He had seen a lot in this place but most of his experience with foreigners was restricted to male customers, *gweilos*. Were all *gweipor* women like this, or was this one mad? She must be mad. She had white foam at the corners of her mouth. He shrugged and poured himself a whisky. She withdrew a tiny plastic bag from her purse and waved it at him.

"You buy?" she said in sing-song English. Fang knew no English but he understood the international language of dealing drugs. He took the bag from her and squelched the contents around, studying it with a practiced eye. He grunted and tasted it before taking a handful of notes from the till. He threw them across the counter at her. She smiled and counted it. There was only a tiny amount of powder in the sample bag and he had paid her two thousand for it. She took the money and waved another, bigger bag at him: "More?"

At this he put his glass down on the counter and beckoned her away from the bar to the door that led upstairs. If this mad woman had a bag full of heroin she would last about ten minutes in this place, once word got out. He grunted at her again and gestured that she should give him more. He examined two of the larger bags of the stuff she was selling and saw that the powder was of the same quality. He pulled ten thousand dollars from his jacket pocket, gave it to her and again gestured her towards the narrow staircase.

"More?" she said.

*

Fang Li had heard of the legendary Red Bird Summer or Phoenix heroin. Few traffickers in Hong Kong and its precincts could have failed to hear of the tragic loss to the drug market of the finest quality heroin ever produced in the region. It was the Hong Kong chiu chau chemists' triumphant entry into the Asian drug market and was intended to be a bid to seek dominance of the world distribution market. When it was confiscated in a spectacular operation by the Hong Kong Police, it also shut down the major regional processing laboratory and stalled Hong Kong's emerging pre-eminence as the world centre for heroin trafficking by years.

*

He thought about that particular brand of heroin now. He had handled many packets of heroin but had never seen anything so fine in quality as this, so pure, pure white. It was high-grade stuff and for his customers it would be the experience of a lifetime, the chance to inject or ingest something akin to the legendary "999" even if it wasn't really the real thing. He nodded at her. She had become even paler, if it were possible, and she had broken out in a profuse sweat. She clutched the money and climbed the stairs without questioning him. She walked unsteadily and clung to the railing for support, hauling herself up the narrow, steep staircase.

Fang Li could see that she wasn't going to be much of a problem, to him or anyone else. She looked ill. Clearly she had taken enough of her own stock to almost immobilise herself. If she had a good supply of the stuff, he would end the night a rich man and she, well, she may survive. He smiled a little. Yes, she would survive, but he would have to make sure she could not talk.

Friday 10 September: just about midnight

Albert manoeuvred the See family's boat into the sampan village at Tsim Tsa Tsui, made a phone call from a nearby phone-box and then hailed a taxi for outer Kowloon. The driver baulked in fear at the sight of him until he saw the HK$100 tip Albert offered, at which he clipped the car's gears smartly into action. Even if this passenger was a ghost, the driver was not about to pass up a one hundred dollar tip.

Albert had been able to board the *Jiang Li* because of his disguise, which was so dramatic that no-one doubted that he was anything but one of the more high-need patients, rarely seen around the hospice, their conditions whispered about but poorly known. Clothes abandoned, he had bandaged his torso, legs, arms, neck and face and also shrouded his torso in a hospital gown. He had wrapped the bags of drugs up in plastic and bound them around his midriff. The leg bandages had now worked a bit loose, but he was still tightly bound around the body, neck, face and arms. He had some other possessions with him too, also wrapped in plastic and stored in one of the hospital's pillow cases, and modest though they were – money and the four statues he had stolen from the museum's bestiary collection – they were the passport out of his present dilemma.

He sat in the back seat of the cab, his graceful form evident even though swathed, one leg crossed easily over the other, hands resting peacefully in his lap. He was peculiarly resigned to the downfall he had inflicted on himself – almost casually so – from that of a respected member of Hong Kong's intellectual society to one who would be safe only in the confines of the Walled City of Kowloon, or as a recluse somewhere like Hei Ling Chau. He would wait for the chance to buy his way out to another place altogether. The sale of the bestiary collection would guarantee him a rich life somewhere, perhaps in Singapore or even Thailand.

His days as an archaeologist were over but Albert had no regrets about it. His career would soon have been over in any event. When Herbie Proust had arrested him for possession of drugs, Albert could still have found a way out of his overpowering addiction, if he had faced the charge squarely and paid the legal penalty. But he didn't want to relinquish his addiction to heroin, and it was precisely that which had driven his actions during the past twenty-four hours. His career would have been over for lesser transgressions, so it might as well be sacrificed for much more. When news got out that he was a heroin addict, it would have led to other questions, such as how he managed to pay for his long-term habit. His affairs and the affairs of the museum would not survive that sort of scrutiny.

It was better to creep forward on the plank, peer over the edge and see what lay on the other side.

Albert's inner animal howled gently in delight at the prospect.

When the cab drew to a halt, he created a minor sensation on the street. People scattered or peered at the ghost who walks, from behind their thinly-curtained windows as he passed the rows of poor housing that fringed the Walled City precincts. He walked the last half mile in the unlit darkness that marked the perimeter of its walls and finally entered through the southern gate – the infamous, dangerous southern route of which Albert would be master tonight, even if he encountered fellow-ghosts.

He finally arrived at the *Emperor Inn* at one o'clock in the morning, unscathed, unchallenged, but exhausted and craving.

*

The *Emperor Inn* accommodates the Walled City's nocturnal revellers, the early morning recoverers and the all-day-all-night smoking-room patrons and drinkers. Fang Li was not the owner of the *Emperor* but he had made a good living from his twenty years there as barman and now looked forward to retirement with Mrs Fang in Greater Kowloon, where he planned to rent an apartment with a view of the water. He would buy a caged bird and sit with the other old men in the park and compare notes about birdsong. Mrs Fang would cook his meals and make clothes for herself if she wished. He would be free at last, twenty-five years after arriving in Hong Kong from China, with the time and money to enjoy his sunset years.

But for the present he had obligations to his masters and now he discharged them with a phone call to the landlord's representative. If the shadowy men who manipulated the spine of the Walled City knew that drugs such as these had entered its confines without being informed, Fang Li could kiss his retirement, and his life, goodbye.

*

He put the phone down and was about to go upstairs and take his commission from BJ's stocks when the ghost entered the bar. Tonight was indeed a night of firsts. Fang Li had seen many ghosts, of course, usually in one or the other of the smoking salons as they metamorphosed from human to other states under the influence of opium smoke, but he had yet to encounter one as it walked through the door.

This ghost had a mouth which smiled at Fang. It had eyes that coldly twinkled. It asked for a whisky and said "make it a double, Fang, for I am very thirsty". Case-hardened though he was to the whims and wiles of those who stalk the Walled City's night alleys, Fang Li felt a hint of dread. This thing knew him. He nodded and poured the drink and handed it to the creature, which tossed it down in a gulp and slapped the glass back on the bar.

"More!"

Fang Li reached for a new bottle and this time as he poured – with his back to the ghost – he added some of the contents of the second bag of heroin he had paid BJ for. The ghost downed the drink and immediately slurred at him for more. Fang Li repeated the operation. It finished the drink and smiled. "I will ascend and take repose," it said, "For I am expecting company."

Fang Li nodded gravely. He knew this ghost after all. It was the one who spoke high Mandarin, the one who had come to the *Emperor* the previous night dressed in ordinary street clothes and disappeared well before light. Under its wrappings it had the same height, the same slender build as the other. It was The Owl.

"You are the owl, the harbinger of death, are you not?" queried Fang Li of Albert in high Mandarin, for Fang had been a scholar before he murdered his tutor's wife.

The ghost nodded imperiously and ascended the staircase.

*

Hew Nuttingsall frowned. The late night call was from Albert, at him for money again. *Twice this week.* Screw that man! He wished he had killed him. When would there be any peace from his demands? He had been summoned like an errant schoolboy to attend on Albert in that god-forsaken hole in Kowloon that should have been burnt to the ground years ago. Like Albert, Hew was also a familiar of the Walled City. It was there, many years earlier, that he and Albert first commenced their on-again off-again passage towards drug addiction, which, for Hew, as he rose in importance in the business and social world, finally came to include blackmail by Albert.

It would be unthinkable, in the business environment of a place like Hong Kong, for the Chairman of the Hong Kong and Shanghai Banking Corporation to be revealed as a drug-addicted homosexual. Hew had paid and paid for his secret to be safe with Albert. Generally, Albert wanted money only and although Hew would pay a little back from time to time, it was only ever a gesture, nothing near the amounts Albert demanded. Hew constantly tried to recoup his fortunes, but in doing so had run up heavy gambling debts, which he had frequently settled by embezzling funds from the bank. In order to pay those back before they were discovered, he took loans at high interest from Yip Yee Koon, a money broker with astounding resources and scant interest in the financial morals of his customers.

Everyone in Hong Kong loved money – it was the mantra for success and tonight was no different: *Bring money with you*, Albert said. *Lots of it, Hew. This is the last time I'll ever ask, I swear.*

Hew showered and changed from his dinner suit into a pair of casual slacks and a loose cotton shirt. He opened the bedroom safe and took out the wads of cash he had set aside to pay off a block of one of his many loans from Yip Yee Koon, before Yip cancelled the debt in its entirety and left Hew with the cash he had stolen from his own bank vault. Hew looked at the money and sighed. There could be no going back to Yip for further loans. He had intended to return this money to the bank and thereby have a clean slate for the first time in nearly fifteen years. Hew packed the notes into a roomy briefcase. Albert had said this was a buy and sell situation. Perhaps whatever he was going to buy would be worth something and he would be clear of his debts after all.

Then again, there was that hot tip for the 1.30pm race at Happy Valley tomorrow afternoon .... Hew gulped down a glass of whisky and took a cab to the quiet end of the harbour near Wanchai, where he caught a water-taxi for the short ride to Kowloon Bay. It was now a still and beautiful night. On Kowloon side, he hailed a cab and ignored the look of surprise on the driver's face when he told him the destination. As the vehicle whizzed through the emptying streets, Hew swore this was the last time he would get involved in such a venture, whatever the cost.

*

James was asleep when Yip approached the Mandarin Hotel's reception desk and asked that Sir James be called urgently to the phone. Five minutes later James was grumbling his way to the hotel room door.

"What has happened, Yee Koon?"

"Bad things are happening, James. We have to go to the Walled City immediately. I'll explain along the way. I have been trying to stop the contracts on Pearl and Dr Henderson, but without success. I have to go there and leave instructions directly."

James grabbed his jacket and followed his old friend back out into the night. Yip did not tell James that he thought that either Pearl or Dr Henderson had been shot. If there was to be grief, it would have to come later. The contracts had to be stopped, so that at least one life could be saved and even Yip Yee Koon had never entered the Walled City alone.

*

Pearl sat on a bench outside the operating theatre and unravelled her woolly hat row by row. She wound the twisted strands around her clenched fist, made it into a ball, threw it up in the air, caught it, then hurled it across the waiting-room floor. She huffed with impatience. Kaz and Drew sat on either side of her. They were silent. It was two hours since Ben had been shot and the bullet that had lodged under his left shoulder-blade was already being probed and its safe extraction evaluated. But the three people felt as though they had been frozen in time, in that space, for many many years.

The initial cries of alarm and fear and sympathy and outrage all lay silent. The cry that lay between them in the room was the silent cry of hope, but the early morning hours of Saturday 11 September crept into being, dragging with it only the rank aftermath of the previous day.

Saturday 11 September, 2.30am

BJ came to at 2.30am. Or rather, she was able to open her eyes. There was something in the room with her. It saw that she was awake and stood up and came towards her. She made sure it saw her flinch. It had to be a man. It was very tall and seemed to be covered in bandages. It must have some terrible disease or perhaps it was a fetishist. Did they like women to flinch, this sort of thing? Flinch and crush your eyes closed and then when they do whatever they are going to do, bite your lip so hard that you draw blood? It amuses them so much that sometimes they stop? Never cry? Crying brings out their ugly side whereas a little spontaneous reacting and retching gives them the jollies? She kept her eyes closed, but there was nothing. No striking, no plunging, no pinching, twisting. Nothing.

The voice was slurred but smooth. She felt it more as a caress than a sound. "Are you BJ Cresswell?" She nodded.

"I want more of the heroin you supplied to John. I want a lot more."

BJ lifted her head and tried to nod but it hurt, hurt so much that she grunted with the pain. The night hadn't been a total waste after all. The ultimate punter had come along at last, so it seemed. "Where am I, she asked. "Where have you taken me?"

Albert processed the question for what seemed a long time. If she was in the room when he arrived – and he was certain she was – why did she think he had brought her here? She struggled to sit up. Her features were blurred, hard to make out and her skin was so translucently pale that she seemed only to have shape because of the definition of her hair and the clothes she wore.

Albert looked at her carefully. He had even talked himself into hating this woman. *Why? Look at her!* She was common, a tart. He had let a street-walker ruin him. She was garbage. "You must have been sampling your own wares to excess, Miss Cresswell. Now, to business! Drugs! I know you have supplies and I can pay. How much do you want?"

*

Fang Li paused outside the door and heard his two customers conversing in almost companionable terms even though he could not understand what they were talking about. In the room, BJ was telling Albert about the provenance of her drugs. "...and my adviser said that this is genuine Red Bird "999", famous in its own right, identifiable down to which chemist processed it by the marks on each block. Each block is probably worth $20 million on the street, but I've got to get rid of it. You can have it for three. Here, try a little. Taste it. It's heaven." Albert nodded appreciatively.

So did Fang Li. He heard the woman say "999". Eveyone knew what that meant. He knew how much heroin he'd given Albert and the *gwaipor* was clearly mad with it. He thought about the two mismatched people in the salon, how strange they each looked and how so obviously and badly drug-addicted they both were. Both were garbed in white, but the woman was fading away, while the owl's feathers were only disguised by his white wrappings. As Fang Li well knew, white symbolized the white tiger – kirin – the guardian of the West and it was September – Autumn – the tiger's

Red Bird Summer 235

time, when the phoenix, guardian of the summer months, relinquishes its season of hope to more warlike times. The tiger is clairvoyant and has the power to change into a witch, but the owl is just the harbinger of death – no deals can be done with the owl. *Clearly*, thought Fang, *this is a no-win situation*. He carefully considered all the signs again, descended the stairs, picked up his packet of Camel cigarettes – the camel signifying nothing so far as he was aware – tucked the wallet carefully into the side pocket of his cotton jacket and walked from the *Emperor Inn* to the house he shared with Mrs Fang in Lotus Lane.

No point locking up. Death did not respect locks.

*

Hew could hardly believe his luck. He peered into the bar of the *Emperor* to see how best to navigate his way upstairs but there wasn't a soul in sight, no customers, not even that foul old barman. Upstairs, Albert had said. *The usual place.*

*

"You need to be careful with it." BJ had warmed to her subject. "It's strong and that must be because it's so pure, not like what they say, that it's the cutting agents that give the high. This is pure heaven. But there have been times during the past few weeks when I have a bit of trouble recalling where I've been after taking a hit." She frowned and bit her lip in her familiar gesture of submission. "Or in remembering what I've done. I want to give it up. That's why I want to get shot of all of it. It's a bargain for you if you want it."

"I'm selling assets tonight," said Albert. "Depending on the price they raise, I'll let you know. Where are you staying?"

BJ looked distressed. *What does he mean, where am I staying?*

"Well, I… I'm staying here, aren't I? Aren't I staying with you? Isn't this what John intended weeks ago? Didn't he organise this? If he didn't …." She faltered. *What if John didn't organise this? How had this bloke, the one I refused to meet because he seemed so creepy – and that was before I met him.* She resumed with difficulty, "If John didn't organise this, how did you know where to find me?"

Albert didn't answer her. She was such a boring tart. Fancy wasting strong emotions like hatred on something like her! He walked to the door and checked that the corridor was clear. No sign of Fang Li. Good. He closed it and turned to her. "If you would like to wait here for a little while, I'll have the cash for you. Then I'm sure you can find somewhere to stay, Miss Cresswell." He saw her shoulders relax. She cupped her chin in her hands and rocked to and fro on the edge of the bed.

Albert settled into a chair. "I'm selling these. He withdrew each of the four statues from the pillowcases and placed them in compass-point order on the small round table that sat in the centre of the room.

"The turtle guards the north and is the black warrior – the shell – armour, get it? The white tiger, kirin, guards the west and this time of the year is his time. Autumn. He is the king of all animals and is also the god of war. The phoenix, the red bird, guards the south and its symbol is fire. The phoenix appears only when times are good, so its appearance here tonight is propitious, perhaps. Then we have the dragon and the dragon guards the east. For an animal that gets so much bad press, the dragon heralds spring, the colours of blue and green and its medium is wood. These particular statues are more than a thousand years old and are very valuable. You will easily have your three million."

"Except that the set is incomplete, Albert."

Hew Nuttingsall stepped into the room.

"Ah, Hew! You are of course quite right. I didn't feel it any loss to omit the final element from the array."

BJ looked up at Hew's kindly face and unconsciously straightened her clothes and patted her wig into place. He ignored her. She frowned, unaware that she was now all but invisible.

"What's this about, Albert? Being here, like this, with her? Are you mad?"

"Yes, I think so, Hew! I really think so! This is Miss BJ Cresswell. The initials B and J are a mystery – and alas – the only mysterious thing about her. She traffics in drugs and is a prostitute, so I understand from my good friend, Mr Simons. I had her hired to drug Dr Henderson early in August in an attempt to recover an object I believed the good doctor had filched from the museum. She botched that well and truly. But more recently she has had the good fortune to score some of the rarest heroin in the world, the legendary Red Bird "999". We are negotiating a price, so your arrival is doubly propitious, as the issue of payment has come up."

It was too late for BJ to size up the room they were in. It was tiny and the two men blocked the exit. She was well and truly trapped. She drew her handbag towards her and gently eased the clasp open and at that moment remembered what she had been straining so hard to recall. "The Peninsula. That's it. I'm staying at the Peninsula. If you gentlemen are ready to do business, I'd like to get going." She peered into her purse and extracted the flick-knife in its cylindrical case instead of her lipstick. She flicked it open and said, "Lipstick. I must put on some lipstick."

Albert regarded the knife and picked up the statue of the phoenix. "Observe this creature, Miss Cresswell, do. It's a very interesting classical rendition of the phoenix by a Song Dynasty sculptor, who regrettably, is completely unknown. Sad, such wonderful work!" He hurled it at her. The phoenix, the portent of good times, was made of solid bronze and the blow struck BJ with lethal force on the side of her head. She did not even so much as gasp as she fell back on the bed. Albert rose to his feet and grabbed the knife from her. As she feebly struggled to sit up, he picked up the statue and hit her again, hard, on the front of her head this time. He looked at the deep depression that appeared on her forehead with almost clinical interest.

"It seemed a shame to do anything but put the poor cow out of her misery," he said to Hew. "Look at her."

BJ was a cruel sight. Her wig had come adrift and her over-dyed hair was stuck to the side of her head in mousey-brown clumps. There was a dull ooze of blood on her left temple and myriad wellsprings of blood were erupting from the wound on her forehead. Her face was streaked with the heroin she had consumed, dipping into her bags of drugs and eating them like packets of sherbert. Her dress had ridden up and exposed her torso to the ribcage. With her legs agape, BJ looked as she had done so many times in life – used and thrown aside like a rag doll.

Albert opened the handbag, a beautiful oblong object about fourteen inches long and eight inches wide and found it stuffed full of bags of heroin, topped up with a fat wad of notes. Hew saw what Albert saw and, standing not a foot apart, they looked deeply into one another's eyes.

"Well, Hew, this could be a fine time for both of us." Albert smiled and picked up the white leather tote bag from the floor near the bed and held it open for Hew to inspect. There were more bank notes rolled and placed in neat layers inside. He kissed Hew firmly on the lips. "We've shared before. Want to share again, lover?"

Hew drew back. "I always think how very elegant all white can look, Albert, but I must say you go beyond doing it justice in that get-up. Really, very fancy! And as for your Miss BJ Cresswell here, well I can see that she possibly did white well once. But, Albert," and Hew tapped one of the packets of heroin, "If we share this, I will still be at your beck and call. Buying my way out of our shared history is why I came here tonight, not the lure of this stuff. Truth is, I'm not so lured by it any more, old boy."

Albert was used to Hew's long-winded speeches and he smiled at him fondly: "I know you killed the man who was in my house early yesterday morning too, Hew. I saw you leave when I returned to pick up my collection there. I left your tiger paw on the body as a calling card for the police. Didn't want to make it too hard for them. So, red bird trumps tiger, I think."

Albert's voice slurred again. The drugs Fang Li had slipped to him in his whisky took hold in full strength at last, and now he was too slow, too drugged, too exhausted to be quick enough to duck when Hew elbowed him off-balance and smacked him soundly in the lower back with the exquisite statue of the bronze turtle, before swinging his arm in his distinctive left-handed short-drive style and wedging the object firmly in the back of Albert's head.

Albert's body buckled and he slumped to his knees. Blood oozed from his head through his bandages and his last mortal sensation was dread, as he felt Hew pick him up and throw him across BJ's prone form.

Hew admired the turtle, the symbol of the black warrior. *It really is a magnificent collection.* The pair in white looked aberrantly peaceful. He wasn't sure the woman was dead but he certainly didn't intend touching the creature. In any event she certainly wasn't going anywhere in a hurry. In Albert's case, he was prepared to make sure. He took BJ's knife and stabbed at Albert's back, delicately jabbing at his kidneys until he was convinced that there was no response from the owl. He wiped the knife and put it on the table.

He patted Albert's bum and said, "And you're right about there being something missing, old boy. It's the centre. You can't have four points of a compass without having a centre, otherwise there's no sense in anything. The centre represents benevolence and that's why it's missing. Not much benevolence around here tonight, eh, Albert?

He emptied the contents of BJ's handbag and tote bag into his briefcase, added two of the statues and made a parcel of the tiger and the phoenix in Albert's pillow-case. He tucked the parcel under his arm and scanned the room swiftly. It would present a pretty puzzle to anyone who tried to reconstruct what had happened in here. Time to leave.

"Bronze turtle trumps red bird, I think. Cheerio, both!" He closed the door on the dead white witch and her final acquisition, the rare, white, masked owl.

Saturday 11 September: 4.30am

Early on Saturday morning, there was the unusual occurrence of people walking loudly into the Walled City's confines through the northern entrance. Torchlight made the place lighter than any daylight had done for many decades and many saw a tall *gwailo* policeman with hair of flame, accompanied by four others who wore the uniforms of Hong Kong Police officers. Fang Li missed the unique sight. He slumbered at his wife's side in their small mudbrick house in Lotus Lane, a place he rarely visited after his long working days, when he would usually just bunk down at the *Emperor Inn* to avoid making his way home through the dangerous narrow alleyways.

But at 5.30am Fang Li and many others heard an even rarer sound as the city walls reverberated to the sound of vehicles making their way carefully through the main thoroughfare. The alley wasn't wide enough for a regular vehicle and those who had the courage to peer out from behind their papered or curtained windows saw strange motor bikes pass by, bikes with three wheels and narrow trailers attached to them. At 6.00am, the bodies of Albert Ho and BJ Cresswell were removed from the *Emperor Inn*.

Few bodies had ever been removed from the Walled City so overtly in recent years. The place throbbed with a silence informed by fear.

When Fang Li returned to work at 7.00am there was no sign that the early morning noises were connected with the *Emperor Inn*. Nothing was missing or disturbed. A regular sipped whisky at the bar and a small pile of coins showed that the man had not abused the hospitality of the place in the absence of the barman, who, many vowed, had never before left the bar in the twenty-five years he had worked there. All was quiet upstairs and when Fang Li checked the salons, they were empty. The only sign that there had been some disorder was the bed-cover on the floor, which, as he noticed when he picked it up, had two patches of blood on it. He hurriedly bundled up the object and put it at the bottom of a cupboard. Later he would dump it.

Of his clients from the previous evening there was no sign.

He went downstairs and made a casual swipe at cleaning down the bar and sweeping the floor. It was then he saw the crumpled note. He smoothed the piece of paper out on top of the wooden bench-top and in his scholarly way, easily deciphered the characters.

"You are informed that the contracts issued for the targets Green and Henderson are cancelled. The contractor is dead and cannot pay the premium. On Monday 13th September at 7pm, you will be given compensation for the cancellation. Here. Be on time.

There was a small decorative chop depicting a rearing horse stamped on the bottom of the note. The note had been read and discarded. Fang Li smiled and lit the first of his many cigarettes of the day.

*

At 7.30am John Simons was brought under escort from the holding cells at Central Division to the Police Morgue where he identified the two bodies that had been transported from the *Emperor Inn* as being those of BJ Cresswell and Albert Ho, the former his dealer, the latter his client, the former Director of the Hong Kong Archaeological Museum. Without any jurisdictional authority in the Walled City, the Police had technically acted beyond their powers in retrieving the bodies, but once it was done it was unlikely there would be a counter-challenge by the Chinese mainland authorities.

When Chief Superintendent Smythe and his men met James at *The Emperor* and prepared to remove the bodies of Albert and BJ Cresswell, they found no sign of the weapon which seemed to have caused the deaths of both victims – both had been bludgeoned with a heavy blunt object – but there was a knife in the room and there was some evidence that it had been used during the violence.

The way Smythe saw it, it appeared that Albert Ho and BJ Cresswell had fought violently and died as a result of injuries sustained during the struggle. Albert had a lot of superficial, almost nonsensical stab wounds. Chief Superintendent Smythe initially held the view that it was a violent sexual encounter gone wrong, but as he followed that line of enquiry, the absence of the murder weapon cast doubt on the idea that Albert and BJ Cresswell battled to their mutual death. *Unless,* he thought, *there was a third party who removed it.*

The Emperor was wide open when CS Smythe and his men had arrived in the early hours, just as it had been when Yip and James entered the bar an hour or so earlier. Anything could have happened and anything could have been removed without being noticed while the place was open to all-comers.

The most appalling aspect surrounding the deaths, in the view of CS Smythe, was that both victims had died without being brought to justice for the murders they had both almost certainly committed in the previous twenty-four hours. The list was long: Detective Sergeant Herbert Proust, Miss Annie Cheung, DS Michael "Sandy" Fraser and Mrs Emmeline Franklin.

There was now firm evidence that BJ Cresswell had stabbed Herbie Proust to death in the early hours of Friday morning and that same day, in the evening, had strangled Emmie Franklin to death in the ground floor ladies' powder-room at the Peninsula Hotel. CS Smythe fully expected the pearl-handled flick-knife found at the murder scene in the *Emperor Inn* to be identified as the weapon that was used to kill DS Proust. As for Albert, he was surely guilty, at least, of the killing of Annie Cheung and the attacks on Dr Henderson, as well as being in the frame for the murders of DS Fraser and BJ Cresswell.

The whole case was connected to the theft of the drugs from the Narcotics Bureau. Tommy Smythe fully expected the pathology report to show that both Cresswell and Ho had drugs in their systems. Somehow, Cresswell and Ho had come into close contact with one another in an encounter that resulted in their mutual death. Smythe recalled the comment from the Chief of Police – hell, was that only yesterday? – that if the whole matter only boiled down to drugs, it would be a welcome relief.

Well, it had turned out to be about drugs, but on this grim early autumn morning there was little comfort to be had from that knowledge.

*

At 12 noon the desk clerk checked the Observatory Hill Hotel register and noted that the guest in room 8, Miss E Jones, had not checked out. Discreet knocking produced no result. At 2pm the door was forced but there was no sign of Miss Jones. She had left a spectacular room tip however, more than three million Hong Kong dollars in the room safe. At 3.30pm, PanAm Flight 812 from Hong Kong to London left without one of the passengers aboard, a Miss B J Cresswell, who had booked a seat in first class.

*

Pearl sat on the side of Ben's bed and fed him soup. He spluttered and choked and she wiped his chin lovingly with a handerchief and pushed more liquid into his mouth.

"For God's sake Pearl, the man's choking. Fine mother you'd make." Kaz took the spoon away. "Talk about killing someone with kindness. Here. You do it like this." She held the spoon with a small helping of soup to the edge of Ben's mouth and he sipped at it gratefully without taking his eyes off Pearl. Now past post-operative nausea, he was starving. The bullet had been prised out of his ribcage where it had lodged with glancing, minimal damage.

James laughed. "Kaz, it is so wonderful to have you back. I didn't know you'd taken mothercraft lessons. You've never struck me as the maternal type." Pearl smiled at her father and smiled at Kaz. James was of the opinion that if the Jabberwocky itself stormed into the ward she would have been happy about that too. Had love made her lose a bit of her edge? But he underestimated her.

"Right, Dad. Dish it up! Tell us the lot. And don't rush it."

James uttered a loud sigh. "I was hoping Yip would come by and help me out with that, but he sends his regards and wants you to know that the danger is past and that the contracts on you and Kaz are negated."

He added to himself that he had no intention of telling them the whole story of how he and Yip had found Barbara Cresswell and

Albert Ho's bodies at four thirty that morning, when they finally arrived at the *Emperor*, where he and Yip had been forced to go so that Yip could be sure that the death contracts on Pearl and Kaz really were dropped. He would have to describe the death scene if there was ever to be a hearing into the affair, but until that time it was something James was trying to erase from his mind as much as he humanly could.

"It may not cheer you to know, Ben, that a financial reward has been offered to be paid to the Contractor for the cancellation of the contract on Pearl and Kaz, to make up for any inconvenience caused to him. But because he will turn up to claim his compensation, I am happy to tell you there is also the opportunity for some rough justice to be measured out to him, Walled City style. Nothing for any of us to be involved with of course. What will be, will be, in this case. Bringing him to justice as we understand it just ain't going to happen, I'm afraid. The Hong Kong Police are rarely willing to push their luck in the Walled City by mounting a legal case that has originated there. They seem satisfied that the major matter is closed."

Ben smiled and shrugged. "Once again, I don't know what to say, James. If that's the way it goes in Hong Kong, I suppose I just have to accept it. Everyone is safe but there was luck involved and accepting a jurisdiction-free area where this type of crime can flourish, without there ever being any hope of achieving justice for the innocent, strikes me as fundamentally wrong."

"Spoken like a true human rights lawyer. I applaud your view. By the way, I haven't said how deeply grateful I am to you for what you did last night, Ben. Who knows what we might all be doing today, if it weren't for you. But, as for the entire story, that must wait till later. I simply must sleep now. The full story has to be later. Except for this part. You won't believe …."

There was total silence as James revealed that Emmie Franklin had issued the contract on BJ after BJ humiliated her in the lobby of the Peninsula on Wednesday night. Although Yip had been shocked at how she had so easily talked herself round to ordering BJ Cresswell's death, he went along with it by pretending that he would put the contract out around the traps. He intended to teach Mrs Franklin a lesson, but a crueler irony was at work when BJ killed Emmie instead.

"It seems that Mrs Franklin recognized BJ in her disguise as the mousey Christine James. What must have gone through her mind as she died at the hands of that deranged young woman! – Truly ghastly! In addition," James continued, "the knife that was used on Albert is confirmed as the weapon used to kill DS Proust. It must have belonged to BJ. Her prints are all over both death-rooms, but interestingly, not on the knife. When it was found in the salon of the *Emperor Inn*, it had been wiped. Albert's prints aren't on it either. Neither BJ nor Albert could have wiped it posthumously, hmm? I'll see you all later. Don't want to tire Ben."

He patted Ben's arm, kissed Pearl and Kaz and shook Drew's hand. If he didn't get some food and sleep – James wasn't sure of the order of need – he thought he might fade away, much as BJ had.

Saturday 11 September: 5.30pm

"It was the notes, James. I always keep a record of the bank note numbers on cash loans. Today at the races I won a lot of cash from someone I know and it struck me how unusually new and untouched the notes were, so I checked the numbers against my records" – Yip tapped his pocket – "and they were part of a loan I made to John Simons last Sunday."

James mentally shut down his conscience. Yip had never come so close to revealing his business affairs.

"As a cautionary measure, I like to see what my clients spend their loans on. As I had suspicions about Mr Simons's activities, I had Hua Leung keep him under surveillance. On Sunday evening, Simons used the money to buy goods from the young – lady – whom we found dead in the *Emperor Inn* this morning. Then today, the cash came back to me. How good is that James? I knew that tip on the 1.30 Autumn Festival race was a good one. I made…" he pulled up short. He had almost become animated.

James looked at Yip, one eyebrow raised. *So that's what makes you tick is it? Gambling.* "You made an amazing leap of logic, Yee Koon. No wonder you are the businessman you are. But how does that help us?"

"Ah, James, that is the magic of keeping such records. I of course know to whom I gave the money, but as for who gifted it back to me, well, the police need a case, James, and my records may be evidence. Without evidence beyond the precincts of the Walled City, they have nothing with which to mount their case. We should give them evidence that is valid in Her Majesty's legal jurisdiction, don't you think? Pay respect to Her Majesty's laws?"

Yip smiled and James was enchanted. The man whose immense wealth was rumoured to be based on the anonymity that the Walled City gave to at least some of his activities was betraying its sanctity and seemed happy to do so. Yip reminded him of Pearl. Pearl rarely smiled, but when she did, she lit up the city. Yip's smile had much the same effect. Perhaps that explained their mysterious bond.

"Do you know what this will cost me personally, to enter Police Headquarters, James? That is how important I think this is. Will you ring Chief Superintendent Smythe? I don't think I can quite do it."

"Tommy. James Gates. Yip Yee Koon and I are ready to give you a statement about our role in the events of this morning and we have another matter to discuss with you as a matter of some urgency. Are you available now?"

Tommy Smythe was more than available, he was jubilant. He would have filmed Yip Yee Koon's entry into the Central Division Police Station for his own present and future enjoyment if he possibly could. Yip and Gates had indeed found the bodies of Albert Ho and Barbara Jane Cresswell in the Walled City in the early hours of this morning and as yet there had been no formal statements taken. Their explanation as to why they were there was plausible: simply that the *Emperor Inn* is where contracts issued from the Walled City are settled and that is where they went to track down the man sent to execute James's daughter and her friend Dr Henderson.

The advice from the legal coppers was that because the bodies were found in an area free of any British legal jurisdiction, technically a crime hadn't been committed under the Crown, so technically there could be no call for statements. It was intriguing, but as Albert Ho and BJ Cresswell had probably killed one another, Smythe thought it pointless to pursue it.

*

Yip replaced the telephone receiver and informed his wife that he would be out for some hours. Mrs Yip smiled and thanked her husband for the information and enquired if he would return for dinner. She had ordered fish fried in sesame oil and eschallots. He smiled gently in return and told her to go ahead without him.

Yip had other fish to fry. He met James outside Hong Kong Police Division Central and James courteously assisted him through the door. Yip was like a man fading fast and James was heartily amused.

*

It was six o'clock when Hew returned to his apartment. The phone rang almost immediately. He barked into the hand piece: "Yes? Is something wrong?" *What a day* .... He listened and paled. "I'll meet you there at eight, Yip." Yip's voice annoyed him, brought back events of a most unsatisfactory afternoon at the track. He had hoped to launder part of the money he had taken from BJ Cresswell's handbag at Happy Valley by setting a bet directly with Yip Yee Koon on the 1.30 but he lost and had to hand part of his windfall over. That was little compared to his overall losses for the day, which amounted to nearly half the money he had helped himself to from the wretched woman's tote bag, close to two million Hong Kong dollars.

Hew felt sour and hard done by. The last thing he wanted to do this evening was go out again. Especially to spend time with Yip after the successful day the businessman had clearly had at the turf meeting. He had rarely seen Yip Yee Koon smile, but that afternoon he had been in extraordinarily high spirits for such a generally conservative sort of chap.

Hew remembered the bestiary collection he had relieved Albert of and cheered up a bit. It was boxed up and stored away in the bottom drawer of the guest-room wardrobe, safe until the day he could sell it. Albert had intimated that it was worth a small fortune but he would wait to see what sort of public storm might break out over Albert's demise. Albert had been a man of influence in Hong Kong. If anything came out about the collection, well, who knows? Clearly, Albert had stolen it. Hew needed to be very careful.

Hew was oddly detached from his murderous outbreak of the early hours. He didn't even acknowledge to himself that the call from Yip Yee Koon could in some way be connected with the death of Albert and that odious young woman. Yip had simply said the meeting was important for their future association. On the other hand, he had concluded that association just this week. *Damn the man. What can he want?*

*

Pearl and Ben argued with a fierce intensity. Kaz and Drew tried to get Pearl out of the room. "He's in no state to argue. How can you do this to him? Look at him, Pearl. He's barely conscious."

"Well, I'm sorry of course. I love him and owe him my life, But. I have to go. I have to see how Danny is and he's trying to stop me. He's got no right...."

"Ben *saw* Danny," said Kaz. "How do you think he'll be? He'll still be devastated and you won't make any difference drifting into his grief like Mother saintly Theresa dispensing beads of hope. But Ben needs you here."

Pearl drew herself up to her full height and glared at Kaz. It was Saturday. She had a foundation to run, and what was left of her staff to look after. There were things to organise. She didn't even know how the move to Lantau had gone yesterday. *Yesterday.* She sat down on the visitor's chair, hard. Yesterday, Ben had been wounded by a bullet intended to end her life. Yesterday, Annie had been killed. Albert Ho was dead. BJ Cresswell was dead. It all seemed an aeon away. How could she have been so stupid? She burst into tears. "I'm sorry, I'm sorry. I'm just trying to go back and somehow, make it right."

"There's no going back, Pearl." It was Ben's voice, calm, level. "When you turn up for work on Monday, it's going to be just that. Regardless of what's happened, you'll just be turning up for work. It will be horrible, but Danny will cope and you will cope and we'll all have grown up a little more. Put a line under it!"

Pearl didn't know where the words came from but they were there. She thought they had been there for a long time: "I can't *go* back to work. My whole life is nothing more than a monument to my mother. I've spent all these years working at it to keep her alive in my memory. I haven't really lived. I haven't tested myself against what my own intellect can achieve, or can't. I've just used influence and I only have influence, because I have money and a title. "I want to be an archaeologist."

Kaz spluttered and Drew sat down rather quickly. "Not another damned archaeologist to blight the planet," he said unkindly.

Ben laughed. There was immense relief in it. "You'll make a great archaeologist. You already know how to dig up trouble. Any room in your life for someone to carry your shovel?"

"How about you, Drew?" said Kaz sarcastically, "would you like to be an archaeologist?"

"No thanks" said Drew. "I'm happy being a political scientist. Being married to one is bad enough."

Kaz and Pearl and Ben looked at him.

"Will you marry me, Kaz?"

"Not unless you get me a beer. How many times does a woman have to ask?"

Saturday 11 September: 7.00pm

By the time Pearl reached her Connaught Road apartment it was thirty-six hours since she had opened the door to Mr Yip and heard him spell out the hard facts about the death contracts that had been issued during the night. She was exhausted. Ben had fallen into a deep sleep in his hospital bed and even Drew had given up his three-day vigil and planned to stay at Kaz's flat overnight.

Pearl paused at the door, key in hand: *Dammit. I forgot to tell Drew that Mrs Chan will be there. I'd better call her. She'll think he's an intruder.*

The thought of what Mrs Chan might be capable of doing to an intruder was not one to be trifled with and Pearl hurried to the phone. The message light flickered in the gloom of the unlit apartment and the voice that came through the speaker brought the past crowding back into the sitting-room so vibrantly that it filled and spilled outside to the penthouse's colonnaded verandah, cascaded into the streets and flooded the harbour. Her mother and her friends were there, all of Pearl's old friends were there, and the penthouse was alive with music and flowers and art and laughter. In an instant Pearl was a girl again, a nineteen-year-old girl:

"Pearl. This is Peter Benson. I'm in Hong Kong and need to see you. You'll understand why, when we meet. Meet me at Stormy's at eight o'clock tonight. I hear it's Hong Kong's best restaurant these days and I have a deep need to eat tea-smoked duck. Be there!"

Pearl played the message again, rang Mrs Chan, then sat down at the desk and stared at the phone. Peter Benson. The man who had run Hong Kong's covert operation for the Home Office for fifteen years, the consummate academic, humanitarian and devious bastard of a man-about-town, the former lover of her mother, and when she was still pretty fresh out of school, even Pearl's boss for a time.

It was odd that she should be so overwhelmed by nostalgia just by hearing his voice. She had never even sorted out if she liked him. One thing she was sure of: she certainly didn't trust him. But he was a link to her past, a past she was now only beginning to acknowledge that she had to let go, if her own life was going to be healthy. Peter was a last hurrah for the old days. She smiled at the framed photograph of her mother that stood on the desk, blew her a kiss and said aloud: "I know what you would say, mother: 'It's about bloody time too, mooning about over things that can't be changed. Really, Pearl!'"

*

Stormy's was crammed with diners. The familiar concept of large round tables crowded with up to twenty diners and common to most Hong Kong restaurants was not evident at Stormy's, which allowed a maximum of four people at each table. The owner and chef considered that more than four diners led to a lack of concentration on the food and too much general conversation; and that was not the point of Stormy's. Stormy's was all about the food, the very exceptional food. Tonight there were eight courses on offer. The only free choices were drinks. Pearl took the dry martini she had ordered and smiled tightly at the waiter. The smile switched off as she turned her gaze back to her dinner companion. "Well?"

"You could be a little more chummy, surely?"

"I'm here to hear what you have to say. If you'd chosen anywhere other than this restaurant I'd not have bothered. You do know I bought your apartment?"

Peter Benson nodded and smiled. "Complete with everything I owned in the world except for my watch and the clothes I stood up in."

"It was your choice. You broke the rules when you disappeared."

"I disappeared, as you put it, because I was held under so-called restraint on Hei Ling Chau by that maniac Matron for six months. Officially, Pearl, I was kidnapped."

Pearl looked a little guilty.

"During that time I was also diagnosed with leprosy."

Pearl gulped a sliver of goose meat down rather more hastily than she intended and spluttered into her napkin. She picked up her glass and swallowed the martini in another, rather awkward gulp.

"Great! Did anyone bother to tell you that leprosy's infectious and perhaps eating in a crowded restaurant is possibly not in the best interests of public health?"

"It was a mis-diagnosis but it took two years for a full clearance. During that time I stayed in the Maromji Monastery in Japan and started to get interested in Zen Bhuddhism. I spent the next seven years as a novitiate and carried out post-doctoral research at the same time. I'm on leave this year. I can enter the monastery and spend my life there as a monk if I go back."

"Why do you want to see me, Peter? Do you want to talk about my mother? My father?"

"I don't even know who your father is. I didn't think that you did either, Pearl."

"Times change! Well?"

"I want to talk to you about what I should do next."

Pearl ducked her head a little and tried to cover the smile that gathered around the edges of her mouth despite her intention to remain distant from him. Dr Peter Benson, Ph.D. in Asian Political Studies, wanted her advice about what to do next? *My my*, thought Pearl, *times have changed.*

"I will not return to the monastery. I have money, enough at any rate to live quietly here or back in the UK. I've heard about the Bowen Foundation of course and I would like to offer you my services. There is a history of old hurts between us – no need to spell them out – and I owe you, Pearl. You will find that they are very particular services and come free of charge.

"I speak fourteen languages, I'm now something of an expert on the history of the great marine trading routes in and out of China and I am recognised, in Japan at any rate, for my post-doctoral research into the voyages of the great exploration fleets of Zheng He. I have been able to establish shipping routes, cargo loads and the voyage configurations of all the great exploration journeys south from Taicang to Macau, from the fourteenth to the seventeenth century. During the past three weeks while in Hong Kong, I have also done some field work that confirms that another rather surprising theory of mine is correct. Not, I realise that such a specialist area of research would necessarily be useful to the Bowen Foundation, but I have other skills too, of course."

Pearl thought about the sleek black head that had emerged from the waters of Squid Cove when she and Kaz were there in late August; the diver who swam away at speed when he saw Kaz and her on the grey sands of the little beach. She thought of Kaz and the years she had spent protecting her archaeological site. During all that time, in Japan, this man, Pearl's old boss, her mother's former lover and her father's former senior operational man in Hong Kong, had been studying texts which had led to impressive results. He could not only theoretically corroborate Kaz's field work but had the cargo lists for the sunken ships. He could probably make up an inventory for Kaz.

Pearl would have laughed out loud if it hadn't meant her deep fried oyster would end up on the other side of the room. She said, "And you don't have leprosy?"

"And I don't have leprosy. Though I'm damned if I see what amuses you so much about that."

"I can also presume that going back to Hei Ling Chau for a spot of work there wouldn't pose any problems for you, physical or psychological?"

"Oddly enough, no. Though you may think me mad for saying so."

"Yep. But not as mad as Kaz is going to be. Have a piece of steamed jelly-fish. By the way, you still dive, I notice, don't you?"

*

Dinner proceeded more companionably. Pearl took a close look at Benson but could not see a great difference in his appearance in the eleven years that had gone by since they had last encountered one another. It had been a night when there was betrayal abroad, driven by the wild winds of Cyclone Marita and fed by the uncertainty of treachery; a night when Pearl had come to suspect him of having turned on her mother, and her.

He was in his fifties now, still a tall, elegant man, but much thinner than he had been. He wore a lightweight grey lounge suit with a white shirt and a dark blue tie, a far cry from the eccentric academic rig he affected in his role of Head of the external Loweth School of Political Science, South-East Asia Faculty, the cover operation for the British Home Office presence in Hong Kong during the 1960s.

Pearl thought hard as she ate her way through the courses, relishing each dish as it rolled by. "I so love bêche de mer. Poor things. So ugly. So delicious. I'll have to talk to my colleagues and the JBF Board about your proposal and I certainly will at the first available opportunity. I think I have a project for you, Peter. Work that you and Karen Henderson have in common, I believe, and work that Kaz won't be able to manage in the immediate future. But don't you have to square things up with your London masters?"

Pearl could have mentioned that James was in town but she didn't and Benson ignored the question. Clearly, he no longer considered that he had London masters. They continued eating. Pearl glanced around the room. It was full of smoke and talk and the clip of chopsticks and a rattle of plates and it took her a moment to register that one of the faces in her view was the familiar one of Yip Yee Koon.

Yip was dining with Sir Hew Nuttingsall.

Yip was his contained, very usual self, and she could see his mouth just moving as he spoke. Yip seemed to make no effort to speak but he neither mumbled nor spoke softly. Words just seemed to flow from him. He took a mouthful of food, placed his chopsticks across the bowl, half turned his head to wipe his mouth, glanced at Pearl and very gently shook his head.

She quickly looked away and saw Peter Benson's gaze upon her.

"Your expression was quite odd, then, Pearl. Is everything all right?"

"Sure. Everything's just fine. Now what are we going to do next? Where are you staying?"

Saturday 11 September: 8.30pm

Chief Superintendent Smythe and James contemplated the front door of Hew's apartment. Tommy knocked. When there was no response after the third try, he rifled through a bunch of keys. "It's an Everlock. Let's see what we can do with this." The door opened easily and Tommy grinned at James. "This is like Special Branch stuff, eh, James? Now, let's see if we can put some clout behind your suspicions about this chappie."

Hew's apartment was a double penthouse but it had only three bedrooms with most of the space set aside for reception rooms, libraries, display rooms, a music room and the biggest dining-room James had ever seen outside of a palace. James entered the apartment after CS Smythe and looked around. Old Hew had certainly set himself up well and this place complemented his spectacular career very nicely. Not bad for a lad who'd been sent down for some undisclosed college crime, leading his family to despatch him to the colonies. He was now a long-term Hong Kong celebrity of some clout, respected in the banking profession and a highly valued guest among Hong Kong hostesses.

Hew had even been rumoured to have had an affair with the famous American film star Amanda Clift, whom he met when she came to Hong Kong to star in a movie. It was said that when it ended, he was so broken hearted that he swore off marriage, although he was frequently photographed escorting a variety of women through the endless rounds of Hong Kong parties.

James let the atmosphere of the living-room wash over him. What did it say about the man? The lighting was recessed behind deep cornices and the artworks were each lit up in their own little pools of light. Ebony stands were placed at regular intervals around the walls, bearing objects or statues. Then it struck James what was bothering him. It was a museum. It didn't say anything about Hew Nuttingsall. It was a showroom, a display. Like Albert's place. It was on a different scale and Albert's house definitely had a certain uniqueness that this room lacked but even so ....

Is Hew a cook? James put his head around the kitchen door and saw a utilitarian Hong Kong kitchen of open shelves and acres of small square white tiles on the bench-tops and walls. *No. Not a cook.* He wandered into the master bedroom, a room just as staged and decorated as the living-room except for the crimson glazed wall behind the matching bedhead and the crimson velvet bedspread. A mahogany built-in cupboard lined one wall from floor to ceiling. CS Smythe was systematically going through the contents.

The second bedroom was a surprise, undecorated, utilitarian. It seemed Hew didn't encourage guests. A double bed was pushed against one wall and there was a heavy oak desk, a chair, and a free-standing wardrobe. With the way the bed was shoved against the wall, the room looked bare, temporary in some way. James looked through the desk drawers and then opened the wardrobe, which was full of clothes and shoes.

"Tommy. Come in here a sec."

DS Smythe came into the room.

"Nothing in the bedroom or the library, far as I can tell. Man's got a million books, though. I expect some of them could be hollow. What have you got here, James?"

"A dominatrix, I believe, Chief Superintendent. Take a look."

The clothes were beautiful, delicate, even though they had been cleverly made to fit a tall and big-bodied person. Everything was black, the capes, cloaks, frocks, leather slacks, halter tops, stiletto-heeled shoes, leather manacles and underwear. Even the collection of cruel-looking masks. The accessories were all steel studded – belts, cuffs, neckpieces and whip-handles. The whips themselves were of plaited black leather and there were seven of them, all different sizes.

Chief Superintendent Smythe's mouth tightened. *More perverts.* He almost flinched at the sight of some of the masks. They were clearly modelled on early Roman battle-masks and were pure cruelty etched into metal. He edged the clothing aside and looked in the back of the wardrobe, but there was nothing else to see. Then James opened the large bottom drawer of the cupboard and saw a box. It was heavy and when they placed it on the desk and opened it, it was clear to James why.

"These statues are exquisite", said Tommy Smythe. "I wonder ...."

"I've had the pleasure of seeing these particular items before, at Albert Ho's house, old man" said James. "Don't touch them. They're evidence."

The four statues were laid side by side in the box, fine tissue-paper wedged between them. James peered at them and sniffed. "Odour. I can smell something. Blood? Look!"

The bronze was faintly dulled in a couple of places with a barely discernible discoloration of some sort. Closer inspection showed that some hairs were stuck to the discoloured material on the statue of the phoenix. Attached to the statue of the turtle was the tiniest piece of white gauze thread. It could have come from a bandage.

"Yip," said James a little dreamily. "Yip is with him now. Hew is our murderer. This is the evidence for the case Yip wanted to help you build, Chief Superintendent. We've got to get him away from Hew. Have you got enough here to arrest him?"

Tommy Smythe was struck by how strange a world it was, when a man like Yip Yee Koon could help him build a case – or was it that James was asking if he had enough evidence to arrest Yip? How Tommy would love to arrest Yip!

"I will take these to HQ for technical examination. But no, this in itself isn't enough to arrest Sir Hew, James, not yet, not without conducting tests, establishing they are the stolen goods and so on. It will take a little time. I'm sure it won't be long before I can return with a warrant for Sir Hew." He waited for an argument from James but didn't get it.

James shrugged and took his leave. "Leave you to it then, old man. I have to get some more sleep. Don't know how you keep on going! You'll lock up?" He saluted Chief Superintendent Smythe and walked happily away. If old Tommy wouldn't bail out old Yip after all, it seemed as though old James was going to have to oblige. Probably better to do so without a copper about the place in any event. He thought of the time back in 1964 when he and Yip had been involved in a stand-off on Sharp Island. He had a faint sense of déjà vu as the lift descended to the ground floor of the building. He stepped out into the night and breathed deeply. He sniffed again. There was change in the air.

Tonight, at last, autumn really had arrived.

Saturday 11 September: 8.40pm

Yip's encounter with Sir Hew Nuttingsall was not going well. He folded his napkin after giving Pearl a nod, and returned to contemplating a dish of eel jellied in agar agar and sesame oil, a delicious concoction of smooth-textured fish supported in a smoky, jellied medium. This place certainly could turn on the food, but Yip thought of Mrs Yip sitting down to her fried fish and wished he was at home with her.

"I'm not satisfied, Yip." Sir Hew's voice was peeved. "Our business was concluded this week, debt cleared, you said. Thought it was very generous of you, sorry to find you seem to be having a change of heart." Hew spat out the observations in his usual style, stuffing up the context and making Yip's job more difficult than it was already. Somehow Yip had to trick this man into connecting himself to a murder based on the movements of some bank notes.

"It's a matter of currency, Sir Hew, not a matter of renewing surrendered debts. We had a one on one bet this afternoon at Happy Valley. – You do recall that?"

"Yes, and your point is?"

"The notes you gave me..."

"... are perfectly legal notes."

"Yes. They, ah, belong to me."

"Need you rub it in man?"

Yip's reputation for subtlety had been won by his ability to maintain a silence, a fearless capacity to stonewall his opponents. Now, he was in the position of having to create a verbal scene. He remained silent and Hew became impatient:

"Well. Spell it out, will you?"

"Try the deep fried oysters, Sir Hew. They are quite remarkable." After a brief pause, he added, "Excuse me a moment, Sir Hew, if you will."

Yip left the table and headed for the Gents' restroom. He needed a moment or two to regroup and think.

*

James hesitated. He didn't know where Stormy's was, for God's sake. He turned to go back into the building to ask Tommy but the automatic door had locked behind him. He hailed a cab and gave the destination but the cabbie just shrugged. He tried two more taxi-

Red Bird Summer

drivers but no-one had heard of Stormy's. Stormy's was new and obviously word hadn't got around about this particular new eatery. He finally took a cab to Pearl's apartment and began to feel uneasy when there was no response to his ring.

She must have gone back to the hospital, he thought, but there, all he found were Kaz and Ben in deep sleep in their neighbouring rooms. No sign of either Pearl or Drew. *Ah-ha*. They had obviously gone to Kaz's apartment, but as Mrs Chan pointed out very firmly to James, Mr Drew was asleep and no, Miss Pearl certainly was not here. Goodnight, Sir!

James could do nothing. Yip would have to look after his own affairs and if the police wouldn't commit to taking Hew Nuttingsall's involvement seriously until they had clear evidence, then James could do nothing about that either, unless he went over Smythe's head. James wasn't about to do that. Mrs Charlton might not be amused.

The Hong Kong Police would love to get Yip on something and James could tell from Tommy Smythe's fixation on Yip during that afternoon's interview that he was more absorbed by that thought than by Sir Hew Nuttingsall's role in this whole business. And since when did Yip Yee Koon need protection anyway? Wasn't he supposed to be in the business?

James eventually took his own advice and went back to the Mandarin, but he couldn't sleep, so he showered and shaved and toyed with the idea of going down to the hotel dining-room for a meal. He couldn't live Pearl's life for her either, he lectured his soapy reflection. How could he stop worrying about her, though? He waved the razor at the mirror and said, "This must be what true fatherhood feels like James m'boy. It's been a long time coming."

*

Yip Yee Koon returned to the table. During his absence Pearl saw that Hew Nuttingsall's face had become contused with anger and as Yip sat down, his voice was raised sufficiently for her to hear Hew say, "You're back. Good. I'm tired of this, Yip, and no, I will not have another poached eel steak thank you. I've had a long day and I'm going to leave. I'll…"

"Sir Hew", Yip interrupted, "I know my request sounds very odd, but the bank notes that you returned to me this afternoon are part of a run that have brought me a great deal of luck, and not just today." Yip took a gulp from his glass of water.

Pearl saw that he was nervous and she also saw that Hew's expression changed as he watched Yip drink from the glass of water. It reflected something like pleasure without the happiness of pleasure. She became more and more intrigued. Hew Nuttingsall had Yip Yee Koon in a state of nervous agitation. This must be a first.

"There were more notes in the same transaction which included this run of numbers, Sir Hew, and I merely wondered if you would oblige me by making a cash exchange, so that I can retrieve some more of the original sequence. It's for luck." He waited for Sir Heew's response.

Pearl watched Hew's colour flush to deep red across his cheeks and forehead. He dabbed at his mouth with the napkin, nodded and carefully placed his chopsticks across the rice bowl. The chair scraped loudly as he rose to his feet. With palpable control he said a few words to Yip and made his way out from the restaurant. Pearl watched the scene, and her mouth tightened. She looked at Yip, but he ignored her, threw money on to the table and followed Sir Hew Nuttingsall out into the night.

"I know something's going on in here. The air is thick with it." It was Benson. "Well, are you just going to sit there or are you going to follow them?" He moved to the back of her chair and helped her to her feet. "Come on, Pearl, what's the matter with you?"

"Oh nothing," said Pearl. "Tonight's not right, though. I wouldn't be surprised if there's a mother of a typhoon brewing outside."

"Or," said Benson and looked at her closely, "perhaps some other explosion, of nuclear proportions perhaps."

She ignored yet another reference to their shared past and followed him downstairs.

*

Tommy Smythe was at the door and about to lock up Sir Hew's apartment when the flash of a camera lens dazzled him. He put the box on the coffee-table and walked to the far wall of the sitting-room, opposite the entry. He stood on a splendid French Empire chair and felt along the recessed cornicing. Sure enough there was a camera mounted on a flat angled wall-bracket that just peeped over the cornice's ornate edging. There must be a trip-switch in the entry somewhere that activated the mechanisms for it.

He wondered why he and James hadn't noticed it earlier. It had a pretty obvious flash. He detached it, pulled a plastic bag from his pocket, bagged it up and put it in the box with the statues. It was when he picked the box up that he noticed what it was that had bothered him about this room ever since he had walked into it. Something was not right in here, in all of the splendid order of its well-curated contents. The coffee-table sat on the skin of a Bengal Tiger whose massive head and magnificent ivory teeth faced the living-room door, guarding the master of the house from intruders. The tiger's eyes were large faceted garnets, but one was missing. The tiger's left front paw was missing too, up to the second joint.

Tommy thought he had a match for it.

Saturday 11 September: 9.30pm

Peter Benson and Pearl reached the footpath just in time to see Yip and Hew get into a taxi. Pearl stepped out into the street and flagged down a cab and Benson told the driver to step on it in his impeccable Cantonese. "I've asked him to follow Yip. Your play, Pearl."

"I don't know if there is any play. Perhaps they have a business arrangement to sort out and Hew is understandably miffed about leaving his dinner to fulfil it. I honestly don't know what's going on. Why don't we go back to Hong Kong side for a coffee and I'll bring you up to date on what's been happening here in the last month or so? It's been rich."

"Are you kidding? I haven't had the chance to trail anyone for more than ten years. Give me a break, Pearl."

The vehicle continued to follow Yip and Sir Hew's taxi through the back streets of Kowloon. If they had business to sort out, it was in an unusual part of town for two such high-flyers to frequent. The vehicle left Argyle Street and wove through a maze of back streets. Pearl began to recognise street names that she hadn't seen for years.

"They're heading for the Walled City. That's where the rumours have always said that Yip's power base is," said Benson.

Pearl looked at him sitting back in the passenger seat, relaxed and happy. The Dr Peter Benson she knew had always affected a relaxed air but he had never exuded happiness.

When the taxi reached Spring Festival Lane, Pearl leant forward and spoke to the driver. "We will get out here."

They walked quickly to the end and turned left into Dentist Street. "Look!"

"Sshhh."

They caught the merest glimpse of Hew Nuttingsall and Yip Yee Koon as they disappeared into the arched gap between the two shops selling dental prostheses, which marked the safest entrance into the old urban maze. The two men seemed to be having difficulty walking.

"Come on," whispered Benson.

But Pearl baulked with pure dread at the thought of going in. It was there that her mother had been killed, there where Benson had betrayed them, or so she had thought. It was there where she might as well have forfeited her own life, so bad was the pain when she found her beautiful mother lying on the floor in the health clinic where she had done her regular volunteer work, her life snuffed out for nothing more than shallow greed.

"You never said ..."

"I never had the chance. I had a nervous breakdown, all right? Come on. Let's see what your friends are up to. I could do with a bit of sleuthing and I know you are worried about Yee Koon."

"Do you *know* Yip?"

Peter Benson crossed his middle finger over his index finger and held it up. "Like that."

*

Chief Superintendent Smythe booked in the articles that he had removed from Sir Hew's apartment for forensic examination as circumstantial evidence pertaining to the cases of Cresswell, Ho and Fraser. He added the camera, with written instructions for the film to be developed and dropped off to his office as quickly as possible. He put in a request to examine the material forensic evidence into the death of DS Fraser and sat down with the box of evidence that had been removed from the crime scene in Albert Ho's house in Ong Hing Terrace. He removed the plastic bag containing the tiger's paw that had been found posed near the wound in DS Fraser's throat.

Tommy turned the bag over and looked at the under-side of the paw. He was tired, had hardly slept for two days and this whole case seemed to be getting more and more complicated. Then he saw the garnet. It was a fine stone, large and beautifully cut, worthy of display, but it was lodged under one of the animal's claws. *In this context it looks like a drop of blood but is actually the tiger's missing eye, and it comes from the rug in Sir Hew's apartment.* DS Smythe gave a loud whoop of pleasure and the desk Sergeant jumped in alarm. That would be something to tell the morning shift! Old Smythe being jolly about something.

The Chief Superintendent had what he needed – circumstantial evidence true, but evidence nevertheless. Combined with the haul of statues, it was enough to arrest Sir Hew Nuttingsall. Tommy took a deep breath, picked up the phone and called his wife, who assured him quite pleasantly that she barely remembered what he looked like, let alone had any expectations of ever seeing him at home again. Then he called James at The Mandarin.

"Developments, James!"

James, yawning, arrived back at Division Central. Tommy held up the tiger paw in its plastic bag and related what had happened when he went to secure the apartment after they had parted company. "And there's a surveillance camera. – I saw the flash of it when I was about to leave. – It's been sent off for examination and to have the film developed."

James was very quiet and it took a moment for DS Smythe to realise why.

"Sorry, James. I should given Mr Yip more credibility for what he said in his statement. And James, I think it's time we went to Stormy's."

"So you do know where Stormy's is," said James pensively. "Wish I'd thought to ask before I left you earlier."

Saturday 11 September: 10.00pm

James looked wistfully at the diners in the little restaurant. He still had not eaten. The smells in the room were magical and there was a woman at a nearby table eating his all-time favourite dish, Peking Duck. He salivated. The waiter beamed and said there would be a table free in half an hour if they wished to go next door to Sunny's for a drink while they waited. James wished it were other, sunnier days and he could do just that.

Chief Superintendent Smythe was brisk. "Has Sir Hew Nuttingsall or Mr Yip Yee Koon been in the restaurant tonight?"

The waiter nodded, his face less than happy. "Yes, Sir. We are very fortunate tonight to have had many high profile Hong Kong figures in the restaurant. But Sir Hew and Mr Yip did not finish all the courses. In fact they left very suddenly."

"Why?"

"I do not know, Sir. I am sure it was not the food, but they did not look happy. And then as soon as those gentlemen went, Lady Green and her dining companion left. They also did not complete the set menu. Chef is very upset."

"Father is very upset too," muttered James as they descended the steep stairs to the street. "What's going on? My daughter is mixed up in this now, it would seem."

CS Smythe didn't reply. His failure to credit Yip's part in this business could have serious repercussions. He radioed in to HQ and ordered immediate surveillance on the apartments of Lady Pearl Green, Sir Hew Nuttingsall and the home of Mr and Mrs Yip Yee Koon.

"Ring Mrs Yip first. She's reclusive, and if Yip isn't there, she'll think … well, I don't know what she may think. When the officer arrives – send two, come to think of it and make one of them a female officer – speak to her very carefully. I don't want the poor woman alarmed. Then when you have done that, I want another search warrant issued for Sir Hew Nuttingsall's apartment. Post two officers outside. Wait until I arrive, but if Sir Hew returns do not obstruct him in any way. Understand? I'm on my way back."

HQ were agog. The Duty Sergeant battled to get down the instructions and then read them back on demand.

"In that order, Sergeant!"

*

There were a few yellow lights showing from the mudbrick dwellings that lined the ground level of the main thoroughfare through the Walled City, but little light illuminated the cobbles. Except for the dull occasional gleam of Benson's cigarette lighter, they walked in deep blackness.

Benson and Pearl needed little guidance in this place. They had both stalked its alleys before. Although the upper canopy was in a continual state of change, the ground floor byways through the original old fort were so narrow that all they needed to do was keep a hand on each wall. So doing, they walked in single file with careful, even steps, making their way deep into the city's heart, where the network of alleys – aerial as well as at ground level – dissolved into a maze, from which many people never emerged.

The quiet was total except for the rustle of rats moving along their own walkways in the intricate canopy of interconnecting buildings. Pearl heard them, the noise as familiar to her as if she had been here yesterday, not eleven years earlier. Had she grown up at all? She fervently hoped that her so-called maturity would not be tested by the creatures that scurried opportunistically around in their own ratty urban maze.

Of one mind, Pearl and Peter Benson turned left where the main alley terminated and halted as one outside the *Emperor Inn*. It was the only place in the city they knew of that was even marginally safe for outsiders. It was also where one could find out what was going on in the city. They could regroup here.

It must be said, however, that the relative safety of the place was a matter of individual luck rather than anything else. *The Emperor* was a bar and an opium den. Many Hong Kong residents were said to shelter in its legal and geographical anonymity. Benson knew something more about it. Yip Yee Koon's name had been linked to the *Emperor Inn* on more than one occasion. Some even said he owned it.

*

Fang Li baulked as the *gwai-lo*s entered the bar and he announced loudly to his customers, "See! The Rat Woman is back after all these years! Not only that, but she is the second *gwai-por* to come here for a second night in a row. This is a bad omen indeed. Are they a race of demons?"

Pearl and Peter Benson towered over the other customers. Pearl was dressed in a floor-length black evening-gown, the sleeveless fitted top attached to a full skirt of chiffon and silk that reached the floor. She wore elbow-length black gloves and black high-heeled shoes which were beginning to make their presence felt on her calf muscles after the walk from the northern gate. Her hair was piled up on top of her head and she wore long diamond drop-earrings. She looked magnificent. She was so strangely exotic in this exotic place that no-one could see that she was actually scared stiff.

The customers quailed. The story of the mad "white witch" who had terrified the regulars in the *Emperor* the previous evening was all over the Walled City; and tonight, lo, a Black Witch comes among us. Many gulped their drinks and fled. Fang Li was sufficiently intimidated to stub out his half-smoked Camel.

Fang Li took a big gulp of whisky and looked closely at Benson. He knew this man.

Benson said in his clear and precisely intoned high Mandarin: "In all existence there is sorrow. All existence results from attachment to life or desire. Existence may be extinguished by extinguishing desire."

Fang Li, who had recovered sufficiently to light a fresh cigarette, exhaled and replied to the familiar refrain in his own meticulous high Mandarin: "And desire may be extinguished by following the path to Nirvana." *Oh yes, just another old customer.* He pointed upstairs. It was none of his business if the place was going to be taken over by mad *gweilos*. They are all ghosts and vanish by morning anyway, just as the owl and the white witch had last night.

Fang Li looked around the bar, comforted by the alarmed expressions of those who had stayed. At least he could be sure he wasn't having visions.

*

The staircase was steep and dark and Pearl removed her shoes and trod as quietly as she could manage behind Benson. Walking quietly was not Pearl's strong suit. The first door off the landing was open and a candle burnt on a table in the centre of the small, empty salon. They crept forward. The door to the second room was closed but they could hear a voice.

Even though his tones were subdued, Hew Nuttingsall still had the voice of a member of the ruling English classes. "It was the tiger that finally did it, you do see that, don't you Yip?"

The door panels were made of starched paper and Benson and Pearl heard what he said easily.

"He tortured me for years, literally and metaphorically. Turned me into an addict and a pervert just like himself, all the while threatening to expose me for what I am. A simple homosexual man. Nothing wrong with that is there? Eh, Yip? No-one understands ...."

His voice slurred a little before settling into a silence that went on and on. If Yip was talking, they couldn't hear him. Pearl gripped Benson's wrist and shook it gently. But he shook his head hard at her.

Hew began speaking again. "Six weeks ago he got into a rage when I couldn't meet one of his demands for a 'loan' as he used to put it. He hacked off the foot of my tiger skin rug. When I still refused, he gouged out its jewelled eye. He said that is what he would arrange for me if I didn't come up with the goods. That was the end. I had to get free of him, he was getting uglier and uglier in his moods and his habits and I'd had enough. When you absolved my debt a few weeks back, Yip old man, it was such a relief to me. But I knew it wouldn't last long, he'd be back for more and he was, just this week. I decided that he had to be dealt with. You gave me a chance to square off my debts. See what I mean Yip? If I could be free of him, if I didn't have to keep feeding him money ...."

They heard sobbing. Pearl and Benson heard a faint sound from Yip. Pearl bit the side of her hand. She wanted to scream.

"I went to his house on Thursday morning, well before light. The door was open and I went in. It's like a tomb in there, you know. I heard him moving around upstairs and I went up the stairs and I killed him. I just walked into the room and cut his throat from behind, but when he fell, I saw it wasn't Albert at all. It must have been one of his fancy boys. I ran. Then as though my prayers were fated to be answered, early in the hours of Saturday, he rang me. He wanted more money, the second demand this week. He was staying here, in this hovel of a place and I was determined this time to sort it all out for once and for all. *Bring money Hew,* he said, *bring lots of money.* I intended really to kill him this time, with no mistakes."

Then Yip's voice, in far from its usual soft tones, cut Hew short. "It was you in this room last night, Sir Hew?"

"Yes. It was like magic in here last night. Not a soul in the place. Not even that foul old barman. And there was Albert looking like nothing on earth. I thought for a moment that he had planned a fancy seduction and intended to stage some horrible tableau with that cheap little tart he had with him. He'd got himself done up into one hell of an outfit –"

"Let me describe it for you. His body and head were bandaged and he wore a shroud." Yip's voice was faint. "The shroud would not have been bloodied at that stage, so I fancy, Sir Hew?"

*

Benson nudged Pearl. They had heard each word clearly through the paper-panelled door.

"Get help," mouthed Benson at her. But Pearl ignored him. She could see Albert, fully bandaged, his torso covered by a shroud – a white gown – a white hospital gown, which he must have taken from the hospital on Hei Ling Chau and used to disguise himself with after he had killed her poor Annie.

And that's how he escaped from the police. He boarded the "Jiang Li" with the other patients. How he escaped after that is immaterial. He killed my friend first and then concealed himself among some of the most vulnerable people in the world. She felt hatred well up in her.

Benson elbowed her sharply. She was off somewhere, just like she used to drift off at the office, all those years ago when she was a girl. He pointed to the stairs and this time she took notice of him and made her way down to the bar and used the phone. The barman didn't even look at her. She rang James at his hotel and when there was no reply from his room she called Central Division Police HQ and was astonished when the desk staff seemed to know what was going on.

"I will radio the Chief Superintendent for assistance immediately, Lady Green. Oh, and Lady Green … ?"

"Yes, what is it?" Pearl's voice was just a whisper.

"I saw your photo in the *Sunday Hong Kong Social* recently, when you attended the Governor's Ball."

Pearl hung up. You had to love Hong Kong. Social chit-chat crossed all boundaries and situations, serious, social or criminal. She crept back up the stairs and settled down beside Benson. There was more sobbing, much louder sobbing now.

"Let's go in," she mouthed at him. She longed to barge into the room.

"Sshh." Soundlessly.

"How do you know what Albert was wearing, Yip?" The crying stopped and Hew's voice was suddenly remarkably normal.

Red Bird Summer

"I found the bodies, Sir Hew. They were removed this morning. Did you expect them still to be here this evening? Of course not. Or, for your purposes, did it not matter to you if I saw them? You know this place absorbs as much as it radiates evil, and you also know that it protects its secrets."

Pearl stood up. This had gone too far. Yip had said too much. Benson hurled himself through the door and she fell behind him into the room, barefoot and brandishing her heels like six guns.

Sir Hew looked at them benevolently. "Lady Green, how very lovely to see you." He put his head back and howled like an animal.

Fang Li heard the noise and concentrated even harder on placing several clean glasses back on the rack above the sink. *Owls, witches, and now wolves. In the morning, I will hand in my notice. The neighbourhood has gone to the dogs.*

*

It was an hour before Chief Superintendent Smythe and James Gates arrived at the Walled City's northern gate. They had two police cars for back-up, one of which was sent to the southern entrance. CS Smythe, James and the two Police Constables who accompanied them had torches and made short work of the walk to the *Emperor*. The two PCs were posted at the front door, their instructions being to permit no-one to leave or enter the premises. James smiled and didn't bother to tell Tommy that there were at least three other exits from the little inn that he knew of, one aerial, one through the cellar and the third achieved simply by removing the end panel in the upstairs hallway and stepping into the house next door.

For the second time that night, the bar emptied. Fang Li arched an eyebrow at them but said nothing, nor was he invited to. The doors to both salons were open, the first one empty, the second containing a tableau of what could have been a group of old friends having a reunion, nostalgic, tinged with sorrow.

Fang Li had cleaned up the room during the day. The bed had a new mattress and the table and dining-chairs had been replaced. The bed covering was also new, salmon pink silk. A large candle sat on the table and cast a gentle yellow glow around the small chamber.

Pearl sat decorously on the edge of the bed, resplendent in black evening-wear, her long diamond drop-earrings glittering to the dance of the candle's flame. She sipped a small whisky. Even though this chamber looked starkly different to the sight that had greeted Yip and himself last night, James recoiled at the sight of Pearl, sitting exactly where BJ Cresswell had died in the early hours of Saturday morning. He rushed across the room to her, pulled her to her feet and hugged her wordlessly. He wrung Yip's hand and beamed at him.

Pearl was surprised, but smiled warmly at him, kissed him on the cheek, and offered him her whisky. He sat her down in one of the dining-chairs and took her place on the edge of the bed. Really, it was insupportable ... he could not ....

It was only then that James noticed that Sir Hew had been firmly tied into another of the dining-chairs, his shoes and tie removed. These sat neatly beside Peter Benson, who sat on the floor in an apparently meditative pose, although truth to tell Peter was riveted by the display of affection between James and Pearl.

As for Hew, tears rolled down his cheeks and he crooned and laughed like a babe entertaining itself while waiting helplessly for attention. When he saw CS Smythe and James, he smiled and said, "I seem to be in a bit of bother one way or another. Tied up again. Ha ha. I enjoy that sort of thing sometimes. Ha ha. Sorry, Yip old man, I wouldn't really have done for you. You know that, don't you?"

Yip seemed quite composed, nursing a potion that Fang Li had given him. He did not know what Sir Hew had given him but it must have happened in the restaurant and he still felt sick. He thought he might even have been out of it for a time in the cab. He remembered feeling surprised when they ended up in Dentist Street, but had been too weak to do anything but allow Sir Hew to half-drag, half-push him to the *Emperor Inn*.

Hew never did say why he wanted Yip in there, although if he thought Yip was on to him, he had nothing to lose, after killing twice in a period of just over two days. Their conversation had not got that far. Perhaps it never would have done, even if Dr Benson and Pearl hadn't burst into the room when they did.

Hew looked quietly at Pearl and James. James had looked stunned when he entered the room and saw where his daughter was sitting. The colour was only just returning to his face.

James and Yip had exchanged glances before James rushed across the room to Pearl. The glance shared again the sight that greeted them the previous evening in the room, to which tonight they had been fated to return. *So be it,* thought Yip. *I didn't seem to be doing so well with my approach to Sir Hew in the restaurant. At least CS Smythe seems to be taking the matter of Sir Hew's involvement seriously at last.*

CS Smythe was very quiet as he went about the business of cautioning Sir Hew, pointing out that, because they were in a jurisdiction-free zone, the caution was only a formality and would be repeated for the purposes of due legalities when Sir Hew arrived at Division Central HQ, Hong Kong Island.

Sir Hew smiled at Smythe and asked what they would be doing there.

"Spot of chat, Sir Hew, we'll have a bit of a chat."

"Oh lovely," said Sir Hew and to anyone's best recall, they were the last lucid words he ever uttered.

Saturday 9 October

The assembly point was at the southern end of the harbourside covered food market in South Connaught Road. The invitation stated that departure time was 12 o'clock and lunch would be served on board. The guests slowly turned up and greeted one another from eleven thirty onwards when they were welcomed on board by a smartly turned-out crew. The vessel was one of the glamorous tourist junks so often seen around Hong Kong harbour these days, kitted-out to give cashed-up tourists a taste of what it would be like to roam the South China Sea in luxury.

The guests sat down to eat. Pearl leant across Ben and spoke to James. "Dad, do you want to do a quick wrap on the case before I make the announcements?"

James nodded and tapped the side of his claret glass, calling for order. Karen Henderson, Drew Pierson, Peter Benson, Mr and Mrs Yip Yee Koon, Danny Tsiu and his sister Irene, Matron Cheung, Mae Lim, Lily Wong, Ben Sanders and Pearl turned to him.

James stood up: "Most of us here today know much of what has happened during the last two months. I'm happy to say that now, even after such a short lapse of time, a great deal of ugliness and unhappiness has gone from Hong Kong. The summer of the Red

Bird is over and autumn is here. Autumn is the time when wisdom reigns, or at least so it says in the old stories."

Yip Yee Koon doubted that wisdom ever reigned anywhere for very long but he liked the sentiments that James expressed and smiled his rare, brilliant smile.

"The police have all but finalised the case that most of us here today have been associated with in one way or another, with two important exceptions. A man associated with Miss Cresswell, the man she referred to as her adviser, has not been found. The only information the police have about him that may be useful is from an Interpol Report circulated via Tokyo concerning one Jonathon Abbott, wanted for fraud in England, who arrived in Japan in May and in Hong Kong in June. John Simons introduced him to Miss Cresswell and thinks he took on the role of mentoring her into her new, ah, career in Hong Kong.

"We know that Jonathan Abbott had Dr Benson's watch in his possession because he turned it in to a pawnshop in Causeway Bay and because of the particular engravings on the back of the timepiece, the pawnshop owner was obliged to notify the Police, who were able to establish Dr Benson's ownership of it through various, ah, channels between government departments.

"I was aware that Dr Benson had not been heard of for several months at that time and it was feared that he had been killed, but as all here can see, Dr Benson is with us today. Dr Benson was robbed in Tokyo about six months ago when he was on a visit to the National Library. The watch was one of his few personal possessions and that is why there were concerns for his safety. My Department had been concerned about Peter's whereabouts for some time and our concerns for his safety seemed valid, up to a point."

James smiled at Peter, a little grudgingly, Pearl thought. Had they not yet solved their differences?

"The other outstanding mystery surrounds the small funerary clip, or pin, that we think initiated Albert Ho's violence against Karen. It remains missing and it seems unlikely that Albert was the thief. We all know about the objects that comprised the rest of the theft on the day Karen was attacked at the museum. Albert Ho was undoubtedly the thief and the objects are being held as part of the forensic evidence in the case. However, the Police have not been able to shed any light on the matter of the pin.

"In hindsight, Albert's paranoia about it is understandable, obviously, because he stole the bestiary collection that morning in early August, but not the pin. Who was the thief? Clearly, he reasoned it must be Karen, who in his view opportunistically seized it after he had struck her on the head while she worked on her pot in the archive room. He accused Karen of being less debilitated by the blow than she gave the appearance of being later that day.

"It seems reasonable to assume that there was someone else in the museum that morning; someone who perhaps saw Albert remove the bestiary collection from the cabinet in Gallery One before he attacked Karen; someone who was able to admit themselves into the archive room, remove the artefact, walk back past the unconscious Karen and let themselves out of the room into which Albert – remember – had locked her. Very puzzling, I am sure you will agree. This person saw what Albert did and very coolly capitalised on it."

As James spoke, he saw Yip Yee Koon shudder. Yip's greatest nightmare since Sir Hew's arrest was that he would have to be a witness for the prosecution in the case of The Crown versus Nuttingsall. As James revisited the facts of the case, Yip was obviously revisiting that particular horror associated with it, one which he had been learning to live with up to the previous week, when the panel of Psychiatrists responsible for assessing Hew's mental health state declared him to be criminally insane. Hew would spend his life in a suitable institution back in England. Yip's relief was as intense as his dread of sitting in a court-room and giving evidence, even though the decision meant that Hew Nuttingsall could never be tried for the murders he had committed.

For his part, James did not want to dwell on the clip too much, although it seemed to him to have been the genesis for everything else that had happened. It had dissolved like a gas, unable, even after much investigation on his part and on the part of the Hong Kong Police Service, to be slotted into the overall picture of this case.

"For the rest of it, we know that BJ Cresswell became delusional as she ingested large amounts of heroin during the last three weeks of her life. The autopsy report states that she was very close to death from organ shutdown at the time she was murdered. There is firm evidence that she took the lives of DS Proust and Mrs

Franklin, violently and deliberately. We should also be careful of assuming that it was her delusional state that caused her to act so violently, however. – She is also thought to be responsible for the deliberate murder of a man in Tokyo in a drugs-associated act of violence that occurred the night before she left for Hong Kong in early July.

"Albert Ho took the life of dear Annie Cheung – accidentally or not, we will never know – and he murdered BJ Cresswell in cold blood. Sir Hew killed DS Fraser because he mistook him for Albert and he then finally killed Albert two days later, after he watched Albert murder Miss Cresswell.

"I think I am in very little danger of second-guessing the Hong Kong Police in saying that this whole affair is one of the nastiest series of events ever recorded in the police records of this colony and it all came down to drugs. Even Sir Hew's financial enslavement to Albert was essentially about drugs.

"It all happened when BJ Cresswell scored a substantial quantity of a legendary drug, the Red Bird "999" shipment of heroin. When that product was removed from the streets back in 1964, it was a great triumph for the Hong Kong Police Department.

"All of this misery has been caused by the theft of just three blocks of Red Bird. Nearly seven thousand blocks of the stuff have now been destroyed. Imagine what might have happened, what could have been let loose on the streets of this beautiful city, if those drugs had ever found their way back into circulation. The phoenix got its timing wrong this summer. There was not much in the way of good times." James paused. "It has been an extraordinary time. And now please join me in a toast to our absent friends."

"To absent friends!" The toast was solemn.

*

It was a magic day on the water and the mood of the party gradually picked up. Pearl smiled at her father and squeezed his hand. Her face was vitally alive with beauty and love. "Wait till they hear what I've got to say. It will blow their socks off," she was thinking. She smiled again, took a sip of champagne, kissed James on the cheek, then turned to Ben and kissed him with a markedly different emphasis. Danny saw the kiss and blushed. He wished his old boss would come back, the one who was interested in looking at columns of figures, but he was afraid she was gone forever.

*

As the guests relaxed and the party warmed up, few noticed that the junk was heading south, except for Kaz who was all too aware that they were getting ever nearer to the familiar, low-lying shoreline of Hei Ling Chau.

She leant across to Pearl: "What's going on?"

Pearl tapped her nose and then tapped the side of her glass. "Please everyone, if I may …. There are a couple of announcements now. It's time for some good news."

She waited for the conversations that had started up across the table to pause.

"We all agreed that life had to keep going somehow, despite everything that has happened since August. The first task was to make things good after I learned that one of the families in Silverwater Bay had their fishing boat stolen on the day that the patients were moved to Lantau. This family has received compensation for their loss and I think the people of Lantau Island will be more welcoming of their new neighbours from now on. The patients are all very happy in their new home and, despite this incident, it seems that the move has been for the good after all."

She dabbed at her eyes, where tears for her lost Annie had risen, unbidden. The regretful thought arose yet again, *If I hadn't initiated the move at all ….*

"Now. Charge your glasses please! We have good news and congratulations to offer. First I would like to announce that I have relinquished my position as Director of the Bowen Foundation for three years, in order to take up the study of Archaeology at the University of Hong Kong."

The audience was stunned. Mouths gaped and eyes widened. The clapping was no more than a confused spatter.

"I have also been asked to announce that Karen and Drew plan to re-marry when the time is appropriate and that Drew will run the Bowen Foundation in my absence for the next three years."

Some surprised clapping this time.

"Dr Benson has agreed to manage the scholarship arm of the Foundation and he will do this on a part-time basis as there are other plans afoot connected with his post-doctoral research into the voyages of the great exploration fleets of Zheng He."

Kaz frowned.

Peter Benson decided to add a comment: "I want to thank Pearl for the opportunity this gives me to return to mainstream life. I also want to thank Dr Henderson for her illuminating work on the marine archaeology of this region which has complemented the post doctoral thesis I have been involved with for the past several years, namely the establishment of previously unknown shipping routes and cargo loads and voyage configurations of all the great exploration journeys south from Taicang to Macau between the fourteenth and seventeenth centuries."

Kaz looked worried now and turned to Pearl. "Pearl?"

Pearl patted Kaz's hand and resumed speaking. "Karen would also like you all to know that she has accepted the position of Director of the Hong Kong Archaeological Museum on a contract basis for three years. She will suspend her post-doctoral research for that period of time, as the museum will be a full-time role for her.

"Kaz?"

There was a more enthusiastic level of applause for Kaz, and no small amount of speculation about how she was going to cope with taking over the role of the man who had tried to ruin her reputation and almost succeeded in taking her life.

"I know this will be a challenge," Kaz said. "But with Drew and Pearl's support I can do it. There is a huge job to do here, to build up the morale of the staff again as well as the reputation of this fine museum. It will regain its former status. It is an opportunity that will only come along once. I can't say 'no'."

The boat drew closer to Squid Cove. Pearl said, "As you see, we are now approaching Hei Ling Chau Island. I would like you all to know also about a proposal that the Bowen Foundation Board has accepted. I have recently purchased the island on a ninety-nine-year lease arrangement with the Hong Kong Government. It is my intention to demolish the hospice and build a new community hospital here, within the next five years. The foundation stone will be laid on 30th June next year to commemorate the construction of the *Ann Cheung Community Hospital and Health Centre*. This is my personal dedication to Annie. I will finance it from my own resources and it will be managed by the June Bowen Foundation."

The clapping was now overwhelming. Matron and Nurse Lim cried into their napkins.

"And finally ... I swear, finally ... Ben?" He shook his head and indicated that she should go ahead. "Ben and I are getting married on the 15th December this year in the grounds of the new hospital on Lantau Island and you are all invited to attend." She threw her notes in the air and hugged Ben as she finished the sentence on something approaching a squeal.

Thunderous applause. Much kissing. Much hand-shaking. The boat reached the cove and they felt and heard the grating of the wooden hull as it scraped the sand. They turned as a single person. Kaz screamed and pointed. "The cove, the beach. Ohmygoddddddd!"

On the narrow stretch of grass that rimmed the grey sands of Squid Cove was a sign, mounted on two wooden posts, which simply said, "Benson's Salvage Operations"

Pearl looked at Benson and said, "This is *not* what I meant by seeking your involvement. I own this island, you know!" She felt the old familiar hint of treachery, which she always associated with Peter Benson, poke at her guts.

Benson was back.

"I know that, Pearl, but you don't own the waters." He was very calm and turned to the gathering. Except for Kaz, Pearl, Ben and Drew, most looked perplexed. "In relation to what I briefly mentioned earlier, I have been successful in accurately pinpointing the location of several wrecked vessels in this cove from two very disparate periods of Chinese exploration history. I took the precaution of invoking salvage rights over the site to protect it from interlopers six years ago.

"I became aware of Dr Henderson's work only when her book was published late last year. She did not identify her site but it was clear to me that our different research techniques had almost certainly identified the same location."

He looked purposefully at Kaz, but it was lost on her. She had sat down heavily on her chair and was literally wringing her hands.

"As Dr Henderson is no longer able to dive and with you all as witnesses today and – if necessary, Pearl, until death us do part – I will, under Karen's supervision, do the field work for the second phase of her post-doctoral research. This is work that will ultimately benefit the world community of scholars from many disciplines who are interested in the great exploration trails of the past. I hope my contribution will be of assistance. Thank you."

There was wild clapping from Drew and Pearl. Ben scowled at Benson. *What was he on about? "Until death us do part, Pearl" – that's my line.* Danny, Matron, Mae Lim and the Yips were mystified and all Kaz managed to say before she fainted, was, "For Christ's sake, will someone get me a beer?"

*

James regarded the small company in his usual pleasant but detached way. Sunken boats and the promise of treasure and enhanced knowledge were all very well, but he was thinking about the past months and everything that had happened; how easily the actions of those two flawed people had altered the lives of everyone here today forever.

Perhaps some good was to come from it indirectly. Pearl was in love and was about to marry. Peter Benson had been brought back into mainstream life. Karen and Drew were re-united. Everyone else was safe, even if grief still shared their company. He thought about the words to a poem he had heard somewhere once:

> *From ashes the phoenix rises*
> *to bring hope at summer's end;*
> *but only the fires of winter*
> *let the red bird rise again.*

He looked out at the beach of Hei Ling Chau and thought again about how the place had only ever seemed to generate unhappiness. Then he turned and saw Pearl's face, as she watched Ben who was tending to Kaz.

Pearl had the power to change it.

And she would, one day.

Red Bird Summer 278

**We are interested to know how you enjoyed reading
Jan Pearson's** *Red Bird Summer.*

Write to our email address, giving us a few sentences which you
are willing for us to publish,
describing your response to this book.
If your comments are chosen to be included
in our E-Newsletter or website,
we will select another title published by Proverse
and send you a complimentary copy.
Please include your name, email address and mailing address
when you write to us, and state whether or not we may cut or edit
your comments for publication.
We will use your initials to attribute your comments.

ABOUT PROVERSE HONG KONG

Proverse Hong Kong (PVHK) is based in Hong Kong with long-term and expanding regional and international connections.

Proverse has published novels, novellas, non-fiction (including autobiography, biography, history, memoirs, sport, travel narratives, fictionalized autobiography), single-author poetry and short-story collections, children's, teens / young adult and academic books. Other interests include diaries, and academic works in the humanities, social sciences, cultural studies, linguistics and education. Some Proverse books have accompanying audio texts. Some are translated into Chinese.

Proverse welcomes authors who have a story to tell, wisdom, perceptions or information to convey, a person they want to memorialize, a neglect they want to remedy, a record they want to correct, a strong interest that they want to share, skills they want to teach, and who consciously seek to make a contribution to society in an informative, interesting and well-written way. Proverse works with texts by non-native-speaker writers of English as well as by native English-speaking writers.

The name, "Proverse", combines the words "prose" and "verse" and is pronounced accordingly.

THE INTERNATIONAL PROVERSE PRIZE

The Proverse Prize, an annual international competition for an unpublished single-author book-length work of fiction, non-fiction, or poetry, was established in January 2008. It is open to all who are at least eighteen on the date they sign the entry form and without restriction of nationality, residence or citizenship.

The objectives of the prize are: to encourage excellence and / or excellence and usefulness in publishable written work in the English Language, which can, in varying degrees, "delight and instruct". Entries are invited from anywhere in the world.

The Prize
1) Publication by Proverse Hong Kong, with
2) Cash prize of HKD10,000 (HKD7.80 = approx. US$1.00)

Extent of the Manuscript: within the range of what is usual for the genre of the work submitted. However, it is advisable that novellas be in the range 35,000 to 50,000 words); other fiction (e.g. novels, short-story collections) and non-fiction (e.g. autobiographies, biographies, diaries, letters, memoirs, essay collections, etc.) should be in the range, 80,000 to 110,000 words. Poetry collections should be in the range, 8,000 to 30,000 words. Other word-counts and mixed-genre submissions are not ruled out.

KEY DATES FOR THE PROVERSE PRIZE IN ANY YEAR
*(subject to confirmation and/or change)

Receipt of Entry Fees/ Forms begins	No later than 14 April
Deadline for receipt of Entry Fees/ Entry Forms	31 May
Receipt of entered manuscripts begins	1 May
Deadline for receipt of entered manuscripts	30 June
Long-list announced	July-September of the year of entry*
Short-list announced	October-December of the year of entry*
Winner(s) announced	March to November of the year that follows the year of entry*
Winning book(s) published	Within the period, beginning in November of the year that follows the year of entry*
Cash award made	At the same time as publication of the winning work(s)*

More information, updated from time to time, is available on the Proverse Hong Kong website: <www.proversepublishing.com>.

The free Proverse E-Newsletter includes ongoing information about the Proverse Prize. To be put on the E-Newsletter mailing-list, email: info@proversepublishing.com with your request.

NOVELS, SHORT STORY COLLECTIONS AND OTHER FICTION
Published by Proverse Hong Kong

Those who enjoy **Red Bird Summer** by **Jan Pearson** may also enjoy the following (all titles in English unless otherwise stated):

A Misted Mirror, by Gillian Jones. 2011.
A Painted Moment, by Jennifer Ching. 2010.
An Imitation of Life, by Laura Solomon. 2013.
Article 109, by Peter Gregoire. 2012.
Bao Bao's Odyssey: from Mao's Shanghai to Capitalist Hong Kong, by Paul Ting. 2012.
Bright Lights and White Nights, by Andrew Carter. 2015.
cemetery miss you, by Jason S Polley. 2011.
Cop Show Heaven, by Lawrence Gray. 2015.
Death has a Thousand Doors, by Patricia Grey. 2011.
Hilary and David, by Laura Solomon. 2011.
Instant Messages, by Laura Solomon. 2010.
Man's Last Song, by James Tam. 2013.
Mila the Magician, by Zhang Jian 章简. 2013. (English / Chinese bilingual)
Mishpacha – Family, by Rebecca Tomasis. 2010.
Odds and Sods, by Lawrence Gray. 2013.
Paranoia (the Walk and Talk with Angela), by Caleb Kavon. 2012.
Red Bird Summer, by Jan Pearson. 2014.
Revenge from Beyond, by Dennis Wong. 2011.
The Day They Came, by Gérard Louis Breissan. 2012.
The Devil You know, by Peter Gregoire. 2014.
The Monkey in Me: Confusion, Love and Hope under a Chinese Sky, by Caleb Kavon. 2009.
The Monkey in Me, by Caleb Kavon. Translated by Chapman Chen. 2010. E-book. 2010. (Chinese)
The Perilous Passage of Princess Petunia Peasant, by Victor Edward Apps. 2014.
The Reluctant Terrorist: in Search of the Jizo, by Caleb Kavon. 2011.

The Shingle Bar Sea Monster and Other Stories, by Laura Solomon. 2012.
The Village in the Mountains, by David Diskin. 2012.
Tiger Autumn, by Jan Pearson. 2015.
Tightrope! A Bohemian Tale, by Olga Walló. Translated from Czech by Johanna Pokorny, Veronika Revická & others. 2010.
Tightrope! A Bohemian Tale, by Olga Walló. Translated by Chapman Chen. 2011. (Chinese)
University Days, by Laura Solomon. 2014.
Vera Magpie, by Laura Solomon. 2013.

OTHER GENRES

We also publish in other genres, including autobiography, biography, children's illustrated books, educational books, Hong Kong educational and legal history, memoirs, poetry, teenage / young adult books, and travel. Other genres may be added.

**FIND OUT MORE ABOUT OUR AUTHORS
OUR BOOKS OUR EVENTS
AND THE INTERNATIONAL PROVERSE PRIZE**

Website
<http://www.proversepublishing.com>

Visit our Hong Kong based distributor's website
<www.chineseupress.com>

Follow us on Twitter
Follow news and conversation: <twitter.com/Proversebooks>
OR
Copy and paste the following to your browser window and follow the instructions: https://twitter.com/#!/ProverseBooks

Request our E-Newsletter
Send your request to info@proversepublishing.com.

Availability
Most books are available in Hong Kong and world-wide
from our Hong Kong based Distributor,
The Chinese University Press of Hong Kong,
The Chinese University of Hong Kong, Shatin, NT,
Hong Kong SAR, China.
Email: cup-bus@cuhk.edu.hk
Website: <www.chineseupress.com>.

All titles are available from Proverse Hong Kong
and the Proverse Hong Kong UK-based Distributor:
Email: chrisp@proversepublishing.com
We have stock-holding retailers in Hong Kong,
Singapore (Select Books), Canada (Elizabeth Campbell Books),
Andorra (Llibreria La Puça, La Llibreria).
Orders can be made from bookshops in the UK.

Ebooks
Most of our titles are available also as Ebooks.